HAPPY AFTERLIFE

PART ONE

BY

STEPHANIE HUDSON

Happy Ever Afterlife - Part 1
The Afterlife Saga #11
Copyright © 2020 Stephanie Hudson
Published by Hudson Indie Ink
www.hudsonindieink.com

Happy Ever Afterlife - Part 1/Stephanie Hudson – 2nd ed.
ISBN-13 - 978-1-913769-28-4

Dedication

When thinking about who I was going to dedicate this book to, I didn't have to think very hard. This person was the one who planted the seed in my mind, and from that the Afterlife saga grew from ten books to twelve and to what I hope you will all think is a beautiful Happy Ever After...life.

Claire Boyle, my wonderful PA but above all my fabulous friend. I dedicate this book to you as it is only fitting for it stemmed from an idea that found its way into two more books.

I would be lost without your constant support and can't thank you enough for all your hard work.

Love Stephanie.

X

Being There.

A true friend is sometimes hard to find,
To have your back, when you're in a bind,
Finding patience, when my life's a mess,
To bringing round wine, and classing PJ's as being dressed.

To knowing what to say when times are the worst,
Holding my hand and being the one to call first.
Making me laugh or giving me a big hug,
When my deadlines are due and all I do is shrug.

You accept me for who I am and my quirky ways,
Even when I drive you nuts when my mind's in a daze,
You never cast judgment or comment on my messy hair,
You are always there for me, my wonderful friend Claire.

Author Insight

I want to start this book by explaining the reasons behind its very existence. As many of you know I don't usually do things in the 'Normal' way and although a lot of you may think that some of these chapters should have made the last book, I made the decision to do things this way to give people the option to choose. Which is why I think you, the fabulous fans of the saga, deserved this explanation.

When writing the last book in the saga I knew I wanted it to end with an epic bang, one I think it deserved after all this time. But in doing so, I had to make the heart-breaking decision to leave out all the 'fun chapters' which could have only happened after the 'Near end of the world as we know it' ending.

However, not long after starting to edit these chapters I once again became lost in the story and before I knew it, there was not just one book, but two.

So, make yourself a cuppa, grab a few snacks and sit back and enjoy this little slice of heaven for our girl Afterlife Heroine, Keira Draven.

After all, I think she deserves her very own...
Happy Ever Afterlife.

WARNING

This book contains explicit sexual content, some graphic language and a highly addictive Alpha Male.

This book has been written by a UK Author with a mad sense of humour. Which means the following story contains a mixture of Northern English slang, dialect, regional colloquialisms and other quirky spellings that have been intentionally included to make the story and dialogue more realistic for modern-day characters.

Please note that for your convenience language translations have been added to optimise the readers enjoyment throughout the story.

Also meaning…

No Googling is required ;)

Also, please remember that this part of a 12 book saga, which means you are in for a long and rocky ride. So, put the kettle on, brew a cup, grab a stash of snacks and enjoy!

Warning!

Thanks for reading x

PROLOGUE

Holding your child in your arms after you had felt
them growing inside you for nine months was a
feeling like no other. It was like meeting the rest
of your life with the biggest smile on your face and tears in
your eyes. And suddenly boom, your glorious life played out
in the form of a flicker book of things you saw yourself
doing years ahead of that moment. It was everything from
getting splashed when giving your child a bath, pushing your
child on a swing, playing in the snow or watching as their
father helped them learn how to ride a bike.

They might seem mundane and seemingly unimportant in
the grand scheme of things. And trust me, once you have
saved the Earth from Titan destruction and Heaven and Hell
damnation, then changing a nappy or getting splatted with
baby food really did put life into perspective.

But it meant that because of these things it made the
personal world you had created for yourself even more
precious. Because, in reality I had spent far too long
believing that one day soon I would die and miss out on

seeing the life I had helped create with the love of my life. That I would miss all the little things that when combined, help paint a perfect picture of blissful happiness…

My Happy Ever Afterlife.

Of course, being that this was me and Draven I was talking about, then the reality was, well, as always…

Things were never going to be that simple.

CHAPTER ONE

THE THRONE CLUB

"Well I think another new table is top of this week's shopping list," I remarked after finally being able to walk back into the club part of Afterlife. I had not long given birth to our beautiful baby girl, only twelve hours earlier and currently had her nestled fast asleep in my arms.

After the emotional birth on Draven's council table I couldn't help but sob with a mixture of both happiness at what we had been gifted, but also sob with grief at what the Gods had deemed it necessary to be taken away.

This had happened after Draven had picked me up with our baby in my arms and taken me back to our room so that we could share in this moment together. Then he simply took over as was his husbandly duty, something he informed me softly when I told him to stop.

But in hindsight I knew why he acted this way…it was his own way of dealing with his own grief. It didn't matter that our babies' souls didn't have vessels to gaze upon after their birth. They had both touched our souls and they were all loved equally. Our only solace now was the hope that we would see them again soon and find ourselves a family three times blessed. But right now, well it was a simple case of all too much, too soon.

So instead I looked to our perfect little bundle of cute baby pink skin and tiny features, thanking the Gods for allowing us this…our own slice of Heaven on Earth.

Our gift.

It felt like the perfect ending to all we had endured. All the years of heartache and pain inflicted from both sides just to get to this point in our lives. Because saving the world aside, all we both wanted sounded the most basic of things, but something that people all around the world were granted each and every day…

A chance at happiness together.

That was all either of us ever asked for. It was all each of us ever wanted…*needed.* Just the simple chance to be together and live throughout the ages creating our own history hand in hand. And fingers crossed doing so without the doom and gloom of an apocalypse hanging over our heads. Of course, hearing what came next from Draven shortly after he had cleaned me up, had me believing another 'end of days' was on its way,

"By the Gods! There must be something wrong, for such a thing could not be produced by a being so tiny!" I frowned, sitting up quickly from the bed and groaning in the process from still feeling slightly tender. Draven growled and I rolled my eyes at his over-reaction.

"Draven, I am fi…"

"Don't you dare finish that sentence, little wife of mine," he warned making me shake my head at him. Then I shifted closer to the edge and saw what he was doing. He had our little baby's legs up in one hand and was currently looking down in disgust at what she had produced. Of course, being around Libby and her first experience of such things, I knew what this was…

"Let me guess, is it black and looks like something an Alien from the X files produced?" I asked on a giggle. He looked up at me and said,

"I don't know what the X files is, but it does look like something a spawn of Azathoth produced."

"And who is Azathoth when he's at home?" I asked in my very Northern way. Draven raised an eyebrow in that sexy way of his and said,

"He rules all time and space at the centre of Chaos and when he is at home, he no doubt does so from his black throne," Draven said answering me in his very 'Master of his domain' kind of way.

"Ah another one that has a thing for thrones then… seriously are you guys all in a club or something?" I asked on a giggle. He rolled his eyes and said,

"No, not yet but I am thinking of starting a new club."

"Yeah?" I challenged knowing this was going to be good.

"Yes, and I think it should be called, 'husbands who like to punish unruly, vixen wives on their thrones' club." I laughed with an unfortunate added snort and said,

"I think that's a little long for a club's name, honey...maybe you could just go with the 'Game of Thrones' instead," I joked. He paused looked down at our tiny baby and told her,

"You know, that's not half bad, I think your mummy is a clever little Queen indeed." I couldn't help the beaming grin at hearing him calling me this. And although it had the word 'little' and cringeworthy 'Queen' attached to it, I still couldn't help but love the sound of him calling me a mum for the first time. I bit my lip as I let the moment wash over me, then I laughed as I put on my dressing gown. I quickly slipped out of bed and walked over to him trying not to show the wince in my tentative steps. Once there I patted him on the arm and said,

"Honey, we really need to get a TV for home." He raised an eyebrow at me and said,

"If it shows things like this on TV, then I think I will pass," he replied nodding down at the dreaded 'first black baby poo'. I laughed picking up the new-born wipes and said,

"Draven, you're a half demon with a front door key into Hell, I think you can handle 'first time baby poo'…now step to it, Mulder!" Then I slapped the wipes to his chest with a chuckle.

"And what exactly is a Mulder may I ask?"

"Well, you would know that if you watched awesome TV like I keep suggesting," I told him smirking making him roll his eyes at me. Of course, so far, the only thing I had managed to get Draven to watch on a TV was my favourite movie of Jane Eyre. Of course, I had been naked at the time, so this might have been why he was so accommodating in my request for a TV in the first place.

"And as I keep telling you my dearest, if you promise to do so naked again when it's switched on, then I will get one." I laughed shaking my head as this wasn't the first time we'd had this conversation.

"And as *I* keep telling *you* in reply, that if I did that then knowing you your eyes would be elsewhere…*again."* I teased back, helping him with the tiny nappy and unfolding it ready to slide under the cutest bum in history.

"Then I would call it a win, win, wouldn't you?"

"How so?" I asked discarding the dirty nappy into the nappy genie Libby had bought us, declaring it a godsend. She was then left wondering why half the people at the baby shower had nearly choked on their drinks or burst out laughing. I guess if she had known what had been happening underneath the wedding tent seven months before that moment then she would have thought very differently about the Gods…seeing as for a short time I had become a scary bad ass one.

Thankfully all the guests had little clue as to what truly happened that day. And even when they were ushered back into the tent, they swiftly had their memories of being kept safe in the ruined mansion at Witley Court erased. I don't think I had even asked what was said to them to get them to go there in the first place. But after returning from Hell, well let's just say, there were other matters to attend to and trying to pretend nothing had happened in front of my mortal family hadn't been something I was able to do. Not after so much heartbreak.

Because in the end the fight hadn't been without its losses. For not only did we have to say goodbye to Ranka, who gave his life for a cause so great, it pained me to think of it without getting upset. Just knowing that millions of lives owed the fate of the world to what we did, but to know the sacrifices made by Ranka would forever go on unknown as the hero he should be remembered by. But only our kind knew and for me, it just didn't seem enough. I remember crying about it one night in the first few weeks after the Janus War. A name given to it by Draven, and I had to say, it fit considering we pretty much nearly destroyed the place.

But stone could be reset, wood carved, marble and doors replaced. The temple could be rebuilt, however the lives lost couldn't and there was one life that still hung in the balance...

Jack.

Not only had we returned to find Ranka hanging on to life just for one last good bye, but there was also Jack. I couldn't help but blame myself for what I had unknowingly brought Jack and RJ into by just being my friends. Of course, Draven wouldn't hear of any blame I cast back at myself, telling me blame was only saved for those who caused actionable force inflicted on others knowingly. Therefore, I was not to blame for what I didn't know. I understood this, I really did but still the sight of ripping Cronus from Jack's body wouldn't leave me.

Seeing his lifeless body becoming his own for the first time in months and all so he could drop to the floor like a heap of bone and flesh, was a nightmare I now faced. Because even though Jack wasn't yet dead, it also didn't mean he was living either. No, he was sort of caught in between two places, this world and the next, suspended in his own mind's prison.

Draven tried to explain it to me, so that I might be able to explain it to his poor sister. He told me that Jack was so strong in his hopeless fight against Cronus, that instead of giving him full access he simply closed off his mind and locked himself away inside it. I guess it was similar to being in a coma, being kept alive in the hopes that one day he would make it home again. I would never forget seeing RJ's face, first full of hope at seeing her brother again, to then be quickly ripped away by the reality of her new situation.

Her cries of anguish could be heard like a tormented wave crashing through the halls of Afterlife. I had heard it and bolted from our room to where she was so that I could catch her shaking form in my arms. Thanks to my new vampire speed, I made it before she hit the floor. In that moment I couldn't help feel for not only her but also for Seth. He was stood a few steps away looking as if he had unknowingly just delivered the killing blow himself. He reached out to her and whispered her name only to have RJ scream at him. She cursed ever knowing him and told him to leave her alone. I bit my lip just to hold in the regret I wanted to voice that I knew she would feel later. But right then that wasn't my place. So, I held her head to my shoulder as she sobbed out her grief and I mouthed the words, 'Give it time' to him before he left the room. He did so asking only one thing of me…

"Take care of her." And then he was gone and as far as I know, he hadn't been seen since. Jack still hadn't woken up and RJ still hadn't lost hope or left his side, now living in Afterlife with only that hope keeping her sane. In the end both Draven and I had each made a vow that day, mine was to keep her safe and Draven's was that he would do everything in his power to bring Jack back to the land of the living. So far, we were both still working on those vows.

But for now, right at this minute another life needed our

attention and I smiled at the sight of Draven carefully re-dressing our little girl. It was one of the sweetest sights I had ever witnessed and I momentarily lost my train of thought as to what we had been talking about.

"You get to watch your unrealistic shows and I get to watch my *very real naked and beautiful wife.*" He whispered this last part in my ear with our baby cradled to his other shoulder. Then he placed a sweet kiss on my cheek and in that one blissful moment, life seemed utterly complete.

"Now back into bed with you," he demanded, making me try and hide a smile before giving him a fake groan. Once I had been carried back into our bedchamber he had made sure I was comfortable, ignoring me when I complained about getting blood on the sheets. He had been placing a pillow at my back and then once I said it, he promptly gave me a 'Draven Look', one I thought best not to argue against. I had wanted to point out that I was now a vampire and therefore healed quite quickly but I stopped myself, knowing how I couldn't take this away from him. Taking care of me gave him pleasure, so I didn't want to spoil this moment for him.

So, he left me with our sweet girl in my arms so that he could tend to me. This didn't only mean washing the blood from me but also examining me and playing doctor...and not in a good way. More like in the most embarrassing way possible. I made the mistake of asking him wouldn't it be better to see an actual doctor, to which he started his response on a growl, followed swiftly by a lecture...

"Keira, do you really think there is someone better qualified out there when I not only hold a Medical Doctorate and have for quite some time now, but also spent the last nine months learning everything there is to know about giving birth to a child...*including aftercare?"* he said sternly and I had to agree with him. Following medicine, I found out, had been a kind of hobby of his and when he found out that I was pregnant, well it kind of opened up the baby medical gates, flooding my life with annoying pregnancy facts. If anything, I had just wanted to burn most of the books he read and one argument we had in only the first trimester was exactly what I did one day in the library.

He had been explaining to me how there wasn't one single reason for morning sickness and he asked if he could study me for the weeks ahead to see if he could find the reasons why. My answer had been quite blunt as I had simply plucked the current book from his hands, walked over to the fire, thrown the book into it and said,

"No." Then I had walked back out of the room again. He found me minutes later throwing up in the toilet asking me if I wanted a ginger biscuit...my look had said it all.

Okay, so had I mentioned about the angry pregnant lady bit, right? Well thankfully Draven did know the reasons behind this and let's just say, that he definitely *didn't* want to 'study' me for it.

So back to post first nappy change and that was Doctor Draven issuing his orders making me groan as I did so. He placed our girl in her swinging crib that was next to our bed and before I even had chance to bend my knee to step up, he had me in his arms and was lowering me down like I was fine china.

"You do know that I am not going to break...right?" I asked in an amused tone, telling him that I found his actions sweet but unnecessary.

"Yes, but I also know the changes that a woman's body

endures after the strain of having a baby and these include…"

"Seriously Draven if you continue that sentence and it includes words like, vaginal, pain and discharge then I am going to stop you right there before I swear off sex for life… and I have been told…*it's a very, very long life together.*" I said this last part leaning in closer to him as he fussed with my pillows again. He paused mid fluff (not a sentence I would have ever have thought to have put together in my mind when referring to Draven) he then leant closer to me and said with a smirk,

"I have told you once before, lying is a sin you know." At this I laughed and retorted with,

"Yes, and so is pissing off your wife, so quit being a pussy and man up, Commander!" I teased back looking down at his man package with a naughty wink. I couldn't help but bite my lip when I heard that aroused growl I had been waiting for.

"You play with fire, little Vixen," he warned and my smile grew.

"Oh, come on, you know I have already started to heal and besides…" I paused so that I could grip the front of his shirt and pull him close enough so I could speak over his lips,

"…This kick ass Vampire Warrior Queen likes her King sexually demanding…*and hard.*" Then I licked out along the seam of his lips before he finished the action in a bruising kiss, one that had me releasing a moan in his open hot mouth. Then just as he banded an arm around my back pulling me tighter to him the sweetest little cry alerted us to the fact that in this room, we were no longer alone and wouldn't be for quite some time. My smiled ended the kiss and it turned into a perfect moment to speak the words that I knew he would hold with him for the rest of our lives…

"Someone wants her daddy."

After hearing himself being referred to as 'Daddy' for the first time the look on his face was one that I would never forget for as long as I lived…thankfully, something that was considerably longer than what I had thought it would be nine months ago.

It was a different tenderness that I had never seen before, one reserved for only one person…*his child.* It was a beauty beyond words and it took my breath away. Draven turned towards our little girl and lifted her from her crib with the level of care that only came from an adoring love that knew no bounds. Draven might have been a King to the rest of the world but in this room, he was simply a man who felt as though he had been bestowed the greatest gift from the Gods…

A family to love.

Back in Afterlife

"I am not getting rid of the place you had our child," Draven said in reply to the first comment I made when walking back into the club with our baby girl to present to our unique world.

"Yes, and I am not having everyone we know sat around the place… *I had my legs spread wide with my vagina on show as I pushed our baby from a place only YOU know intimately."* I leaned into him and whispered this last part so only he would hear. He had looked as though he had been about to argue but the second the whispered words left my mouth he firmly locked his jaw before saying,

"I will have it moved into storage immediately."

"Yep, thought so," I commented dryly as we both stepped into the room to announce our sweet Amelia Faith Draven to the rest of the Family.

In the end, asking Draven what we should name our child wasn't as hard as I thought it was going to be. But then again, I suppose with nine months to think about it, then for most parents who don't know what sex they are having, it only really comes down to two names. Of course, during my pregnancy and one of my 'softer' moments, we had spent one evening thinking up names.

This was after I had convinced him to help me put together the crib by hand. At first, he thought I had been joking and with a simple swipe of his hand it was complete. Then the irrational side of hormonal pregnancy kicked in and I began to cry.

Draven had looked as though he had been caught competing in a kitten kicking competition and with a horrified look the crib instantly crumbled back into a million pieces. Okay, so that was a slight exaggeration but hey, it was from Ikea, so it was close.

I admit, once again I had got it into my irrational pregnant mind that I needed to go baby furniture shopping. I also knew I wouldn't have got away with dragging Draven around the reasonably priced Swedish megastore, no matter how many tears labelled emotional blackmail I shed. So, instead I dragged my personal time travelling posse, Pip and Sophia with me.

I would have also asked Ari if she had been around,

which unfortunately, she wasn't. I wasn't bitter or upset about this as I knew her and Vincent were currently dealing with their own 'Fated' issues. Or at least this was the most my overbearingly protective and stubborn husband would tell me. I knew something big was going on with them but with me being pregnant meant Draven had deemed everything too much for my overemotional state to deal with. And thanks to the damn baby book, stress was a big no, no.

So, Ikea it was and to make it 'Stress Free' we had also declared it a 'No Husbands Allowed' occasion. Or at least I tried to, but the most I could get away with was doing it without *my* husband around as Zagan and Ragnar were sworn to protect me whenever Draven wasn't there. And as for Pip, well since her unknown disappearing act 2000 years into the past, well let's just say she was lucky she didn't find herself shackled to Adam's wrist for the next thousand years as punishment.

No instead he just forbade her to go anywhere without him. Pip had sulked for weeks and did so up until the next big thing happened to take her mind off it, which just so happened to be me giving birth.

But before the baby arrived there was something else to take Pip's mind off overbearing demon husbands...

Lots and lots of shopping.

CHAPTER TWO

A COUCH CALLED OLIVER

TWO MONTHS EARLIER...
BEFORE THE BIRTH

"I am going to buy every damn smelly candle in the joint just to piss him off!" Pip moaned secretly to me as we followed the arrows around the showroom with the three men looming close behind looking utterly depressed. The looks they got were priceless and I was half tempted to get Ragnar to walk in front as everyone was giving him a wide berth anyway and that would make it easier for us to get the trolley through.

In the end it turned out to be a good thing that the men had come along as buying one thing in Ikea didn't necessarily mean one box. So, buying an entire nursery set meant a shit load of boxes that meant muscles certainly came in handy.

Now I knew that being the supernatural bad ass chicks that we were, meant lifting a few boxes would have been a piece of cake. But on the other side of that supernatural spectrum, I was also dealing with high maintenance Sophia, who was wearing a tight pencil skirt designer dress that wouldn't have survived it…her words not mine. And as for our naughty imp, well she had just spent about two hours doing her nails as rude unicorns complete with willy shaped horns that I quote…'were easily 'wacked off''.

She burst into a fit of giggles after saying this, so I gathered she had meant it as a sexual pun. Either way I wasn't willing to risk a tiny willy flicking in some innocent child's direction or Sophia mooning a family when splitting her skirt by picking up box number 46!

Okay, so there weren't that many boxes, but by the end of hauling my big belly around the place, it certainly felt like it. This had been the main reason I had collapsed into a stained couch in the reduced section close to the tills. Once there I had simply watched with my cheek resting in my palm with a smile on my face as my supernatural family fully immersed themselves into the human world. I didn't know it at the time but the moment would stay with me and become a secret smile every time I would open the small wardrobe to get out one of Amelia's tiny outfits.

I don't think I will ever forget seeing a giant Viking, an Albino warrior and Hell's deadliest beast who looked like an accountant, arguing about which aisle was which and which section was where the right box was located.

"And pray tell, what is that smile all about?" Sophia asked teasingly as she came into view. I grinned up at her, squinting a little as the powerful overhead lights were in my eyes.

"Yeah Preggy Toots, spill the beans not the Cheerios," Pip said after first falling backwards onto the couch with a bounce. Normally I would have tried to make sense of what she said. But well, in truth after knowing Pip for a few years, you kind of stopped asking yourself why and just rolled with her brand of crazy. I shifted closer to her and patted the couch for Sophia to sit down as well. She wrinkled her nose up at the sight of the couch as if it had been condemned to a city tip in Hell or something.

I laughed and said,

"Seriously, after all we have been through, you're wussing out of sitting in a used Ikea couch?" Pip snorted a laugh granting her a scowl from Sophia, which only managed to turn her giggle into a snigger.

"I am not 'wussing' out of anything but just so you know I have seen cleaner seats in the Third Circle of Hell." I frowned in question until Pip leant into me and muttered,

"Greedy little bastards…" Then she filled me in when she whispered who the Third level was reserved for,

"Gluttony."

"Ah but of course," I replied with a roll of my eyes making Sophia huff before sitting down gingerly as if any minute the seat would split its seams, open its disgusting mouth and vomit human germs all over her. I think she barely even had her butt cheeks on it she was perched that close to the edge.

"So, come on, what was that smile all about?" Pip asked and Sophia quickly added,

"Yeah spill it, it's the least you could do before I catch

something from sitting on this thing," Sophia said looking around her as though she was currently being coughed on. Pip laughed again, winked at me and then said,

"Oh, look here, I found a brown stain…wonder what that could be." I burst out laughing at the sight of Sophia jumping up as if the rabid couch had bitten her ass with disease riddled springs. Pip nearly fell off the couch she was laughing so hard. She was holding her belly and rocking back and forth shaking and trying in vain to wipe away the tears.

Her plaited pigtails were swinging like jungle vines and the short floaty skirt she wore dipped down to her knees. It was a pretty material that was covered in dripping rainbow trees that looked like a watercolour painting. To this however, she had added a plain black vest top with white writing on the front. When first seeing her that morning I of course had to ask what 'Dolor sit amet, sunt bonum et melius, sed irrumatus' had meant. Not that I had actually said the words, because let's face it, most of the time with my accent I sounded as if I struggled with basic English. Of course, get me back to good old Liverpool and no one would have any difficulty understanding me.

"Why it means …carrots are good for you, but dick is better," she said with a wink.

"But of course," I said turning from her and giving Sophia a 'this girl is crazy' look. This was when I noticed the back of her shirt that said, 'It's a shame you can't speak Latin, 'cause my shit is funny'.

But getting back to the couch and the brown stain Pip just freaked Sophia out with.

"That was not funny, Winnie!" Sophia snapped making

me join in the laughter as well. Because let's face it, Pip had a point, it was funny.

"Seriously, what is it with you and germs, I mean it's not like you can even get ill?" I asked giggling. Sophia curled her lip at the thought, folded her arms and then said,

"I just don't like the thought of it." I tried to hold back my grin and said,

"Well if it makes you feel any better, I'm someone who's afraid of heights."

"Oh, that's nothing, loads of humans are," Sophia argued.

"Yeah and how many of them are married to a guy with wings, eh?"

"She makes a good point'damundo," Pip said waving a thumb my way. Sophia shrugged her shoulders and said,

"Alright, you win, *weirdo.*" To which we all burst out laughing.

"Come on now, sit your pretty designer ass down and watch the show." I said pulling on her hand and making her fall down next to me, looking horrified.

"The show?" she enquired. I nodded to the guys as they emerged from the aisle with three extra boxes added to the long flatbed trolley. A trolley where Zagan was currently slumped over the handle looking as though he wanted to shoot himself just for something more interesting to do.

"Next on the list is the changing table and my 5's look like S's." I informed them making Sophia frown in question and Pip cock her head at me like a dog and say,

"Huh?"

"Just watch," I said as Adam pulled the little piece of paper out of his pocket and read out the next item that I had added to the list.

"Aisle twenty, section I.S," he said looking at the others with a frown.

"Yes, and the section…*is* what?" Zagan asked after first mimicking the way Adam had said it.

"No, not the word *is,* the letters I.S…it's in the section I.S." Adam said again making Zagan groan and throw his head back as if now he wished he was back battling demons in the Janus Temple and asking any God out there to grant him this.

"I not understand. I.S is not here," Ragnar said looking around as if he had lost his book on 'How to Deal with the Human World in Ten Easy Steps'.

"You're right, this is funny!" Pip said laughing and Sophia shook her head in shame and groaned a muttered,

"Idiots."

"Gimme that!" Zagan said snatching the piece of paper out of Adam's hand making him shout in panicked tones,

"Careful! You might have ripped it!"

"And that's a bad thing because…?" Zagan asked as if ripping it was the answer to all his current problems. Adam grimaced, looked around as if making sure the coast was clear before hissing,

"Because if you rip it and we lose the location of where these things are then she might make us go back through the whole damn showroom again to find the godforsaken number, that's why," Adam said in way that make it sound like this was torturous just thinking about it.

"OMG, this is just priceless!" Pip said crying now she was laughing that hard. Thankfully, the men couldn't see us thanks to the middle of the walkway being full of furniture displays, but we had a perfect view of them and were hearing

22

this all play out thanks to supernatural hearing. One thing I might add, I had been very happy to discover after turning into a human vampire hybrid…that and not needing to feed half as much as regular vampires, because let's face it…*ewww*. Thankfully though, I had a very willing husband on tap who liked to think of it more as foreplay than as my starter before the main course.

Zagan's eyes widened in panic and he quickly started smoothing out the paper as if it held the secret location to the lost Ark, Holy Grail and the Fountain of Youth. Then his eyes widened at the paper before he rolled them as if now asking for strength.

"Hey Genius, it's not section I.S, it's section *fifteen"* Zagan said clearly exasperated and frowning before slapping the paper to Adam's chest. He fumbled to catch it before it fluttered to the floor and then said,

"What?! No, it definitely said…oh, yeah, I see it now." He added this last part after catching it and turning it side on making me wonder how that helped in reading my bad handwriting.

"Geez, just how bad is your penmanship, Toots?" I growled and said,

"Well excuse me if I didn't get taught calligraphy in school when the first quill was invented!"

"Not sure feathers were invented there, angry preggy bird," Pip replied making me growl again only this time with a gritted teeth warning,

"Will you please stop calling me that!" Pip just giggled of course before smacking her lips together blowing me a kiss.

"Anyway, shouldn't you know what most of this crap is!"

Zagan said to Ragnar now making *him* growl, only when he did it people quickly left their loaded trolleys and hastily made for another aisle…like ones on the other side of the warehouse!

"The last time I heard the word Sundvik it was meant as a family name not the name of a slab to wipe shit off baby skin," Ragnar replied.

"Wow man, that was deep," Zagan said pounding a fist over his heart with a smirk. Adam pushed up his glasses and said,

"I would think less slab and more sensible table to place the child safely whilst changing its diaper." Zagan looked at him side on and said,

"Seriously, explain to me again how you can be the scariest mother fucker on the planet and still know about this shit?" Adam smirked and shrugged before saying,

"I also know about tax returns and what pneumonoultra-microscopicsilicovolcanoconiosis means." Then he gave him a cocky grin before knocking the trolley from his hands as he passed making Zagan growl.

"What the hell does that mean?" I asked wondering if it was even a real word…of course Pip knew.

"Pneumonoultramicroscopicsilicovolcanoconiosis is a word that refers to a lung disease contracted from the inhalation of very fine silica particles, specifically from a volcano. Medically, it is the same as silicosis…I bought him a 'ridiculously long word of the day' toilet roll…I think this one took up six sheets, so we all know what he was doing when he learned this one, eh…?" she said nudging me with a snorted laugh.

"Eww Pip, too much information there, love," I told her making her giggle yet again.

"Aww but that's my man, he's got such a clever brain and such a smushy heart!" Pip said this time tilting her head in a 'isn't that cute' kind of way. Then of course by doing this it put her head closer to the stain on the armrest making her lose her train of thought to another one...

"Oh look, it's only a Coke stain, not poop, like I first thought...you're all good Sophia," Pip said making Sophia look her way and when her eyes widened in horror I looked back to Pip to see her licking the couch.

"Yep, definitely Coke, we're all good people." Needless to say, this made it extra memorable as after that I found myself running to the toilets when laughing so hard I came very close to wetting myself...damn weak preggy bladder.

When I had finished (just making it in time) I came out to find not only Ragnar standing guard but also poor Adam lugging the stained couch through the checkout as Pip said, and I quote 'I just had to have it as now it has memories and it was all sad there on its own with no one to love it.' Therefore, it was quickly dubbed 'part of the family' and swiftly bought.

"Well, that was memorable," Sophia commented dryly as we walked from the building, making me chuckle. I nudged her shoulder and gave her a grin.

"Ah come on, it wasn't that bad," I said making her look at me sideways as if I had lost my mind.

"Well, I thought it was awesome sauce with extra jalapenos, baby!" Pip shouted, fist bumping the dinosaur glove puppet she had on her hand. She also had a massive cactus under one arm and a giant pencil under the other, both were soft toys she bought in the kid's section, which of course had been her favourite bit. She also had a giant toothbrush, shark, robot with a heart on its belly and a set of three mice that she explained were going to get glued to the side of an antique grandfather clock made by John Taylor in the 18th Century. Now I didn't know who this John Taylor was, but I was pretty sure he would be rolling around in his grave screaming Pip's name into damnation if he knew she was about to glue three stuffed mice to the side of his time keeping masterpiece.

"Yes, and two days ago I found you dragging a broken rocking chair covered in bird shit, into Afterlife, one that you found on the side of the road," Sophia said after first rolling her eyes, which she skilfully combined with a look of disgust.

"And your point is?" Pip asked cocking her hip out with a glove puppeteer hand to her waist. I had to say but if she was going for bad ass then she needed to rethink her choice of 'bad ass' pose as I didn't think cute stuffed objects were going to cut it. No-one was going to be intimidated by a stuffed cactus, no matter how many fake spikes it had or having a giant pencil stuck out of your armpit.

"Uh…I just made my point," Sophia stated as if it was obvious, which considering this was Pip she was talking to, then it really wasn't.

"Alright ladies, let's not get our knickers in a twist over an Ikea couch," I said playing referee and calling time out.

"Hey! What's wrong with my couch?!" Pip said making me wince. Sophia turned to me with an evil grin, folded her arms and said,

"Yeah Kaz, what's wrong with her coke stained,

orphaned 'I need a home, please sir, can I have some more', Oliver couch?"

"Oooh I like that, it's catchy," Pip said making me think I was in the clear, that was until she said,

"Yeah, so what's wrong with Oliver?"

"Oliver?"

"New couch name," Pip stated still with her hands on her hips. I looked to Sophia with a scowl and then masked my features before turning back to Pip and saying,

"Oh, don't listen to me, I am pregnant and talking crazy preggy talk... I love your new couch...*Oliver.*" I added his new name tentatively when she didn't look convinced,

"Pulling the pregnant card again, are we?" Sophia said leaning closer and whispering next to me.

"Yes well, when your ankles are as fat as mine then you can comment, but until then, I am using the preggy card as much as I can!" I growled at her side on, making her laugh. Just then the men came through the doors thankfully saving me from a Pip meltdown as Adam bounced the giant toothbrush on Pip's head making her giggle before he began to chase her with it shouting on about him being the new naughty tooth fairy. Of course, our Pip loved it.

"Ambrogetti should mean 'Big Kids' not Immortal," Sophia muttered with a shake of her head before Zagan snuck up behind her and wrapped a giant heart with arms around her neck for a hug. She jumped before bursting into a fit of giggles and turning around to take her own soft toy gift in her hands. Then she looked up at him as though he had just handed her the biggest diamond before kissing him passionately.

Needless to say, the whole scene made me cry and in turn

made Ragnar panic. He left the trolley instantly making it crash into a stone bollard and before I could utter a word he was in front of me, holding on to my arms checking me over.

"What is wrong, what has happened?! Are you unwell, is the baby…?"

"Ragnar it's fine, I am just over-emotional and happy," I told him after rubbing my nose. He looked down at me as if trying to detect a lie before disbelief made him frown.

"You be happy?" I nodded with a little laugh.

"I don't understand you women," he muttered grumpily as he let me go. So, I patted his arm and then reached up as far as I could whilst pulling down at his jacket so he would get the hint. He let me pull him closer so I could whisper,

"You're not supposed to, big guy." Then I kissed his cheek making him grunt to hide how much the gesture had touched him. I knew it had because he actually blushed before hiding his face by turning back to retrieve the trolley. By this time Zagan had taken his own trolley off towards the car leaving me and Sophia standing there alone together.

"So, you know once Dom finds out how cheap this stuff was he is never going to let you put it in your bedchamber, don't you?" She informed me with a smirk but I just patted my big belly and said,

"Maybe we should have a bet on that…preggy card remember." She looked down at my belly and smiled before patting it herself. Then she looked back at the still blushing Ragnar and replied,

"Well considering you just turned a Viking King to putty, then I guess I will give you that one but just so you know…" She paused so that she could look at me and said something that filled me with dread,

"I am not sure all that baby furniture is going to match what Pip got you." After hearing this I decided to just rip the band aid off in one swift move by asking,

"Why, what did Pip get me?" Sophia had started walking ahead and stopped to tell me over her shoulder...

"That condemned rocking chair she found on the side of the road of course." Then she continued towards the car, only this time with a huge evil smirk on her face.

There was only one thing left for me to mutter at her back...

"Damn evil sister Demons!"

CHAPTER THREE

GUILT IS A BEAUTIFUL THING

I had to say that when the boxes continued to pile up in our bedchamber Draven's face was a picture. I didn't know what was funnier, Draven's shock or the guys' pitying looks they gave their King as they walked through the room. Draven had his hand on the door holding it open as Zagan, Adam and Ragnar continued inside each carrying as many boxes as their arms would allow. Draven's eyes would follow one box after another and just as he was going to close the door, in walked Pip swinging two big, blue bags full of even more stuff.

I knew it was bad when I saw him gripping the bridge of his nose between his thumb and forefinger before closing his eyes and muttering something in another language. I looked to the door and now saw Sophia leaning casually against it looking at her nails with a smug grin she wasn't even trying to hide, damn her!

"Is that the last of it?" Zagan asked Adam who after first

looking to Draven, decided to quietly shake his head indicating no, it wasn't. Unfortunately for me, Draven saw it and after taking a deep breath released it again on a big sigh.

"Gentlemen, I think I need a moment alone with my wife," he said, and I swear it was almost comical the way the three men nearly ran from the room.

"Not a problem," Zagan said quickly, obviously in a hurry to make it to freedom.

"But of course, My Lord," Adam said following suit after first bending slightly so that he could pick up his own little wife by putting her over his shoulder.

"Sure thing, Boss man!" Pip said giving him a salute as Adam walked them both past. I nearly groaned out loud when I saw Pip mouth the words, 'You're screwed' at me.

"Certainly, my King," Ragnar said bowing his head as he too made a swift getaway, patting me on the shoulder as he passed. And his own parting words,

"Good luck, little apple." This time I finally did growl making him chuckle as he left the room. Jeez, was everyone a bloody comedian now!

Well one look at Sophia and the answer to that was no, just half of them were reborn into bloody demons, so really what did I expect?! I rolled my eyes at her when she mouthed the words, 'Told you so,' before she was swiftly grabbed from around the doorway by Zagan, who snagged her arm and thankfully for me, dragged her out of the room. The eruption of laughter from all of them could be still heard even after Draven had closed the door.

"So, I went shopping," I blurted out and Draven made another quick sweep of the room, that currently resembled a small warehouse and replied,

"Yes, so I see." The hint of sarcasm couldn't be missed.

"Oh, come on, it's not like I spent a fortune as it was bloody Ikea for God's sake, not imported from Italy and besides, I hardly ever spend any money and I didn't even use that fancy gold card you gave me." I said in a hurry which for some reason caused him to tip his head back and look up at the Gods as if they held some of the answers.

"I know I am going to regret asking this but please tell me you stumbled across my treasury and paid for this the old-fashioned way?" I gave him a questioning look before asking,

"The old-fashioned way?"

"In gold, Keira," he informed me wryly and I nearly laughed. Okay, so with this question I couldn't actually tell if he was joking or not, so I asked the next question that popped into my head.

"You have a treasury?!" He released a sigh and muttered,

"Well, there's my answer...yes my Love, *we* have a treasury," he replied after first talking to himself and then making sure to emphasise the word 'We' in that sentence. What can I say, money was still kind of a sore point with me as I hated spending what I myself hadn't earned.

"Oh," was my simple whispered answer.

"Now for my next question," he said sternly, stepping around each box and coming closer towards me with clear determination in his strides. I backed up a step knowing this dominating side of Draven well and that somewhere along the line I had said something to frustrate him. This usually meant one thing and that was whatever was said next was going to end with a demanding, toe curling kiss...or at least I hoped it would.

I ended up against his desk by the time he reached me, and I placed a hand on each side of the carved wood at my back to steady myself as he leaned closer into my body... well as much as my baby bump would allow anyway.

"Um...shoot," I said after first having to clear my voice making him smirk down at me in that bad ass cocky way of his. Seriously, would I ever get used to how sexy and gorgeous this man was or the even more shocking fact that I was actually married to him?

"Alright sweetheart, now I suggest you think really hard about the next answer you give me, for it could push me over the edge if I hear the wrong one." I swallowed hard making him put a hand to my throat and stroke down its length leisurely. His other arm was positioned above me, pinning me in with no escape. I swore, if he carried on like this I would end up a puddle on the floor with a baby in the middle asking what the hell just happened!

"O...kay," I said or at least tried to, as to be honest, I couldn't tell how it sounded. It could have just been a squeak for all I knew. His smug grin told me as much.

"Pray tell me, my dear sweet girl, for I so wish to know how you paid for...all of this," he asked, pausing so that he could sweep a hand out at the floor indicating all I had bought.

"Ah, well..." I started, now knowing what this was all about. He laughed once only it was done so out of mockery, not humour. Okay, so I knew I was in trouble here because as much as I hated spending his money, he equally hated me spending my own as he had quickly declared his vast fortune as 'ours'...a sentiment I didn't share I might add.

"Well wife of mine, let's hear it," he said knowing he

was backing me into a corner and not just physically. Oh yeah, I was going to get broody demanding Draven alright. And from the look of the way those large shoulder muscles were punishing the material on his t shirt, then it looked as though I wasn't going to be making baby furniture tonight as I had thought. I got wet just thinking about it and had to bite my lip to prevent a moan from escaping.

"Okay, so don't be mad but well…"

"Yes…?" Draven purred knowing I was stalling for time.

"I kinda used…well okay so if you must know I used my savings to buy it all," I told him just blurting it out and making him growl at me. There had once been a time that hearing Draven's reaction to something he didn't like would have had me flinching in fear. I knew he would never hurt me, but back then it was still something that took some getting used to. After all, Draven was as famous for his temper as Lucius was for keeping his icy, deadly cool.

But the difference now was that I knew how to master it and what I did next would have made people ask if I was crazy or if I had a death wish. I raised my hand to his cheek, gently slapped it twice and then raised on my tiptoes and said,

"Suck it up big man, your wife doesn't like spending other people's money, so deal with it." Then I kissed his cheek and ducked under his arm moving about half a step before I was in his arms again. Now I was the one smirking to myself as I heard yet another growl in my ear before I felt him nip at the lobe.

"How am I ever to win this war against your stubborn mind, woman?" he asked with his lips at my neck and with a voice that was thick and gruff thanks to his growing arousal I also felt pressing into me from behind. Well, it certainly had to be said that the once held notion I had that Draven wouldn't find me sexy when pregnant was once again proven wrong, like the hundreds of times before now.

It also seemed that the bigger I got, the more and more he cooed over just how sexy he found me. He also relished in this new challenge in finding positions that worked with a big belly in the way. I had to say, that like anything else where it concerned Draven, he certainly knew how to conquer the battle and conquer he did… *often in fact.*

He soon cottoned on that with the release of endorphins with every orgasm he gave me, my bad mood pregnant hormones would just float away and become lost in a sea of happiness. The reasons he gave for then having the excuse to do this as frequently as possible. I think if it had been left up to Draven then he would have preferred we just spend the whole nine months in bed! But as I continued to remind him, we did have other stuff to do and in my case, shopping for the baby. Thus bringing me back once again to dealing with a sexually hungry beast of a man growling at me.

"Well, you could let me have my way and win the war that way," I suggested with a smug tone making him bite my neck playfully. The next thing I knew I was being swept up into his arms and instead of trying to navigate around all the boxes he decided on a better way. I squealed when his wings suddenly burst from his back just long enough to quickly propel us forward towards the bed in one of the quickest flights I had ever had with Draven. His wings hit either side of the bed posts to stop us from going too far and I yelped at the sound. I was still amazed how he could do such things with me in his arms without jarring me once in his hold.

"I think I know a better way to win the war you wage on my heart, wife of mine," he said as he lay me down as gently as supernaturally possible. I then sat up quickly grabbed his t shirt and yanked him hard to me.

"Don't you mean the war I wage on your straining manhood?" I teased looking down to see it currently trying to immortally imprint its silhouette onto the denim that was still keeping it prisoner. I had to say that from the size of it, then I doubted the denim was up to the task at keeping it contained for much longer!

He followed my gaze down before looking back up again slowly in a predatory way. I was met with an intense purple stare that told me he was close to the demonic edge. Now being pregnant we hadn't yet had chance to play at it rough and try out my new vampire body. Well okay, so not much had changed in the looks department, in fact nothing had changed other than having to learn to get a handle on my fangs and creepy black eyes thingy.

I still even got split ends! I remember being outraged in the bathroom when finding them...Draven thought it had been hilarious at the time when racing in to find me stomping my foot and ranting on about the injustice of it all. I mean is that what I get for saving the world, not even a break from split ends and chipped fingernails?

Okay so yeah, looking back at the grand scheme of things then this wasn't really anything to moan about but at the time, well let's just say raging bitch hormones were winning ten billion to one on the nice, bad Keira scale!

"Are you trying to get punished, little Vixen of mine?" Draven asked in a demonic purr. I shuddered beneath him after he lowered himself down over me, holding himself from crushing me with his weight with both fists pressing into the bed either side of my head.

"Ah now I see that threat worked," he said in response to my gulp.

"Good, it's about time I had you back under my control and we both know there is only one way I can achieve such a thing." To this I was about to argue, but then he held all his weight with one hand freeing up his other. This was then used against me like he first threatened…and holy crap had it worked the sneaky bastard. He simply had to dip his hand under the stretchy waistband of my maternity pants and hey presto, he was in. I sucked in a sharp breath at the first feel of him parting my wet folds, only to let it all out in a whoosh when he skimmed slowly across my sweet spot.

But I wasn't lost yet and I wanted to show him that his vixen still had a few sparks left in her.

"Are you going to pull a rabbit outta there?" He grinned down at me, leant in that little bit closer and said,

"Oh, I am not going to pull anything *out* of there…" He paused for effect before suddenly plunging two fingers inside me making me scream with the pleasure of it. I raised my body up, arching my back just as he whispered the rest of his lingered sentence,

"…Put in however, now that's a different story." He accentuated his point by curling his finger up slightly and stroking on my inner G spot. I cried out again and he chuckled before whispering in my ear,

"Now there's my good girl," Then he released his intimate hold on me before gently lifting me up so that he could slowly remove my clothes before doing the same with

his own. I smiled knowing he did this just to tease me and make me wait as was usually 'my punishment'.

Then he shifted me around into one of those easier positions that put me on my side, so that he could still see my face as I came. He was like a man obsessed and sometimes I had to wonder if most of the pleasure found for him in the bedroom wasn't down to forcing orgasms on me. He liked to watch my face the moment I came, telling me once he had never seen anything more beautiful than that of my soul lighting up the way it did just for him.

"Now it's time I take care of my well-behaved wife for being so good for me," he praised and right there surrounded by unopened Ikea boxes, he kept his promise and took care of me...

Over and over and over again.

"You know, this doesn't mean you can get out of helping me put this stuff together," I said leaning over his bare torso and looking at all the cardboard that currently still littered our bedroom. He didn't say anything but simply started to raise his arm as he was about to click his fingers and it would be done. I quickly grabbed his hand in mine and stopped with a screech,

"No! That's not what I meant." His lips twitched as if he found this amusing but was trying to rein it in. Instead of laughing he raised an eyebrow in question and encased my little hand in his much larger one.

"And may I enquire as to why I am not to utilise the gifts the Gods deemed upon me on this occasion?" He asked with a smirk as if he knew this was going to be good.

"Because I am still human...or at least some of me is," I amended. At this he gave me a soft look before running a firm hand down my naked back and then featherlight caresses back up my spine. I shuddered at the feeling and couldn't help the small moan that rumbled out.

"Yes, you are but I think we should fully explore just which parts are...*for scientific purposes of course.*" He teased this last part over my lips before sucking in the bottom one and holding it dangerously in his teeth. I moaned again louder this time, and he let it go so that he could inform me seductively,

"I think we just found our first piece, Mrs Draven."

Shortly after this I found out that Draven hadn't been joking when he said he wanted to explore me, as 'explore' was just what he did. Every inch of me for that matter and there were both tears of laughter from tickling fingers, and tears from pleasure he inflicted upon those 'found human parts'...which according to him, were pretty much everywhere there was skin.

I could have sworn that sometimes it was as though Draven was trying to brand the memory of every inch of my body to his memory. I think it all stemmed from him seeing me die that day back in the Janus temple. I knew from experience that there was nothing more crushing in this world than believing your loved one had died, but for him, not only was he forced to see it, he was also forced to be the one that committed the act against his will.

This, for Draven, had snapped something deep inside him and I couldn't help but think back to that night after the war had been won...

After Draven had killed me.

But what I was soon to discover was that our troubles

were far from over and like most stories, this one needed to be told from the beginning.

A beginning that meant our Happy Ever Afterlife would have to wait and something I would have to fight Hell for...

Again.

CHAPTER FOUR

LOST, FOUND AND FATE IN BETWEEN

BACK TO THE BEGINNING
OUR WEDDING NIGHT

After the war in Hell had been won I would never forget waking up in Draven's arms and taking my first breath as myself again. Lucifer had taken Pertinax's blood from me and thankfully gifted me my humanity back. It wasn't exactly the first person I would have ever thought would have done this, as wasn't he supposed to be the bad guy? Well, he must have a soft spot somewhere under all that hard, scary muscle, that's all I am saying and also…

Who knew the Devil was a sucker for a love story?

But at the time all other thoughts were insignificant compared to what faced me now…

"Draven?" I spoke his name seeing his face now above

me, looking at me like a man who had almost lost his everything. Hearing me speak must have cracked something deep within him as I saw the unshed tears in his eyes finally give away to releasing one...two...three of them.

Then suddenly he pulled me closer to him, gripping the back of my head and holding it to his chest as he finally broke. I was in his lap and it was as if he had carried me back from Hell and then collapsed to his knees with relief the second we were back on Earth. He rested his head down on top of mine and let his tears of relief flow down his cheeks getting lost in the sea of my hair...his golden fleece.

"I thought... I had lost you...I thought...by the Gods Keira, I thought I'd killed you!" he whispered desperately into my hairline. I could feel him almost shaking and it was the most emotion I had ever witnessed from Draven. It nearly broke my heart to witness and I knew right now, I had to be the strong one for him this time as I knew this trauma wouldn't leave him for a long while to come.

So, I reached up with a hand that was free and placed it on his wet cheek, feeling the evidence of his heartache for myself. He finally released some of the tension in his hold so that I could move back enough to look up at him. The sight nearly undid me as my own tears seeped to the surface.

"But you didn't," I told him and just as he was about to argue I placed my fingers across his lips and told him more forcefully this time,

"But you didn't."

"How can you say that? I wasn't strong enough for you... I wasn't...I couldn't help..." he started to say but his pain wouldn't allow him to finish. It broke my heart to see him this way.

"Ssshh and listen to me when I say this Draven, for I love you and therefore I need you to understand what I am telling you." He finally stopped trying to fight my words with ones of his own when he lowered his head in defeat.

"You didn't kill me, you saved me, don't you see?" He finally looked back up at me in surprise and I swear in that moment I had never seen him looking more vulnerable.

"It wasn't only me you saved, but Draven, you also saved the world," I told him softly. He blinked a few times as if trying to process what I was telling him.

"No, you're wrong, I didn't save the world, Keira, *you did* …it was all you…it's always only ever been about you," he told me sincerely making me shake my head slightly.

"You don't see it, but I do…I do!" I shouted this last part compelling him to listen to me even when he turned his face away. I placed a hand upon his cheek and forced him to look back at me.

"Our fate, everything we ever did all led to this moment. And if you hadn't plunged that dagger into my heart then there would have never been a force strong enough to defeat him. He would have released the Titans and that would have been the end…the end of this world, our world we built, everything we hold dear…it would have been dust at our feet before we even had a chance to say goodbye to each other in it…there would have been nothing left in this world or the next…there would have been no Afterlife for us," I said trying to get him to see but he shook his head stubbornly and said,

"You are never going to make what I did right Keira, it just isn't…"

"Ssshh…I can always make it right, *because I have you,*"

I said stopping him mid flow by then placing my lips on his for the last of my words, finished with my own branding kiss, one he couldn't have stopped even if he had tried. I sat up and took his face in my hands holding him to me whilst his own hands anchored my body to his.

And it was in that moment that he finally let go of his guilt, one that could have been powerful enough to destroy a man. But love was what kept him with me and the sight of our future together was what anchored him home in the safety of my arms.

Once the emotional storm had subsided I pulled back and whispered over his lips,

"I was always fated to die and the gift you gave me meant I came back stronger…I fought for you Draven and I don't just mean the war, I mean much more than that."

"What do you mean?" I closed my eyes for a moment as my own emotions washed over me. Then I told him.

"You don't understand what it is you give me…*what you gave me."* He looked confused and before he could ask again I told him,

"I fought for you. Don't you see, I fought being a God and having all that power so that I could keep not only my humanity but mainly so that I could *keep you with it.* I may have fought the war for the rest of the world, but I fought against a God for you… *I fought against myself for you, Dominic."* The second I told him this he crushed my body to him and held me close so that he could breathe me in deep before letting out the last of his tears on a shudder.

"By the Gods *I love you,"* he told me fiercely and this time I let myself cry freely against his shoulder.

"And by the Fates, I love you too," I told him with just as

much strength in my words as my crying would allow. He pulled back and just as he lifted me so that we were no longer sat amongst the crumbling mess that was left of the temple, I tugged on his hand to get him to step back into me.

"However, I do hope you have enough of that love to go around?" I asked him with a smile and then looked down at my stomach before touching it with my hand. I had just remembered what the last thing he had been told before I passed out in Hell and now I wanted to see his reaction to the news myself.

He looked down at my hand and his eyes widened as if he too had just remembered what he had been told.

"Then it's true…it's…" He was suddenly lost for words and fell to his knees at my feet. Then he framed my belly with his hands as if he could see for himself the life we made. He kissed my belly and said,

"It's my child… *you carry my child,"* looking back up at me as if still stunned any of this was happening. Of course, seeing him this way soon made his astonished face blurry from my tears. But thankfully I didn't miss the beaming smile that quickly followed when I shouted,

"Yes! It's true, we are going to have a baby!" Then I threw my arms around him after jumping up into his arms just as he stood ready to catch me. And catch me he did…

Just like he always did.

After this blissful moment then came the difficult stuff. Everyone had witnessed our not so private moment, but in the end, it didn't matter to me or to Draven. As far as we were concerned, they were family and deserved to witness a small slice of the happiness they too had fought for. But there were those who didn't make it to the end and gave their life for the fight…

Sacrificed their life for the fate of the world.

The second I saw Draven look over my head his eyes said it all. I didn't need to ask or to see, I just felt it…

I just felt his pain.

"Ranka." I spoke his name and ran from Draven's arms over to where I could see Sophia and Vincent knelt by a lifeless looking body. By the time I got there I skidded to the floor and grabbed his face, now looking down at the woman his other side preferred to portray to the world. But it didn't matter now which side he wanted to show as this was where his journey was to end.

I had no idea where his final destination would be, but I just hoped for two things. One that as he left for it he was doing so being true to himself, for this was his last opportunity to do so. And the second, was that wherever he found himself he would finally find the happiness he had been fully denied by committing himself to a one-sided love.

But in the end the most shocking thing of all was that Draven had always known who he really was behind his mask. And I could say with absolute certainty that when Ranka did pass, he did so after finally finding peace.

But my heartache didn't have long to recover before another lost friend was seen. Because after Ranka came Jack and I found not only one body to cry over but two. I remember my shocked gasp when seeing Seth moving aside and looking down at Jack's lifeless looking shell that had been used and abused for all this time. Seth looked as though he had failed in his own private mission and I knew the truth of this was down to his love for RJ.

But as for my own heartbreak, well that was down to seeing my friend trapped between two worlds... a personal Hell he was imprisoned in and where his body remained. And worst of all there was nothing I could do to help him...*not one single thing.* I knew this when I felt the weight of Draven's hand on my shoulder as he didn't need to say a word. I just lowered my head and cried for my friend. It was only the sound of Seth's voice that cut through the moment.

"I...I failed her," he said, and my head shot up to face him before I raised myself to my feet.

"No, we all failed her. For there was nothing any of us could have done," I told him, but he turned his head away and replied,

"She is my responsibility."

"Yes, and he was mine. So don't take this away from me, for if you wish to point blame then that only ever belongs to me to carry because without me, he wouldn't have been here in the first place...and neither would RJ," I reminded him placing my hand on his arm and getting him to turn back to me. It was strange, but I could feel the pulsating of immense power that lay buried beneath the surface of his vessel as if kept firmly on lock down. He looked down at my hand on his arm before looking back up at me, showing me his death mask that flickered over his handsome face. I didn't even flinch at the sight of that living skull and I knew I probably wouldn't react to such things ever again...not after all I had seen.

He nodded his acceptance before shocking me with his next action. After a quick look to Draven, who must have given him the go ahead, he placed a hand at the back of my head and pulled me slightly forward so that he could kiss my forehead. Then he whispered,

"She is lucky to have you in her life little Queen, as are we all." Then he was gone by the time I looked back up and I didn't know how as I hadn't even seen him take a single step.

After this Draven found my hand and pulled me back to his side, then he turned me so we both faced the room together.

So we both now faced our people.

Because it was then that I realised something. I was no longer the outsider in all this. I was no longer just the human girl that was chosen to be loved by Draven, by their King of Kings. No, now I was something more. I was one of them, a Vampire, a Demon, an Angel all wrapped up into a Human host that was always mine to own from the very beginning. One born as me, not *for me* like the others. But that was all right, because I would take that and hopefully do wonderful things with it for all the years I know I now had ahead of me. I would take my given power and I would only use it to do good in this world...and the start of that would be keeping our family safe at all costs.

And speaking of family,

"My brothers, my sisters, my Kings at arms, I simply say this to you, for all you have done in keeping my Queen safe I can never repay you for such actions taken. I know this, for there are no limitations, no boundaries my gratitude would not reach and therefore nothing I do in this long lifetime would ever be enough."

"Well, there was that little added plus about her saving

the world we live in and everything, so I think we can call it even," Marcus said making Smidge groan before elbowing him.

"Yes, but I care little for saving a world Keira isn't a part of for she... *she is my world."* Draven had paused before saying this so that he could do so looking down at me. Hearing this perfect declaration of love once again had my tears finding a new home down my cheeks as I gripped his hand tighter. I then had to bite my lip to try and stop the girly sob that wanted to escape at one of the most beautiful things he had ever said. Then the unbelievable started to happen and it all started with Jared.

"I think I speak for us all when I say that we would follow you both into battle blindly for only to keep her soul alight would be worth dying for and My King of Kings, well, it has been a privilege protecting it for you." Then just as I had sucked in a sharp breath, he continued to shock me as he lowered down to one knee being the first to start the wave that followed him. First his own people all lowered to one knee, bowing their heads to us making me gasp behind my hand that flew up to cover my mouth in shock.

But the surprise continued as then even Sigurd bent his knee and keeping his eyes on me, lowered as did his father. I smiled through my tears as he winked at me, mouthing 'Little Apple' my way. Even Sophia and Vincent bowed down to us and I squeezed Draven's hand needing him right then to keep steadying me. I nearly buckled at the sight of so many important people in the Supernatural world all bowing for the first time to another. But this wasn't what pushed me over the edge as every single person lowered showing us their alliance.

No, it was the sight of Lucius that finally did it. He had been a face in the crowd I had tried not to search for but when he stepped to the front, then there was no way of getting away from it. I still remember seeing the utter heartbreak on his face when he too had thought me dead. The pain in his eyes had matched that of Draven's and thinking someone loved you with that level of intensity was one thing, but now *knowing* they did left you feeling breathless. Because my proof may have only happened in the seconds it took for me to draw in my last breath, but that's all love ever needed...

A single breath taken.

My lips started to tremble, and tears now followed the path of others soon finding the cracked floor beneath me.

Lucius only came to a stop when he was in front of me and Draven did the unthinkable. He took my hand and passed it to Lucius to hold. I looked back up at him questioning his actions, but his slight nod told me that Lucius needed this. So, I looked back up at my maker and held my breath at what was to come.

"Lucius, I..." I started to say when suddenly after taking a deep breath and closing his eyes as his beautiful phoenix erupted from behind him. A forbidden breath left me staring at him in awe but if I thought this sight a shocking one, then what was to come next nearly made my heart stop beating for the second time that night.

He started to lower himself so that he was kneeling at my feet. With my hand still in his, he brought it to his lips and before he granted it with a kiss he spoke gently over my skin,

"I would give my life for you, now and till the end of time...*my Queen.*" After this I threw my arms around him and lowered to my knees, crying into his shoulder. I knew this must have been hard on Draven, but he also knew how much I needed this too. We both owed so much to him that like Draven had said, the amount was immeasurable. Then I lifted my head and whispered back in his ear,

"As would I my friend."

After this emotional moment was witnessed by everyone, I knew it was all at an end when I once more felt my husband's hand weigh upon my shoulder. This was where he must have found his limit of seeing me in the arms of another man. I stood after Draven upturned his hand so he could help me up and the second I was on my feet, he pulled me possessively to his side.

Lucius also raised back to his feet in one effortless move and smirked at the sight of us, obviously knowing he could still get to Draven, as forever would be their love/hate relationship. Okay so it was mainly based on hate with let's say a sprinkling of mutual respect. But if Draven could stop himself from trying to rip Lucius' head off, then that was good enough for me. However, secretly I was still holding out for the day that I found these two sharing a drink together in friendship. But let's just say, I wasn't going to hold my breath or anything, new Vampire lungs or no Vampire lungs.

This was quickly the signal for the rest of them to all rise and for Draven, well he saw it as the time to take me away from all this chaotic aftermath.

"But what about all the people..." I started to protest

making him quickly yank me to his side so that I fell into him before he tipped my chin to make me look up at him and without saying a word he simply growled down at me. I turned to the rest of them and said,

"Okay, so we are just going to go now." This made most of them laugh and I looked to Vincent, but before I could ask he read my mind with just a look.

"We will take care of everything here." I watched as sadly this didn't just mean with dealing with the living above but also the two bodies below. However, only one of them had any real chance at living again and I just hoped and prayed that the key to that was discovered soon.

I mouthed the word thank you to them all and let Draven lead me out of the broken remains of a place that would now and forevermore remind us of victory. A new start this time not gifted by any Gods, but one conquered by humanity. So, with my hand in his, I let him lead me away, putting more and more distance between the evidence of the horror of what could have been. But when I looked back at everyone, the sight nearly took my breath away.

One look was all it took to almost have the tears back again. For looking back over to the small army we had lead into battle, one thing became clear. It wasn't one they had all fought just to save the world they lived in but also the people that meant the most to them in that world and it was the proof of this that I found so beautiful.

There was Jared who was stood ahead of his own people looking proud of all they had achieved and happy in the knowledge that he hadn't lost any of them in the fight. Marcus even had his arm around Smidge, who he had tucked to his side and given his jacket to so that she was warm. He was also currently looking down at her adoringly and her blush was the only indication she gave that she knew it too but chose to hide from it.

Orthrus came up to his brother and slapped his back before gifting him a look that said it all...another victory won together. I looked to each of them all, smiling at the couples like Otto and his husband Chase, Sophia and Zagan and even the usually pissed of Caspian was looking happy as now he had his oiled-up wife Liessa in his arms.

Sigurd was stood by his father and it was the first time I saw that there was an amused glint in their eyes that looked very similar, as if they had just shared in a joke together. Takeshi nodded to Hakan in respect after he had been slapped on the back by Ruto in excitement and the adrenaline that no doubt still coursed through his supernatural veins. The only people missing were Pip and Adam and I kind of felt sorry for her that she had missed all the action.

Of course, she would never know it, but her part played in protecting those dearest to me was what gave me the strength to do what was needed. To know at the time that they were being kept safe and protected by the strongest of us all was a hope that drove me forward. It gave me courage.

But knowing Pip as I did, this wouldn't matter as she would only see it as a missed opportunity for a kick ass fight. Maybe one day I would make her see what it had meant to me. However, I think I would wait until she was holding our baby in her arms, as it would only drive my point home more.

Now this was a thought that had me looking back up at

Draven to see him bow his head at the others in his own respect shown.

"Go be together, we will deal with things here...go and take care of each other." I heard Sophia say in my mind and I granted her a smile in thanks. And, of course take care of each other we did. I was surprised to see that our private doorway back into Afterlife was still intact making me wonder if it didn't have some kind of protection spell on it or something.

Of course, this was when I noticed something in the rubble making me grin uncontrollably. I remembered that night when I tried to convince a badass Hellbeast biker to lend me his jacket. The look on his face made me laugh out loud and before Draven could ask, I said,

"Just give me a second."

"Oh sure, it isn't like we just survived the end of the world or anything," he replied sarcastically making me laugh and I blew him a quick kiss before I started digging through the mess at what I had found. Then I dragged it up in triumph and shouted back at Jared,

"Well, would you look at what I just found!" Then I waved his precious leather jacket at him making the whole room erupt into laughter despite what they'd just faced.

His look said it all as first he looked down and shook his head as if he couldn't believe what I was doing. Orthrus slapped him on the back and muttered something I couldn't hear making him nod in agreement before he started walking towards me. Once he got close enough he took it off me, examined it for a second before speaking,

"I don't think you can class that as survived..." he said poking three fingers through the slash in one side before looking to Draven for a second. I don't know what he found there but after it he stepped closer to me and took my arm so that he could pull me to him. Once there he finished off his sentence on a whisper over my skin,

"...but I sure am glad you did, Doll." Then he gave me a kiss on the cheek before saying,

"You've got one *Hell* of a girl here Dom, but do me a favour, try and keep her out of it in the future," he said referring to having to help me get into Hell himself. Draven laughed and said,

"Oh, don't worry Hellbeast, I fully intend to." Jared laughed and muttered, 'yeah right' before walking back to the others, taking the ruined jacket with him and throwing it back over his shoulder casually as he went.

"Mrs Draven, if you please," Draven said holding out his hand for me to take so that I might get myself out of the rubble. The second I took it he pulled me free and spun me in his arms until my feet were slowly lowered to the floor. Then without another word he tucked me close to his side and walked us both back to our home...

Our Afterlife.

CHAPTER FIVE

NEVER ENOUGH

The second we were through the door into our bedchamber Draven spun me round to face him and pulled me tight into his embrace. He didn't speak but instead just held me to him as if he needed this moment. It was as though he had needed this more than I think I would ever fully realise but it didn't mean I couldn't show him what it meant to me. I did this by finally letting go of my captured emotions freely as I broke down in his arms. He didn't say anything but just held a hand to the back of my head, cradling me to him where I held on and gave him everything I had bottled up.

"I...I thought..." I tried to say through the tears, cutting the silence when he stroked a hand down my hair and said,

"Ssshh now, I know...I know Keira...*because I thought it too."* And right then in that one moment we didn't need any more words to say what we had both thought because we could feel it. We could feel the utter relief wash over us at knowing my death wasn't coming like we both feared. It was no longer a threat for us to see playing out in our nightmares like some macabre opera.

"Why didn't you tell me?" He had whispered into my hair before pulling back to look at me and after some time had passed. I knew what he referred to when he brought his hand down to my belly and ran the back of his knuckles down the centre. I swallowed down the emotional lump and bit my lip as I thought of how to word the reason why. When I imagined Draven finding out about me being pregnant it certainly wasn't by the Devil himself telling him after ripping a God's blood from my chest, that was for damn sure. Way to go on ruining that one for me Lucifer, I thought wryly.

"Because I was afraid. I knew that you believed as I did that by being pregnant was what would kill me. But now we know it has to do with the future." And it did. Lucifer's words had confirmed that. Our child would be the start of the Infinity war, one that the next generation would face and we would be ready for it right alongside them.

"I can't believe it's possible!" he said obviously getting used to the idea quickly and finally able to rejoice at the news. Then I giggled as he bent slightly so that he could lift me up by wrapping his arms around the tops of my legs and spinning me round before letting me go. I gasped just before he caught me again making me laugh.

"You won't be able to do that when I have a big bump in the way," I said breathlessly which made him stop dead and look down at me as if he was seeing it for himself. I bit my lip at the heated look he gave me. Wow, okay so what was that about? Did Draven like the idea of seeing me heavily pregnant…as in really, *really* like it?

*"I…*um…I look forward to seeing that," he replied after first having to clear his throat, something I rarely heard from Draven. It wasn't often he was stuck for words so when he was it shot a thrill straight to my core.

"Really?!" I asked him astonished. He gently pulled my bottom lip from my teeth and bent slightly so that he could be level with my eyes. Then he answered me in a deep rumble,

"Greatly." Then he swept my legs from beneath me and swung me up in his arms so he could carry me to the bed. A place I was thankful to say we spent the rest of our wedding night in utter bliss.

I could barely believe that we no longer had all the 'what could have happened' bearing down on our time together. No now, it was only filled with endless possibilities of what we could do together. What we could accomplish or seeing what our child would. Just to know that we would have each night like this. In each other arms finding our own happy rhythm in day to day life, which prompted me to ask,

"Do you think you will ever get bored with normality?" At this he gave me a quizzical eyebrow raise as he was currently on his side with his head leant against his hand propped up by his elbow. We were both naked after making love and he was currently running his fingertips lazily across my collar bone as if lost in his own thoughts. He laughed once and said,

"I think I recall telling you once that you belong to a Demon/Angel King who has to control the supernatural world, I think you can kiss normality goodbye, Sweetheart."

I smiled remembering this for myself which seemed like an age ago now. It was not long after Draven and I had become a couple. I almost laughed thinking back to that time. If anyone had ever told me back then that I would still be lay in his bed years later, married to him and carrying his baby I think I would have called them crazy.

But then I thought back to everything I had been through after that point and I think I would have then called them insane. Because looking back on all the things I had done in the name of love was insanity but of the best kind. After all, that's what love is all about. It's about sacrifice, it's about taking risks and having faith that somewhere in the dark depths of uncertainty then someone would take your hand and lead you to the light.

That they would lead you home to your heart.

Of course, at the time normal to me had simply been dating a man like Draven and trying to fit him into my life. But unbeknown at the time, this was never going to be the case. A being such as Draven wasn't ever going to fit that 'boyfriend' role within my world as I had first hoped. So, instead it was only ever going to be about fitting myself into his world and finding my place within it, which just so happened to be right where I was now, by his side.

Although like I said, at the time I was oblivious to all this and would be until first being taken by the one King who had kicked started my journey…Lucius.

But I didn't focus on that, no instead I simply informed him,

"I think you're forgetting something." Draven looked intrigued and obviously wanted to see where this game we played was going to lead so he asked,

"And that is?"

"You said King but back then I think you will recall that at the time that was something you had kept from me." He smirked and then replied,

"Well I knew that after a while of hearing others calling me their Lord that sooner or later you would catch on…my little wife is clever like that," he teased giving my nose a little tap.

"It was Sophia who told me!" I yelled making him feign mock surprise,

"Was it now, well I guess I gave you too much credit, I would like it back please and will take such in way of a kiss…tis a fair payment I think." I laughed as I smacked him playfully on the arm that was on perfect show and making my mouth water at just the sight of that naked muscle.

"I think being a married man has gone to your head and made you too cocky," I told him making him laugh again.

"Keira, I was already married to your heart, soul, body and mind the very first second I met you…you just didn't know it." I couldn't help but melt into his side when he said this. Then to hide my true feelings on what this did to me so that we could continue this playful banter, I muttered into his hard pec,

"See, totally cocky." I felt him start to shake as this time he laughed even harder, a sound I relished in and always would.

"Alright little one, let's hear it, what brought this on?" he asked all jokes aside. I lifted my head from his chest and pushed my hair back before taking a deep breath.

"Well according to the Fates, it's now over, the threat of the end of the world is gone."

"Yes, and I would say thank the Gods for that but in this case, I believe my thanks are given to only one Goddess, one I am looking forward to worshipping in this 'world of normality' of which you speak," he replied, and I groaned making him smirk.

"Oh, come on! Jeez what is it with you, before you met me, did you like take a 'smooth talk the Electus' class or something!?" I asked this time making him throw his head back and really laugh.

"Seriously my Love, if for my many lifetimes this is what you call normality then sign me up to drown in it because I can guarantee that I shall never tire of it!" I threw my hands up and moaned a dramatic,

"AH! There you go again, with the perfect answer! Can't you just fart at least once or something, just so I know you have at least one flaw!" Okay so I was getting weird, I knew this, but he still didn't seem to be bothered by it. No, if anything I was highly entertaining. He chuckled and said,

"So, body flatulence is what does it for you is it? Why, my little goddess you shock me! But I will make you a deal, for if you wish to show me how it's done... on our wedding night I might add... then please do, for I am as intrigued as you to hear the sound..." he then paused and leant in closer to me to whisper for dramatic effect,

"...but tell me, should I rate it accordingly and should we do so by sound or smell?" he teased tugging my body closer and in turn I kept trying playfully to get away from him, but he simply kept pulling me back making me laugh even harder.

"Alright, alright, you win but just so you know this, right

here, is normality," I informed him after motioning between us with my hand. He raised a brow and said,

"Talking about expelling bodily gas on your wedding night? Tell me sweetheart, is this a mortal custom or one of your very own you wish to start?" I tried to not to laugh and instead said in my own cocky swagger,

"I don't know, do you think it will catch on?" He tried to contain his smile as he quickly pulled me beneath him and said,

"With you in their bed, then I imagine there isn't a husband out there such as I who wouldn't do anything for his duelling vixen." At this I bit my lip and gave him a shy blush just before he homed in on my lip and told me,

"I believe I have warned you about that lip of yours many times now, for it belongs to me and therefore is only *mine to bite.*" This was my only warning before he swooped down for the attack, taking my lip for himself like he threatened. I moaned in his mouth just before he took me whole and consumed my senses with a mind-blowing kiss. I raised my hands up and embedded them into his hair to anchor him to me, never wanting to let go. I knew in that moment what my soul was telling me. So, I pulled him back making him release me on a growl so that I could tell him,

"I will never get enough of you..." I said fiercely holding onto him before bringing my hands round to frame his face, then I leant up and placed my forehead to his and whispered,

"Never enough Dominic, my husband." And if I thought Draven couldn't have fallen anymore in love with me until this point then I was wrong, as with that one look given I knew for him that this was his breaking point. I very briefly only managed to see the tears glistening in his purple eyes

before he crushed me to him and in one quick action, entered my body. It was as if in that perfect moment he needed to join our loving souls together and nothing in the world could have prevented the action.

This time no other words were needed. There were no demands or acts of dominance. There was no control or power shift between us. It was simply the two of us making love and using our bodies to communicate how we felt for each other. One hand framed my face as the other was holding my hand above, with his long, thick fingers firmly entwined in my slender ones. He looked down at me as if I was the most perfect and precious gift to him and that look alone brought tears to my eyes at the intensity of it all. Then he kissed me and we came together, tasting the sweet moans of our pleasure as we stepped over the edge of euphoria together.

The last words heard that night was after Draven placed his forehead to mine and whispered his own admission,

"Mine...*At Last.*"

And I was. I was his now and forevermore. Because I hadn't just gone to Hell and back for him, but went beyond the realms of the boundaries set against us. I broke every rule and destroyed every enemy in our way just to have this single moment in time. I said fuck to the Fates and walked my own path hand in hand with hope at seeing him on the other side. The Fates hadn't given me this, I had. I had done this and journeyed not only to the past but now with Draven's child growing inside me, had also touched our future. I had reached out and brushed against the endless possibilities, gifting me a glimpse into my perfect world.

A life with the man I loved.

That night our bodies remained connected to each other and we finally found peace in each other's arms, for nothing could come between us now.

And it was like Draven had said,

It was our…

At last.

CHAPTER SIX

TENDER LOVING NEEDS

I woke the next morning to the feel of fingertips caressing my naked back and the sensations made me moan and stretch out like a cat. I heard Draven chuckle before admitting,

"I love it when you do that." I raised my head up from the pillow I had been smushing my face into during this morning ritual of mine, so that I could look at him. I was just about to push all the wild hair from my face when he beat me to it. Then he leaned into me, kissed my forehead softly, and said,

"Good morning, Mrs Draven." Well after this the question I was going to ask him went right out of my head and was replaced instead with a massive cheesy grin. Then after a quick nibble on my bottom lip, I let it go so that I could reply with a blushing,

"Good morning, Mr Draven." I think the flash of purple flames in his eyes and the sexy growl I received was a good sign he liked hearing this, but the morning sex he gave me after it was confirmation that he *really* liked hearing this.

After our lovemaking I swiftly found myself being carried to the shower where I was thankful it was more than big enough for the two of us. But in Draven's mind being in the shower together didn't just mean getting clean together. Oh no, it was more about him first getting me dirty again before he took it upon himself to 'clean the mess he made'.

"I think being married to you will certainly have its benefits," I commented as I started towel drying my hair, bringing it all around to one side over my shoulder. I was currently in an oversized fluffy bathrobe that felt like heaven on my skin. But then the real heaven was what I was now fixated on and that was the sight of Draven in nothing but a towel hung low around his hips.

He had been looking at himself in the mirror and obviously debating on whether or not to shave as he ran a hand over his jawline as if testing the length of stubble there. Christ, but even the sight of him doing this was making me wish we were back in the shower. Jesus, but would I ever get enough of this man? Well as I had told him last night, I would never get enough of him and I smirked to myself knowing the truth of my words and his reaction to them last night.

"Be careful little wife, for that look alone speaks of sinful thoughts that will only manage to rouse my demon…*again,*" he warned me with a bad boy grin I could now see was dominating his lips as he looked at me sideways through the mirror. I smirked before walking up to him after casually throwing the wet towel off to the side and then when I was within reach, I raised myself up on my tiptoes and kissed his stubble covered cheek.

"Well lucky for you, I like it when your demon comes out to play…or should I say, *lucky for me.*" I added with a wink before turning to walk away…as usual with Draven, I didn't get far.

"You play with fire, Vixen," he growled in my ear before playfully nipping at my neck just below the lobe. He had picked me up in his arms and was walking us back into the bedroom with long steady strides. I giggled like some blushing adolescent teen in the arms of her first lover and the thought of what was to come.

But then my hopes of making this morning a sexathon hat-trick were doused in a bucket of ice. Draven lowered me to the bed, tapped me on the nose twice and then straightened his dripping muscular frame to walk past the bed frame. My mouth dropped open in shock and I mouthed silently 'What the hell just happened?' to the sight of his wide back.

"But have no fear, for I have something to cool you off, lustful wife of mine," he said over his shoulder before he whipped off his towel, baring his utterly delicious behind and making me inhale a sharp breath. Just the sight of that perfect tight ass connected to a pair of strong muscular thighs was enough to have me squeezing my legs together and biting my lip to keep a moan contained.

Then unbelievably he threw me his towel so that it landed on my nearly heaving chest with a wet slap. Then he turned back around and walked into his closet room chuckling as he went. My mouth dropped open making a perfect O shape before I frowned down at the wet towel.

"Not cool, Draven!" I shouted back in annoyance as I threw the towel on the ground in frustration making him laugh harder, the bastard!

I growled crossing my arms over my chest, angrily pushing back a few wet strands of my hair that had stuck to my face. Of course, then he walked back out of the door and all my anger morphed into desire at just the sight of him. He now had on a pair of fitted grey jeans, a slim black belt with rectangle silver buckle and a crisp white shirt he was still buttoning up over his eight-pack abs…Yep, I had counted them this morning.

I felt like looking up at the Gods and asking 'Why me?' because I felt as though I had no hope of surviving such a sight without becoming a puddle on the floor.

He was casually leaning against the doorway as he continued to cover up that heavenly Adonis body of his. Thankfully he stopped, leaving two buttons at the top so I could see his sun-kissed corded neck, one I just wanted to latch my lips on to. Oh, and didn't his smirk just tell me that he knew it!

"Still need cooling off, sweetheart?" he asked being cocky and then laughed when I snapped my gaping mouth closed and snapped back,

"Absolutely not!" Then after looking down to try and hide his secret smile, he pushed off the door frame, and circled the bed like a predator. I tried not to look at him, holding on to my annoyance at being turned down. Okay, so I failed only by the one glance I gave him and in that single look it was obvious he wasn't taking me seriously. Then I jumped when he finally pounced. He was on the bed and before I knew what was happening he was dragging my body down underneath his large frame by fisting the robe's belt that was still tied around my waist.

I slid down and after running a firm hand up my inner thigh did he speak.

"That's not what this hot little body is telling me, Keira," he told me, stopping just inches away from the sweet, sexual junction between my thighs. I took a deep and needed breath before I was just about to give in to him, seeing as he'd reignited the flames of desire once more. Then he lowered closer to my eager lips before whispering cruel words above them,

"A pity then that we have somewhere to be and a cooling off is all you will get." After this he quickly shook his head at me, making the last of the water droplets that clung to his hair shower my face in a spray.

"AH! Draven!" I shouted making him laugh before he kissed my cheek and got back off the bed. I sat up with my arms behind me as I watched him walk over to the seating area still chuckling to himself.

"That was mean!" I complained, and he just shrugged his shoulders and said,

"Demon remember…besides, as much as I would like nothing better than to spend the day in bed ravishing that delectable body of yours, we do in fact have somewhere to be." I frowned at the sight of him picking up a newspaper and folding it out as he sat down. In return I just folded my arms again and snapped,

"So, you thought it would be funny to see me getting all hot and bothered when you had no intention of doing anything about it?" At this I could tell he was trying not to laugh again as he was clearly enjoying himself. He shook the paper to straighten it and said without looking at me,

"I believe my intentions were known this morning… *twice,"* he added with a *knowing* look. At this I decided to play him at his own game knowing that I wasn't without my own powers against him. So, I huffed and slapped a hand to the bed before getting up. I noticed his lips twitch as he held the smug grin at bay and his eyes slid to the side for a second to watch me. Oh yes, this was going to be like taking candy from a baby…or better still, a plaything from a demon.

"Alright Draven, we will have it your way but just remember… *you started this!"* I warned him before whipping around, giving him my back and making my way to the walk-in closet without another look. Then once inside I decided to fight fire with fire and Draven was about to realise pretty quickly that payback was a bitch…or in this case, I was hoping for a sexy bitch!

So, with what I knew was a mischievous smile on my lips I undid my robe and gave my body a little shake to let it fall to the floor. Then instead of going to my side of the shared closet I walked over to Draven's. Once there I drew my hand across all his hanging dress shirts and grabbed a white one off the hanger saying,

"Oh yes, I think this will do nicely." Then I threw it across the velvet armchair situated in the corner and got to work.

After a rushed twenty minutes, I had dried my hair like a mad woman, knowing parts of it were still damp and therefore wild and curly. I even flicked most of it over to one side giving it wicked volume. Then after finding some black stockings that gripped the tops of my thighs without the need for a suspender belt, I found a black thong to match. I even managed to find some black stiletto heels that I thought would add that nice touch.

After this all that was needed was Draven's shirt that I barely buttoned up. This meant leaving the bottom loose, leaving the tiny black triangle in between my legs to be seen barely covering my modesty. Then I did up two buttons over my stomach and left the rest, so in between my breasts could be seen. Then after quickly making sure my nipples were hidden I stepped towards the door, took a deep breath and faced my next foe in battle...*Draven's willpower.*

I stepped into our room to find him still sitting in the same seat reading the newspaper. I decided to clear my throat to get his attention and the second I did I found it hard to keep a straight face. He turned his head slowly to find me leaning against the door frame like he had been earlier. I looked down slowly at myself and then seductively crossed my legs by the ankles trying to act casual.

Then I looked up to see him swallow hard before slowly folding the paper and placing it down next to him. Then he turned to me and the liquid fire I saw in his eyes made me want to cheer in my victory. But I knew I wasn't yet finished in my revenge...oh no, not yet, not by far.

"Come here," he ordered sternly, motioning me over with a flicker of his index fingers. This was when I knew I had him right where I wanted him.

"I am sorry Mr Draven, didn't you say we needed to be somewhere...only I forgot to ask whatever should I wear, for I am at a loss," I told him making a show of licking my lips and playing innocent. I saw him visibly try to get a handle on his reactions, as he took a deep breath and clenched his hands into fists a few times by his sides. I had been tempted to ask if that helped but from the next carnal look he gave me, well I would have said that was a big fat no!

I tried not to flinch as he slapped his hands to his knees before standing. He definitely looked to be fighting with himself and I had to wonder if it was in fact his demon that wanted to take control? Every single movement of his looked strained and precise.

"I think if you went anywhere looking like that I would tear the whole fucking room apart, along with anyone in it that witnessed that sinful body of yours," he told me with not only a deep huskiness to his voice but also a growl lacing his every word. Hearing this I blushed, one that I knew wasn't only confined to my cheeks. No, I felt the heat of his words bloom over my body making me want to squirm under that intense stare of his. Okay, so maybe this hadn't been a good idea because it was like he said, if I hadn't been playing with fire before, then I was definitely playing with it now...Hellfire!

When in Rome, I thought with an inner shoulder shrug. So, I paused by putting a finger to my lips, cocking my hip and faking innocence once more before saying

"Well, if you think I should go change..." Then I turned around showing him what I hoped was the enticing view of my bare cheeks just peeking below his shirt. The groan I heard made me smile to myself before I looked back over my shoulder at him. Oh yes, I was making him pay all right! He looked as though he didn't know what to do first, chase me down or chain me to the bed to punish me.

Then I made it even worse for him and asked seductively,

"What's the matter Draven, need cooling off?" I followed this through by turning back to face him before bending a leg to place it back against the door frame I still leant against. His eyes widened in shock as I then let my leg fall open slightly granting him the view of my barely covered sex. The cherry on the top was sucking in my bottom lip slowly and thus completing my payback.

He smirked looking off to one side before shaking his head as if he could barely believe I would have the guts to be doing this. After this he muttered something to himself in another language before his head snapped back up and he stalked towards me. He quickly closed the space between us and soon I was looking up at him. He stretched out, resting his forearm above me and started drumming his fingers against the wooden frame as if he was deciding what part of me to eat first. He looked like a hungry wolf and for a second I had to look down to check I wasn't wearing a blood red cloak.

His other hand came up and started to gently skim his knuckles down in between my breasts, moving the shirt out of his way as he went. It was tantalisingly slow and torturous, making me hold my breath just so I wouldn't shudder against him.

"And just when I thought I had seen it all, she goes and does this to me," he said this time making me swallow hard.

"I…I'm not sure I know what you mean?" I said clearing my throat and pushing through my nervousness, so I could follow through with my plan. He leaned further into me and said,

"Oh, I think you know exactly what it is you do to me…

Vixen." He growled out my sexual pet name this time making me unable to hold back my shudder.

"Is that so?" I asked putting my leg down so I could reach up higher on my tiptoes. His eyes were completely lost to a purple abyss and they burned brighter with my question.

"Yes," he forced out through gritted teeth making me smile because I was about to complete my plan, happy I was seeing it through to the end.

"Then it's a shame you won't get to show me... *My Lord,"* I said calling him this over his lips but just as he was going to kiss me I pulled back and went to turn my back on him. Seeing this his hand stopped its gentle journey down my stomach so it could fully flatten over my belly, quickly holding me pinned to the door. He placed his lips to my cheek and let his demon growl at me. My only answer to this was a simply cocky reply,

"Your plans and your rules remember." At this he yanked me to him hard making me gasp against him. Then he tipped my chin up so I was looking at him before he ground out the last of his restraint,

"Fuck my plans and fuck my rules! *You're all mine!"* And as if to prove this he quickly grabbed my ass with both hands and lifted me so I could wrap my legs around his waist. Then he pushed me into the closest wall, holding me trapped there. Okay, so this was the part of my plan that was quickly flying out the window and it was all because he had his hands on me. I wished I could have said I was stronger than that but who was I kidding, this man could shred my willpower to pieces like a tornado could rip through a tissue factory!

Once he had me where he wanted me he yanked his shirt

off my shoulder so he could get to my skin, quickly sinking his fangs into my neck. I cried out at the pain but was seconds later crying out at the pleasure that first suck on my neck caused me.

"Yes! Yes! YES!" I shouted holding his head close so he could continue to feast on me. It was a sexual taboo that felt as right as it did wrong. The forbidden was being unleashed and my head fell back helplessly when I felt my own warm blood dripping down in between my breasts. It was such a carnal act of lust that I almost expected any minute that Draven would throw his head back and howl in victory at the pray he had caught.

But then something within me clicked and this was when I wanted to get in on the action. So, before I knew what I was doing I fisted his hair and snapped his head back, forcing him to release his prize. He snarled at me and the sight of my blood still dripping down his chin made my mouth water. Oh yeah, I was a changed woman alright, and it was time he saw a glimpse of her.

"My turn!" I snarled back before I attacked. I fell on to his neck like my life depended on it and the second I sank my own fangs into his neck and tasted his blood, it was like tasting Heaven's wine. The roar of pleasure that rippled through him made me suck harder and for a moment I wondered if the pleasure of it would bring Draven to his knees.

His hand snapped out quickly bracing himself against the wall and I vaguely heard the crumbling of stone next to me. In the end Draven must have thought it wise to utilise the bed before he did something very out of character like drop me. The thought made me smile around my hold of him.

He gripped me tighter so he could stumble a few steps backwards until the edge of the bed hit the back of his legs. Then I decided to up this control I had over him a notch or two…or maybe ten, if what I had in mind went to plan. So, the second his ass touched the bed I launched all my weight forward, taking him off guard so he fell backwards.

I pulled my teeth from his neck and looked down at him, making a show of licking his blood off my lips.

"By the Gods," he hissed at the sight, gripping my hips in a tighter hold as if this was a natural reaction. I grinned down at him as I sat back feeling this newfound power raging through me as if igniting my veins. Then I grabbed his belt buckle and told him on a growl,

"I'm still hungry." This was his only warning before I ripped it open then doing the same with his jeans. His eyes widened at seeing this new side of me and before I gave it thought on how I was going to take his pants off without leaving him, they suddenly started to disappear. Like every tiny thread was being erased from this world and soon I found him lying beneath me completely naked.

"I think it's only fair you do the same," he informed me with his voice still thick with desire. I looked back up at him as I slowly climbed up his frame. I placed a hand flat next to his face and lowered my lips to his and after sucking in his bottom lip to bite, I told him,

"Fuck your rules remember, now it's time for mine!" He tried to nip at me as I moved away, looking more and more like the beast he was in Hell than the gentleman he could be on Earth. I smiled again, knowing what I was doing to him.

"Now stay still while I take what's mine…and like I said, *I am still hungry my King,"* I said seductively before looking down at the feast laid out hard before me. His eyes widened in surprise and just as he lifted his body further up the bed, I crawled backwards positioning myself over him, ready to take that first sinful taste. I looked up at him as his eyes were glued to the sight. I was surprised that I no longer found myself shy when keeping eye contact with him as I normally would have. Especially not when I took his hard long, thick shaft in my hand. The second I touched it he shuddered, but if I thought this was a good reaction then the second I licked up its full length from base to tip... well let's just say that he went crazy.

"Fuck!" He swore, letting his head fall back at the intensity of it all as his back bowed off the bed. Oh yeah, my King liked that. I smirked to myself. I couldn't believe the high I was getting from this. It was unlike anything I had ever felt before. The power of being able to do this to him was unlike anything I had ever experienced, and I fucking loved it!

So, with this in mind, I suddenly cupped his heavy sack and took the full length of him in my mouth this time making him roar at the ceiling. He had his hands fisted in the sheets that he was tearing apart with the intensity of it all. I knew he liked that, so I upped the game and gripped him more firmly in both hands running them up the full length of him. Then I sucked on the top, paying extra attention to the wet slit that was currently feeding me a delicious pre-come. I couldn't help my reaction to the taste. I suddenly sucked him down again this time moaning around his solid shaft causing him little vibrations all up the sides.

"Fuck...FUCK! Keira! Gods woman what it is you do to me!" He growled with his eyes closed and his neck straining back as he threw his head back once more. The sight had me nearly coming and I shamelessly started rubbing myself against his thigh. This was when I started going crazy on him, making a meal out of him and when he started to try and stop me, I only let him go long enough to snarl back up at him.

"Mine." The only word hissed from my lips before I took him back into my mouth. I was like a woman possessed and when he started to try and warn me that he couldn't hold it back much longer, well then this just drove me on. I wanted him to explode and I wanted to drink him down like an orgasmic elixir. I knew I needed it because just the idea of him finding his release this quickly was like feeding a new addiction. I wanted to do to him what he always had the power to do to me. I wanted him wild and begging, which was precisely what he was doing.

"Please...have mercy on me Vixen, give me...give yourself to me..." But I wouldn't stop and give him what he wanted. So instead I gave him what I wanted! Soon his begging was being swallowed by my actions as I lowered enough to do something I hadn't ever done before. I licked down his soft sack, bringing my tongue up the length of him before suddenly swallowing him down again, this time more forcefully. And this for Draven was what did it!

"Give me...No, Stop...Oh fuck Keira...AHHH!" He suddenly roared his release as if it had hit him so unexpectedly the strength of his actions couldn't be contained. He quickly gripped the bedpost in one hand crushing a chunk out of it with the force of his hold. Of course, I wasn't helping as I made a meal out of swallowing him down and humming out my pleasure from the brazen act.

"Fuck me…Gods be damned!" He cursed again, and this was no doubt down to taking even more of his length and using my tongue to swirl around the head. I felt his hand at the back of my head, holding me there terrified that in that moment I would move away from drinking down the next burst of come that flooded my mouth. The action along with the taste of him bursting across my tongue was what made me come, finding my own release shamelessly against his leg.

"YESSSS!" I screamed as I rode his leg shamelessly after first burying my head into his thigh. After this I couldn't help but go back to my meal for one last taste and it was only after I had swallowed every drop and licked him clean that I would finally let go of my prize.

That and after he begged me to,

"Have mercy upon my tortured soul sweetheart and release me," he begged making me let him go. The second I looked up at him I finally saw the damage my act had caused.

"Oh," I uttered in shock as it was obvious, I was back to being me again and all signs of feisty Vampire bride was now gone. Draven however had very nearly destroyed the bed. One of the posts had chunks out of it that littered the bed with large splinters. The sheets had been torn and Draven even had what looked like a self-inflicted bite mark in the side of one hand as if he had at one point put a fist in his mouth. There was blood trickling down his hand and I watched as it started to heal slowly.

"Come here my shy Vixen," he told me softly and I

looked down at myself knowing what I would find if I moved. So, I decided to do something very out of character because let's face it, after what I had just done, what was stopping me now. I got up and said,

"Okay, so don't move." Draven sat up and gave me a questioning look with his usual eyebrow raised at me.

"Please just stay here," I said again pulling my shirt together a little as I got off the bed.

"I have to say, I am not liking this part, Keira" he forced out telling me I had about five seconds to get what I wanted before he would start becoming demanding.

"Just give me a sec...okay." I then quickly ran into the bathroom, grabbed a cloth and dampened it under the tap.

"You have three seconds left darling and then nothing will stop me from coming to get you!" I heard him bellow from the bed and I jumped at how much it sounded as though it had come from his demon side.

"Coming!" I shouted grabbing the cloth and running back to him. I couldn't help but bite my lip, holding back my satisfied smile as I saw he hadn't moved for me. Then he nodded to the cloth in my hand and I couldn't help blushing shyly before telling him gently,

"I wanted to take care of you," I told him before kneeling on the bed, so I could wipe his leg, one I had shamefully left a wet patch on from finding my own release. I sneaked a look at him, seeing his soft eyes watching me, all signs of earlier frustration long gone. I felt my face get hot and looked away from his intense stare, so I could clean the other part of him. And this I did with shaky hands, which was ridiculous considering what I had just done to him. But I

CHAPTER SEVEN

FACING YOUR YOUNGER DEMONS

After this I found out that Draven's plans had been for us to go back to the hotel, so we could spend some more time with family seeing as we didn't get much chance to do this on our actual wedding day. I remember laughing at the pained expression Draven gave me when I got up off the bed still wearing just his shirt and declared,

"I'd better go change then."

"I fear I made a mistake making such plans, for I can think of better ones I wish to choose instead," was his reply and I looked back to see his eyes solely focused on my bare behind. I decided to be cruel and I lifted up my arms faking a yawn and a stretch as I knew it would give him a better view as his shirt rose higher up my bum. I saw his eyes widen before a ring of purple flashed brighter making me giggle and give up the game. His eyes shot to mine to see I had been teasing him and his growl made me chuckle.

"You are cruel to me," he complained, and I let out a quick laugh before informing him,

"That's not what you were saying a minute ago." His lips twitched as he fought a smile before he shifted off the bed. I couldn't help but marvel at the sight of him naked and watch as his muscles danced with each movement he made. The erotic sight made me momentarily forget our sexual banter and just made me think about sex. He walked the few steps to me and lightly grazed his hand across my bum, looking down at it as his hand made the curvaceous journey. It was as though he wanted to spend the time admiring the view, a thought that made me blush and restrain myself from looking down to see what it was he saw.

"Keeping this exquisite body from me is always a cruelty, Keira," he told me and now my lips were the ones twitching to hold in the massive, victorious grin I was trying to hold back after hearing this.

"Ah, this pleases you I see," he told me, and now I had not only to try and hold back a smile but also a laugh as I feigned ignorance.

"I don't know what you mean."

"What I mean is that smug, contented grin you are failing at trying to hide tells me all I need to know." Ah well I guess I was busted then. I decided if this was the case I might as well give up the game and instead did something cocky by reaching up and kissing him softly on the cheek.

"What can I say honey, but I learned from the best." Then I patted his chest before walking away, although Draven had other ideas. He snagged my hand and yanked me back to his body.

"Where are you going?!" he demanded and once I was

back tucked tightly against his large body, he kissed me, showing me that my statement meant far more than just teasing, as I certainly learned to kiss from the master who currently had me in his arms.

After this it became even harder to get Draven to let me go so I could change, and I found that this also included him following me into the closet to watch me as I found a new outfit. One more fitting for a social event with my mortal family. Of course, doing this when he was so confidently unashamed of his naked self then I had to say it wasn't the easiest of tasks.

"I have to say, I look forward to the day I have to take you shopping of a different kind," he said finally moving to his own side and putting me out of my lustful misery by putting on some clothes.

"Don't you want to…uh…like…well…you know…" I said being as eloquent as always.

"Words, sweetheart," Draven said smirking to himself as he picked a pair of jeans from the shelf.

"I just thought you would want to shower first…you know before…I mean well after…you know," I said rolling my hand around trying not to say it. Then I decided to put my chunky knitted sweater over my head just so that I could hide from his obvious amusement. In the end I felt it being pulled down over my head but not by me.

"You know I find it utterly astonishing that out there, only moments ago, I was rendered half a man and imprisoned with just the sight of you." He pulled me to him, used both hands to lift my hair free of my sweater and then after leaning in, his husky voice came to my ear,

"The way you took my cock into your hot demanding

mouth and sucked me deep, milking every last drop of me to swallow down like a greedy little Vixen that spoke only of her hunger for me." Hearing this made me shudder and close my eyes as the erotic memory assaulted me.

"And now you can barely even speak, stumbling on your words like I had just ravished a virgin wearing white," he said pulling on my white sweater, so it slid off my shoulder making his point, as it just so happened to be the same colour as the shirt he now wore once again. I gave him wide eyes looking up at him and this time he bit his lip at the sight.

"Gods woman, I don't know which look has more power over me, the sex kitten that shows me her claws and makes me want to punish her body or this one that looks up at me now, a look that simply makes me want to worship at your feet." This time I joined him in biting my own lip before I said,

"I honestly couldn't tell you which one I would prefer but both sound nice." At this he laughed before kissing me on the forehead and speaking in my hairline,

"And there's my girl." The squishy, mushy love feeling I got hearing this made my toes want to curl…if this was a cartoon and that was physically possible.

"And in answer to your cryptic question, no I don't wish to shower, for that would rid me of your scent, *one that I am quite enjoying knowing is still marked along my thigh,"* he said before moving away to continue getting himself ready. The second he turned his back to me I mouthed the word, 'oh god' looking up to the ceiling wondering if there wasn't in fact a sex god up there that had educated this man in the art of seduction. I even felt the need to cover up my shoulder to protect myself as I hugged the big knitted fold up to my neck.

"You look like you fear I will soon pounce on you and sate my animalistic lust for you," Draven said after giving me the once over and finding the sight of me both an amusing and arousing one. I laughed anxiously when he decided to play with me, first slapping his hand on the marble topped island in the middle of the room. I jumped, shrieking and once again laughed nervously. His look said it all... *he wanted to chase.*

I looked to the door to see how far I could get before he reached me, then I glanced back not expecting the demon that was now looking back at me. I vaulted back a step and his demon liked the submissive action as he grinned, showing me a slight lengthening of his fangs.

The rush of adrenaline that flooded my sexual addiction for this man was almost making me lightheaded. But then he raised an eyebrow at me as if questioning what my next move would be. I did the same back to him, shrugging my shoulders as if I would do nothing, then I shrieked in excitement before I ran for it!

Actually, I was surprised I made it out the door and to the other side of the bed before he reached me. He swung me up making me yelp breathlessly and once he had me he pretended to be a wicked beast. The sight of him with his wings glowing freely along with the pulsating purple glow beneath his veins was enough to make me come undone. He then gripped my neck in his hold, securing my flesh in his teeth before growling as though he was about to feast upon me. I laughed and giggled at the playful noise he made, knowing this game was all simply to make me smile and not in a sexual way as it had started out. I loved the feel of his smile against my skin and soon he was peppering the length of my neck with little kisses that tickled.

"But wait, what did you mean when you said about shopping of a different kind?" I said thinking back to what he said earlier and now making him burst into laughter.

"Only you," he responded now being cryptic himself before answering me,

"I was referring to the joy of watching your body swell as our child grows inside you." He looked down at me and I couldn't help my reaction.

"What you mean is how funny it will be so see me get plump and waddle around like a duck." At this he laughed again but now with the added shake of his head. I patted his cheek and said,

"But if it helps, you made it sound a lot nicer." Now this had him roaring with laughter and I shook from still being in his arms.

"I look forward to seeing it all," he told me sweetly walking us into the living space.

"I do have to wonder though at how this happened or when we conceived for that matter," Draven mused and I couldn't help it as I went rigid in his hold... *he didn't yet know*.

He paused mid step, so I knew he had felt my 'oh shit' moment for himself and I found I couldn't look at him as he placed me gently on the couch.

"Look at me, Keira," he demanded softly, and I shook my head telling him all he needed to know. I felt his hand at my neck before his thumb pushed my face up as he forced his command on me. I don't know what he saw in my eyes, but I knew guilt was definitely one emotion that was going to be on the table.

"Okay, so I think we need to talk." Draven frowned down at me before taking his own seat, replying with a curt,

"If that guilty look is anything to go by, then yes, I would say that we do." I knew it was a cop out, but I couldn't help but try my luck when I said,

"But aren't we going to be late, I mean this can wa…"

"No, it can't wait but the rest of the world can, so I suggest you start talking, heart of mine, for I believe this conversation is long overdue," he said swiftly interrupting me. Okay, so I guess there was no getting out of it then, I thought with a gulp.

"Well, you say that but technically I only got back from Persia yesterday…so it's not really that…" I never finished that sentence as the rumbling of displeasure coming from his chest told me it was time to stop. That and the sight of him closing his eyes as if he was trying to ask the Gods silently for patience.

"Okay, so it's not that bad but can you at least try to promise me that you will try and not shout at me and rein in that temper of yours?" I asked making him groan aloud before saying,

"Well, if you are asking this of me then that question alone tells me the first part of your statement to be false, for I doubt it is *far from good.*" Okay so he had a point there, but I decided to ignore this little truth and just dive right in with a question, as it would be nice to know how much his sister had actually told him…as in the little details, oh say, first meeting him with a blade held to my throat.

"So, can I ask first what Sophia told you?" His look said it all, but his words only confirmed it,

"I will tell you what sweetheart, why don't you explain to me what really happened and then I shall see if it matches her very brief and extremely vague recollection of the last seventeen days." Oh yeah, so this was definitely an oh shit moment. I laughed nervously and shifted around on the seat.

"Do you think this sweater is too much, I mean it's warmer here but I'm not sure about when we leave, you know what English summers are like, one day it's sunny and then the next it rains for a week and I think…" Draven finally took pity on me and placed two fingers over my lips,

"You're stalling, love." Well at least he was looking less pissed off at the sight of my nervous rambling.

"Who me?" I said trying to sound innocent and hoping my next stalling tactic would mean at least ten minutes worth of banter.

"Yes, *you*," he replied tugging me closer to him obviously hating going too long with any space between us. If anything, you would have thought that he had experienced those seventeen days without me for himself. Not the few hours it had been.

"You think by now I would know better," I teased making him fight a grin. Oh yeah, he knew what I was doing.

"You would think so, yes but considering you were exactly seventeen days and one hour late for our wedding, then I think you would agree that we can call this a lesson not yet learned," he replied sternly, and I hated his damn logic! But then he pulled me closer still, so he could push back some of the hair from my face. Then as he concentrated his gaze on his own action he said,

"But have no fear wife of mine, for there is no time like the present to rectify this failing, starting of course with the next words out of your mouth being the very thing you are still keeping from me." The last of this sentence was said with his gaze firmly back on me and his eyes spoke of only one thing….my time for stalling was well and truly over. So, I took a deep breath and then another one for good luck before just getting it all out in one go.

"Alright so here it is…the real reason for me going back in time was so that I could trick your younger self into getting me pregnant because the oracle told me that would complete the prophecy and I knew that *you* knew this, but you refused to…well…give up the goods shall we say, as you believed it would mean my death. So, I thought the only way was to go back in time and well…get knocked up." Of course, his first reaction to this was to stand up and shout,

"You slept with him?" He seemed outraged and my mouth dropped open in shock. Had I just heard him right… had he just referred to his younger self as someone else?

"Uh no, I slept with *you*…big, *big* difference here," I said holding my hands out like I was holding an imaginary box that kept getting bigger.

"So, you cheated on me!" he yelled accusingly, raking a hand so violently through his hair I was surprised there was anything left, and he didn't now have a palm full of silky black strands. All I can say is he must have had supernatural strength roots and I wasn't talking about his mother and father.

Upon hearing this I laughed, quickly ignoring his scowl on hearing it.

"No, I didn't cheat because that's kind of hard to do when it's sleeping with the same person," I informed him calmly, thinking this would help him see things straight. Or so I had hoped.

"I have no memory of this and *definitely no* say in the act, so therefore it is very much classed as cheating," he informed me, folding his arms across his wide chest and this was when I stood up and matched his defensive stance for one of my own.

"Oh sweetheart, you may have been in the world a lot longer than I, but you've obviously still got a lot left to learn if you think sleeping with the same man in a different time zone is classed as *cheating!*" I said starting this argument off with sarcasm and ending it on a hiss.

"Different time zone…really Keira, that's what you're going for?" He asked after shaking his head once as if trying to make sense of what I had just said and coming up empty.

"Look, I know what I did wasn't cool but…"

"Not cool! Not cool?!" he shouted repeating this twice as if he couldn't believe it. However, I just ignored it and carried on, more forcefully this time.

"…*But*, I am not going to stand here and listen to you try and make out like what I did was cheating on you!" I shouted making him frown back at me.

"You slept with another man!" he snapped back and that was when I lost it,

"I slept with you, you big ape!"

"Did you just call me a big ape?" he asked incredulously.

"Well if the hairy ass shoe fits, Mister!" I replied angrily now making him fight a bloody grin once again. I couldn't believe it and he knew it when I asked,

"Seriously Draven I am starting to think you have multiple personalities or is it just your Demon that's pissed off with me for missing out on sex?" I asked making him growl this time and I knew it wasn't Draven but the Demon in question.

"Careful Keira, you tread on thin ice with that one." At this I threw up my hands and shouted a dramatic,

"AAHHH! Men! Jesus Christ, they can be Angels, Demons, bloody lost creatures from the blue lagoon, but if they have a penis then they are all the bloody same!" I shouted and just before he said anything about the Jesus Christ comment I held up my hand to stop him,

"Oh no, don't say a word for I think this time you can bloody well give me this one! And as for threatening me with your Demon, well if you think by now that shit scares me then you don't know me very well, because as far as I am concerned he is a damn pussy cat compared to this pissed off wife!" I yelled at him shocking him, although I don't know who was more shocked in that moment Draven or our little audience that we hadn't realised had opened the door.

"Well okay then, I guess we will just be going," Vincent said backing up and trying to pull Sophia along with him. She smirked and said,

"Wow they don't do things by halves, do they? I mean what was that, all of nine hours of marital bliss before their first fight as a married couple?" Me and Draven both turned to the door and shouted different things, his was one word roared,

"LEAVE!" Mine on the other hand was,

"He thinks I cheated on him WITH HIMSELF!" I screamed this last part and both Vincent and Sophia looked at each other awkwardly before saying,

"Righty, okay, so we will just go and…" Vincent didn't finish, and I just heard Sophia as she said,

"I guess this means a family dinner instead of family lunch it is then."

"Anyway, what did you think was going to happen in the past Draven, because trust me, you certainly weren't living life as a damn priest. No, your harem full of exotic sluts on tap told me that!" I snapped and for once I wanted to smack that knowing half grin from his perfect lips.

"Oh yeah, how do you think that one made me feel huh!? Do you think that nipping back to the past was like a damn erotic holiday for me? Do you think that when I first saw you holding a blade to my throat was going to be fun for me? Or then finding myself in a pit of jealous vipers that wanted to rip off my head and fill it full of dates!" I said and finally my words hit home, and he started to lose grip of his anger at me in sight of something else and damn if he didn't just home right in there on it.

"What do you mean a fucking blade to your throat?!" Oh yeah, trust him to focus on that bit I thought bitterly.

"Exactly what it sounds like, my first sight of you was with a blade in your hand and one you held to my throat for causing a ruckus in your throne room," I said and once I was finished I knew he was trying very hard for my sake to keep a lid on his temper as he closed his eyes and held the bridge of his nose as if this would help. I also had to wonder if he wasn't counting in a different ancient language as another form of coping mechanism…well he was certainly muttering something, and I had a feeling it wasn't all his fuzzy warm feelings about his pain in the ass new wife.

"Jesus!" he hissed, and I was just about to call him up on now being the one to curse his name, as he usually did with me but then just like I had done, he held up a hand and warned,

"Don't." I had to say, that if we hadn't been arguing I would have seen the humour in it but as it stood it currently looked like Draven was trying not to rip something apart.

"Explain the ruckus?" he asked in a strained tone.

"Oh, it was just some asshole, he called him a Royal Sap... stat... or something, anyway I accidently pushed into him..."

"That doesn't sound so bad..." he started to say but then I finished by adding the worst bit,

"Yeah well then, he grabbed me, so I punched him in the nose."

"You punched A Royal Satrap! Fuck Keira!" Draven shouted in utter shock, swiping an angry hand down, slicing the air. I took this reaction in and gathered this was a big no, no of his time.

"Yeah well, what else was I supposed to do, he grabbed me by the throat and then called me an ugly little whore before pushing me?" Draven's eyes quickly looked murderous when hearing this and he snapped,

"I am surprised I let him live after witnessing it!" Okay so this side of Draven I liked. The one where he was no longer blaming me but the asshole who was nasty to me.

"...But I am seeing where this is headed, for you no doubt left me little choice but to act on the offence."

"Well yeah, the next thing I knew you were at me in a

heartbeat and had your blade to my neck. Although, to be fair to your younger self, you were actually quite nice about it." He gave me a quizzical looked, silently asking me the question.

"Let's just say you were gentle with me and very careful not to hurt me, I think it was more for show than anything else."

"Oh, I know it was more for show, one that as King, I had no choice but to put on. What did I do to the Satrap?" he asked abruptly, and I had to inwardly smile knowing Draven well enough to know he wouldn't have let him get away with hurting me, even back then.

"You humiliated him and manipulated the situation so that he insulted you first, then you basically told him that if he wanted your forgiveness then he would also need to accept mine...I think your exact words were, 'are you yourself willing to extend the same forgiveness to an act against you that was equally as insolent as the disrespect you showed your King?'" I repeated the same words back I'd heard him speak that day, knowing that every sentence said by him that day would be forever imprinted on my memory.

"Yes, well that would do it, but I would be surprised if I let him live for long after that day," Draven commented making me frown.

"I think that would have been a bit drastic Draven, you had only just met me." What he said next confirmed just how much he really didn't know.

"No one raises an aggressive hand to my Electus and lives to see the next sunrise, now or two thousand years in the past! For time doesn't matter, the outcome would be the same." My look must have said it all.

"What?"

"Uh…well…" I stumbled for my words again and saw once more my husband's patience was slipping.

"Just tell me, Keira." he said in a way that told me he was close to reaching his limit.

"Well…okay so, you didn't know I was your Chosen One, Draven," I said tentatively and wincing after it. He was so taken aback by this he took a step back before swiftly taking two forward, coming closer to me to say a disbelieving,

"Come again?" At this I took a deep breath and nodded to the couch, now both our tempers had cooled slightly.

"Can we at least sit down?" I asked and after he bowed his head in agreement, I let out another sigh before deflating into the seat.

"You are going to have to explain that one to me sweetheart, for I am at a loss here." This time I was the one to rake a frustrated hand through my hair, holding half of it back as I said,

"I know." Then I took another deep breath and admitted the last thing he would have ever had expected to hear.

"You didn't know I was your Chosen One because we hid it from you." His looked said it all but that one word hissed spoke it aloud,

"Impossible."

"Not really, not when you have a…"

*"Shadow Imp…*but of course." His reference to poor Pip was hissed through gritted teeth and again I winced, tensing my shoulders.

"And now the reasons become clear as to why she joined you on your…*your quest."* He said this last part so bitterly I had to close my eyes against the guilt it caused me.

"Look, I know this must be hard for you to hear as trust me, it is just as hard explaining it all, but you have to know that everything we did was because of what we believed we *had to do*…it was said that the second you knew about who I was that you wouldn't…"

"That I wouldn't what?!" he snapped, and I flinched before telling him,

"That when the time came you wouldn't have let me go." Hearing this he closed his eyes and finally… *finally* started to understand. I think it helped him knowing that from the very beginning I was ensuring a way to get back to my own time and more importantly back to Draven.

"Alright Keira, I am starting to see your logic, but I am curious for if I didn't know who you were to me, if your true self was being kept hidden, then how did you manage such a feat?" he asked in a strained voice. He looked down at my belly and I knew what he meant.

"Umm…with a little help from my friends." At this he shot me a horrified look and the second I identified what it was, I screwed up my face and said,

"Oh god, not like that! It's not like we popped up out of nowhere, surprised you enough to tackle you to the bed, tied you there and then forced the baby making goods out of you as a team effort!" I said crossing my arms and thankfully seeing him now fighting off a grin was better than him fighting for control on his anger. But then I had to ask myself how long this would last because the next thing I knew he wasn't just demanding more from me, oh no, he was demanding,

Everything.

"Then just how did you manage it Keira, for I think now is the time to explain it and make no mistake my dear for I will not be satisfied until it has been done so…

"In detail."

CHAPTER EIGHT

THE DEVIL IS IN THE DETAILS

Okay, so taking one look at Draven and I knew this wasn't going to be easy. Hell, if his first reaction to me sleeping with his younger self was anything to go by then I would say this was going to be harder than our first conversation we had when I got back through the Janus Gate.

"I see you're struggling with this." Draven's voice pulled me out of my silent dread and he took my deep sigh as my answer.

"Would it help if I asked the questions?" he offered in a now calm tone, one that gave me hope of getting through this without another temper explosion. I nodded after dragging a hand down my face as if the headache that was building was due to the lights or something. The truth of it though was that I felt exhausted. I felt emotionally drained after all I had been through and I think it was only now that Draven was finally getting it. Because in the end, as much as he didn't like hearing what I had done, then the truth of the matter was simple…I liked explaining it even less.

I hadn't asked for any of this. I hadn't decided to do something crazy like skipping out on my husband and taking a trip to the past because I was throwing caution to the wind and saying, 'Ah hell with it, this looks fun!'

I did it because at the time I had no choice. I mean I couldn't even bear to think of what could have happened if I hadn't followed through with my time travelling quest. Because without that blade filled with a God's blood and without Lucius turning me into a Vampire…well, then I very much doubt we would have been sat here now having this discussion.

As it turned out, getting pregnant was part of the prophecy yes, but just not the one we faced a day ago. But right now, well explaining just how I became pregnant to my very possessive and jealous husband felt like having another bloody battle on my hands!

"I think at this rate I will need to learn sign language before I find the courage to tell you everything…*in detail.*" I added this last part giving him back a taste of his own words. Upon hearing this he gave me a soft smile in return. Then he surprised me when he started making perfectly rehearsed signs with his hands.

He lifted his right hand and keeping some of his fingers up, he bent the middle two. Then he brought his two hands together after making fists keeping his thumbs up. After this he flattened his hands, placing one behind the other, keeping them side on and then made another sign that looked like he was trying to hook two of his fingers with his index finger and thumb. The last few signs were created by placing a hand flat against his chest where his heart was before then drawing a shape over it with one finger.

"You know sign language?!" I shouted excitedly making him smile.

"I do," was his short reply but the grin I received with it told me of his satisfaction at making me smile, or in achieving his main goal, in making me relax.

"What did it mean?" I asked biting my lip.

"Do you own this goat?" he said making my mouth drop and with the look of disbelief I gave him, he threw his head back and laughed as it was mission accomplished. I had given him the reaction he had been hoping for and the second I started laughing with him, it was like the last of the tension was sucked out of the room.

"You're teasing me!" I shouted, and he lifted one of my hands up and playfully bit my fingers before saying,

"Yes, I am teasing you, sweetheart."

"Then what did it really mean?"

"It's a secret," he said continuing with his teasing tone. I yanked my hand from his hold and folded my arms across my chest giving him a fake pout.

"I thought we didn't keep secrets from each other." The second I said this I knew what he was playing at here…he had knowingly coerced me into saying what he wanted. I knew it the second I saw his bad boy grin, one he tried to momentarily hide behind his hand that had been resting against his jaw.

"I agree; therefore, I will make you a vow…" I laughed bitterly and said,

"Oh, let me guess, you will tell me after I have told you…right?" He held out his hand in cocky gesture and said,

"Something like that, Pet." I released a pent-up sigh, dropped my arms and bent forward, plonking my elbows on my knees holding my head in my hands. I let out a groan and admitted,

"You know your logic is annoyingly frustrating at times." I looked at him side on to see him smirking before saying,

"When needs must, my dear." I rolled my eyes and this time he laughed. Then he reached for me, pulling my tense body into his embrace before he started to smooth back my hair.

"Look, I will promise you this, I will try to contain my anger, for no doubt hearing all you have to say will rouse it, but I will not direct it at you." I looked up at him from where my head was being cradled against his chest and pulled back enough to say,

"And you can promise that?"

"I can, for I do understand your reasons and they were not the acts committed for the sole intent to hurt but more so out of love…I have my wits about me enough to know that you did what you felt you *had* to do Keira, not what you *wanted* to do." I gave him a sceptical look making him add,

"I may be a jealous fool and allow my hot temper to get the better of me where you are concerned, but that doesn't mean I can't also see your own logic and therefore reason with myself when fighting for it." I grinned up at him and when he took my chin in his thumb and finger, he then added on a teasing growl,

"So, you see, you're not the only one who has annoyingly frustrating logic to contend with." At this I giggled before reaching and kissing him softly before teasing back over his lips,

"Well, we are very smart people, just one more than the other." I gave him a wink making him roll his eyes in jest.

"I couldn't agree more, and I thank you for the compliment," he said making me fake my shock. Then I hit him on the chest and said,

"I was talking about me!"

"Oh, were you now? Once more, tell me wife of mine, how old are you again? For I think you shall find the years I have on you are quite considerably greater."

"That may be true old man but there is only one of us in this room who has ever worked in a library." I teased back, this time making him throw his head back and really laugh. I had to bite my lip at the sight. He suddenly pulled me forward, gripped the back of my hair so I couldn't escape and told me in a husky voice,

"I much preferred the job you had before that."

"Oh, and which job was that, I often forget?" I said faking ignorance. He gripped me tight and answered me in a throaty growl over my lips,

"The one where you served me!" Then he crushed his lips to mine for an all-consuming kiss. I don't know how long we spent battling it out in the best way possible but as always Draven came out of it the victor as I panted and shook in his hold. What this man could do to me with his hands alone was nothing short of heavenly but what he could do with his mouth was equal amounts sinful!

Draven ran his thumb across my now slightly abused lips with a smirk he didn't even bother to try to hide.

"You look happy," I said as I tucked some hair behind my ear now being shy.

"I must say the primal need to have you seems only to increase the more I am with you and now seeing the brand I had unknowing placed upon your lip, well then, it makes me want to… *devour you further.*" I swear his Demon practically purred this last part at me and I raised my own fingers to my lip wondering what he meant by 'the brand'. So, before he could act, I jumped off the couch and ran into the bathroom to take a look. Staring back at me was a stunned face I knew well as it was my own and the new thing I had never seen before…a purple reddish bruise on my lip.

"You gave me a hickey!" I shouted from the bathroom in utter shock. I heard Draven's laughter before walking back out into the room to witness it.

"And what, may I enquire, is a hickey?" I pointed at my lip and said,

"This is a bloody hickey! Draven, you gave me a love bite," I said in astonishment but the mirth I saw dancing in his eyes told me he wasn't taking this seriously.

"Yes, and if I recall I am not the only one that likes to bite, my dear." I flustered turning red and arguing,

"Yes but…but…well, that is different!"

"How so?" he asked clearly enjoying himself as he leant back against the couch, resting an arm casually along its back, tapping the material with his long fingers.

"How so?" I repeated this time making him give me a one side grin.

"I, well I…well for one this is not a bite, bite!" I said making him raise an eyebrow at me and I wanted to damn him for being far too sexy for his own good…or should I say for my own good, as sometimes I couldn't bloody think around him!

"Then pray tell me my love, for I can't seem to recall, just what constitutes a 'bite, bite' again...you know, this *old man* needs re-educating on such worldly ways, something that shouldn't be a problem with the help of my wife's extensive knowledge, *one that stems from long hours working in a library,"* he replied coolly after rubbing a hand along his jawline for effect and whispering the last of his sentence as if it had been a secret. I had to say, my husband was pretty funny, and I had to try damn hard not to laugh at that one. I failed slightly when he could obviously see my lips twitching, fighting a grin.

"Then let me educate you and your old bones, husband of mine..." I said walking back over to him and he shifted to face me as I placed a knee either side of his thighs. After I had situated myself on his lap, straddling him, I pointed to my lip and said,

"This is not the result of an animalistic need driven on by sex..." I purposely shifted my hips when I said this, grinding myself against the length I could feel growing. He moaned as he too shifted after closing his eyes for a few seconds at the feel of me.

"This right here, is the work of *horny teenager copping a feel of some girl behind the bike sheds at school!"* I hissed without malice that just added to our playful teasing.

"Well, what can I say beautiful, other than you make me feel both young at heart and obviously more human every day!" He finished this with pretending to reach out and bite me again as I continued to try and get away. So much so, we ended up play fighting on the couch like a couple of teenagers I had accused him of being. The rules of the game were simple. Draven would try and get to every bit of bare skin to nip, suck and kiss and I in turn would try and get away from him, so that I didn't end up looking as if I had been ravished by a love biting beast.

Needless to say, Draven won this game with flying colours and a bike shed full of piggy snorts.

I was just trying to catch my breath again, thanks to the very unsexy appearance of Miss Piggy, when he spoke.

"As much as I love the sight of you unravelling in my arms, I must also point out that time is not on our side," Draven reminded me after we both looked to the large grandfather clock that chimed, telling us that it was now two o'clock in the afternoon.

"I guess we missed lunch then?" Draven dismissed my worries first with a wave of his hand and then with his words,

"Vincent and Sophia have handled it." I raised an eyebrow at him in question.

"Care to elaborate?" He smirked and this time the sight of him trying hard to hide an even bigger grin had me worried, not just turned on.

"Oh no, what did they do?" Just as I said this I heard the ringing of a phone and neither of us looked as if it was a welcome distraction. No, in fact it now looked like Draven had been busted.

"I think that's yours," I told him, suddenly being shot back into the past and the first time he had driven me home years ago. Of course, the sound of Abba filling the car had promoted the same dry response from him. From the looks of him it looked as though he too had just been transported back to the same memory, if the purple tinge that fired his eyes was anything to go by.

He reached around to the small table at the side of the couch and picked up his expensive phone, sliding a finger across the panel to answer it.

"Yes?" was his smooth reply. I frowned as I tried to home into what was being said and to my astonishment, I found myself being able to hear the more I concentrated. Well, it looked like new Vamp hearing was certainly going to come in handy, I thought with a grin. Of course, that grin lasted all of about five seconds when I heard the rest of the conversation.

"Just thought I would give the heads up to my new brother in law and all, but there are some pretty restless English folk here all waiting for the happy couple to arrive," Frank said with gritted teeth. I winced thinking this wasn't good and started pulling at the sleeves of my sweater just so that I didn't start biting my lip. However, Draven didn't look at all bothered by this and simply replied,

"I believe my brother and sister should be there any moment to explain."

"Oh, okay well what should I...oh wait, here they come now," Frank said and then obviously covered the phone his side as the last thing I heard was his siblings each speaking separately,

"I will go and speak with Libby," Sophia said just before it was Vincent's turn to talk.

"Frank, if I may..." Then there was a pause where I could now grab Draven's attention.

"What's going on?" I whispered after tugging on his arm. He gave me a teasingly vacant look and shrugged his

shoulders, but the second I crossed my arms over my chest he knew that he was fooling no one. He knew exactly what was going on. And soon so would I.

"Dom? You still there, Man?"

"I'm here, Frank."

"Right, so your brother just…uh…*explained things.*" The way Frank said this instantly had me on edge and Draven felt me tensing even though there was space between us. Just exactly what was he up to this time?

"So, it won't be a problem?" Draven said, and I wasn't really sure if this was a question or he was just stating a fact.

"Well, I don't think people can complain considering you're about to offer to buy dinner for over fifty people and book out the restaurant for the entire evening," Frank said on a laugh making Draven smile. Meanwhile, I was still stuck on the whole part about buying everyone dinner.

"Thank you, Frank."

"Oh no need to thank me, besides, I am sure our father in law was in the same boat years ago, eh!" Frank said trying to sound light hearted but also strangely sounding awkward mostly. I started asking myself what the Draven siblings were up to this time and what did Frank mean by that statement about my father?

Thinking all this and getting lost in my thoughts, I couldn't help the new impulse as it happened before I knew it. My nervous lip biting had a new friend as I started playing with my wedding ring. I hadn't even known I had started doing it until I saw Draven's eyes intensify into two flaming pools of purple fire. He was fixated on the sight and I looked down to see what he saw.

I don't know why but I think for him, it was like the

ultimate sign I finally belonged to him in every way a woman could belong to a man like him. It was his claim on me for the world to see and from the look of things he liked seeing the proof against my skin that he owned me. If I was honest, then I couldn't exactly say I was immune to the sight myself. No, because the truth was that seeing my own mark of ownership on his finger was doing funny things to my insides. And shamefully, I was getting wet just thinking about it.

These thoughts made me think back to the beginning when my obsession first started to take root. Over the years he had slowly taken every piece of me he could, capturing me first with my growing fascination of him. What came after this was a series of events that there wasn't a power on Earth, Heaven or Hell that could have stopped it. Trust me, they had bloody tried enough times! But nothing was strong enough to prevent him from quickly taking my heart and imprisoning it, surrounding it with his own love for me.

"Goodbye, Frank," he told him in a strained voice that almost sounded as if the polite custom had to be first dragged from his Demon. Then without waiting for a reply he ended the call, never letting his eyes leave me for a heartbeat. It was almost as if for a short moment he could hear my inner thoughts and by touching that ring, was connecting to him somehow.

I let it go instantly and watched as he closed his eyes for a second as if something had snapped whatever hold I had just had on him. I was about to ask if he was alright when suddenly he was on me. He had moved so quickly that even my extra senses hadn't fully registered it until he was breathing heavily above me. It looked as if he was trying to fight his Demon again, only this time, he was closer to losing.

"Hey, come back to me, handsome," I cooed softly as I gently raised a hand to place against his cheek. He turned his face into the touch and held himself so still above me it was as if he was scared any sudden movement and I would be fighting to get away from him. I couldn't really understand where this was coming from, but I knew it had something to do with my ring.

I remembered back to the early hours of this morning and what he had told me. I momentarily looked to my hand against his cheek and saw it; the half symbol that was embedded there, one seen in better detail after he had taken off my ring to show me. He had twisted them round until a symbol I knew well had appeared. Of course, never in a million years had I expected to hear what it meant, and my mind now once again took me back to the conversation...

"Simply put, it means us."

"Us?" I asked, my confusion obvious.

"You and I, our union." I frowned, shaking my head a little before asking,

"What, you mean like a man and woman coming together, that type of us?"

"No, Keira, what I mean is..." He stopped talking a second to get closer to me so he could whisper the truth across my skin,

"Just you and me...*together.*"

"Okay, you are going to have to explain this to me," I complained making him smirk before kissing my temple. After this I was just thankful that he took pity and started to enlighten me. He started to tell me about the first shape that was engraved in his own ring, one wider than my delicate one.

It meant the Alpha and simply put meant the first, representing himself as the first and only of his kind. Then came the Omega, which was shocking to hear meant…well, like he had said, *it meant me.*

I was the last and therefore completed our souls. I had wanted to ask more but then he beat me to it and spoke, explaining it in such a beautiful way, that I would never forget what he said to me that night,

"It means I was the beginning, but you were my end… my everything, my only…it is like Sophia said in her speech…*you complete me.*" After this, he finished his sentence as he thrust inside me making me cry out in unexpected bliss. Now once seated at home within the warmth of my body, I knew he was only half right.

So, I had reached up and touched his cheek, whispering back…

"We complete each other."

But now, after the way he had just been looking at me, I was overcome with the feeling that it meant so much more. Something even Draven didn't understand. Which was why I was currently reaching out to his Demon and trying once more to tame him. I felt him shudder above me, as if he too was trying to sooth this volatile side of him and forcing him to submit.

"And there he is," I whispered tenderly to him the second he opened his eyes and after I had released a relieved sigh as his beautiful dark eyes met mine.

"I don't know what came over me," he said after sitting back up and no longer caging me in. He dragged a hand down his face and I couldn't help but notice the slight tremble in it. It was as if the action was done in hopes of taking away the invisible veil of uncertainty from sticking to his skin. I put my hand to his shoulder and shifted closer.

"Hey, are you okay?" I asked and without looking at me, he replied,

"I'm fine." My lips flattened into an unconvincing line.

"Now you sound like me, when you ask me that question and if I remember correctly, it used to piss you off," I informed him, finally making him look my way. He was arched over with his elbows to his knees and his head in his hands before my statement.

The second I spoke he dropped his hands and turned his head my way, making all his hair fall forward. It was a primal look of a man that was close to the edge and was trying to talk himself off a ledge and from making that doomed first step. Thankfully, with the sound of my voice and it being one of reason he took a deep breath and said,

"You're right. I am not fine, but I will be…" I frowned and asked,

"What do you need Draven, tell me." I implored reaching out to him. He looked down at my hand and the harsh glint I saw there actually had me stopping before touching him. His eyes snapped up to me the second I started to retract my hand and before I knew what was coming he had my wrist shackled in his large hand, putting a swift stop to my movements.

Then the next words out of his mouth had me gasping and not just from the raw sexual current I could feel coming from him in waves. Nor was it from the fire in his eyes or the deep growl of his Demon speaking to me.

No, all that fear I felt was down to one name spoken.
One gifted to me by another love,
By another King.
By another Draven.
"Where do you think you're going…"

"My Little Lamb?"

CHAPTER NINE

PEELING BACK THE YEARS

I couldn't help my reaction to him as I tore my hand from his and dug my heels into the couch so that I could move back, putting space between us. I lifted my hand up to my pounding chest as if feeling the beating of my heart beneath my palm would bring me comfort in knowing I was still alive in this world.

"Wh...what did you just say?" I asked in a tone that was barely above a whisper. Draven looked as though something was trying to reach him in his mind, as though he was chasing a memory and in a flash, it was gone. He shook his head as if this would help in bringing it back or getting rid of it, I didn't know.

"I...I don't know what just happened," he admitted, and the sound of his uncertain voice made my body relax, knowing that none of this was his fault. So, I decided to be honest with him.

"Janus told me you wouldn't remember." My voice was

so quiet, it almost seemed far away. As if shouting the words across the sea and through a storm. Looking down at the space between us now and the heavy emotions playing out in Draven's eyes, then those words seemed closer to the truth than I would have liked.

"Are you telling me what I think you are telling me, Keira?" he asked as if almost afraid to, for fear of what my answer maybe this time. I nodded and said,

"I met the God Janus when coming back, it's why the others arrived before I did, that and…" I faltered a moment when thinking back to the devastating look of agony on Draven's face just before I left his world. Draven looked at me as though he knew…as if he himself had felt it but he didn't say anything, not even when I finished off my painful sentence. No, his reaction was enough.

"…and I was saying goodbye." I saw him wince as he closed his eyes and his muscles tensed. In that moment I had no clue as to what he was thinking. I tried to place myself in his shoes. Just how many times since he had known of me had he been forced to say goodbye in one way or another? How many times had he had to endure the pain of leaving me or watching me being ripped away from his side? At the very beginning he had done nothing but vow to protect me and for a man like Draven, to know he had only failed at this time and time again looked to be eating him up inside.

I watched as he once more found solace in cradling his head in his hands as he bent over to place his elbows to his knees. I watched as he ran his hands through his hair, stopping so he could fist them, holding himself as if tortured. So, I did the only thing I knew I could do to help him. I slipped off the couch and lowered myself in front of him on my knees then I rose up enough to hold his face in both hands. I placed my forehead to his and told him with tears in my eyes,

"I am so, so sorry for what I did, Dominic."

After saying this to him his reaction was sure and swift, for he grabbed me under the arms and lifted me into his embrace. There he held me to him, fisting his hands in my sweater as if any moment the Gods themselves were going to come in here and take me away from him.

"You are never to leave me again... do you hear me... never!" He told me this through gritted teeth and a demonic growl, one I would have been stupid not to take seriously.

"And you, do I also get this promise from you?" I asked him, knowing that he wasn't the only one that needed to hear the vow being made. He pulled back slightly so he could look at me from his tight embrace.

"I left you once and it ripped apart my heart and tore at my soul, both of which were only pieced back together once you were mine again...I could never leave you, for next time there would be no pieces left to fix...no...next time I fear... well, I fear that it would *simply kill me,"* he told me holding my face and commanding my eyes with his intense gaze. The second his last words were free I couldn't bear the weight of his dark thoughts any longer. I closed my eyes and found tears falling, cascading over my lashes as the emotions were too great to handle without showing the evidence.

"So yes, this I can promise you, Keira," he told me after using both his thumbs to wipe away the pain his words had caused. I opened my eyes just in time to see him tasting one from his thumb as if this would help in taking the hurt away.

"Now it is your turn," he commanded me, and I nodded, not trusting my voice from not breaking in that moment.

"I need your words, my love," he whispered over my cheek before giving into the impulse to kiss it. I swallowed down the heavy lump in my throat and tried first testing my voice, surprised to find it was still there at all.

"I...I promise never to leave you again, Draven."

And it was done.

In that moment we had both admitted our greatest fears and had them cast into the nightmare world that was full of our past tortures. We had given each other a peace that was only found in a promise spoken aloud, so that it may be heard and stored away to be kept forever.

He closed his eyes as he bottled up my words, sealed them and then cast them into the sea of his mind, no doubt praying they were never to be needed again.

Once this had passed, then came the time for difficult conversations as I knew if we were ever going to do this then now was the time. Not tomorrow or next week or even a year from now. No, we had both declared a promise to each other that today marked a change for us both. No more secrets and no more lies we'd both labelled as protection. Now was the time for honesty and I knew that it started with me.

"I went back in time with the sole purpose to get pregnant as I was led to believe that it was the only way to prevent the end of the world," I said bravely, taking the first terrifying step.

Draven listened to me and even though I knew he tried very hard not to react to make it easier on me, I could still see it. Every time he tensed his shoulders or that grinding of his teeth seen as a tick in his strong jawline. But I also knew that he needed this as I did, so I continued.

"I lied to you yesterday, when I said I let it lead me down a path in hopes of finding the outcome to be part of the Fates' plan. I knew why I was sent back…of course even that turned out to be wrong," I said with a small laugh that was void of humour.

"Why didn't you tell me about the baby?" he asked, and I gave him a sad smile in return before answering him.

"I wanted you to be happy, but then I knew you would see it as a sign that I would die because of it. I just could bear to see your devastation because of the life I now carry inside me…I just…" I couldn't finish and when Draven took both my hands in his I knew that I didn't have to.

"I understand and maybe even that too was fated."

"What do you mean?" I asked frowning.

"Well, who knows how differently things would have played out if I had known…I am sometimes rash and hasty in my decisions, which could have meant a different future." One look at my face told him that he needed to explain this further. He raked a frustrated hand through his hair once before coming right out and saying it.

"If I had known Keira, then I would not have married you that day." Hearing this I bolted up, my back going tense as if someone had zapped me with an electric wire. His eyes homed in on my chest as I now found myself clutching my heart as though he had just crushed it with his own fist. He looked pained by the sight.

"Hear me out, please," Draven said in a stern voice when I started shaking my head in disbelief.

"How could you…"

"Keira, listen to me! I wouldn't have married you that day because I would have simply picked you up, against your will no doubt, and carried you back to Afterlife. Once there I would have flown you to my cave and left you there for your protection. Your life means more to me than vows spoken in front of mortal people or the Gods they trust. It means more to me that my own life or those of my people! And knowing that the reason you might die because of the foolish choices you made, then it would have forced my hand in making my *own* choices...ones you would not have liked." I couldn't believe what he was saying.

"You wouldn't have...you..." I started to say but my words felt like lies the second they were formed by my trembling lips...his look alone told me that.

"Oh, you may have hated me for it at the time but at least you would have been alive to feel the compulsion to do so!" he snapped ceasing my argument and daring me to challenge what I knew was a losing fight.

"But none of that matters now as the Fates accomplished only one thing."

"And that is?" I almost feared to ask.

"That we were all wrong." I thought on his words for a moment and he was right. Nothing either of us had set out to do had been for the reasons we first thought, yet the outcome was all we could have ever asked for.

"Everything that happened to us...every single..."

"...last grain of sand built the shores in which we fought upon. The second you came into my life, it was as if our story was written before it was even told. If Lucius hadn't taken you, if the Triple Goddess had never happened, then he wouldn't have found himself in love enough to change you into what you were always destined to become. You would have plunged that dagger into your heart and it would have ripped your vessel apart before the blood of a God had chance to take hold." He told me all of this as if he had spent the entire night playing it out in his head.

"And you...if you hadn't died in my mind, then I would never have come looking for you." I added in awe.

"If you hadn't fought your way through the darkness, like a flickering candle in the night searching for me, then all the moths you collected along the way wouldn't have followed you into battle." I shook my head and disagreed.

"No, surely they would have fought..." Once again, he interrupted me.

"They fought for *you Keira,* not for me," he said sounding so sure.

"But you are their King," I argued but he just shook his head and told me,

"A King does not fight for another King, but they would fight for their rightful Queen, one who is prophesied to aid them when finding their own." This made me gasp and my first instinct was to deny it. But Draven placed his hand on mine, squeezed it once and said,

"Think about it." So, I did. I thought back to all that had happened when everything started to fit together like some endless jigsaw puzzle that wasn't yet finished. One that's image appeared first from its centre, not it edges.

There was the girl on the plane, one I knew was destined somehow for Sigurd. Even her warning all that time ago was fated to be heard. Then there was RJ, who was my first friend here and the one thrust into this supernatural life by my doing. I knew her own destiny lay with Seth in some way, but how and why, well that was her journey to take.

And now there was Ari. A girl thrown into my life for what felt like since the beginning. But in reality, it hadn't yet even been a year. A sister to me in every sense of the word, but lacking so only by blood. She was meant to be with Vincent, for there was little doubt of that from where I stood. Her own doubt however, well no one could account for her reasons to distrust this, other than her own tormented mind.

I didn't know how or who, but I knew even Jared and Lucius were linked with me in some way. For what other reasons were there for the connection we shared? Lucius was someone I had fallen in love with despite fighting the constant battle of my own heart and now I knew why. It was written in our destiny…no, not mine anymore…*but his.*

"I see now it has started to all fit into place." I nodded looking at Draven to see him struggling with this himself and when he spoke I now knew why.

"I once told you that I didn't share, but I guess the joke is on me for I ended up having to share you with everyone involved in this damn prophecy!" I couldn't help but laugh a little and when I did, he shot me an incredulous look.

"Tell me you're not laughing at this," he warned with no malice to be wary of.

"Maybe just a little," I confessed making him growl, but then I jumped at him, taking him off guard as he caught me. Then I lay half across him and told him something I knew he would very much like to hear.

"Yes, that may have been true, but do you want to know the best bit?" I asked him, running a fingertip across his straight annoyed lips. He didn't reply with words but with a little nod of his head.

"Now it's finished you no longer have to share me anymore, for I am all yours... *today...tomorrow and... forevermore,"* I said kissing him in between each word, until the very last was consumed by his own kiss.

After this I shared with him everything that had happened since leaving the hotel and passing through the Janus Gate. I knew most of it was hard for him to hear and the beginning was most probably the worst. Hearing how I was attacked meant the next set of questions asked were done so by his Demon side.

However, I continued and realised he had only calmed slightly by the time my tale got me to Draven's side, even if he was strangely jealous to hear it.

"I am surprised I didn't just pick you up and take you to my bedchamber, keeping you behind lock and key," he commented sounding surprised.

"You didn't know I was your Chosen One at the time remember," I informed him, but his huffed laugh had me soon frowning in question.

"That wouldn't have mattered, Keira," he told me as if I should already know this.

"Well, if it helps I think if Ranka hadn't intervened then you most likely would have, even against the strong wishes of your sister," I replied, and his look of acknowledgement told me that this was another part of the story he knew.

"Sophia was very different back then. She didn't yet

know what it was like to love," was his argument. I laughed myself this time making him raise an eyebrow my way.

"And what may I enquire do you find so funny?"

"Only that she said the same thing about you…it seems you were both destined at some point to argue the point for one another." Draven nodded his head slightly, taking note of my words.

"It's true, that before you I had no clue what it meant to love or to watch yourself fall without the aid of my wings to catch me. Back then I was a selfish being that simply took what I wanted and thought I had the right to, thanks to my high position of power…I see now of course, what a fool I had been." I blushed at his admission and couldn't help but bite my lip because of how sweet it sounded. To be the first person Draven had ever fallen in love with was a gift I was blessed to have bestowed upon me by the Gods… that and I was one lucky bitch!

"You'd better continue on with your story before I give in to the urge to strip you of that beautiful look of innocence and make a meal out of your body again…*doing so sinfully,*" he warned on a growl and my blush only managed to deepen. I almost felt like pushing him but as he had said, time was not on our side and I had a feeling Draven wasn't letting me out of this room until he was satisfied.

So, with this in mind, I continued on, telling him of my short time in his harem. I was at least grateful that he had the inclination to look uncomfortable when hearing how I felt about first encountering his room full of waiting and willing beauties.

"Come now, for I know full well that once I first laid my fortunate eyes on you, that no other had the power to take them away from you and that beautiful and enticing body of yours."

"And how would you know that exactly, as I don't recall you hitch hiking a ride back to the past with us?" I teased.

"I may not have been there Keira, but I know enough of myself and my past character to know that one look at you and I would have considered myself a claimed man." I couldn't keep the grin from my face hearing this.

"Maybe that's why you got so pissed off when I ran from you," I said dropping my next bombshell. Draven looked shocked for a moment and by the looks of him clenching his fists, then I would say that the very thought of it was something Draven would always struggle with.

"Undoubtedly so, I can imagine I was as murderous as I usually am now, and I can promise you, two thousand years of etiquette, laws and high society would not change that impulse."

"No?" I challenged, and his lips curled up in a bad boy grin before he commented,

"No, now I am just better at hiding the bodies." I laughed at his joke, silently praying it was just that...a joke.

"So, tell me my little time travelling intruder, what did I do when I caught you?" he asked almost humming the question my way as I could see that no doubt he liked the idea of chasing me. Well, if that mischievous glint in his eyes was anything to go by.

"Who said that you caught me?" I challenged making him give me a disbelieving look.

"You are fooling no one sweetheart, if you try and have me believe that I wouldn't have caught you, for I know from experience that I would have torn apart my whole damn city in order to find you. So, tell me what happened when I did, I can image there were chains involved." I thought back to that time and shuddered before saying,

"Oh yeah, there were definitely chains involved." He gave me a look that told me he was getting impatient to know so I decided to tell him…his reaction of course, was the very last one I would have expected. He started laughing.

"Why are you laughing, Draven?! I was terrified!" I shouted smacking him on the arm.

"Oh, sweetheart you were never in any danger. I would have undoubtedly cut off my own arm before seeing you hurt in any way," he told me running his fingers down my own arm after pushing my sleeve up and out of his way.

"But you were going to have me whipped!" I argued but he just shook his head.

"No, I was an angry King who was dealing with a mortal girl I was in love with and had claimed as mine. One, who in my eyes, needed to be taught a lesson in what would happen if she tried to escape me again. I did it to frighten you love, that is all." I thought on what he was saying and when I must have looked even more confused he asked,

"This whip, did you once feel its bite upon your skin?"

"No, because you got in the way and took the hit," I told him, but his eyes told me that he already knew the answer to this.

"As was always my intention. I gather at the time I was also trying to get you to explain to me the reasons for your attempted escape?" He raised both his eyebrows this time expectantly.

"Well yeah, but I refused to tell you." He laughed and commented to himself,

"Of course, you did." I decided to ignore that comment, as let's face it, he had dealt with enough frustrating 'Stubborn Keira' moments in the last few years so it wasn't as if he didn't know what he was talking about.

"I would ask what happened next, but I think I have a fairly good idea." I folded my arms across my chest and said a cocky,

"Oh yeah, you think so, do you?"

"Well, to begin with I would have kept you in those chains, raised your shackled hands over my neck and carried you from the harem making sure it was the last time you ever saw it!" he told me firmly, shackling my wrists with both hands so he could yank me closer to him, making his point. He knew when he saw me swallow hard and look anywhere but at his eyes, that he had his answer…damn him and his cocky all-knowing ass!

"What happened next, Keira?" he asked in a hard tone, obviously thinking he was getting closer to the part that would make him jealous. He still had hold of me as if letting me go now would mean so much more than just a space between us on the couch.

"I don't know, why don't you tell me seeing as you are so good at this," I snapped unable to help myself.

"Well, I can very well imagine that considering the bounty I had secured in my arms…" he said pausing as he lifted my arms still imprisoned in his masterful hold before continuing,

"…I most likely carried you off to a private room in my palace, somewhere that we couldn't be disturbed." The strain it looked like it took for him to say this made me feel bad for him. The second he let me go and sat back I ran a frustrated hand through my hair.

"You know technically speaking here, you also kind of had sex with a different version of me, so I would say we are…" I was about to finish when Draven thought to do it for me…*again*.

"Don't you dare say *even,* as that was *not* the same thing, Keira," he stressed to get through to me, but I wouldn't be deterred.

"No, you're right, I went back in time and slept with your younger, more barbaric self and you slept with me when I believed myself to be someone different…tell me Draven, where exactly do you want to draw the line in the sand here, because I think at some point, we both stepped over it?" I knew I had made my point when I heard him sigh, inhaling deep and only letting it go when he had to. For long moments he didn't speak but I knew I had won him over when I watched his gaze soften.

"Come here.," he ordered gently, and I had to admit that I loved the way he could issue a demand and still do so with a tender tone that should have counteracted his authoritative nature. Instead however, it simply strengthened it in a way that also showed his love for me. For there was only one person Draven was like this with and yes, once again I found myself thinking, I was that lucky bitch!

"There is that frustrating logic of yours again," he told me once I had shifted closer so that he could play with my fingers, as was another habit of his.

"Yes, and one that will be forced upon you many times over no doubt, *as I hear an eternity is known to be quite long,"* I said teasing him with this last part as I reached up to whisper it in his ear. His chest rumbled, and I could tell by his smile that he certainly liked the sound of this.

"Now you can answer me something," I said.

"Well, it seems I can deny you nothing, so ask away, little wife." He laughed when I growled at my new nickname.

"I think I prefer vixen," I grumbled making him laugh. Then he pulled me closer and spoke over my cheek,

"Ask me your question, sweetheart." This time I smiled knowing he had said this in place of the 'little wife' comment.

"What was it that Sophia and Vincent told Frank. What reason did they give him why we were late?" His first answer to this question came as a smirk and in that very moment I knew it was bad. But then it only got worse when he suddenly started to look sheepish.

"What did you do?" I asked, now using my own authoritative tone. He laughed once and held up his hands to say,

"I did nothing, my brother and sister however I cannot account for."

"Draven," I said his name in warning but again he just laughed.

"They told him the truth, of sorts." I released what I didn't know yet was a premature sigh of relief and said,

"Oh, so they said we just had to talk about stuff?" Draven looked at me side on and with a one-sided grin replied,

"Not exactly." I frowned so hard I could feel my eyes squinting.

"Just tell me!" I shouted, and Draven grabbed my dramatic hands as they flew up in anger and pulled me closer to him, so he could whisper the dreaded, embarrassing words in my ear,

"They told him that I couldn't keep my hands off you and that I planned on keeping you in my bed for as long as possible." I sucked in a shocked, mortified breath and voiced the first worry that came to my mind,

"Oh God! Please, tell me…" I paused so I could swallow hard first and continued with my eyes closed…

"They haven't told my Dad that." I hissed as I felt my cheeks were lighting up with my shame.

And Draven's reaction to this…

He burst out laughing.

CHAPTER TEN

SOME THINGS NEVER CHANGE

The rest of the afternoon came and went in a conversational whirlwind. I continued to tell him all about my time in Persia and he tried to listen without judgement. Of course, this didn't help when he started to demand the details from me. It almost felt like one of those cringeworthy conversations you find yourself having to go through when you first started dating someone new. But we weren't a new couple, we were married and in one way or another had been together for years. But more importantly this wasn't some ex-boyfriend I was having to talk about or some one-night stand…no, *this was him.*

This was the Persian warrior King that was, on some level, as far away from the man in front of me now, wearing denim jeans and a crisp white shirt, as you could get. Gone were the deadly weapons, armoured shoulders and heavy breast plates. Gone were the battle scars, callused hands and bearded face. But even in sight of it all, it was still the man I fell in love with, just a rougher version. The heart, soul and mind were still the same, with just a different shell to house it all.

"Why can't you understand, it was still you I made love to, it was still you that…" I couldn't finish as I looked down at my belly that I knew one day soon would start to show the wonderful life we made growing inside of me. I had said this after hearing him growling when asking about out first time together.

"I know that my jealousy may seem irrational…"

"It *is* irrational," I corrected. He gave me a pointed look but before he could continue I told him,

"Do you know how you found out that I wasn't from your own time?" He shook his head as if it wouldn't matter but I took his hand in mine and gave it a firm squeeze until I got his gaze back.

"Draven listen to me now when I tell you this. When we finally made love, it was *your* name I called out, not *his*. *You* were the one that was forever in my mind and he knew it." I paused and huffed a laugh before saying,

"You were murderous. You promised me that you would hunt down this Draven and make me watch as you killed him, you told me when you were finished with him, there would be nothing left of him to love." His eyes widened in surprise before finally he started to understand. I knew this when he asked incredulously,

"You called out my name?" It was as if he needed to hear it again, so I happily gave him this.

"More than once and trust me, if I thought your temper was bad in this time then it was nothing compared to what it used to be…I can see the years have definitely helped in taming the beast." I joked and the small smile that played at his lips as he looked down at his hand in mine told me he had something else on his mind.

"Not years Keira, only you...it is only you that has the power to tame my beast of a temper." I smirked knowing he was right as I remembered back to when we first were together. It was after my nightmare in the bathroom where Samael attacked me with his deadly spiders. Vincent had just read my past and told Draven of its dire outcome. I had bravely walked straight up to Draven and pleaded with him not to be angry. Even his brother had been shocked to see the outcome and couldn't help but comment on it at the time.

I suddenly looked down as a touch at my belly drew me out of the past to see Draven's hand flat against my stomach.

"I just..." he paused and closed his eyes as if he could see something for himself. Something that he desperately wanted but was too far out of his reach to grasp. And now, with a gust of time blowing past, it was gone, and the moment lost to him forever.

I covered his hand with my own and finished off his wish, with one of my own.

"I know, and I would wish it too."

After this bittersweet moment had passed I took his hand as he led me out of the room and back towards the library. We were ready to go back through the Janus door that would lead us up through the temple and into the grounds of Witley Court. It was obvious that Draven was trying to protect me from the sensitive sight when we walked back through the temple. I knew this because as soon as we were through the bookcase doorway, he swung me up into his arms. Then he ran through the space kissing my neck and making me giggle as he effortlessly jumped and manoeuvred his way through the rubble.

The second we were up topside and through the fountain's hidden entrance, I couldn't help but take a deep breath, loving the smell of the English countryside. I looked all around and couldn't help the depressing thought seep its way into my mind. I just found myself asking what would have happened to all this beauty had last night not gone our way...had we not won the war?

Thankfully, it was a fleeting thought, one that was cast away when Draven held me from behind. Feeling his large arms wrapping around me as we both gave ourselves a moment to take in the view had me sighing in happiness and relaxing back into his body.

"I think back to when I lived here, and I cannot tell you the pleasure it would have brought me to have been given the chance to share it all with you." I grinned before biting my lip at the sweet thought.

"Yes, and I bet back then if someone had told you the first time you would see your Chosen One in this place, she would have been dressed like a biker clown and hitting your ex-girlfriend over the head with a giant penis. You would have called them insane." At this he roared with laughter behind me, making my whole body shake with him.

"I think if I lived for another ten thousand years I would never forget such a sight! I think in that moment I was asking about my own sanity and if my immense love for you had finally driven me to madness." I laughed at that and moved to walk away but was stopped when he tightened his hold around me.

"Draven?"

"Stay... I just...I just want to hold you for a moment longer," he admitted on a broken whisper and I couldn't say that the sound of both his velvet voice and sweet request didn't do funny things to my feminine parts.

"I remember I would walk these grounds after some tedious day of mortgages and accounts, or worse, some damaged soul that needed my lawful judgement being cast, all the while wondering when I would finally do so with my own soul intact." Hearing this I turned around and looked up at him. He tenderly ran the backs of his knuckles down my cheek before tucking hair behind my ear.

"I don't think you would have been able to cope with my 'frustratingly annoying logic' back then," I teased thinking if I didn't speak in that moment I would only be tearing up again.

"Oh, make no mistake of it sweetheart, I think we both know that recent evidence suggests that I could 'cope' with your wilful ways, no matter what time period we are given to live through." I gave him an 'is that so' look prompting him to say,

"From the sounds of it, then it wasn't long ago that you had my *barbarian self* putty in your hands by your own admission...and after all, I did walk these grounds as a gentleman back then," he teased back, pretending to bite my nose, or at least trying to.

"Mmm, makes me wonder what to call you now, as I think you are somewhere in between," I said playfully making him fake a growl at me in return. I laughed again when I started to walk backwards and he in turn started to stalk closer.

"Is that so, pet?" he challenged coming closer, waiting for me to make my move. I bit my lip once and then winked at him as his only warning before I turned and sprinted the other way. I was actually surprised to find I was quicker than before and when I really pushed, I soon found myself around the side of the building before he finally caught me.

"Got you, little rabbit!" he roared making me squeal in surprise and fright as I was quickly lifted up and placed over his shoulder. Then he continued to walk with strong purposeful strides along the side of the building, quickly eating up the space.

"Alright, alright king of the cavemen, you win, you can put me down now," I said out of breath and panting.

"Oh, I don't think so! Not with such an unruly wife, for it's time I showed her just what I would have done in my gentlemanly days," he replied enthusiastically and when I wriggled on his shoulder he turned his head into my thigh and warned,

"Behave, my little captive." Then he bit my bottom making me yelp and cry out.

"Oi!" I shouted in fake outrage when in truth I was getting more turned on by the minute. Then I tried to push up a little, so I could see where he was taking me when I finally noticed a fancy blacked out car waiting for us. The driver stood to one side holding open the door for us watching this little barbaric scene play out.

"Draven put me down, people can see us," I hissed in horror, feeling the blood beneath my cheeks start to boil. But Draven simply laughed in sight of my shame and instead,

turned with me still over his shoulder to acknowledge the driver.

"Thank you, Thomas," he said before finally letting me down, plastering me to his front. I swear I could feel every raw muscle tense as my breasts were pushed and lifted against his torso. I was about to complain teasingly of my heavy-handed treatment but the sight of purple lust seeping into his eyes stopped me. Then he pushed all my hair back and nearly snarled his next words,

"Fuck me, Keira."

"Wh…what is it?" I asked shyly given the passionate and fierce way he was looking at me.

"You looked so beautiful, so pure and innocent, it makes me want to ravish you…"

"Draven." His name left my lips on a breathy whisper and his eyes flashed a deeper shade of violet flames.

"Get in the car!" he commanded sternly as if he was on edge and needed to be obeyed in that moment. I sucked in my bottom lip making him growl down at me and his eyes slid to the open door he looked close to crushing in his unyielding hold. I quickly did as I was told and tucked myself inside.

"To the hotel." I heard Draven give the order before slipping in beside me. Once there he promptly pressed a button above his head and a privacy screen started to slide up between us and the driver.

"This is a nice car, what is it…" I started to say when suddenly I was grabbed and pulled roughly to him.

"Fuck the car Keira, I need your mouth!" he hissed before taking what he wanted… *me.* He gripped the back of my head and held me captive to his lips as he started to

143

devour me. It was as if he couldn't get enough of me. Couldn't get enough of my taste, the feel of me or the battle we fought. I felt him shudder as I ran my tongue over his teeth, feeling the fangs that started to lengthen.

He started to pull at my sweater as if duelling with his demon on whether or not to tear it from my skin. So, in the end I took the option from him as I grabbed a handful in each hand before tearing it up over my head. He even growled at having to break the connection for that brief second before he was back. I had on a little black vest top underneath and this time I felt him fist it, bunching the material at my belly. I knew where this was going so I pulled back and asked breathlessly,

"How long do we have?" Draven looked pained for a moment as if trying to work out how long he would need to slake his thirst for me. And then without answering me, he pressed another button above him and spoke in a harsh voice,

"Make the journey last the hour, Thomas." He didn't wait for a reply but my own was a naughty grin that told him I approved. Well, if the smile didn't, then me tearing the vest over my head certainly did, that and when I desperately tried to pull his belt free. Thankfully, he got the hint and soon he was freeing his length for me to take hold. The silky steel I felt beneath my fingers made me moan at first touch whereas Draven sucked in air through his teeth. Then I pressed my body up against his side as I started kissing my way up his tensed neck. I sucked and nipped at him making him groan like some pained animal. In that moment I chose not to just grip him harder but also bite him, holding his skin in my teeth. His reaction to this was to suddenly grip the back of the waistband of my jeans near my bum. His hold started to rip the seams at the sides and I felt the painful tug pull at my aching clit as the material rubbed against it.

He pulled back enough to snarl at me,

"Fucking addictive!" Then suddenly I was up, and denim was being pulled down my legs, before he quickly had me on top of him. I placed my knee either side of his thighs and with his hands at my hips he started to lower me down over his hard erection. I couldn't help but look down at the sight as he did, needing to know what he saw. The end of his thick shaft was beaded with pre-come and I had the sudden, most insane urge to taste it. So, before he could bury himself inside me, I reached down between us.

His eyes shot to mine in astonishment that quickly hooded in lust when he saw me bring my dripping finger to my lips before I sucked it in deep, moaning around it in my mouth. I felt so wanton, so sinful that I couldn't help but make a show of it. And boy did he like it.

"Mine!" he barked demonically before suddenly yanking me hard down over his ready length, making it hard to take its full size. I was about to cry out, but it was soon swallowed up and consumed by Draven's mouth, as he devoured it in a demanding kiss. It felt as though with every drive of his cock, he would also drive his passion home with his tongue in my mouth. His hands bit into the flesh at my hips as he used it to plough my body down on him and each time I would feel him surging up inside me, making my body feel blissfully full. I felt owned, completely and utterly owned by him.

"Draven...Draven I am so close," I told him in a desperate tone, only spoken over his lips before I bit at them in my restless need.

"Not yet, for I am not done with you and your tight little hold you have quivering around my cock," he growled back and then proved his words to be true…

He wasn't finished with me.

All I can say I was thankful the plush looking car had blacked out windows or the other drivers would have got more than they bargained for when sat in end of day traffic waiting to go home from work. I even slapped my hand on the window at one point, very sure I was close to cracking the glass I was so far gone in my passion. I let my head fall back, my hair raining down with it as I cried out with every rock of my hips. Draven wouldn't allow the space this created for long as one of his hands left the hold on my hip. Then once free, he snaked his hand up under my hair, caressing my back as he went before he found my shoulder. Once there he held on to it in a tight grip and used its hold to force me down on him, taking the most I had of him into my body. Then, his eager mouth latched on to my nipple and I screamed out, unable to help the orgasm that suddenly tore through me. I erupted so violently I nearly passed out from it. This reaction soon became the catalyst for his own release and he too roared out, as if it had been robbed from him prematurely.

My head fell forward onto his chest and his hand held the back of my head there, cradling it as we both tried to calm our raging hearts. I could feel his release slipping down my soaked channel and around the length of him, making me squirm.

"Wife, have pity on your husband," he groaned making me giggle, which also made him groan seeing as it made me squeeze my inner muscles and shudder around my tight, internal hold on him. After this he wrapped a strong arm around my waist and lifted me off him, making me moan out my loss with a small pleading sound. His chest rumbled as though he liked the sound of my neediness for him but instead of putting himself back like I wanted, he gently lifted me up and over to the seat.

"Keira my love, what are you doing?" he asked after pulling up his jeans and seeing me kind of half sat at a funny angle, so I wouldn't get any of his 'man juice' on the expensive looking upholstery.

"What does it look like I am doing, trying to save you an expensive and embarrassing detailing job!" I snapped making him laugh. Then before I could issue a warning he produced a handkerchief out of thin air and slipped down to one knee in front of me.

"Then allow me, sweetheart," he said playing the gentleman once more. However, his next actions counteracted the notion. He sensually took my leg in his hand and then lifted it over his elbow, making sure to run his fingertips down the length of my thigh. He kept his eyes to me the whole time and just as I was being lured in by his gentle hands, he suddenly yanked me forward. I had no choice but to slip down until my back was flat on the seat and my ass was now literally in his hands.

"Draven!" I squealed in shock making him laugh before telling me,

"Relax love, I am just cleaning you up." He said this with an easy-going tone lacing his words as he set about doing his husbandly duty and cleaning up the mess he had made. I didn't think I would ever get used to the embarrassment I felt, no matter how sweet the gesture was. Which is why I flung an arm over my face and groaned into it making him chuckle.

After this it didn't take us long before we were pulling up outside the hotel and just in time considering I was just now pulling my big chunky knit sweater back over my head. Draven had thankfully mended the tear he had made in my jeans and the rip in my knickers I hadn't realised was there. I think from the looks of things his fingers had gone straight through lace in his haste to get me free of them. I tried in vain to straighten my hair and make myself look at least somewhat presentable, when Draven took my hands in his to stop me from fussing.

"You look beautiful, Keira," he told me kissing my cheek and then before I could even say a thank you, the door was opened. Draven got out first and then turned around to hold a hand out to me. I let him help me out of the car and the second my feet were on the ground he pulled me to him and said,

"Oh yes, you look perfectly ravished." Then with a wink he started to walk me into the hotel, leaving my mouth hanging open in shock. By the time I came to my senses we were almost at the front desk.

"That is not exactly the look I was trying to go for, Draven," I hissed through an angry jaw as Draven approached a door on the right. Then, just as he pushed it open to reveal a room full of family and friends, he leant down to my ear and whispered...

"No, but I was."

CHAPTER ELEVEN

FAMILY AFFAIR

As it turned out our late arrival combined with the way Draven said I looked seemed to go hand in hand as the second I got inside Sophia quickly stole me away. I thought this was sweet for all of thirty seconds before she told me why she was dragging me off to one side. But once she opened her mouth and then yeah, not so much on the sweet but definitely much, much more of the...

"Oh my god, are you Ffffing crazy!?" I hissed the second she confessed and now was self-consciously looking around like a paranoid android with a few circuits short of a functioning motherboard!

Of course, Sophia didn't even try to contain the smirk that made her look more primeval than cute as she held up her hands in feigned surrender and said,

"Don't shoot down the demon messenger honey, it was your new husband that gave the order." Hearing this I couldn't help but say to hell with keeping this conversation on the low down as I screamed,

"You're shitting me!" Just then my great aunty Jean decided to walk past and instead of looking mortified she simply patted my arm and said,

"Don't worry deary, it happens to us all… I find eating three prunes a day helps keep things flowing down the pipes just fine." I first gave her a vacant lost look wondering what on earth she had heard me say or taken from my shouted comment, now knowing she obviously thought I had problems with my back plumbing. Oh great, that was all I needed, to be the next topic of conversation at her weekly WI meeting. I was still in my early twenties for Christ's sake and what I liked to think was a long way off from wearing big beige knickers the size of a cape and asking for a blue rinse at my next hair appointment!

I gave her a strained smile that was more of a wince as she limped passed us on her three-wheeler walker, trying not to groan aloud and smack my forehead in frustration. So instead I turned my attention back to the current cause of my mental anguish only to see her fighting off a grin.

"Hey, it's like I said, this one isn't on me this time, so take it up with the big man," she said looking as if she was enjoying this far too much and if anything, just waiting to become a spectator in the next Keira/Draven showdown. Of course, when Draven had first told me what they had told my dad, I had of course believed he was joking and simply teasing me. Because surely that wasn't exactly the smartest thing to tell your new father in law…was it?

Well, for a man like Draven then who the hell knew, as it wasn't exactly as though he went by human convention on a daily basis. I turned around and looked about the room trying to find the culprit and not having to look far. I saw him standing near my sister and Frank, deep in conversation whilst little Ella was trying to swing from his arm like he was a climbing frame.

I guess, given his great height and strength, it was like begging a wild child like Ella to just grab a hand and have a go. I even saw Libby try to contain her but with a small shake of my husband's head, she continued to let her daughter use him as she saw fit. I found myself smiling at the sight despite my annoyance and I looked down to see a hand cradling my stomach. I bit my lip at the thought of seeing that very sight with our own child and tears nearly sprang up, pushing my pissed off state to one side and my baby hormones giving it the elbow. But then my sister's eyes found mine and that barely contained smirk had my heckles back up again just as quickly.

"Excuse me Sophia, it's time to teach my husband a very important life lesson." I said scornfully walking away.

"And that is?" I looked back over my shoulder at her and said firmly,

"A happy wife means a happy life."

"And an unhappy one?" She just couldn't help herself from asking with another knowing grin and this time I found myself joining her when I answered with two simple words,

"Blue balls." Then I walked away to the sound of her laughter and the second I got within distance of Draven it was as if he felt me before he even needed to look. He snaked out a hand without confirming it was me and quickly tucked me into his free side... the one not being used as a play thing for a toddler.

Libby gave us both a warm smile obviously enjoying the sight of me being next to my new husband so sweetly. Then she gave me a knowing look that also held a mirror smirk her own husband was also currently gifting my way. I wanted to roll my eyes before elbowing Draven in the gut knowing it would do no harm but in letting him know I was not happy.

He leant down closer to me so as he could kiss the top of my head before whispering so no one else could hear,

"Blue balls, is it?" I growled in response making him chuckle.

"Excuse me, I just need to borrow my husband a minute…sorry Ella Bella," I added looking down at my niece who was dressed like her favourite Disney character, hence where her nickname first stemmed from. She even had a small beast doll hanging by his leg that she had held firmly in her little fist. At first, I thought she was going to cry and so did Draven as he quickly bent down and whispered something in her ear. I didn't hear what it was, but it made her suddenly drop to all fours, growl up at him like a little cat and go crawling off at a quicker speed than Libby would have liked.

"Aunty Pip, Pip!" she shouted quickly getting Pip's attention. Pip saw her coming and just as quickly dropped to all fours and started chasing her. I think Hilary and her mum, who she and Adam had been speaking with, actually did a double take when she did this. Adam however just looked down at his now crawling wife like he wanted to snatch her up and cuddle her for how cute he found it.

Of course. there was something to be said at seeing a small green haired woman crawling around the floor of what was essentially a posh place. But then add this to her wearing pink frilly dungarees that were a skirt and make to look like a 1950's housewife's apron, was enough to get you looking twice. You could actually tell who was used to the sight as the only supernatural being staring at her was her husband and that was in his usual adoring way.

The rest of us were just so used to Pip's amazing brand of crazy that this was considered normal. Now, maybe if we had walked in and found Pip dressed like she had just walked out of the Gap and was calmly making normal chit chat, then we would have probably questioned if another apocalypse was upon us.

Which brought me back to the now and that was Ella currently pretending to be a wild beast, using the cute Disney doll as a chew toy and shaking it in her mouth like it was her recent kill.

"I swear she gets it from your side of the family," my sister moaned to Frank before making her way in the same direction as her unruly daughter. Frank just shrugged his shoulders before following her and I couldn't miss the way Draven commented under his breath, saying,

"Not likely." I would have asked what he meant by that but right in that moment I had my own agenda for storming over here. I grabbed his sleeve and practically dragged him over to the side of the room, unfortunately walking past my great aunty Jean yet again.

"Remember the prunes dear, three a day to keep any blockage away," she said as if humming a merry tune making me roll my eyes and nearly asking for God's help out loud. But instead of letting my instincts kick in the second she passed, I forced myself to grant her an obligatory smile I felt was close to cracking my face it was that strained. I also tried to ignore Draven who obviously was trying very hard not to ask if I had an issue with my bowels he was unaware of. However, with one hissed warning, he wisely refrained when I said,

"Don't you dare say a word."

"Not to say that I am not enjoying being dragged forcefully away by my wife, but I must at the very least enquire as to why?" he asked once I had found a safe distance between us and the rest of the room. One look told me this was supernatural bullshit, as with his hearing he knew exactly why…which is exactly what I said…well sort of anyway.

"You know why! Draven how could you allow your brother and sister to tell my family that the reasons we were late were…well, were…were… you know!?" I asked letting my anger strain my voice. He looked down at me and even bit his bottom lip to aid in holding back the smile I already knew was there ready to break out. Then he ran a single fingertip down my cheek and purred my name.

"Keira." I wanted to frown back up at him but instead I foolishly allowed his voice to affect me as he knew it would. So instead, I closed my eyes and breathed in his touch like a drug I needed to feel the hit from flood my system. I felt him getting closer to me and only when his lips were at my ear did I shudder against him.

"Are you embarrassed that people know you belong to me?" he asked me with dangerous calm. But I knew Draven and therefore knew him well enough to answer his question with care. Of course, the way his teeth found my neck also told me without words to be careful with my answer.

"Nnn…no," I stuttered, and I felt his lips turn up into a smile against my skin.

"Right answer, Sweetheart," he praised, squeezing my side and tugging me even closer to his large muscular frame. Then his hand shamelessly snaked under my sweater and found contact with my skin, making me shiver against him.

"Draven, not here." The three pleaded words were whispered through gritted teeth as I frantically grabbed his hand and tried to push it away. His growl vibrating the length of my neck loosened my grip on his hand instantly.

"Damn the room Keira, you are mine whenever I wish it, do you understand?" he told me, and the first half came more from his demon side speaking directly to me.

"You don't mean that, Draven," I told him knowing he knew I was referring only to him damning the room full of people we cared about.

"Then you are not right of mind if you question me on this, for I can quite assure you, Love of mine, that when you are in the room, that is all that consumes my mind, body, heart and soul…so yes, my demon would damn all that kept me from you and my hands from your body… *one I owned from the first day I met you,"* he said with such intensity it had me questioning what was happening with him. Even his hold on me had become rough and hard.

Yes, so Draven had always been the possessive type, but this new behaviour was…well it was a little unnerving.

I didn't really know what to say to this so instead I let my head fall forward until my forehead was resting on his chest. Once there I muttered his name as a single worded plea,

"Dominic." Upon hearing this he finally relinquished his

firm hold of me and instead started to sooth where his fingertips had started to bite into my skin.

"I am sorry, I don't know what came over me," he confessed, and I looked up at him in time to see him shake his head slightly as if to try and make sense of his behaviour himself. I decided to just put it down to what it was and that was surviving the end of the world after nearly losing everything…that everything being mainly each other.

"Are you alright?" I couldn't stop myself from asking as I reached up and placed my hand to cup his cheek. This seemed to bring him back to me and for a moment he looked lost in my eyes. Then he covered my hand, dwarfing it in his much larger palm before pulling it down to his lips to kiss.

"With you forever by my side, then how could I be anything else but alright?" He told me sweetly, however I wasn't convinced. But instead of going with my impulse to push, I fought against it and decided to let it go…*for now*.

"Good, does this mean I can go back to telling you off now?" I only half joked making him laugh. And just like that the tension seemed to roll off him like an invisible dark veil that slipped from his shoulders and back into the shadows where it belonged.

"I can't believe my family now thinks that we were late because you couldn't keep your hands off me!" I complained blushing even now at the thought.

"Well then, that will teach you not to underestimate the Angel side of me," he said teasingly, and I cocked a hip to the side resting a hand there and asked,

"And what is that supposed to mean exactly?" From the look on his face he was pleased I had asked this as it was obviously something he was expecting. He smirked down at me before lowering his face closer to mine so that he could whisper over my lips,

"It's a sin to lie, Sweetheart." Then just as my mouth had dropped open I heard Draven speaking my parents' names, addressing them as they approached us from behind.

"Joyce, Eric, please forgive us for our late arrival but as you no doubt gathered by now, the love I have for your daughter comes above all else," Draven said smoothly as if his part time job was writing books titled, 'How to get parents in law to fall in love with you in ten easy steps or less'. I felt his hand find mine and as he tugged me to him, I half fell into his side just as he delivered another bombshell to me in a whisper,

"That's a little long winded for a title, beautiful." Then he kissed my cheek, so it looked to my parents that was what he intended all along. This then leaving him looking like some cool, Greek God nicknamed Casanova and me looking like a fish out of water, flapping on the ground and drowning above sea level. Life just wasn't fair sometimes. So, I giggled, hit his arm lightly and said,

"Oh, would you listen to him, such a smooth talker I married...no the real reason we were late was you had a little business to deal with, *didn't you, honey?"* I almost hissed the last three words, telling him silently that he'd better go along with it or there would be hell to pay!

To say the least, I wasn't exactly thrilled with the idea that letting my parents believe now we were hitched we were a couple of rampant bunnies that couldn't even make it to a meal on time thanks to our lustful ways. Okay, so we did have sex in the car on the way here and I had lost count how many times in the last 24hours we'd had sex but that was beside the point. Just because we couldn't keep our hands off each other didn't mean my parents needed to be in the 'very private know'. As in, not at all!

"Oh dear, that's such a shame that even the day after your wedding you had to work," my mum said softly, although one look at my dad told me he was less convinced.

"Should we take our seats now, I think they are ready for us…oh look, so they are," I said in a rush thankfully noticing the woman who was working front of house opening the door into the restaurant and looking around for whoever was in charge of this large party.

Draven looked down at me in shock and the second I smirked back at him I knew he was suppressing a growl. Then a purple glint flashed in his eyes once and his wicked grin was back in place when it was obvious an idea had just struck him.

But instead of freaking out, I decided now was a perfect time to make my getaway and thanks to my new Vampiness skills, (Yes, I am sure it's a word) I managed to twist out of his hold without falling over and sneaking away before he could stop me. I giggled when hearing him growl as I quickly strutted away.

I walked into the large room that had now all been set up ready for what looked more like a stately dinner than a casual meal with family and friends.

The long table had been decorated with flower arrangements with what looked like every purple flower known to man. And each were created in low diamond shapes that sprayed out against the long white table runner with large silver candelabras at their centres. Each of these then held five long purple candles that stretched up like flame lit fingers reaching up to Heaven. Even the chairs were covered in pristine white, tied with deep purple sashes...all expect two.

These were two high backed chairs of highly polished black lacquer positioned opposite each other, situated in the middle of the long table, reminding me too much of thrones. If anything, the whole opulent room just reminded me of another wedding, and suddenly I was wishing I was wearing something less casual than a chunky cream sweater. But then as I caught Draven's eyes search me out when he swiftly entered the room, I no longer felt self-conscious. If anything, the way he looked at me right now made me feel like the most beautiful girl in the room, one he was currently and shamelessly undressing with his eyes.

He briefly took in the room and I soon realised he wasn't doing it for reasons as I had, which was to take in the beautiful setting. No, I was soon to find out why...in the most embarrassing way possible. I watched as the girl who was front of house approached Draven and asked if everything was to his satisfaction. I was just taking my seat when he found what he was looking for and sternly replied,

"No, but it soon will be." Then just as everyone else entered the room and started to fill the long rows of seats, Draven positioned himself opposite me, grasping the back of his chair tightly. His eyes burned into me with that strange intensity back in his flickering purple gaze. It was almost as if he was silently challenging me and I couldn't help raising an eyebrow in question. Just what was he up to this time?

Unfortunately for me I soon found out after he had waited until everyone had pretty much taken their seats and he had the attention of the room. Only then did he make his intentions known. Frank was just about to take his seat next to me, which would have put him opposite my sister, when Draven gestured to him with a shake of his head. Then I couldn't believe it when Draven took hold of his chair and raised it up easily over one shoulder.

"Excuse me Frank, I am sure you understand, but if you wouldn't mind, I think others would agree I have been without her beauty by my side for far too many years than I wish to count," he said as he swiftly spun Frank's chair out of his way so that he could position his own next to mine. Frank's grin was huge as he slapped Draven on the back and said,

"You got it Dom, besides, now I get to sit next to my own beautiful wife." Hearing this made Libby blush just like I did but her own beaming smile couldn't be missed. I glanced towards my mum who was leaning into my dad and whispering something that I knew was no doubt soppy and proud. I knew this when my dad granted a sweet kiss on her forehead making me realise how much love was flowing freely in the room.

I watched as Frank lifted his own chair over the other side, squeezing my dad's shoulder as he passed, a gesture that spoke of the closeness of our family unit and now it was only getting bigger. I couldn't help but look down at the table to see not only my own family members but also my adopted supernatural family, starting with Vincent who sat next to Draven and Sophia who sat opposite him. This was when I noticed that there was a definite divide as one side of the table was all human and the other was all supernatural. Almost everyone from the wedding was still here and I was touched to see that everyone close to us, still wanted to celebrate our union.

"Everyone is still here," I said nodding down Draven's end of the table seeing everyone from Jared and his crew, to Lucius and his own council. Even Leivic, Draven's best friend was still here, along with Sigurd and of course, his father Ragnar.

"They too want to celebrate the battle won with us, and this day marks the end of the end of days." Draven replied, and I couldn't help but give him a sceptical look in return. It wasn't that I didn't believe him, but I knew him well enough by now to see that he was keeping another reason from me. Thankfully, he also knew me well enough to know that with my one look that was all it took for him to fess up.

"We also have a council meeting set for tomorrow after the party tonight," he confessed, and I couldn't hide my knowing smile.

"Party?" I asked with a raised eyebrow. He first had to clear his throat before answering and only when he spoke did I understand why when he said,

"In Sophia's playroom." I felt my eyes get wide before having to quickly clear my own throat before saying a murmured,

"Oh." I felt him grip my thigh under the table to get my attention and say,

"We will be celebrating on our own, sweetheart...*in private,*" Draven told me quietly but obviously not quietly enough as Sophia quickly and very clearly, disagreed.

"Oh no, you two are not getting out of it and will definitely be there..." Sophia was interrupted by Draven's low growl, one that didn't go solely unnoticed by the humans it should have been hidden from. I laughed trying to ease the tension and squeezed his leg to try and get him back to the room, one filled with humans.

"Not going to happen, Sophia." Draven said sternly obviously not liking the idea, but Sophia had an ace up her sleeve, or should I say a Royal.

"Shame then that you must, as it is after all your place… being that *you* are the boss and it is *your* business," Sophia reminded him of his duty in a way that could be argued in front of the unsuspecting humans.

"Oh, that's a shame, work again Dominic…You kids sure do need a honeymoon," my mum said giving me a sympathetic look.

"That's ok mum, we don't need one and besides, we spend a lot of time together, don't we Dra…Dominic?" I said almost forgetting myself and calling him by his last name again.

"Well that's not strictly true, Sweetheart," he said making me wish I could get away with kicking his shin like I would have done had we been sat opposite each other. No, instead I had to be content with just digging my nails into the inside of his leg, hoping it didn't just feel like being tickled by a kitten. Of course, the bastard didn't even flinch, but he did at least look at me, so I knew he felt it.

"I believe your mother is right, lately work has occupied too much of my time and I think now is the right time to set aside my commitments to one far more important to me… you, *my wife,"* Draven said making me silently panic inside…what the hell was he planning this time? I gave the room and him a fake smile as I leant into him to whisper something only he would hear.

"If this plan of yours includes a tall tower in the middle of nowhere with a lock on the door, then me and you are going to have words, Draven." I threatened all the while still smiling. He let out a booming laugh making the whole table wonder what I must have said to prompt such a reaction. Then he grabbed the back of my neck and pulled me in for a kiss that was closer to being classed as X rated than the 'family function' peck on the cheek it really should have been. Even Marcus and Orthrus had been wolf whistling towards the end.

"Kissy, kissy!" Ella shouted, and my dad was clearing his throat whilst my nan was fanning herself with a napkin. I finally felt Draven's hold ease on me and I pulled back to see his eyes hooded with lust that only spoke of his need for me, not the same shame I was feeling at our carnal act into front of everyone.

"Draven." I hissed through clenched teeth that even felt as hot as the rest of my face did. Jesus, but I think my blush could even be found on my toes, I was that embarrassed. But one look at Draven and he didn't care, nor was he taking my reaction seriously. I knew this when he simply winked at me before standing up from his seat and announcing to the room,

"As host, I feel it is my duty to say a few words…much to my wife's obvious dismay," he added, this time making the whole room laugh…other than me of course, who was trying hard not to scowl at him.

"First, I would like to thank you all for not only sharing in our joyous union yesterday but also joining us today in celebrating its aftermath. For me personally this day was far too long in waiting and as you have no doubt noticed, now I finally have her, the Devil himself would be questioning his sanity if he were to try and take her from me, as would anyone else," Draven said, more for his side of the family than mine and even though his words must have sounded strange to my human side, well let's just say that they soon got the picture of Draven's love and devotion.

"As simply put as it can be around her, as I am sure you will all agree with me on how blessed we all are to have her in our lives…" he added making me blush scarlet that was very close to verging on the very unsexy 'strangled purple' colour.

"No simply put, she is my life… for nothing else matters to me but the heart she grants me, the soul she entwines with mine and the beautiful mind she gifts me every day. No, nothing else but my love for her and for the love I am extremely blessed and grateful to share with you all, that now quickly grows and extends to another…" He paused to look down at me smiling when seeing the tears of joy overflowing down my cheeks, then he continued and started to tell everyone dear to us,

"Keira, my beautiful wife…" he stopped and took a moment to look down at me once more before taking my hand, pulling me up to stand next to him. Then still looking down at me he cupped my cheek, swiped a single escaping tear from my skin, before announcing to the room,

"…is pregnant with our child."

And he did this without once…

Taking his eyes from mine.

CHAPTER TWELVE

WISHED WISHES BEING MORE THAN WISHED FOR

After this announcement the next few minutes all happened in a whirlwind of well wishes and congratulations. Suddenly we both found ourselves out of our seats, along with the rest of the room. Then we were separated, pulled from each other so that my human family could show me their love and affection upon hearing the good news. But I wasn't the only one, I thought with a smile when I saw that he too was receiving his own version of affection. Manly back slapping and heavy handshakes were in place of my family's cheek kissing and belly rubbing.

I couldn't help but look back over my shoulder at him when I was yanked forward by my tearful mum only to find him looking back at me doing the same when being embraced by his brother.

The poor hotel staff didn't know what to do when they

had been about to serve the first course but thankfully Sophia, already knowing the happy news, took charge and told them to wait. But during all of this I couldn't help but be drawn to one person in particular, and this time for once it wasn't Draven. No, it was the sight of Ari nearly in tears that had me suppressing a frown when being hugged by my dad and being told,

"Well done, Kiddo."

"Thanks dad," I said still looking at Ari who was now desperately trying to get my attention, even though she already had it.

"Well it's not like she had much to do but just lie back and enjoy it and my oh my, but with that man I would say enjoy it she certainly did...oooweee!" My horny old grandmother said making my dad groan and my mum choke out an outraged,

"Mother!" My sister and Frank burst out laughing and I looked down at my nan, giving her a wink when no one was looking. She let loose a cackling laugh gaining another stern look from my mother making me and Libby giggle. Then my mother's scowl landed on my quiet granddad expectantly. Oh yeah, this was going to be good I thought with a hidden grin. He didn't disappoint.

"Don't look at me like that Joyce, you wouldn't have been born if your mother hadn't forced herself on me that night," my granddad said smirking and winking at his wife, who faked a blush. It had to be said that when my family loved, we did it wholeheartedly.

"Dad!" My mother shouted this time, letting half the room know that my grandparents were once again causing my mum embarrassment.

"Congratulations sweetheart and well done," my granddad said winking and reusing my father's words on purpose, that being his new sport in winding up my mother. I smiled and leant down to kiss him on his cheek.

"Thanks Gramps," I said but there was the other side of this conversation that I couldn't exactly have. No, I am not sure they would have understood it from my side if I had started to explain just what I had to do exactly to get pregnant by Draven. I could just picture it now...

'Well actually, it is well done me as I had to travel back in time to fool my two thousand year old younger husband's self into sleeping with me, in order to get me pregnant to save the world from ending, so yeah...yay me!'

Thankfully however, I didn't say this or the hundred and one things I wanted to say right then. Like how their granddaughter, daughter and sister was now a Vampire, demon angel human hybrid. Oh, and had basically saved the world with her husband and his band of merry Demons and Angels by my side. I also wanted to tell them how I also wouldn't age from this point on and how they never needed to worry about me ever again...or ever buy me anti-wrinkle cream for my birthday...which let's face it, was a shitty gift to receive on your birthday anyway. I mean getting older sucked, so why then make someone feel even worse about it by pointing it out with a gift?

But getting back on track, yeah, there were so many things I wanted to tell my parents right now, but thankfully good sense was on my side, keeping me from saying anything but,

"Excuse me a minute mum, dad, but Ari needs to speak to me." And it was more than obvious that she did. In fact, it looked as though if she didn't get to speak to me soon then she would just end up bursting into tears. This was when I really started to get worried. I knew we weren't sisters in the biological sense but after our time together at the colony and our implanted memories of growing up as sisters, then that had forever forged our connection.

The second I was within grabbing distance of her she frantically took my arm and told me,

"I'm so sorry!" I frowned not understanding what she was so sorry for, but the tears that were now spilling over her long lashes told me that she certainly felt like she had reason enough to be feeling bad.

"What on earth could you be sorry for, honey?" She didn't answer me, and it looked for a moment that she couldn't physically get the words out. But with her one guilty look down at my belly, it had me taking a deep breath and taking Ari ten times more seriously. So serious that when she took my hand in hers I followed her without question as I was lead quickly into the women's bathroom.

The second the door closed behind us she let go and the flood gates opened as she burst into tears.

"Oh Ari, come here," I said pulling her into my arms and letting her get it all out.

"I am so…so, oh God I am so sorry, Keira!" I felt her shuddering against me as she started to sob out her confession.

"Ari, I don't know…" I started to say when she quickly interrupted me as though she couldn't contain the guilt any longer.

"I wasn't there!" she shouted, and I gently pulled her back to look into her beautiful but now haunted blue eyes.

They shimmered under the veil of tears ready to overspill, following others in their path.

"Ari?" I said her name in what could only be described as broken desperation, fearing like never before what she could mean by that. I started shaking my head as if trying to rid myself of the paranoia but one look into her eyes before following them down to my stomach and I couldn't help it. I let out a gasp of horror as my hands flew to my belly, that suddenly felt empty of all hope.

"No...it...it can't be...the prophecy, it was said that..." I knew I was rambling out whispered excuses that would never be enough.

"Oh God Keira, I am so sorry, but I wasn't there! That night I didn't know, I just thought by me being there would be enough but when I woke and found myself in his bed, then I knew...I knew I had failed you." I looked up at her and all I saw was pain brought on by an emotion I knew all too well...*guilt.*

And like all those years I was burdened daily with the feeling, I knew just like now, it wasn't her fault as it hadn't been mine all that time ago. No, I couldn't blame her for this, I couldn't blame anyone for this. So, as I looked at her beautiful face masked by worry and sorrow, I knew there was only one thing left to do...mourn together.

"Oh Ari!" I said pulling her back to my embrace, so we could cry as sisters.

"Why didn't you tell me, honey?" I asked once our joint tears had calmed for the moment.

"I thought I would get another chance to help. I was so angry at Vincent for stealing me away that I demanded he take me back to the room just in case. But then when I heard you had gone missing, I was so scared I wouldn't get another opportunity…and well, it looks like I was right." She looked down at her feet and I hated how broken she was because of it all. I wanted to say all the right things to ease her pain and anguish but right then all I could do was hold onto my own. And instead of finding my own feet, I found my hands cradling my stomach instead.

"After we got back I wanted to tell you so badly but how could I…? What type of sister would I be to ruin your big day like that? I just couldn't do it to you and now I hate myself because now there is a room full of people out there that believe you're pregnant along with your husband...he looks so happy, you both do and now I have taken that all away from you and…"

"Ari, stop," I told her firmly taking her tear-soaked face in my hands and framing her face to get her to look at me.

"Please don't do this to yourself, you're not to blame and I never would…*never,*" I said pulling her to me and before we knew it we had both slipped to the floor to cry just like we did that day in the desert.

"I love you, sister," I whispered in her hair making her grip onto me tighter.

"I love you too, my Kaybear…always, my Kaybear," she told me back making me smile through my heartache. Just then two of my other sisters burst through the door and we both looked up to find Pip and Sophia looking panicked and ready to either kill someone or call the cavalry for the army they thought might be crammed in here.

"What in the girly Hell PJ party are you two doing down there crying like a couple of screeching bobcats?" Pip asked, and I reached up a hand knowing she would get the hint in helping me up. Sophia did the same for Ari, only ending up cradling her head to her shoulder as she burst into another fit of tears. It was in that moment that I hated what my next words would have to be, knowing that they wouldn't stop there. No, the hardest part of all of this was having to tell Draven he wasn't going to be a father... *That would very nearly kill me.*

So, I told them what had happened, to the background sound of Ari's misery, which broke my heart even more.

"Show me," Sophia demanded and at first, I frowned not understanding what she meant.

"Drop your shields. Drop everything," she said again, this time more forceful. She looked almost as desperate as I did, but it was in that desperation that made me do something I never thought I would do ever again. I remember what it felt like to learn that as Katie I had been so vulnerable in their world, with them knowing my every thought.

So, I took a deep breath and for the first time since this all began, I started tearing down every wall I had ever built. I was destroying them, no longer caring about preserving my mind, protecting it or anything. I just needed to know right at that second if Ari was right. But in the end, it wasn't Sophia who saw it. No, it was another being that had a piece of my heart...

It was Pip.

"Oh my god! I see it! I feel it!" she shouted excitedly, and my face shot up to hers in utter disbelief and asked,

"Really?!" The hope in both my eyes and voice was testament to how much I wanted it to be true.

"Oh Gods, I can see it too! Oh Keira, you're going to have a baby!" Sophia said with pure joy lacing every word.

"I am? I really am?!" I shrieked out in shock and astonishment.

"YES!" Both Pip and Sophia shouted together. Then I turned to Ari and grabbed her to me as we cried together… this time in overwhelming happiness.

"You did it! I don't know how but you did it!" I told her flinging my arms around her once more. However, our joyous moment quickly came to an abrupt end as someone suddenly burst into the room.

"Draven!" I shouted and before I could control myself I threw myself into his arms. Instantly they wrapped around my torso like a comforting cage he needed to keep me in. He tangled a hand in my hair to hold my head to his chest and he leaned down as if to take in my scent to calm him.

"Keira." He whispered my name as he lifted me off the floor, so that my feet were dangling mid-air.

"Come on girls, let's give them some time alone," Sophia said softly and one quick glance at her face told me that she was so touched by the sight of me in her brother's arms, that her small smile really held the weight of a mountain of happiness behind it. One by one they left the women's toilets and I felt Ari's hand touch mine that was gripping onto Draven's shirt, giving it an acknowledging squeeze before she joined the other two.

"Keira, why can I…" I didn't let him finish his sentence as the second he lowered me back to the ground I took a step back and placed my hands to where our baby grew inside me. Then I looked up at him with tears still in my eyes and said,

"I…I thought for a moment that I wasn't…" I didn't need to say the rest as Draven looked down at my belly and then suddenly dropped to his knees. I watched in awe as this mighty king looked up at me, kneeling in front of who I knew he considered as his queen, with sheer love and astonishment. Then he lowered his head as if first bowing to me before placing his forehead to my stomach.

It was such a profound moment that in his actions I became lost in a world of love for this man, thinking it impossible to have fallen even more in love with him. But there it was, this one fraction in time now burned to my memory forevermore. And just when I thought he couldn't add any more depth to the feeling, he spoke. Voicing the most beautiful words I had ever heard coming from a father to be…

"Our child, I can sense our child," he whispered in such a way it was almost barely heard but completely felt in every way possible. I felt it in my heart as if it started to beat a little harder, a little faster. I felt it in my soul as something within me seemed to light up and glow. I even felt it in my fingertips as I buried my hands into his hair, holding his head to my body. And he felt my response thanks to having destroyed my walls and letting him in.

He stood swiftly and had me back in his embrace before I could take my next breath.

"Gods I love you!" he told me fervently before crushing his lips to mine in a beautiful untamed kiss that felt like he was once again branding his soul to mine.

· · ·

After this, I explained why I had been so worried, telling him of Ari's gift. At first, he had been surprised but quickly understood my concerns, which begged the question of how and when? We were on our way back into the dining room after our emotional moment in the bathroom.

"I don't understand when this could have happened?" I mused trying to think back to when Ari could have had her 'influence'. The reply to my question didn't really come from an unlikely source as Draven tugged back on my hand, but more so an unlikely place in time as its answer.

"That night...I felt something, could it be?" he said at first more to himself looking off to the side as if seeing a moment of time all play out in his mind. Then he looked back at me with a grin, prompting me to ask,

"What do you mean?" Suddenly his grin grew bigger and a slight more of a curve to one side told me he was feeling cocky and I soon knew why...it was the very last place I ever expected.

"In Jared's office...the night before our wedding," he told me dropping that baby bombshell.

"Oh my god, on his desk!?" I cried out in utter shock. Draven's grin, if at all possible, got even bigger and definitely more bad boy, bad ass.

"The desk we broke," he reminded me with great pleasure.

"No...it couldn't be...could it?" I said first denying it, staring at my feet before looking up at Draven again for confirmation. His smug look said it all. After this I pulled Draven along with me until we found Ari and this time she was being comforted in private by another Draven.

It was obvious that Vincent was trying to discover what

was wrong with Ari, but she seemed to be giving him a hard time of it, remaining silent on the matter. She was just shaking her head when she noticed Draven and I seeking her out. Vincent looked in the direction her eyes had taken and before he saw who it was the annoyed glare wasn't easy to miss. Thankfully, the second he saw it was us, he calmed but even I knew his smile was still strained.

"Um…sorry Vincent but do you mind if I borrow my sister real quick?" I asked having to first clear my throat just to try and cut through the tension that was like a brick wall between these two. Vincent looked back to Ari and because of where I was stood I didn't know what she saw, but when she flinched I gathered it wasn't Vincent's handsome grin.

"We *will* continue this later, Arianna," Vincent stated firmly, and in that moment, I couldn't help but feel sorry for her immediate future. I wasn't used to seeing Vincent this way and even I felt like flinching myself when I saw his tensed jaw and eyes of blue ice.

"Come brother, I wish to ask you something," Draven said light heartedly obviously trying to ease the situation and his brother's growing tension. Well, if there was one person in the world that could relate to him, it would be Draven and the same went for me with Ari.

I waited till I received a wink from my husband before giving him a nod in return, knowing he was telling me without words that he needed to help his brother.

"Ari, are you alright?" I asked softly feeling like I had lost her to her own mind for she seemed so far away. I nearly asked what it was she saw on the wall behind me. In the end it wasn't my words that reached her but only when I reached out and touched her arm did she finally see me.

"He doesn't know," she said cryptically, and it made me look back over my shoulder at the two brothers. They were across the room from us and Draven seemed to be trying to get Vincent to open up to him, pretty much the same I was doing now with Ari.

"He doesn't know what, honey?" I asked giving her arm a squeeze.

"What I am, where I have been, what you needed me to do...he knows none of it and I can't tell him," she said in a flat tone that told me only one thing...she was barely holding on to the last of her control not to break down.

"Why Ari...why don't you think you can tell him?" I asked gently. This was finally when she looked at me and the red in her eyes told me straight away why Vincent was pushing her...*he was worried.*

"I can't explain it but when I am with him it feels like I am doing something wrong...as if I let myself be free around him then I will only end up hurting him." I frowned not understanding why she would feel this way but at least happy that she was finally opening up to me.

"What would make you think that?" She shook her head as if trying to rid herself of her own thoughts but with that one flash of pain in her eyes I knew she just couldn't manage it.

"I don't know but it's just like...like I have been here before and every time I mess it up."

"You mean you remember other men in your life?" I asked getting excited at the prospect that she might remember something of her past life. But then she frowned, and her lips made a flat line telling me I was wrong.

"That's just it...I don't remember there ever being another man before Vincent."

"Okay, I would be lying if I didn't say I am a little confused right now," I confessed, and the little snort of a laugh told me I wasn't the only one.

"Yeah, welcome to a day in my life," she joked, and I was just happy to see a glimpse of the old Ari back, if only for a second.

"All I know is that I can't tell him I went back in time with you or what it is you think I am," she said but I grabbed her shoulders this time and told her,

"What we *know* you are...Ari, I am pregnant because of you." She didn't look convinced as she turned her gaze from mine to find the floor.

"You don't know that...I don't even know when I could have..." I stopped her by quickly asking her,

"Ari that night, my hen night, after we had been on stage...do you remember it?" Her deep blush told me that she did only I wasn't convinced it was for the same reasons I had. Like standing on stage half naked singing Dolly Parton's 9 to 5 in Jared's weird ass, fight club!

"How could I forget it," she said under her breath and I knew I had guessed right, she remembered it alright but definitely not for the same reasons I did.

"After the dance and after, well Draven went all caveman on me, what happened to you?" I asked hoping to get the answer Draven was obviously hoping for. To be honest I think he would be content with any answer that was in this time frame, not one two thousand years into the past with his younger self. But one look at Ari told me this wasn't going to be an easy answer…for her anyway. Not if that deep blush was anything to go by.

"I would rather not…" I stopped her by grabbing her arm and communicating with not only my words but also with a squeeze of my hand what this meant to me.

"I wouldn't ask if it wasn't important, Ari," I said looking down at my stomach to indicate just how important it was. She followed my gaze and with a released sigh I knew she wouldn't refuse me. No, instead she pulled me closer and said in hushed tones,

"After we…well after our sexy dance and my twirling baton thing, well let's just say that your Draven might have been okay with it but mine *definitely wasn't,*" she told me, and I couldn't say I was surprised. I knew Draven had a possessive streak the size of Texas and I doubted that his brother was any different.

However, the massive difference in all of this was that Draven had claimed me years ago and Vincent was yet to accomplish the task. So, for someone who couldn't yet openly enjoy the act knowing that he could then *act* upon his own wishes and desires… well then, yeah it was a bit like cock teasing a nymphomaniac, control freak that was well known for his possessive and dominating issues…that and like waving a flag with your naked picture on it to a Supernatural Bull! It made me wonder who I actually felt sorrier for in this situation, Nun Ari or Blue Balls Vincent?

"Why, what happened?" I asked, thinking that I already had a pretty good idea.

"Well…" she almost started but then paused when looking down at her sleeve, one she started pulling the thread at out of nervous habit. I decided to take pity on her and grab her hand to take in my own, also saving her cute long-sleeved navy-blue dress from having its hems plucked apart.

"It's okay, I get it."

"You do?" she asked looking surprised. So, I looked back over my shoulder at my own domineering other half and said again without looking at her,

"Yeah, I totally do." Then I looked back at her and told her the truth.

"I remember what it was like you know." She frowned not understanding fully what I was getting at, so I told her.

"I remember how intimidated I was around him. How confusing it was to be drawn to something that scared me, to someone who made me even fearful to speak at times. A feeling so intense that you doubted yourself for it even being reality, like in some way something that powerful just...*well it just couldn't be real.*" She looked thoughtful and then nodded both to herself and to me. But I wasn't finished yet and she knew it when I said,

"I remember how intense he was around me and at first I mistook it for hate, if you can believe that." Hearing this her eyes flew to mine and then after finding Draven's figure across the room, she hissed,

"No, never, how could you ever think that?" Her shock made me laugh and I nodded telling her,

"It's true. God, when I think back to the way he was with me, I will tell you it's a wonder we ended up together at all." Her disbelief was still easy to see in both her frown and scrunched up lips.

"I promise you, I am not exaggerating here. He looked like he didn't even want me in his club half the time and the other half he was playing knight in an Armani suit by saving me in some way. Trust me when I say confused is an understatement." She laughed when I said this, and I could finally see the tension lifting from her shoulders. I wondered at that moment what it would have been like to have had someone like me to relate to. Would it have made it easier or harder knowing what I had in store for me?

"But he adores you," she said in a soft voice, bringing me out of my thoughts.

"Yeah, now he does but before we got together most of the time I think I was just a major pain in his royal ass." Ari laughed again, and you could see it was acting like a natural healer for her burdened soul.

"What you…a pain in the ass…*never,*" she joked back being sarcastic and pretending to look shocked. This time I was the one that started laughing and soon we both were.

I quickly noticed Ari stop suddenly and a blush was once again highlighting the apple of her cheeks. I followed where her gaze had been before she lowered her eyes submissively and saw that Vincent was now looking at her like a starved beast wanting nothing more than to devour his next meal. Talk about lust vibes, jeez but my new brother in law was casting them out like he just activated a pheromone bomb and any second it was going to blow up in Ari's face!

And that was all from seeing her laugh. Oh yeah, man did he have it bad. Now I knew who I felt sorry for more and that was definitely Ari. For she may not know it yet, but she was in massive trouble with that bad boy Angel…the question was, when? From the looks of him, I would say that she didn't have long, that was for damn sure!

"Um…so anyway, getting back to that night…" I said trying to get back on track after first having to clear my throat and my mind for that matter. As thanks to Vincent, I now just had visions of him chasing her down like some wild beast man with wings, plucking her from the ground and flying her off somewhere, ready to have his wicked way with her.

"Well, after he took off his jacket and practically ran up on the stage to cover me up like my body was causing everyone offense or something he…what, wait, why are you laughing?" Ari asked me after I couldn't help it, I snorted a series of giggles.

"Seriously Ari, you really think that's why he did it?" She looked taken aback by the question at first and then released a sigh before admitting,

"Well, I don't know why as other than him hissing at me about looking indecent and having to 'deal with people' whatever that meant, what else was I supposed to think?" Once again this had me bursting out laughing much to her annoyance.

"Oh Ari, seriously, he was annoyed because someone he is obsessing over was just up on stage doing a sexy dance and showing off one hot sexy ass in front a room full of people he no doubt wanted to rip apart for watching," I informed her and by her gasp and now gaping open mouth, it looked as though that thought hadn't even once entered her head.

"Noooo…seriously?" she said after the lengthened word 'no' came whispered through her teeth.

"Yessss…what did you think he meant by having to deal with people?" I asked truly curious to know.

"Well, I just thought he meant like to apologise on my behalf or something, you know in case I had embarrassed him or offended important people or something...stop laughing like that or he will hear you!" she hissed pulling me further away, but I couldn't help it, I was now nearly crying with laughter and she too was trying hard not to let the infectious sound invade her irritation.

"You're funny Ari, you know that! Seriously hun, did you even look in a mirror that night?" She frowned at the question.

"You were hot! As in seriously H.O.T! And knowing the Draven brothers as I do, then Vincent no doubt was battling against himself the entire time from grabbing you the first moment he could and running away with you!" I told her making her snort and reply,

"Well, he did try and that's why I ran from him...until he caught me of course," she said in frustration.

"Run to where exactly?" I asked as now it was clear I was getting somewhere.

"Oh, I don't know, I just ran to the nearest door I could find at the back of the club." Her dismissive tone made me smile as now things, like Draven had said, were making sense.

"A broken door by any chance?" Her wide-eyed look said it all.

"You guys were in there?!" I laughed and nodded, now being the one to blush.

"But when I touched the door... that voice...it was...?" She let her question trail away as if she was trying to recall an answer to her own question by looking into the past. Looking into the past, instead of asking me, who was here right now I might add. I couldn't help giving her vulnerable and naive mind a break as I finished off her sentence softly saying what she feared.

"Demonic?" Her eyes flashed to mine in horror and I couldn't help but give her a small smile in return.

"It was Draven speaking from his Demon side." Hearing this her mouth dropped and I was suddenly reminded just how new to this world she really was. She looked so concerned for me, it was almost painful to see.

Yeah, so she may have been a supernatural being trapped in a human mind, but that didn't mean this was any easier on her. If anything, the not knowing who or what you were made it near impossible to fully understand. For how could a person really understand, when they lived in a world they weren't sure which side they were truly part of?

It was this thought that made me gently pull her into my arms and hug her.

"It will be okay, we will figure this out honey, but in the meantime, please don't worry about me. Draven's Demon would never hurt me. And I know this may seem hard to understand right now, but he loves me just as much as Draven does," I told her and only when I felt her head nod a little did I ease my hold on her.

"Well, at least that answers one thing," I said after pulling back, holding her by the shoulders for a moment longer.

"Yeah?"

"You definitely were the reason I got pregnant." My reply didn't come from the fragile young woman in front of me but from the strong presence now at my back.

"Oh, I think I had something to do with that, Love." Draven's voice hummed before wrapping his arms around my torso and pulling me back to his tall, hard frame. Ari blushed and smirked at the floor.

"But yes, you are right sweetheart. Arianna, how can I ever thank you, for not only blessing me with…"

"Active sperm?" I interrupted making her burst out laughing and with her Vincent who had joined her side. For once it was nice to see the tension leave them both, if only for a moment and by me saying something silly. It was only when Draven growled that I started to join them.

"Sorry baby, should I have said Super Sperm…would that have helped your Man King ego?" I asked sweetly before turning in his arms and reaching up to kiss his jaw. Again, Vincent started laughing and when I looked back over my shoulder I winked at them both. Ari just shook her head in amusement, with a smile on her face.

"Oh, naughty little Vixen of mine, I know exactly what will help my 'Man King ego' and if you are not careful then you will be reminded of it right here in this room for others to witness," he challenged, and this time Ari stopped smiling and looked almost as shocked as I did.

"You wouldn't dare!" I threatened spinning on a heel to face him.

"Try me Sweetheart, because just remember, I have the ability to wipe everyone's memory in the room, so even though they won't recall the act, it should be fun seeing your blush whilst it happens," he dared and even though his bad boy grin was answer enough, his words however, gave me enough reason to be worried and quickly offer him my submission. I bit my lip and lowered my eyes making him growl at the innocent looking gesture.

"Vincent, Arianna, if you'll excuse us a moment, I

believe I have to speak privately to my beautiful, blushing wife," Draven said making me unsuccessfully fight a smile.

"But of course, Brother. As for you my sister in law, as always, it's been a pleasure," Vincent said stepping forward to grant me a kiss on the cheek. I couldn't help but turn my head quickly before he stepped away, so I could whisper one word into his ear for only him to hear,

"Patience." He pulled back slowly and the expression he gave me made me squeeze his arm. I knew that look and it was one that only belonged to a tortured soul. It was the same look I had given him that day on the mountain's edge as I gazed down to Draven's cave. It was when I believed my love was dead and with it the loss of half my heart and the loss of half my tortured soul.

Now I knew who I felt sorrier for and it was no longer Ari.

No, she no longer had my full sympathy.

It was…

Vincent.

CHAPTER THIRTEEN

GRANTED FROM HELL

"Pain in my royal ass, were you?" Draven asked obviously overhearing every word of mine and Ari's conversation. I couldn't help but grimace when I felt him grin against my skin. Cocky bastard!

After Ari was led back to the table by Vincent, Draven also decided to lead me away, only it was in the opposite direction to where everyone else was now re-taking their seats. As we passed one of the waitresses he waved a hand back to the table and said,

"There is no need to wait for us, you may serve the first course." This told me two things, one was whatever Draven wanted to tell me couldn't wait and it also wasn't going to be of the quick variety.

He pulled me through a door that led to a hallway and I noticed signs for the reception and conference rooms. The second the door closed behind us I found myself being swung around and was soon in his arms, being totally captivated by the deep emotion in his eyes. Then he crushed me to his body and whispered fervently,

"My wish was granted." The second the words were out I felt myself release a shuddering breath and soon I felt the tears rising up from emotions too great to control.

"As was mine," I told him, barely making the sounds needed but nevertheless, he heard me...*he would always hear me.*

"I wanted to be the one so badly...by the Gods, you know not what I would have done to be the one to give you this in our time," he told me after gently pulling me back, so he could tip my chin up to look into my eyes. I absorbed his words like a soothing balm to my soul and closed my eyes letting the heavy tears seep beneath my lids and roll down my cheeks. Like lightening he moved so fast I sucked in a startled breath as he caught one before it fell from my chin.

"My child, *our child*...I..." he started but then was lost for words. Something that rarely happened for Draven, but the handful of times it had ever happened made them moments to be remembered and non were more beautiful or profound than in this moment. So, I reached up and cupped his cheek in my palm, seeing for myself the same tears threatening to flow from his own beautiful and soulful eyes.

"I know sweetheart, I know," I told him, easing his emotional struggles.

"It feels like a dream, not only to have you here in my arms after the danger has passed, but now to find that our love, our passion in this time has created life..." He paused to take a deep breath while holding me back at arm's length to look down at my stomach, as if he could still sense that life growing inside me. He closed his eyes tight as if the feeling was overwhelming him.

"It is nothing short of a gift and not one from the Gods or the Fates, but solely from the keeper of my heart, a gift from you my love, my only and my everything... *my Keira.*" Hearing this I threw myself at him, secretly glad he took the hint and caught me before I just ungracefully slapped my face against his chest before slipping back down again. No, instead he grabbed me to him and lifted me, so that our lips could meet in a burning passion that couldn't be contained.

His hand embedded itself in my hair as he dominated the kiss, battling his tongue with mine in a feverous war that was seconds away from getting out of control. I was near panting and it was only when I whispered his name across his lips that he finally registered my increasing need to breathe.

It was beautifully raw and exquisitely brutal. It was as though he was branding the memory of perfection to my soul for all eternity and it was such a profound moment that I felt my body shaking from it. He placed his forehead to mine and right then no words were needed, for there wouldn't have been any to find strong enough to define how we felt. So, we let the solace of silence speak volumes for us both.

Then something happened.

Something that shook our connection to its core and unknowingly cracking the foundations of our combined souls.

And it all started with a simple touch.

Draven's hand was still in my hair, but then as he let it fall through the loose strands, his fingertips traced the curve down my neck. This soft, gentle touch for Draven wasn't something new. However, this time when he touched what I could only guess was my birthmark, I felt a pain unlike any other. His fingers seemed to press in of their own accord as if his fingertips were getting fused with the skin there. I suddenly cried out at the burning sensation that was quickly getting hot enough to scald and singe not only my flesh but also my hair.

"Oww argh! Draven!" I shouted trying to get him to pull himself away, but he couldn't. It was only now that I realised I wasn't the only one in pain or trapped by it.

"AHHRAHH!" Draven roared, and I watched as he threw his head back, neck strained and veins bulging from beneath the skin. And even through my own agony my mind still took in the sight and absorbed what was happening to him. The way red fire lit up under his skin and used his veins as a means of travelling around his body, using his human vessel against himself. I could barely believe what I was seeing for the first time witnessing Draven change into his supernatural self and this was new for me. For it now looked as though his demonic power was trying to rise up within him and overpower him in some way. But that couldn't be right could it?

That wasn't supposed to happen. He controlled his demon…didn't he? But this was when something horrific suddenly occurred to me. What if what I was witnessing now wasn't just Draven battling for control…

What if it was his Demon side…*winning?*

"Draven stop it! Fight it!" I shouted as I tried to pull myself free of his bruising hold. I was fighting with him to get away and I wanted to damn whoever was responsible for ripping our perfect moment from us. I wanted to kill whoever had done this to him and these violent thoughts shook me to the very centre of my human existence.

I even reached up and grabbed a handful of his hair, pulling his head down with what must have been a painful tug, as I felt some of the onyx silky black strands snap free from his scalp. Thanks to my added strength and the anger I now put behind the action, it worked enough to get him to see me but what I found there had me gasping.

"Draven?" I spoke his name like a secret plea for what I was seeing was wrong…wasn't real. But in those endless Demonic eyes of hellfire, there was no mistaking that the Draven I had known was no more.

This was Hell and right now, he was lost to it.

It looked as if I was staring directly into the eternal pits of damnation and Draven was looking directly into the hellish sun and instead of getting burnt by its intensity and strength, he was instead consuming it. He was eating the flames whole and absorbing the power within.

I physically flinched back, and he cocked his head to the side as if this was a strange reaction he was encountering, one he couldn't fully understand. Thankfully, the burning hold he had on me started to ease but the fear that was now replacing that pain was very much real and coursing through every cell in my body. I even shook from the force of it and he must have noticed because instinctively he held me tighter. I looked down in time to see his nails start to lengthen into terrifying demonic claws that were better suited to one of Jared's Hellbeasts.

"No, please stop! Pleeease…" I begged as they continued to grow until they had nowhere else to go but into my knitted sweater, tearing into the tightly bound strands like hands running through grains of sand. Thankfully, they stopped when they felt my flesh at their mercy before cutting through me, tearing into my skin and veins like blood red ribbons.

"Draven, please let me go," I pleaded with him, but again he just looked at me as if studying me for the first time. I didn't know how to bring him back as even the sight of my pain and desperation wasn't working. He looked too far gone in his possession that I felt there was only one option left for me, as I screamed the one name in my arsenal that I knew had a chance at taking him, at stopping him before it was too late, and he did something he would always regret.

So, I did something unthinkable.

I screamed in my mind out to the one other man I cared for most in the world…

My Master and…

My Vampire Sire.

"Lucius, help me!" I used everything left in me to shout out in my mind, calling to him so no one else had a chance to see Draven like this. Then Draven's demon started to snarl down at me as if he too had heard me screaming another man's name. His reaction was almost instinctive as his claws dug in and finally started to pierce my skin. I yelped out in pain and this time I was both amazed and thankful to see that the sound finally made it through to him, reaching beyond the demon. He instantly retracted his deadly weapons and just as his burning eyes started to die down to a smoulder, this was when I was saved and suddenly Draven was…

Gone.

I fell to the floor, cracking my knees as they landed hard and throwing out my hands to save myself from falling any further. Then I lifted my head up and the sight that met me was almost as frightening as Draven's demon.

To the point that at first, I wasn't sure that what I was seeing was real. It took me a moment to get my bearings and take in what was happening. This was when a gasp left me now for a different reason. I was now staring at Lucius holding Draven up by one hand at his neck and snarling inches from his face as if he was ready to rip his throat out any second. It was the first time I had seen Lucius overpower Draven in any way and the sight was utterly terrifying. Now my fear was for a very different reason and was all for what would happen to my husband in these next few moments. It was as though everything up until this moment was now hanging by a single thread, ready to snap and it was rightly named Lucius' control.

So, without thinking about it I ran to Lucius, put a hand to his extended arm, the one currently holding all Draven's body weight, pinning it to the wall. My touch was met with a solid rock beneath my palm that seemed to pulsate with unleashed power. One he was currently taming, unlike Draven had done moments before.

"Lucius, please…*please don't hurt him.*" This time my plea was heard and thankfully acted upon the second my voice penetrated his mind. He released the snarling demon that was still my husband…somewhere deep within and I winced, looking away as the sight lanced through me as though his claws were still attached, only this time to my heart.

Draven was about to attack him, I knew this the second Lucius snarled down at him venomously and demanded in a harsh, demonic voice of his own,

"Stay down!" I was utterly astonished to see him not only obeying but doing so like an obedient dog that had just been whipped. It was a painful sight to witness. This was when a realisation so profound slammed into me that it knocked the air from my lungs, having me staggering backwards, placing a hand at the wall to steady myself.

"You...you always had the power to do that?!" I accused making Lucius' gaze snap to mine. He seemed to absorb my words and after taking a moment to digest them, he decided to take in my appearance, seeing that now my arms showcased five bloody framed holes from where Draven had lost control.

"Come here, my little Keira Girl," Lucius demanded and from the look of things I knew I would have been out of my mind to refuse him. I stepped into his large body, letting him pull me closer. Once there I let my body relax into his safety but one glance around his arm and I flinched when seeing Draven there on the floor looking like a wounded man.

"Don't look at him, look at me, Pet." When I didn't straight away I felt his grip under my chin, forcing me to comply.

"Now, tell me what happened." I bit my lip at his question and suddenly it started tumbling out of me like I was in confession. I told him of the baby, the way he thought...the way we both thought it was from the past but then our happiness at finding we were wrong. I then told him about him touching me and the second he made contact with my birthmark something happened. He started to change, and I couldn't get through to him.

Whilst I relayed all this to Lucius, two things were happening. The first being Lucius rolling up my sleeve to access the damage and the second was he was doing this to the sound of Draven growling like a caged wild beast. This had me jumping in his arms and stuttering my words.

"He…I can't…we…"

"Ignore him," Lucius said sternly, and my mouth gaped open…was he freaking serious?!

"Are you joking, how can I ign…" He cut me off swiftly with his own anger.

"He hurt you, *one of my own*, and right now he is lucky to still be breathing, so for now I suggest you heed my words before I *ignore* your softly spoken pleas…understood?" he told me making me swallow hard and nodding quickly. He sounded so deadly I had no choice but to trust in his threatening words, seeing them as law.

"Good, now turn around," he said his voice clearly still strained and clipped. I decided it was definitely not wise to push him whilst he was this close to the edge. And if my softly spoken pleas were all that was keeping Draven from being mauled by a crazy Vampire, then right now, I was happy to play submissive little Keira girl.

"Right choice Pet, now turn around," Lucius said obviously hearing my thoughts, making me shout out the obvious,

"You can hear my thoughts?!"

"Yes, and right now they are as aloud as you are," he said keeping his frown firmly in place. This was when I wanted to roll my eyes at myself and slap my head. My walls were still down, and I knew that right now they were remaining that way until I had the time and energy to build them back up. Because it was different when you had years to add to them, constructing them with impenetrable layer after layer as my strength grew.

"Of course, you can," I moaned quietly to myself before telling him why, feeling as if I needed to explain why.

"I let them down, so we could see if I was still…well you know…"

"A knocked-up Vamp?" Lucius finished for me and I slapped his bicep, which I should mention was like hitting a metal lamp post!

"Don't say it like that!" I scolded, making him finally crack the barest glimpse of a smile down at me. Then I rolled my eyes at him, but it seemed he'd had enough of waiting for me to do as I was told. Because the next thing I knew he gripped the top of my head and started making a turning motion with his hand as if there was an invisible crank wheel there. I got the hint and turned my back on him, letting him see for himself what had happened. I half expected him to say, 'oh yes, here it is, the trigger on your neck is accidently set to evil demon, not angel boy or even better, the half way point like usual'.

Then I felt him raise a hand ready to touch me, and I sucked in a sharp breath in dangerous anticipation. All other sound seemed to be sucked out of the long corridor and other than the rapid pounding of my heart there was nothing between us but the outcome of what his next action would bring.

"Don't look so scared sweetheart, I won't bite…*again.*" He combined this last word with a playful bite to my ear lobe and I knew when I finally took a breath, it was said for that sole purpose…okay that or it simply amused him but really, who knew with Lucius.

So, I waited for the touch, my shoulders tensed and even though I was no longer holding my breath, I was still ready for it to escape me on a gasp. Something that happened, but for all the wrong reasons.

"Ah!" I shouted as the door to the hallway started to open and my mum of all people was trying to step through it.

"Mum!" I shouted stepping towards the door and holding it so that it wouldn't open fully. That was the last thing I wanted to happen, my mum seeing me being gently touched by another shockingly handsome man, whilst my poor husband was slumped on the floor looking like he had just been dragged up from Hell.

"Kazzy dear? What are you doing behind the door?" she asked sounding surprised and agitated. I looked back at Lucius and gave him a look that said what on earth was I going to tell her!? Then I gawked at him when his answer was given to me in the form of a rude sign made with his hands. I think my eyes bulged when he joined the tip of his forefinger to the tip of his thumb before using two of his fingers from his other hand to penetrate the hole he just made. I think he could most likely have seen my tonsils for how wide my mouth had dropped open.

The simple sex enactment he made with his hands made me nearly forget our current predicament and shout, 'What the Hell, are you effing crazy!' Instead I simply went with a mouthed silent,

"What the Fu...?" I was halfway into mouthing my swear word when my mother said my name again only this time using the big guns...

"Catherine, Keiran Williams, I asked you a question!" I swear it was like she knew! Of course, Lucius' bad ass smirk didn't help, that was for damn sure and I felt like kicking him. The only saving grace in all this was that he was situated at my side, so my mother couldn't see him but after that any other grace did a flying leap out the nearest damn window!

"Um…mum, this is embarrassing but…" I couldn't believe I was about to say what Lucius wanted me to say, which was why I was stalling, desperately trying to find others to replace them.

"Umm…well you see I…we…uhhh…"

"Keira, I saw you come in here and we all heard a shout… what are you…?" My mum started to say, obviously getting impatient herself and this was when Lucius had hit his human limit. This along with Draven deciding now was a good time to growl. But Lucius simply slashed out a hand, cutting through the air and using his powerful mind control to silence Draven swiftly. Then he pulled me back out of sight and clamped a hand over my mouth before using my voice as his own! Then the bastard spoke as me and a very large (Titanic iceberg sized) piece of me died of shame!

"Unless you wish to see how I got pregnant in the first place I suggest staying on that side of the door… mum," Lucius said adding the 'mum' bit, but in a really awkward way that sounded more like an afterthought. I couldn't help but growl into his gloved hand feeling myself close to biting through the leather and tearing straight into the blood sucker! I didn't care if his hand was still healing or not!

"Oh…oh my, yes of course, I mean no! I don't…oh dear!" she muttered utterly stunned by her daughter's behaviour that the pressure on the door quickly disappeared as she scurried away. Finally, Lucius let go of me and I turned quickly to hit him on the arm again shouting,

"Are you freaking insane! That was my bloody mother!"

"Exactly, so I think you will find she is fully aware that to conceive a child, her own daughter would not only have full knowledge of the act of copulation but also be actively engaged in it." I gave him a frown so deep it probably gave me a monobrow! Then I snapped,

"Copulation? What are you, like a million years old!?" He gave me a wry look in return and stated,

"You know exactly how old I am."

"Yes, I do which means you think you'd know better by now and have learnt something useful!" I argued back making him fling an arm out to my now quiet husband and say,

"I think you will find in this case, that *is* my something useful!" he bit back but I wasn't listening. No, instead I was now panicking totally over my mum now making her way back to a table full of my family with God only knows what was in her head or worse…on the tip of her tongue!

"Oh God!" I moaned grabbing my hair with both hands and wrenching it back from my forehead in utter frustration. Then a thought popped into my head that I quickly latched onto and almost screamed my demand at him.

"You can control her mind, so fix it!"

"Excuse me?" he said as if this was an utter foreign concept for him.

"You can control minds, I mean jeez you're supposed to be the freakin' master at it…"

"Supposed to be?" he repeated as if this was a massive insult to his ego, one I didn't give a shit about right now.

Something I decided to make known by slapping him on the chest and saying,

"Look Uri Geller, I don't care what level mastermind you are, just fix this!" I snapped making him growl.

"Fine! I will invade your mother's mind and take away her memories, so she can continue to believe of your misconceived, virginal innocence. That way you can continue to think up a great excuse for the next nine months on how you fell victim to the sinless, immaculate conception that is sweeping the nation…mainly in Catholic schools or so I hear," Lucius replied sarcastically.

"Ha, ha" was my come back and yes, I knew it was no doubt my lamest yet and damn him, but didn't his look just say he knew it!

He opened the door a crack and quickly spied my mother just as she reached the table.

"There! There she is!" I shouted right next to him as I too peered around the door as I had now wedged myself in front of him, popping up like a Jack in the Box. I felt him look down at me before commenting dryly,

"Yes, thank you Sherlock." I rolled my eyes but refrained from jabbing him in the ribs like I wanted to. Then he seemed to concentrate a moment and I watched my mum shake her head a little.

"Oh, and just so you know, Uri Geller bends spoons," Lucius said this time making me bite my lip to suppress a giggle.

"Yeah, well if this works then I will upgrade you to Derren Brown, but in the meantime focus will you, 'cause the last thing I want here is my mum breaking out into the funky chicken dance and telling everyone she just had afternoon tea with Tina Turner!"

"Who the fuck is Derren Brown?" Seriously, out of all I had just said that's what he came away with?

"Okay so how is it you know who the bendy spoon guy is but not the world's most famous mentalist and illusionist?"

"Is he English?" he weirdly asked,

"Uh, yeah."

"Then that's why," he stated making me frown.

"Now what is that supposed to mean, Mister?!" I demanded with my hands on my hips, now I had slipped out from between him and the door, once he had obviously finished with my mother's mind. He closed the door and said,

"I know, let's have a long chat about something inconsequential, like the answer to that question, or here's an idea, we could fix your husband before you start to become the next runner up for this year's worst wife award…um?" Okay, so looking at my poor husband and I had to agree, he had a point.

"Can you help him?" I asked taking a step closer to him only to have my movements restricted now by a band of steel that was firmly across my chest.

"Oh no Pet, I think keeping your distance for now is the smart thing to do." Seeing this Draven suddenly pulled from his mental restraints and lunged at Lucius, which meant because he was still holding me, he also lunged at me too.

"Draven no!" I shouted but by the time it took me to even finish saying his name in panic, I found myself being guarded behind a wall of muscle that was Lucius' tall, imposing frame.

"Enough!" Lucius shouted, demanding that he was not only understood but also now obeyed. I had to say the sight of Draven falling to his knees in front of Lucius had me wincing painfully. I hated seeing him this way, as it seemed not only go against the grain, but more like against all that was the natural world.

Draven knelt to no man but his demon, well it was clear Lucius had the power easily enough to make him yield any time he wished it. Which was why I couldn't help but look up at him and surprisingly found that the harsh look in his eyes and the hard tick in his jaw meant he wasn't enjoying this one bit. Oh yeah, considering their past, then like I said, this surprised me alright…surprised the Hell out of me! (No tactless pun intended of course.)

"Please Lucius, can you do something for him…can you bring him back?" I asked in a pained way that told him of how much I hated seeing him like this. Lucius replied to my plea with an issued command, one I hoped would be his last.

"You will sleep, Demon." And with that Draven suddenly passed out on the floor, meaning it was now safe for me to run to his side. I dropped to my knees and gently pushed his fallen hair back from his face.

"Is he…?" I barely made those two words sound audible as they came out on a broken breath.

"Don't worry Pet, he is fine…*they both are,*" Lucius reassured me but even his words couldn't keep the guilt at bay.

"It wasn't your fault, Keira," Lucius said obviously reading my thoughts.

'Stop reading my mind, Lucius,' I told him back in my head knowing he would hear me.

"Your expressive eyes tell me all I need to know and right now they are nearly drowning from the tears of your guilt, a guilt you need not feel, for you are not at fault," he told me crouching behind me and placing his hands on my shoulders. Then I felt him try and pry me away from his side and after tensing, fighting against his pull, he informed me,

"If you want me to help you I first need to understand why this happened." This was his only explanation as to why he wanted me to leave Draven's side, which I decided right now was something I had to do. He was right, if we were to fix whatever this was, then first we needed to understand it. And for that to happen I needed Lucius to see whatever it was Draven had seen.

So, with this firmly in my mind I let him guide me up from the floor. Then keeping my back to him I felt him shift all my hair off to one side as he resumed his previous exploration before my mother had interrupted us. And once again, I braced myself and briefly had time to ask myself the biggest question of all…

What if when he touched my mark the same thing happened to him?

Oh god, what were we doing?

No, I couldn't let that happen!

I had to stop this!

"Lucius stop… STOP!" I shouted this time with more force, but it was too late as his fingertips connected with what still felt like my burnt skin. I hissed at the sting but it was only after his body tensed behind me and his fingers stilled, did I suck in a terrified breath.

I was too late.

It was done.

The connection was made and there was no going back.

I quickly shuddered against him as his arms suddenly locked around me from behind and a deep guttural growl rippled up through his chest. It felt like my body had once again been plunged into the frozen depths of that lake and a thousand shards of ice were now attacking my nervous system.

Lucius must have sensed my desperation and fearful mind because inside I was screaming. I felt him take a deep, shaky breath as if I had just knocked the wind out of him and he was trying to recover from it.

Then he spoke.

"Well, that's interesting," he commented and even though I couldn't see him I felt him shake his head as if he was trying to rid himself of the sticky remains of whatever feeling was still clinging to his mind.

"What?! Lucius tell me… what…what was it?" I asked frantically and in all the answers he could have given me, none would have floored me the way his next words did.

Just three little words.

Three dark, damning words…

"It was Hell."

CHAPTER FOURTEEN

HELLISH HUSBAND TANTRUM

"I'm sorry, come again?" I asked in utter shock on hearing what Lucius just said to me. I felt him release a sigh behind me as I was still currently trapped in his arms. It was as if he knew the second he let me go I would start flapping my arms around in a mixture of denial and blind panic. Of course, he was right.

"We will figure this out, love," he told me softly, but I was no longer hearing him. No, instead I was just replaying those torturous three words over and over again. 'It was Hell'...*it was Hell*'...I mean what the *'Hell'* did that even mean!

"I think I should explain," he said, and I snorted my snappy agreement,

"Yeah, I think that's a damn good idea, don't you?" Again, he took another deep breath before turning me back around to face him. I watched as a few different emotions flittered in his eyes as he looked at me and because of this I couldn't have guessed what he would say next, only hoping it was something helpful…

It wasn't.

"Seriously sweetheart, I am starting to think you are cursed." At this I growled and would have followed through on my urge to punch him in the gut if there weren't more important things to do than knock the wind from him. And with my new vamp strength I just might have achieved it.

"Oh yeah, 'cause that's what I need right now, your helpful theories on why it's highly likely a bird would shit on me, whilst simultaneously stepping in dog shit as I walk down a road named Shit Street! So, unless you want to see me go *batshit* crazy, I would start talking and I warn you Luc, it had better start with the words, 'what I meant when I said it was Hell is'…" I threatened a tad dramatically making his lips twitch in a failed attempt at containing his obvious amusement.

"Lucius." I hissed his name in warning.

"Alright my little Keira Girl, I will ease your mind, although when I tell you, I am not sure how far that *ease* will stretch," he said, warning me this time.

"Please Lucius, just…" I started to say when he cut me off with the reason for his earlier apprehension.

"When I touched your birthmark, it showed me Hell," he said, and I gasped.

"Wh…what do you mean?" I asked unsure I had even voiced it at first. As if I needed to test my voice before committing it to words. Lucius looked as though he hated being the one to tell me this and when he rubbed the back of his neck in frustration I knew it was bad. Supernatural Kings and men high up on the power front, barely looked frustrated

at the worst of times and on the rare occasion they did, it was…well annoyingly, it was usually because of me.

"I don't know why but the second I made contact I felt something calling to my Vampire side, like it was trying to pull it out and drag it back down to Hell." Hearing this I staggered back and covered my mouth with my hand, releasing a cry of shock behind it.

"Keira, listen now…" I started shaking my head telling him no, there was nothing he could say right now to ease the pain of what I had unknowingly done.

"It wasn't your fault," he said but when I looked back at Draven's still sleeping form I was only left asking myself *why* I did this, not the even more important question of *how*.

"And neither was that," Lucius added when he knew where my thoughts we headed…Hell that's where, as in my own personal kind!

"Keira listen to…" he started to say but I wasn't listening. How could I in the face of what I had done? But then, as my mind started to race, suddenly I knew there was more for him to say and I knew this was no doubt my only opportunity to ask. So, with this firmly in my mind I pressed on through my guilt and inner turmoil in sight of gaining important information.

"What did you see?" I asked with my voice growing cold and hard, becoming a reflection of how I felt about myself. I watched him close his eyes a second and I didn't know if it was in pain at seeing my own or if he was searching the memory so that, he could tell me.

"Keira, I…" Lucius started to say but the second he began to speak in that placating tone I could tell he didn't want to tell me.

"Tell. Me. Now. Lucius," I interrupted telling him with my own tone that I wasn't taking any bullshit here. The second I saw his shoulders slump, I knew the next sentence out of his mouth would be my answer…or at least that's what I thought.

He looked first to me and then to Draven before, at last, his gaze finally settled on me again. Then after muttering something under his breath, which was no doubt a foreign curse, he spoke.

"I saw…" he started to say but it was in that moment that Draven groaned behind us and I knew the effects of Lucius' mind control had started to wear off.

"Draven!" I yelled his name and nearly forgot myself as I took a step closer to him. Thankfully, Lucius' quick actions saved me as he quickly situated himself between us, holding me back with an arm cast behind him. I inched around his impressive torso a little, so I could see Draven, and Lucius was right, he was still not himself.

"What are we going to do?" I asked in a wary voice hoping, no more like praying, Lucius had the power to do something.

"We? Sorry sweetheart but this is a one man show. Now, I want you to do the sensible thing for once."

"And that is?" I asked hands on hips waiting for what I knew was going to be something I would no doubt refuse him.

"I want you to walk back in there and…" I cut him off with an annoying buzzer sound, as if he had just got the wrong answer in some cheesy gameshow. His eyes widened before he started frowning, a look I was refusing to take seriously despite what had just happened.

"I do not cut and run, Lucius, you should know that by now," I told him firmly.

"What I *know* is that you like to swap common sense for stubbornness and self-preservation for what I can only assume is suicidal tendencies!" he snapped clearly getting frustrated. So, instead of giving him any more attitude I decided to go down a different route of action...*puppy wide eyes.*

"He's my husband, Luc," I said in a quiet voice, stepping closer so that I could look up at him. However, instead of getting the reaction I was hoping for, he smirked and said,

"Nice try Pet, but that won't work on this immortal, besides as much as I like the feel of your divine little body pressing up against my own, it is not enough to sway me into putting it in danger." I groaned in frustration making him chuckle, the bastard!

"Well, we both know you can't control my mind and I am not moving, so I think you will find you have another... Hey! What are you...!" I shouted, as I was being tipped over his shoulder after he bent to my stomach level before my eyes could follow his movements. Damn him but he was fast, faster than even my new Vamp senses could take in.

"Put me down!" I demanded, one that was quickly stepped on with a deep resonating growl directed my way.

'Silence,' he ordered and this time it was one that was sounded in my mind. Suddenly my lips slammed shut and I was unable to open them again. This was when I realised just how vulnerable I was as I had stupidly believed that Lucius couldn't control me. And in any other circumstance this may be true, but I was forgetting one major factor now at play

here and that was the loss of my barriers…ones, I myself had lain to waste.

I was in half a mind whether to fight him or just slump across his shoulder submissively until he had finished following through with whatever plan he had. In the end, I went with the latter.

Draven growled and snarled as we passed, and Lucius snapped down at him,

"Et tamen, Daemonium!" ('Be still, Demon' in Latin) This seemed to calm Draven enough to stop him trying to fight against Lucius' power but it wasn't enough to prevent the undiluted rage I could see darkening behind his demonic eyes. It was as if he was trapped behind an invisible barrier, pacing like a feral beast just waiting for the opportunity to strike. And it was obvious that Lucius didn't want me around for when he did. This being another reason why I decided to listen and play the submissive little Vampire hybrid...Of course, not being allowed to talk also helped immensely with this decision.

Damn Vampire.

One I intended on kicking in the shins the second I got the chance, I thought on a silent growl.

"For fear of your wrath, I'd better let you speak now Pet, after all…*I am quite partial to my shins,"* he mocked after pausing and giving my legs a squeeze.

"Of course, you are," I replied dryly making him chuckle, but as I pushed myself up from his back so that I wasn't just faced with his black shirt, I looked back at Draven and my heart twisted.

"What if someone…" Lucius cut off my worries about someone walking in and finding Draven, with the sound of a lock being turned after briefly glancing at the door. Then he continued down the hallway until he found what he was looking for, carrying me as though I weighed nothing but a bag full of air. Unfortunately, as I was staring at the sight of his long powerful legs striding down the hall, it was as if he knew because he gave my body a jerk. This was powerful enough for my hands to slip on his waist and just as my head swung towards his back, he purposely lifted his hold on my legs, so I fell further down the back of his body.

I shrieked in panic as at first, I thought he was going to drop me but then that cry ended up being because my head ended up smacking into his ass as he had fully intended. Well, if his man chuckle was anything to go by that was.

I instantly pushed up to get my face off his ass having no choice of where to put my hands other than on each of his cheeks. I was moaning and swearing under my breath as I fumbled around, trying not to touch him there. Thankfully, in the end he felt pity on me and started to pull my legs back down, so I was now back to staring at his back once more.

"Asshole," I called him making him laugh again, replying with,

"Yes, it was but what a shame you didn't kiss it whilst you were there." My response was a growl and once again something that made him laugh out loud.

I was still muttering my insults as he continued to find what he was looking for. Then he stopped at a door and my first reaction was to question it.

"Really?" I asked disapprovingly, after reading the door plaque.

"Sorry sweetheart, but we are under some tight time

constraints here and I don't think I have the time to whisk you up to your luxury suite for you to wait in comfort."

"Yeah, I get that but really, you want to hide me in a stockroom…what do you want me to do, build a sofa out of toilet rolls?" I only half joked but as he lowered me down his front, I saw his half smile and knew he was fighting a laugh. Of course, he would have to do this painfully slow, so I was mere inches from his face for longer than I would have liked. By the time my feet came in contact with the floor again he gave me a smouldering look and told me,

"You're a bright girl, you will figure something out," he said then, with a grin, he flicked me under the nose.

"Besides, I think it's safe to say you can't get up to too much trouble in here."

"Oh, I don't know Lucius, are you sure? I think they're flammables I spot down there on the shelf?" I said looking back over my shoulder at the metal shelving unit. Again, his lips twitched, which I had to say, Lucius fighting a grin was almost as sexy as Lucius sporting a grin.

"I think you will be fine, Pet." At this I slapped him on his chest and said,

"Well lucky for you I failed my 'How to make a bomb out of household products exam', so I think it should be safe." This time I did get the Lucius full on smile and like I said, the Lucius lip twitch definitely came in second place.

"Well in that case, make yourself comfortable, Doll face," Lucius said making me giggle.

"Wait, what are you going to do?" I asked as he was about to close the door.

"What, besides waste time here talking to you…" he started but I put a hand on my hip and said,

"I need to know." He finally took in my serious face and released a sigh before telling me.

"I am going to force his demon to release his control and then explain to Dominic what happened." Oh no, this was bad.

"You can't do that!" I yelled, and his gorgeous eyes widened a moment in shock.

"I think you must have misread the reasons for me now being in this predicament and hence why I am here right now…'cause as entertaining as I find all this, it isn't my perfect idea of attending a dinner and a show."

"What I mean is, that yes, I agree, please get his demon side to backdown but isn't there anyway to do that and…oh I don't know, like have him not remember or something?"

"Excuse me?" Lucius said clearly shocked.

"Look, you do get how possessive and protective Draven is…right?"

"Well, seeing as you could most likely write a book titled 'how to survive ten kidnappings or more' then yeah, I would say he has good enough reasons to be," Lucius replied sarcastically making me roll my eyes. Yeah, okay so he was right, but that didn't mean I was about to swap my paintbrush for a word document and a laptop. Besides, now was not the time for sarcasm…well, not unless it came from me anyway.

"Well seeing as I don't fancy living eternal life in a pretty gilded prison and giving birth in some bloody tower in the middle of nowhere, then I suggest you make life easier for me by taking his memories away." The frown he gave me said it all, but him crossing his arms across his muscular chest only reinforced it.

"Keira, as much I sometimes don't see the logic in Dom's decisions, being myself a victim of his past indiscretions, I have to say that keeping this from him is not what I would call a wise decision…for both parties." I closed my eyes in frustration for a second before giving it one last shot.

"Look I am not saying that I am going to keep this from him indefinitely or anything, but just until I have looked into the reasons why touching my mark caused this and until then, doing everything I can do to prevent it," I said and even though he gave me a 'Yeah right, I would like to see you try' look, I knew he was also starting to waiver in his decision. However, that didn't stop him from trying one last time.

"Keira, I doubt wearing scarves for the foreseeable future is going to work in this instance and not to mention, look a little suspicious." I frowned up at him before releasing a heavy and frustrated sigh.

"Please Lucius, all I am asking for here is a little bit of time…we just found out that the baby we made was in this time, not his past…which trust me when I say, means a great deal to him." He raised an eyebrow at this and then said in a low voice,

"Yes, I can imagine." I decided to ignore the inner meaning of that comment and decided to press forward with desperation as my last hope.

"Please. Please Lucius… do this for me," I whispered completely unashamed and about to beg if need be. His eyes softened just before the point he nodded at my request.

"Fine, I will do as you wish, but be it on your head when this doesn't go your way, pet," he warned but all I heard was his acceptance, which was all I could focus on right now.

"Oh, thank G…" I was about to say God when he gave me a stern questioning look, making me change that thank you into…

"…Goodness for the almighty and powerful Lucius, ruler of all Vamps and so forth…better now?"

He smirked and said, "It's a start." I huffed as my reply but couldn't keep up the pretence of my fake attitude when I started smiling.

"Right, enough time wasted, you stay here until I come back for you, whilst I go and deal with your husband's demonic tantrum." I laughed at that, thinking well that was one way to put it!

"Thank you," I told him making him once again nod in acceptance.

Then just before leaving me to go off and complete his 'mind altering' chore, he stopped and looked beyond me to inside the room. At first, I wondered what he was looking at but then remembering our earlier conversation, I smirked, knowing what was coming.

"Oh, and Keira…" he said after first looking down at the bottom shelf of the shelving unit.

"Yeah?" I asked as he paused before tapping me under the chin and continuing,

"Don't touch anything, you know…"

"Just in case."

CHAPTER FIFTEEN

GIFT OF THE SUN

"Ha, ha," I said to the door after he winked at me before closing it. Okay, so once again it wasn't my best come back but after referring to my bad luck that obviously lay firmly on the dangerous end of the spectrum, what else could I say.

Then came the most annoying part. Waiting like some helpless little victim whilst God knows what was happening out there. Seriously though, I was starting to think that what Lucius had said was right, was I cursed? Well, it was starting to feel like it, that was for damn sure!

"I just beat back the bloody apocalypse for Christ sake, you would think that would entitle me to a free pass for a few days at least!" I complained out loud looking up to the Heavens and only finding a series of square panels that made up a false ceiling...yep, nothing heavenly about that or the dark damp patch growing in one corner, I thought with a frown.

I had to wonder if life was ever going to get any easier and if one day I would look back at all this and think, 'Oh right, I remember those times. Man, how grateful am I that my life is so peaceful now?'... Yeah, I couldn't see it happening anytime soon.

No, unfortunately I think the only way my luck was going to change was if I was to bathe in a tub full of four-leaf clovers, blessed by an Irish priest, a leprechaun and a shaman wearing a horseshoe around his neck. Then he could wave a rabbit's foot at me after hitting me over the head with one of those nodding fortune cats, that personally I thought looked like they were just mocking you. Yeah, I could just see it now, Draven walking in on me naked in a bath of green mush surrounded by my 'Luck Team' all praying, throwing holy water, sprouting off Irish Proverbs and shaking dead animal parts at me.

I think my luck would sharply end there, along with theirs for that matter, as one look at the door and what now lay down the hall behind it, then I think it was easy to say that my demonic husband would no doubt kill them just for seeing me naked.

Yep, Lucius was right.

I was cursed.

By the time Lucius came back I had no idea how long I had been waiting, but it was long enough to make a tower of toilet rolls that impressively nearly touched the ceiling. I was balancing on a small step ladder as I was just reaching over to grab the smaller tower from the shelf, to join with the one I had started from the floor.

This was when the door opened.

And this, embarrassingly enough, was how Lucius found me.

Me, standing on one leg as I reached out, holding a tower of seven toilet rolls in one hand and trying to steady the tower of many, to add them. I looked as if I was auditioning for a really lame circus act. That, or showcasing a new fun way of teaching kids the importance of toilet hygiene...both of which would not have been on my top ten list of how I wished to be found by a sexy Vampire King.

Damn it, but I knew I should have gone with the toilet roll sofa!

"Uh...I fear the answer to this question but alas, still feel it my duty to ask...what exactly are you trying to accomplish here, Pet?" Lucius asked looking as shocked as a two thousand plus year old Vampire could be. Meanwhile, I probably looked like a doe caught in headlights as I looked to the door, arms out, still frozen mid action.

"I got bored," I stated.

"Yes, Love, I can see that," he responded wryly making me bite my lip.

"How did it go? Is he...okay?" I asked, the concern clearly written in my eyes and the waver in my voice. However, when his lips twitched I knew it was because I was still in this odd position. Thankfully, this made him take pity on my obvious deteriorating mental state. So, he took a step inside the room and wrapped one arm around my waist, at the same time wrapping a hand around my wrist that still held the mini toilet roll tower.

Then, with him guiding my hand, I balanced the toilet rolls on top of the bigger tower, (Obviously he knew how important it was to me to finish and accomplish my crazy task) and all the while I was trying not to let Lucius' devastatingly handsome and amused smile cause my hand to shake. He was clearly finding this very entertaining but thankfully did so quietly.

Once I had finished, he pulled me closer to his side before lowering me to the ground off the step ladder. Then he took my hand in his and finally answered my question,

"He is fine but come and see for yourself." Then just as I was letting him lead me from the room I pulled back and said,

"Oh, wait a sec." Then I looked back at the tower and started to count in my head. Lucius cocked his head to one side as if trying to figure out what 'Insane Lady' was doing now. After a few seconds I was done and said to myself,

"I knew it."

"Again, I am almost afraid to ask but then I fear I wouldn't sleep tonight if I don't…What did you know?" I smirked up at him and said,

"The point of the tower." He frowned once and enquired,

"And that was?"

"To see if it would take more than twenty rolls to reach the ceiling."

"Gods woman," he hissed under his breath making me frown in question.

"What?"

"Keira, you were only in there for ten minutes," he informed me making me blush and want to defend myself, which is what I did with a lame bit of attitude thrown his way,

"Yeah and?" He shook his head at my reply and then threw his head back and started laughing and I mean, really laughing. Then in a very un-bad ass way, he yanked me to him and kissed the top of my head still chuckling. I froze not knowing what was so funny or what had prompted such a sweet gesture other than he must have enjoyed witnessing my brand of crazy.

We started walking back to the door that led into the dining room when I informed him,

"You're lucky it wasn't twenty minutes." He looked down at me and raised an eyebrow in question but again by his slight lip curl I knew he was fighting a grin when he asked,

"And why is that?"

"Because after my tower I was going to see how many rolls it would have taken to turn myself into a mummy," I teased making him once again burst out laughing whilst shaking his head. Damn him but why did his corded, tensed neck look so appealing…it was a neck for Christ sake!?

"Wait, where is he?" I asked the second we rounded the corner and found it empty.

"Calm Pet, he is back in the dining room," Lucius informed me like this was naturally the most obvious place for him right now. I, on the other hand, didn't think so.

"What!?"

"Well, I thought that to be the better choice considering our options were limited." I felt my eyebrows meeting in a frown as I looked up at him.

"What would you have preferred, your husband waiting here for you only to find me escorting you back after we'd just spent time alone together in a broom closet or Dom sat at the dining table thinking you are innocently in the rest room?" I didn't need to consider this for long before I said,

"Okay, good point."

"I thought so," he said dryly after I had just agreed with him. Smug Supernatural bugger!

"So, he doesn't remember anything?" I asked unable to keep the hopeful tone from my voice. We stopped just before the door and I was tempted to peek inside just to check he wasn't in there terrorizing our friends and family like a demonic King Kong looking for his little blonde human.

"No, as requested." Lucius said in a way that made me look up at him.

"You disapprove?" I asked guessing by his tone that he did but couldn't help wondering why. He gave me a stern look as he was obviously trying to find the right way to explain what he wanted to say.

"I do," he stated far too briefly than what I was expecting. So, I raised an eyebrow telling him without words to elaborate.

"I do not relish going against an old friend Keira, no matter the river of bad blood that flows between us." Okay so hearing this struck a nerve in me and I flinched from it.

"Then why did you do it?" I asked unsurely and when he stepped closer to me, *intimately closer*, I wished I hadn't. He lifted my face up with two extended fingers under my chin, so that my lowered eyes could meet his intense steel blue ones.

"Because that same river is bridged because of you," he told me in a velvet voice that took my breath away, because by the Gods, wasn't that just one of the sweetest things he had ever said to me. It was so sweet in fact, that I couldn't help it when my head fell forward and I leaned in, planting my forehead to rest against his chest.

"Oh, Lucius." I felt his large hand come to rest at the back of my head holding me there and I couldn't help but feel the slight shudder of his body beneath my palms positioned at his pecs.

After this bitter sweet but passing moment between us, I knew I would have to be the one to pull away first. So, as I took a step back, I felt resistance from where he held me for only a second, but it was enough to tell me he didn't want to let me go.

Then he spoke and it…well, it shocked me to my core.

"I know it was never meant to be between us, Keira," he told me with an intense softness that seemed to fight against the raw emotions that fed the words spoken. I sucked in a shuddered breath because of the pain that seemed to lance at my heart. I wished I could have just left it there and I knew with everything deep inside me that I should have. But instead I found the words coming out of my mouth being said before I could stop them.

"Then…then why did you fight for it?" At this he looked down at me and I swear I nearly lost myself in their amber depths when I saw them change, losing the steel.

"Because hope can do dangerous things to the mind." I bit my lip and found this time I could only nod. Because he was right, sometimes even though hope could grant you the strength needed to make it through the hard times, it could also become your downfall.

To hope when all you hope for is hopeless is a weakness you can't escape from. Not until your sorrows try to drown you and you come up gasping for air called reality. Only then do you move on from wasted time. I knew this better than most after being allowed to believe I could somehow bring Draven back from Hell. That I could somehow save him. But then finding out he was actually alive and living in the world in hiding was like drowning by my own hand holding me under the black murky water.

A hand called hope.

"You were never mine…"

"Lucius I…" I started to interrupt him, but he shook his head slightly and I knew that right now I needed to give him this. I needed to give him this moment, for I knew it would be now, or never. And never for an immortal was a very long time indeed.

"…After that night at the clock tower I knew…*we both knew*…we knew that neither of our hearts belonged to us to give freely to whom we hoped would own them. You had given yours long before I had even chance to earn it," he said, and I couldn't help it, but a tear slipped down my cheek and I had to look away. But being Lucius, he didn't allow this for long as I felt his hand cradle my cheek and a thumb capture my falling teardrop.

"And what now…what of your own heart, Lucius?" I asked trying to keep the quiver from my voice preventing it from breaking…*barely.*

"That night I kissed you, you didn't gift me the sun, Keira," he told me gently and my eyes found his again as I waited for what he would say next with my breath firmly locked in my chest and unable to get out until he spoke.

"You gifted me a glimpse of my future." My eyes widened as what he said started to make sense. That night, when he took me to his special place, his clock tower, we both knew that in the exact moment before our bodies could join that there was a line there. But not one drawn just in this time but one long ago in the sands of time. One that would impact not only our hearts or those that they belonged to but an act so catastrophic it had the power to change the world and the future for us all.

The fate of the world held suspended in a single night of carnal bliss.

He knew this as did I. We both saw something different that night but it all led down the same path. And for Lucius, well it seemed that path was towards his own Chosen One... which he now knew wasn't me, no matter how much he wanted it to be.

Because his future was already written. It was already set in stone, I just hadn't realised until now that I myself had been the one to carve it there.

I knew this after I asked the question,

"What did it show you?"

"The sun you gifted me when we kissed was never yours to give..." he told me gently but when I frowned questioning him without asking, he continued until I understood the true power and nature behind his words...

"It was hers."

CHAPTER SIXTEEN

A BLANKET OF LIES

Once Lucius had dropped that cryptic bombshell on me I didn't know what to think. On one hand I was happy for him that he had an insight into what his future may bring. And one where he would meet his own Chosen One, no matter who she may be. But then, on a selfish level, I also had to be honest with myself and the feelings I had for Lucius. I would be lying to myself if I tried to say I didn't care about him in any other way than as a friend. But then I would also be lying if I ever said that there was a time I wanted more.

Thinking back to that time in the clock tower, I had been in a different place, emotionally and physically. For starters, not only did I believe Draven maybe captured for it was certain he wasn't in Hell thanks to taking a quick trip there myself to make sure. But this was also after Lucius had rescued me from a tortured time even I had cast so far into the prisons of my mind. I couldn't see it, for the pit it had been buried in was that deep. An endless chasm where I stored all the painful times in my life and being imprisoned in that rotting dungeon was definitely near the top of the growing pile.

So, to be saved yet again by Lucius and finding him as a growing strength in my life was always going to mess with my head, no matter how much I loved Draven. But I knew even now that all I wanted for Lucius was essentially to see him happy and we both knew that if that was going to happen, then we couldn't keep torturing ourselves with questions like 'what if?'.

Because life wasn't about the what ifs. It was only ever about the reasons. It was about everything happening for a reason, no matter how painful or heart-breaking at the time. It was about stepping forward and following your path towards your destiny. Not taking two steps back into your past to torture yourself into seeing where it was you went wrong. That never got you anywhere as it was like trying to run into the shadows expecting the sun to follow you.

At one time I believed the sun did follow me and that I had the power to gift it to others like Lucius. But I didn't. All I had was the ability to cast light onto others to show them the way. Which evidently was what had happened to Lucius and who knows, maybe others like RJ for Seth. Was that what made me important to others? Was that really what had pulled everyone together in the end.

Was it like they said? Was I the glue that held us all together or the light that had shown them the way to a better future? Well, whatever the answer was, it was clear that more than one good thing had come out of the prophecy and I had a feeling that there was plenty more to come.

But at the start was me and Draven and that to me was all that mattered right now, that and our baby. So, after saying an emotional goodbye to Lucius I walked back into the dining room to join the other half of my soul.

My reason.

However, when walking back inside my mind was racing and not only thanks to the personal whiplash labelled 'Lucius'. No now it was also about what was next in the future for me and Draven to have to endure. Because no matter how much this crazy incident was now averted, it was like Lucius had warned me before coming back in here…

———

I had my hand on the doorknob and was just about to open the door hoping to put this all behind me. But it was as Lucius had said, that hope could be deadly and, in this case… *foolish.* Lucius' next words only confirmed that.

"This will happen again my little Keira girl and next time I won't be there to protect you… *or his humanity.*" I looked back at him and took a deep breath because really, what was there for me to say to that?

"Are you really willing to risk that…willing to risk *more?*" he added nodding down to my belly where it had been confirmed not even hours ago that precious life now grew. My hand gripped the handle tighter and I thought for a moment that I would crush it from the force of his warning. I shook my head a few times and lowered my eyes to my feet before trying to find the words…any words that would explain how I felt.

"He wouldn't hurt me." I said in a small voice that didn't

do much to back up the sentence, but only ended up making it sound unsure and weak. He raised a honey coloured brow and snapped,

"Take care of what you choose to put your faith in Keira, for I know from experience what happens when it is misplaced," he told me, and I bit my lip because I knew what he was talking about. After all, his faith had not only gotten him tortured and killed, but also reborn as one of Lucifer's sons.

So now, after that I made my way back to the table, I had to ask myself…was Lucius right? Did I now have something else to worry about, even after all we had just been through? Surely the Fates couldn't be that cruel? But the second I asked myself this I nearly snorted out loud because who was I kidding! Going from past experiences here and what they had put us both through, then people would say it was more believable that they hated us. That punishment was first on their agenda and the fate of the world coming in a close second!

But what else was there for me to believe? That now my husband was too dangerous to be around and now because of me, even he didn't yet know it? I knew why Lucius thought taking his memories was a bad idea and it was something I was already hating myself for. But what was the alternative? Because no matter how much I loved Draven, he had one flaw…

Overreaction.

No, I knew deep down if he thought there was a

possibility of him hurting me then he would do what he had done in the past. And unfortunately, it pained me to say that in this he just couldn't be trusted, not after the great and painful depths he had gone to before.

So, no matter how much it had crushed me to lie, I felt I had little choice than to do just that. Because in his mind, if it was to save my life, then he would do it and damn the consequences.

I mean he had been ready to forsake the rest of the world and the seven billion people in it just out of his love for me for God's sake! That wasn't exactly the actions of what you would call a sane man for starters but then in his own words, there was nothing more important to him than his love for me. And, as incredibly wonderful as that knowledge was, it also meant that it placed Draven firmly on the crazy end of the scale when it came to making decisions based on my safety.

Which meant in the end I had been backed into a corner, having to make the hard decision, even if my own scale was more on the cursed side than that of the fated. Because if there was one thing that I would absolutely not allow to happen under any circumstances, was to let Draven leave me...*again.*

Which was why I walked back to my husband's side and did so with the guilt buried deep, and firm in the knowledge that I was doing the right thing.

Draven followed my every move with his dark eyes, tracking me as I walked across the room, making my way to him. I even noticed how he gripped the arm of his chair and I wasn't sure how many pounds per square inch of pressure he was away from demolishing it to sawdust, but let's just say, it didn't look like much.

But then with the other hand he calmly lifted his glass to his lips, proving just how much of his inner beast he could hide from the world. This thought made me shiver as I made the last few steps towards him, knowing just how close that inner statement was to the bone…*crushingly so.*

"Keira." Draven uttered my name like it was a prayer of thanks to the Gods that he didn't have to wait any longer. He took my hand after releasing his armrest, so he could lead me around him to my seat. A seat that now had a few extra carved indents the length of his fingers in its woodwork.

I averted my eyes and tried not to think about that punished wood as I smiled at my family when they too took notice of my return. This was when my mum smiled at me and I was thankful to see there was no blush of shame that joined it. Yep, Lucius was totally getting upgraded to Derren Brown for that one.

"I was very close to coming and hunting you down, little wife," he told me after granting me with a sweet kiss on my cheek. I closed my eyes at the feel of his gentle touch against my skin and tried everything in me to hold in the tremor I could feel trying to invade my nerves.

"Keira?" This time when he said my name it was as a question and just before I could ask myself why or how he would know of my inner struggle, one put there thanks to his last rough demonic touch, Lucius walked back in the room.

His long strides led him straight up to our table and even though I tried so hard not to react to the sight of him, it became an impossible task after what had just happened between us. I knew this and with it the second that I failed by not reacting to his presence. Because, one minute Draven had questioning eyes on me and then his gaze swiftly followed where mine were now focused on…or should I say *who*. Of course, it didn't help when I let his name escape on a whisper,

"Lucius."

My eyes snapped to Draven in panic when I heard his low growl and saw his bruising grip find the arm rest once again, this time enough for me to see splinters emerge beneath his white knuckled fist. Then I knew I was really in trouble when he leaned closer to me and hissed out a whispered warning of what was to come,

"We will be discussing this later, Sweetheart." My visible gulp was enough to show my guilt, even if my averted eyes weren't. Lucius didn't approach our table like I thought he would but instead he nodded to both of us as a way of silent goodbye. But his eyes lingered half a second too long on mine and I knew in that single look what he was trying to say. It was confirmed when I suddenly heard his voice in my mind.

'Remember what I said, My Little Keira Girl… stay safe.' I nodded back to him and in doing so sealed my fate when I heard even more wood give way in Draven's hands.

"Hey Dom, I think you have some blood on your shirt." The sound of Frank's voice seemed to bring us both slamming back to the room, that and the word blood. I looked to Draven to see him still frowning at Lucius' back and it was only with his neck twisted that I could now see it for myself. Frank was right, there was a few small drops of blood there. I couldn't help my reaction as I reached out to his neck, touching it and trying to see for myself where it was coming from.

"It's nothing, must have cut myself shaving," Draven said in a strained but steady tone to Frank as I knew this was a lie. Frank just shrugged his shoulders and went back to enjoying his meal, one I noticed that was also sat in front of both Draven and I, untouched.

Draven grabbed my hand in his to gently put a stop to my examination of his neck and the second he saw the clear worry in my eyes his own finally softened.

"It's nothing," he told me, this time without the tense tone.

"But the blood…" At this he finally grinned and leaned closer to me so that he could whisper,

"The blood is yours, Keira." Then he lifted my hand to his lips and planted an affectionate kiss at the back of my hand. But it was in this moment that realisation slammed into me and I knew what he was saying. I gripped his hand in a tight grasp and yanked it to me and hissed,

"Are you wearing my shirt?!" Hearing this and the way I said it, managed to grant me my first smile since Lucius had walked past.

"I think you will find sweetheart, it was always *my shirt."* My mouth dropped, and horror struck my face as I only just now realised that he was wearing the shirt I had been wearing when I had come on to him. The very one he had yanked aside baring my neck to him whilst he fed on me and yep, there was my blood to prove it.

"Why are you wearing it?" I asked through gritted teeth looking back at everyone with a fake smile and trying not to act as though I was sat next to my husband who was wearing what only hours ago I was wearing when I seduced him like some wanton hussy!

I felt his fingers capture my chin as he turned my attention back to where he wanted it which, as usual, was solely on him. The second I felt that slight rumble in his chest my eyes fluttered to him and I bit my lip at the growing intensity I saw transforming his heated gaze. Then he leaned in closer and gave me his answer in a deep timbre tone that could only be described as dragged through his demon side to get to me.

"Because every time I take a breath I smell your sex on my skin and feel myself getting hard remembering how it felt to have you swallow me whole." The second I sucked in a shuddered breath his eyes flashed purple fire if only for a fleeting moment. But it was long enough to tell me he was once again on the edge. Which, instead of making me feel powerful and triumphant, now only succeeded in making me wary and bombard my mental state with unanswered questions.

"Draven." I whispered his name as a warning, hoping that it was enough to remind him where we were and more importantly *who* we were surrounded by.

Hearing this his reaction was the one I wouldn't have guessed as he suddenly threw his head back and laughed, making everyone stop and stare at him. But it was obvious he didn't care because instead of concerning himself of such things, he simply placed the palm of his hand to the back of my neck. Then, as I sucked in a startled breath, he pulled me to him for a swift but hard kiss, branding me to his lips for all to see. I gasped again which he took as not only an invitation to sweep his tongue inside to taste me but also his opportunity to deepen the kiss.

Now, if we had been around only his own kind this wouldn't have been a problem. I learnt early on with Draven that he made no qualms about showing his affection for me in front of his people. Even to the point that sometimes I had to ask myself if half of it was done as a clear stamp of possession for everyone else to see. As if to say, she is mine and I may have claimed her long ago, but that brand of ownership is still plain to see for anyone suicidal enough not to take notice of it.

But even this domineering act in front of my family wasn't the reason I had gasped. No, it was the feel of his palm now touching the back of my neck and very close to the newly discovered symbol of destruction that lay under my hairline. So naturally I tensed in his hold as if waiting for the demon that I knew still lurked far too close the surface.

However, the second he felt my response to him, not being what it usually was, he pulled back and now he was the one whispering my name in question,

"Keira?" Now if I was a smart girl I would have known my mistake the second I made it and therefore would have accounted for it. Readied myself for the long list of excuses I could have given him for my behaviour and in some respects, yes, I achieved this…well the words anyway.

"My family," I whispered back saying all the right things but the one thing I didn't add to this was hiding the clear worry from my watery gaze. One that was now studying his eyes half expecting to find the demon there looking back at me.

This was when he knew.

I was keeping something from him.

Under a blanket of Lies.

"Keira." This time when he said my name it wasn't in question, no, it was in warning. This was confirmed when he then pulled me closer to him and informed me in hushed tones,

"We will discuss this later, along with other things," he added and when he looked to the door that Lucius had recently walked through, I knew what he meant.

Oh joy, great times ahead then…

NOT!

After this I was silent for most of the remainder of the meal and it was only when Draven must have noticed that, thanks to his taste of things to come, I was now playing with my food. I had hardly taken a single bite, even though the slow braised blade of beef, roasted red onions, and rich red wine and mushroom jus, looked and smelled amazing. No, instead I had concentrated my time into cutting the beef into small pieces and then hiding them around my plate under different vegetables that accompanied the dish. Of course, Draven noticed.

"Not a fan of the beef or are you just picturing it as a certain part of my anatomy?" Draven asked, half joking. My eyes sliced to him just as I stabbed my fork in a chunk of beef making him flinch. I tried to keep the smirk off my face in sight of what was a very natural and human reaction to the thought of stabbing anything in to a man's shaft. What do you know, it seems as though Supernaturals weren't immune to the age-old practice of a seriously pissed off woman and their sometimes right to deliver a swift kick to the man's jangly bits?

"Don't get any idea's Keira, as if I remember correctly it wasn't long ago that you enjoyed that particular part of me and in…*one, strong, hard piece.*" He said this last part after pulling my chair closer to his with one swift pull, yanking me so his lips were suddenly at my ear and his fingertip was simultaneously running gently down my neck.

"But then, maybe my little queen needs reminding… *in a firm way?*" he hummed in that hypnotic velvet voice of his. This time he was the one smirking when he noticed my heated reaction to his words, as it was clear he felt the spike in my pulse and heard me when I released a small barely audible gasp. Anyone else that had been looking would have simply believed my new husband was whispering sweet endearments in my ear, not painting a sexual picture in my mind like he was currently doing.

This was when I decided to play his game and twist the tables on him. So, I reached down and before he knew what was happening I grabbed his length in a strong hand and said,

"Is that so, my *large* King…then maybe I should help you out, you know…*firmly?*" I said giving him a firm squeeze and with it I grinned openly when hearing his deep groan, one that sounded like it couldn't be contained.

"So, when are you two kids planning on going on your honeymoon?" My dad asked and the second he did all my cool vixen went flying out the window. My hand let go of him and in doing so, I lifted it too quickly, banging it on the underside of the table. I muttered a quiet 'Oww' which only Draven heard and tried to focus back to my dad's question.

"Smooth, Sweetheart," Draven commented after putting his head down and off to my side so only I heard. Then I felt his silent chuckle on hearing me growl in response. I continued to feel his amusement shaking against my shoulder thanks to how close we still were, and I shot him a scowl, one he of course, chose to ignore. Then I felt him take my sore hand in his own and not caring who saw, he brought it to his lips. Once there in his gentle hold, his heated eyes found mine over my hand and burned into me as he kissed the red patch, whispering over it,

"Poor baby." I think I nearly came just from those two spoken words that promised so much more than just a soothing kiss. In fact, it was only when I heard my dad chuckling that it brought me back to the room.

"Sorry Dad, what did you say?" I had to ask again but didn't miss the way Draven smirked over my hand before finally lowering it back to his lap, where he continued to cradle it. I swear if he carried on being this tender and mixing it with his possessive and dominating ways, I was going to end up melting into a sticky mess on the floor with only my soggy knickers there as proof I used to be a living person.

"Newlyweds," my mother whispered to my dad, grinning like a mad woman. My dad just cleared his throat and replied on a whisper he didn't think we could hear, (because let's face it, he didn't know we had extra, superhuman senses)

"Yes, but even we showed some restraint in public." I wanted to smile at this but then when she replied with a whispered,

"That's not how I remember it Eric, in fact I think it was at my mum's dinner table that you..."

"Dad! I uh...you were saying?" I said quickly and *loudly*, because suddenly I was seeing the huge flaw in having supercharged senses. I felt Draven laughing next to me and I used the hand he still had hold of to pinch him, which didn't achieve the right goal as I had hoped. No, instead it only managed to make him laugh harder.

"I asked when you are going on your honeymoon, Kazzy?" At my dad's question I was suddenly stumped. Then my mum piped up and asked,

"Oh, and where, I bet it's somewhere special?" My mum added getting excited for me.

"Uh...well I think we were just going to skip the whole..." I started to say when Draven's authoritative voice cut in and as usual took control, which also ended in me looking like a guppy, as my mouth dropped open in shock.

"We will be leaving for our honeymoon tomorrow," he stated, and I turned towards him and instead of playing along, which might have been what he had silently been expecting, I asked,

"We are?!" Everyone at the table laughed as they all heard this. Draven turned to me and the corner of his lips twitched as if he was close to biting down on the grin emerging.

"We are, Love," he told me, and I looked to everyone else, like Libby, Frank and then to my mum and dad and repeated,

"We are." Making them start laughing again.

"I take it we just ruined the surprise?" My dad asked, and Draven shook his head, telling him,

"The surprise is more the destination, which I will let Keira tell you once we arrive." My eyes widened in excitement and I grabbed his arm and asked,

"We are really going?"

"Well, I think you can include the not knowing bit as part of the surprise Dom, she looks like you just handed her a puppy and a lifetime supply of chocolate," Frank said making everyone chuckle, but I ignored it all as I looked at my handsome husband who was looking back at me in that adoring way. It was as if he was wondering how to make it his lifelong mission to keep that look on my face, because he relished making me happy. I felt like telling him that just waking up next to him every morning was enough to achieve the same look. But still, a honeymoon with just the two of us was what I looked forward to the most, the destination came in second…maybe third if he told me we were going to spend most of the time naked.

After this everyone was chatting over dessert, which I noticed was chocolate because like Frank had said, it was a clear winner with the ladies. Although I didn't think it was as far as being written in our DNA like he thought it was or was currently trying to convince Libby of the fact.

"You eat just as much chocolate as me! Which reminds me, I need to stock up whilst we are here because no offence honey, but American chocolate isn't as creamy or yummy as ours," my sister argued, something that was a common conversation in their household. I knew what was coming next from Frank as he stood firmly on the American chocolate side of the fence.

"I've got three words for you babe, Reese's butter cups," Frank said making my sister scowl because let's face it, he had her there knowing it was one of her favourites.

"Still not as good as a Galaxy bar," she told him after crossing her arms, but this just made him laugh harder and turn to Sophia who he was sat next to and say,

"I swear I nearly bought stock in Reese's when she was pregnant." Libby scoffed at this and was about to argue when he playfully wrapped one of his big arms around her from behind and held a hand over her mouth.

"One time I forgot to buy some from the store and when she found out, she got so angry, I swear I thought she was going to stab me in my sleep…It kept me awake so much so, that in the end I went out at three in the morning just to buy her some and ended up getting every one they had on the shelf. Do you remember Libs, I even woke you up by wafting one under your nose?" At this we could hear the screeched outrage of her screaming,

"FRANK!" One that was barely muffled under his palm.

"And why not! I get my love muffin to treat me all the time, don't I, Sugar man jangles? Doesn't matter what time it is, a woman needs to be woken up with chocolate every now and again…it helps the world rotate," Pip exclaimed in my sister's defence making everyone join in the discussion of what crazy demands have been made over the years by loved ones. But I quickly shifted my attention back to more important things, like my husband.

"I can't believe we are going on honeymoon," I told him making him grin behind the hand that was positioned at his jawline. I found him staring at me of course.

"Why are you surprised Keira, since I met you I have been trying to get you to come away with me?" he reminded me, and I guess this was kind of true. But then I grinned and retorted with,

"Yes, but that was usually because you wanted to lock me in some ancient tower somewhere, so you could ravish me, having your wicked way and keeping me to yourself and above all...*keeping me safe.*" This I thought was a pretty good comeback, but the second I finished I saw his eyes flash purple around the edges telling me there was something he knew that I didn't.

Well, that was until he told me, dropping the honeymoon bombshell.

"And those Sweetheart, are the very reasons for my choice in our honeymoon destination."

"What...where...what?" I asked on a breathy exhale that seemed to be on repeat.

He gave me his best bad ass grin.

Then he told me...

"Locked away in my Scottish Castle."

CHAPTER SEVENTEEN

CAVEMEN AND THEIR BIG CLUBS!

"So, do you actually own a castle?" I asked him once we had said our goodbyes to everyone and we were currently in the elevator on our way to the top floor. He looked down side on at me as if trying to search for something and that something wasn't looking for an answer to my question. No, he was looking for an answer to his own unspoken question.

I knew this for a fact when I felt his heavy presence in my mind and this was when I finally started to realise my major flaw...my mind's barriers had been destroyed! Damn it, but why hadn't I thought of that before? No wonder he was so pissed off after seeing my reaction to Lucius, he couldn't just see that there was something wrong, but he could actually feel it as well.

Damn it Keira!

This was when I started to panic, building them up and concentrating so hard, I felt the pressure at my temple start to mount. Draven must have known what I was doing as suddenly I felt his hand in my hair, using it to pull me back so my head would follow. I looked up at him with wide eyes when he commanded softly,

"Don't do that, sweetheart." But it was too late for him, I had already started shutting him out. I knew my barriers were nothing like they had been, having years to strengthen them, creating a heavily fortified stronghold to keep my mind safe. But now, well they felt more like I had simply zipped up the opening on a tent, one I could still see Draven's shadow behind.

But at least it was something and definitely better than nothing, no matter how much the elements battered against it. Those elements being a metaphor of the strength of my husband's will of course.

"It's my mind Draven and therefore it's mine to protect," I told him quietly. Hearing this he tilted his head slightly and raised a brow at me. Oh yeah, that look said it all and he wasn't happy.

"And is that what you think you are doing…*protecting it against me?*" The last part of his question was said in a way that I knew my words had hurt him. I closed my eyes against the guilt and wished I could get him to understand. Just then the doors opened about to let other people inside when Draven growled at them and snapped,

"You will wait for the next one!" The three staff members all nodded in unison and with a swipe of his hand the doors closed again.

"I have to say, pulling shit like that isn't helping your case here Draven," I said sarcastically making him groan in frustration.

"I do not control *your* mind, Keira," he stated, making me remind him,

"No, because you can't but back when you could, can you claim the same statement?" I asked knowing I had just backed him into a corner this time. His look said it all, but it was cemented when he snapped,

"That was different." I raised my eyebrows in mock surprise and asked,

"Oh really, how so?" The second my question was voiced this time the elevator doors opened on our floor and he was the first to storm out of it, clearly at the height of showing off his Supernatural man paddy.

"I am not discussing the past with you," he said as his only lame comeback.

"Oh, but you want me to discuss the future, one where you think you have the rights to my mind and everything in it. I remember the last time that happened, and I think even with a different name I was still mortified when I found out!" I snapped at his back when he started walking ahead of me towards the room and, damn his long legs, in the end I was practically jogging to keep up with him.

"That was different...you were..." he started to say something but stopped himself and instead focused on opening the door to our suite.

"What? I was what Draven?" I demanded with my hands on my hips waiting. He had a palm flat on the door holding it open and after taking a deep breath he told me softly,

"Let it go, Keira."

"No, I want to know...come on Draven tell me, I was what?" I asked again, this time losing my temper with it.

Okay, so who was I kidding, I had already lost my temper in the lift and now this was like the next level up.

I followed him inside after he had given up holding it open for me and barely took in the exquisite room around us as I was too focused on watching Draven's back tense. He didn't stop walking until it took him over to a small bar area. Once there he poured himself a drink from a crystal cut decanter that was filled with a warm amber coloured liquid. I was almost tempted to ask if that helped when he took a long sip.

"Draven tell...!" I started to yell but he quickly lost patience and interrupted me. He did this by first slamming down his glass after he shot it back in one and then finally shouted the truth.

"You were different okay!"

"Well duh Draven, of course I was! For starters I wasn't used to you and your domineering ways, had no clue who the hell you were, but had been dreaming about you being a demon, kidnapping another version of me and using me as your damn sex slave!" I replied after shutting the door and hoping none of our family and friends were also staying on this floor. Then I took a breath but the second he looked like he was about to butt in, I got there first as I was far from finished.

"And besides, as far as I was concerned I had just lived a life as a bloody nun, never been kissed let alone doing the forbidden polka with someone and having to live out my life in some seriously messed up cult, where all I was allowed to wear was a bloody grey polyester ugly ass dress!" At this point I stopped only to take a breath and barely noticed the twitch of amusement on his lips before I carried on with my very (maybe a tad overly) informative point.

"Then I wander into this gothic nightclub and I am faced with lord of the manor, sex god himself and King of sinful thoughts and you expect me to what...be cool?" I ended this with a question I didn't intend for him to answer and instead of taking note of his reaction (again) to this I just carried on, letting my mind get carried away, after realising we had never really talked about this.

"Just count yourself lucky I didn't just self-combust at the first sight of you and beg you to take me there and then!"

"Stop talking, Keira" His serious voice sliced through the room, but I was too far gone to even listen.

"No, seriously you want to know what it was like for me, then you are going to listen to this. I was different Draven because I was the person that fell in love with you before you knew I had fallen in love with you. I was the Keira you didn't know when I first moved here."

"I said stop," he said again but once more I wouldn't listen and I didn't even stop to ask myself why he would want me to stop talking in the first place. No, I just carried on.

"I was the girl that was faced with the man of her dreams and I was the girl that fell in love with what she thought was the unobtainable... the impossible requited love by the man that consumed her dreams. I was the girl that you didn't know because I was too afraid to show you who I was. I was scared of what you could do to me and my fragile breakable heart, one I gave you long before you even knew the power you held in your hand. So, you may think I was different Draven but in reality, I was just the same girl fighting through different circumstances. My love for you was the same, my love for you…"

"Enough!" Draven shouted again but this time throwing the glass off to the side. The sound of it shattering became background noise, like the heavy rain that now lashed against the window, to what happened next. Suddenly Draven was in front of me, grabbing me to him and capturing my startled cry in a demanding, bruising and devouring kiss.

And that was it. Draven had hit his limit and he showed me this by taking command of my mind and body.

And boy, oh boy, wasn't he just the master of it!

He reached down never letting his lips leave mine but lowering himself enough to capture my ass with a bent arm, lifting me up to his height. Then his other hand ran up the length of my back, securing all my body to his, capturing it and commanding it to stay locked in his hold.

I wrapped my legs around his waist and gave him a squeeze to show him my own impatience, one he liked if his reaction was anything to go by. He growled in my mouth and I swear this made me convulse with a mini orgasm. When I rested my elbows at his shoulders I locked my hands behind his neck, holding on for what felt like dear life. As though any minute I was going to burst out of my skin if he didn't thrust into me soon, joining our bodies as one.

"Draven…I need…I need…" I said pulling back and barely making the words form a sentence.

"I know what you need!" he shouted at me, walking both our bodies to the nearest wall so he could use it to wedge me between it and him. Then I felt his free hand snake back under my ass before one quick and violent tug ripped both my jeans and underwear from my skin. And he wasn't the only one in this endeavour as I was trying desperately to rid him of the same, to free him.

Thankfully, he got the hint pretty quickly as he then ripped open the front of his jeans, tearing them in the process. He didn't even bother taking them off but as he shifted me higher, positioning me ready to take him, I noticed them slipping down his bare ass, and I swear I even licked my lips at the sight.

"You ready for me, little Queen?" he asked me on a growl and this time I knew I would have the upper hand when I brought his face to mine with both hands on his cheeks. Then once my lips were just touching his I whispered something I had never before uttered, letting go my inner hussy.

"Fuck me, my King!" At this he roared and at the same time thrust up into me with a strength that I thought would have broken me in two, that is if it hadn't felt like utter bliss first as surely death could never feel that good?

"YES!" I screamed as I felt the first of my orgasms hit and my insides quivered around his length, drawing him deep into my body. This seemed to drive him into a deeper frenzy, but still with my safety in mind, his hand cradled the back of my head as he pounded me harder into the wall. I heard a smash and looked to the side to see pictures falling to the floor. But it became obvious he didn't like my attention elsewhere, demanding on a demonic growl,

"Look at me!" This was snarled into my cheek, as he pressed into my face before finding my lips. Then he nabbed the bottom one, biting on to it and holding it with his teeth to use it to bring me back around to face him. Then he went back to consuming my open mouth in a kiss so dominating I almost felt lost in it. In fact, I felt like I was drowning by every hard muscle that pressed into me, suffocating me in the most glorious way. I felt trapped. I felt possessed. I felt used and owned. And above all I felt like I was his drug, his addiction and his cure.

It was like a battle he would always win.

One that was *beautifully fucking raw!*

So much so that just the thought of it had me screaming another release inside his mouth and this was enough to push him over the edge and the way he came so suddenly it was as if I had done it with a knife's edge held to his control.

His roar of release was bellowed up at the ceiling and I suddenly knew that it didn't matter what floor our family was on, they would have heard us had we been in the attic and they in the basement of a forty-storey building. Jesus, but it felt like we had shaken the very foundations of the hotel and I don't think I would have been surprised if I felt the floor start to move below us.

A moment after his shuddered climax, I jumped at the sound of his hand slamming against the wall next to me, simply done in order to hold up our combined weights, as I felt his knees start to bend. Well, it was certainly a triumph if I could nearly bring Draven to his knees during sex and I felt my lips turn smug at the knowledge.

Then, after obviously deciding the wall was no longer good enough, he walked me through the living space and into a bedroom, all the while still seated firmly inside me. I swear by the time we got there I was ready for him to take me again.

He lowered me on the bed, this time in a soft and tender

way that spoke of his passing frenzy. As we landed he hooked my leg over his thigh so as not to lose the connection and with the size of Draven, this was achieved with ease.

Then he shifted himself, holding all his weight above me. Now resting slightly on his side, he simply gathered my chunky knit sweater in one hand. I felt him fist the wool at my belly, which became the opposite to his other hand that was currently cupping my cheek and making soothing circles with his thumb at my temple.

"By the Gods you're beautiful...*utterly perfect.*" he said after pushing the hair back from my face and staring down at me in wonder. Then, before I could say anything in return, my sweater was suddenly yanked up and off over my head before I even knew to move and help him. He threw it off to one side as if it irritated him, ridding the offending item that dared to keep my naked body from him.

"Why did you want me to stop talking?" I asked timidly, now all my sass and temper had been dissolved.

"Because my sweet girl, hearing the confessed depth of your love for me from both sides of your soul wasn't something I was able to bear any longer without being inside of you."

"And seeing that blush now only deepens that fact," he added on a soft growl.

"Keira, you speak of your love for me in the beginning as if it was one sided, but you forget something."

"And that is."

"I was always destined to fall in love with you." Hearing this sounded as romantic as it gets but for some reason, his words didn't sit right with me. Which prompted my next question, one that felt like it was first stuck in my throat before I had to push it through my lips.

"Sso…so you would have fallen in love with me, no matter who I turned out to be?" I asked hating the way my voice betrayed my lack of self-confidence. Quickly his gaze softened, and a few lines appeared at the corners of his eyes before he spoke.

"No, what I am saying is that I may have been destined to fall in love with you, but it was all that is you that conquered my heart. Falling in love since the first moment I saw you was always going to happen, Keira." I was about to speak but he shook his head and covered my lips with two fingers.

"…But making it so that love continued to grow into immeasurable amounts every day I saw you, every day I was with you. Every single time you spoke, laughed, smiled and I would witness your reaction to others…"

"Draven I…" I said trying to cut him off once his fingers had slipped away and the emotions became too much for me, exactly as they had for him. But he didn't stop, no instead he continued and with each word his hard length would start to move slowly inside me, igniting my core with his deep touch once again.

"…your kindness and generosity, your humour and even your clumsy inability to stay on your feet. Hell, even when you were finally brave enough to touch me, it all just ended up cementing you for eternity within the deepest parts of my heart and my soul."

"Oh, Draven please…" I begged burying my head in the crook of his neck and shoulder. He held a hand to the back of my head, cradling me there as he whispered down at me,

"You wish something of me, my Queen?"

"Yes, now shut up and kiss…!" I told him fervently and thankfully he didn't need to be told twice or even have the sentence finished before he was granting my wish. And this time when he made love to me, it was slow, and it was gentle, and it was oh so tender that it felt like it had the power to shatter me into a thousand pieces. And when Draven finally let me come, he was there to hold me all together, as he too found his comforting release in my hold.

"My greedy little wife loves the feel of me, does she?" he asked a little time later once we had both showered together. Of course, this had ended up leading to another round of sexual activities thanks to Draven spending an ungodly amount of time 'cleaning me up' only to end it in making me dirty again. Of course, I decided to do the same, only with my mouth *again*.

I think it was safe to say that my husband enjoyed the act of oral pleasure (If the cracked tiles and roaring growls were anything to go by) and now that I knew I obviously didn't suck at it, I too enjoyed it…*immensely.*

So now we were back in bed with Draven on his back and me tucked to his side with half of me draped on top of him. I was currently running my fingertips around his hard pecs that looked as strong as marble slabs.

"Well, you do happen to have a nice body," I told him, and he chuckled before informing me,

"That wasn't what I meant." I rolled my eyes making him laugh again.

"Don't get cocky King, it doesn't become you." At this his eyes got wide, and he said,

"Doesn't become me? Why Keira, if I didn't know any

better I would say my old worldly ways are finally rubbing off on you." He looked far too pleased with himself after pointing this out.

"Yes, well when you have been around since dinosaurs roamed the Earth, I can imagine that's bound to happen… let's not worry and just class it as an unfortunate side effect to being your wife." I joked back and in doing so brutally teasing him. I even bit my lip to stifle a giggle when I saw his jaw drop in mock horror.

"You did not just compare my age to that of being Jurassic!?" he stated this time making me laugh, along with the way his fingers had dug into my naked sides, and I knew any minute the tickling would begin.

"That depends," I replied only just fighting a cocky grin.

"On what?" he enquired as I knew he would, which meant I had him right where I wanted him. So, I rested my weight on his chest and pushed up so that I could whisper by his ear my devious, vixen reply.

"On how big your club is, Caveman!" At this he roared with laughter making my body shake with his.

"Right, you asked for it!" he said grabbing my wrist and yanking me over him before rolling so I was trapped underneath him with nowhere to go. Then he grabbed both my hands as I tried to evade capture, holding them shackled at the wrists before forcing them above my head.

"No! I take it back!" I shouted in panic waiting for the moment before he ruthlessly started stroking under my arms and torturing my most ticklish spot.

"I am sorry sweetheart, but it's too late for that now," he told me with a smug smile gracing his perfect lips and his eyes dancing with mirth.

"No, it's not! Come on Caveman, play nice," I said on a giggle and reaching up just enough to suck his bottom lip into my mouth to bite. The sound of his chest rumbling with a slight growl was like a little victory and once I let go of his, I bit my own lip in anticipation as to what his next move would be in this game I'd started.

"Oh, it's like that now is it?" he asked, challenging me and I nodded slowly with what I could feel was a big daft grin on my face.

"You know I was simply going to let you get away with a snorted defeat but now, I think I have other ideas in mind," he informed me, and I swallowed hard making him grin.

"And…um…as your willing captive, can I ask what those other ideas might be?"

"I can't see the harm, *my willing captive,*" he said putting emphasis on his whispered words taken from my own, when he gripped my wrists tighter telling me without argument that I was far from willing. More like, caught, captured and about to be controlled.

"I was thinking this old man should punish you, caveman style…you know, *with my big club!"* he growled before snapping his teeth at me twice, making me flinch back further into the bed.

After this he proved to me just how well that age old experience went hand in hand with a large club.

And in the end, also proving just how…

Willing I could be.

CHAPTER EIGHTEEN

ALL HAIL THE SWEATER

After this sex filled night, it turned out that Draven didn't deliver on his threat at the dinner table about discussing what had happened between Lucius and me. And nor did he mention the reason I flinched when he came close to touching my birthmark. For obvious reasons I never asked him why, as let's face it, I would have been stupid to press my luck.

I had no idea why he didn't press for it, but I had my theories. Alright, so whatever was going on with Draven in these past few days since the battle, I still had no clue, and this included his little demon freak out. Okay so granted, not so much on the little and more on the huge and that huge being very much the colossal and terrifying variety. But no matter how frightening it had been, I couldn't really risk thinking too much about it, not with Draven around and considering we were about to leave for our honeymoon, around he would be…*a lot.*

But on some level, it felt as though he was too scared to leave me and for the short moments that he did, it was always to come back to me craving my body in a way like never before. It was as if he couldn't get enough of me, which was why I had to ask myself, was the reason he didn't bring up Lucius was because of the love I shared last night?

Was it because he was content with all I had said? Was he now satisfied enough to know his worries were unfounded? Well, whatever it was it didn't look like he wanted to talk about it anytime soon and I was more than happy with this.

But these were the reasons I couldn't chance thinking too much on the subject because I was still unsure on the strength of my barriers I had thrown up in a hurry. And well, Draven still felt like the storm that was trying to tear them down. I knew this for a fact as I would feel him there every now and again, like I did in the beginning, when we first met.

The only difference was, back then I didn't know what that intense presence was, but now I knew...boy did I! And because I knew, I would turn quickly to find Draven watching me with an intensity that could only be described as bordering on obsession.

But like I said, the reasons for this were still unknown to me but the only thing I could put my finger on was that nearly losing me and essentially seeing me die had done something to Draven. It had cut him deep and scarred his soul. And to be honest I couldn't say that I wouldn't have been any different given a swap of our circumstances.

Hell, even the thought of it had me shuddering and trying to shake away the past. Because that's when it hit me. I had already felt that and for a lot longer than the few minutes that Draven had been made to feel it.

Yes, so okay, he did have to look in my eyes as he was forced to plunge that knife in my heart and then watch as the life drained from my eyes. And putting it like that, then I could pretty much say for a certainty that this was reason enough for his strange behaviour. Because no matter how much hearing how Draven had died that day, I still hadn't had to watch as his bloody body fell to the floor. I hadn't been made to watch as his knees hit the ground, all strength leaving his body as his soul started to leave the outer shell.

I hadn't had to live through that particular pain.

But Draven had.

And what was worse, it had been by his hand, like it was always destined to be. His greatest fear come true. Christ, but it wasn't worth thinking about what must have gone through his head.

So, question was, could I really say which one was worse?

No, I could not.

As in, definitely not.

But in the end, it was a moot point because Draven woke up that morning, dragging me up his body for a kiss and after that I knew the rest of my day would be perfect and I was right. This of course, started with the delicious and sensual morning sex and was followed by a slightly less delicious, but still amazing, full English breakfast.

Complete with bacon (English cut, not a streaky piece in sight) sausage, beans, crispy golden hash brown, scrambled and runny yoke eggs, friend mushrooms, fried toast and of course, ketchup because I wasn't a brown sauce type of girl.

This I informed Draven of and he threw his head back and laughed before taking a bite out of my black pudding. Which he knew was something else I didn't like because I had immediately pushed the slice to the side of my plate. This he had also found funny.

"Why do you find me not liking black pudding funny?" I finally asked him directly after the ketchup/brown sauce statement. He put down his slice of buttered toast, something I had done for him which ended up making him smile at me like I had just cured world hunger by inventing a magic bean.

"Because technically, you're half Vampire," he informed me with a half-smile.

"So?"

"It's blood sausage, sweetheart." Of course, being born and bred in the UK, I knew what a black pudding was. But the way Draven said this made me burst out laughing, to the point I had to put down my knife and fork so as not to hurt myself. Which would most likely have happened because as it turned out, being a Vampire didn't end up stamping out the clumsy gene, so the vamp side of the pros and cons table got a big fat zero for that one.

"Now I find myself asking you in return, what it is that *you* find so funny?" he enquired trying to keep a straight face at the sight of my hilarity.

"Let's just say I think we are safe and far from the Keira drooling stage when we watch gory movies together," I told him and soon he was the one joining me in my outburst of laughter. Which was why on this particular morning, sat at our private dinner table in a fabulous suite, sharing breakfast together in our matching robes and laughing about the silly little things just made it to the top five of the best mornings ever. Number one was of course, the first morning when waking up next to Draven. But with mornings like waking on a bed of roses and our morning spent sightseeing in Milan coming in second and third on the list.

This was number four.

Hence, this was why our morning was perfect and after I showered and changed, I looked in the mirror to check all was looking as it should. Draven had told me to dress warm for there would be a chill in the air when we arrived. So now I was wearing a pair of light grey tight fit jeans, a light blue sleeveless top with a cute design of birds flying in a spiral over the chest, which was a shame to cover up. But to this I then added a chunky navy coloured hoodie that had thick white drawstrings hanging from the front of the large floppy hood that slightly crossed over at the neck. This also matched the thick white piping around the ribbed material at the bottom and wrists that I was happy to report, had thumb holes. All that was needed was to zip up a pair of tan suede boots that also buckled just below the knee.

In fact, I was just fiddling with the buckles that were attached to the leather straps that crossed over the boots when Draven walked out of the bedroom and I swear I stopped breathing at the sight. Holy Mother of God but he looked incredible.

When he came out of the room fastening what looked like an expensive watch to his wrist with a strap of dark brown leather I was happy to see his attention was elsewhere so that I could openly gawk at him and drank in my fill of his body.

His long strong legs were encased in casual stonewash

jeans that seemed to mould to his thighs like a tailored suit. Added to this he had on a man's rugged, chunky knitted sweater the colour of oatmeal with darker flecks of brown in the wool. It had a thick ribbed panel down from the neck that ended at his pecs and it fastened with brown stitched, leather buttons.

Only one of these were through the bottom buttonhole as the rest of the large collar was left open, skimming the side of his jaw line. This allowed you just a glimpse of the dark blue and white checked shirt with open collar, he wore underneath.

I swear the whole look just made me want to walk up to him and rub against him like a damn cat, seeing for myself if the sweater was as soft as it looked. Even the sight of his bare neck made me want to pull that collar off to one side, just so I could lick, suck and kiss my way up it. That was if I was standing on a stepladder, so I could accomplish such a task.

He looked so incredible, my mouth actually fell open in what must have looked like a comical way. Once he had finished with his watch his eyes found my admiring gaze and I swear the small quirk of his lips was down to my obvious approval.

He walked straight to me, bent at the waist and tipped my head back with a thumb and finger curled under my chin. Then he planted a sweet kiss on my lips and asked,

"Ready to go?" and what was my cool, calm, collected reply,

"Mmm…mm." This again granted me another lip twitch before he pulled back and offered me his hand. I placed mine in his and after he pulled me up, I blushed when he took a step back to take in the sight of me. He scanned me from head to toe and back up again, deepening that growing blush to a crimson flush.

"Beautiful as always." I bit my lip and said shyly,

"I am only wearing a hoodie, Draven."

"And like I said, beautiful as always," he said more forcefully this time after hooking me around the waist and pulling me into his hard body. My hands rested against his chest and it was now I could confirm that yes, the sweater was as soft as it looked. Then, with me looking up at him, he ran the back of his finger over my heated cheeks and told me,

"I like this best of all." And speaking of my blush, it then turned to neon pink, a colour you could also see from space!

Then he ran the pad of his thumb over my lips and added,

"And your lips...*always your lips.*" He muttered this last part over my mouth making me smile as he lightly kissed me.

Shortly after this we were ready to leave and with my hand still firmly in his, he led me down to the waiting Rolls Royce that was ready to take us to Birmingham airport.

"You look excited," Draven commented once we were on his private jet that was all cream leather and shiny varnished wood. In other words, expensive and not somewhere I would choose to eat anything sticky and dripping.

"I am!" I told him only two dials down from going high pitched.

"Come here, sweetheart," he said after giving me a tender look as though he found my exuberant answer endearing.

"But I can't, not until we land anyway." He chuckled at my serious tone and told me,

"I think we both know you will be safe in my arms... wings remember." I let out a nervous laugh at this and it was the first of many that day I had to stomp out the urge to think too strongly about the hidden factor behind his words. And just how wrong they could be. Because really...was I ever safe in the arms of his Demon?

I would like to think so and that deep down it was impossible to even consider that he could hurt me in anyway. But going by yesterday's events, I didn't think the verdict looked as clear cut as it once had.

"Keira?" He said my name bringing me back to my secret (don't think about it) mission and realising quickly that I was currently failing.

"Sorry, I zoned out then," I told him making him frown before agreeing,

"Yes, so I noticed."

"So, you really own a castle?" I asked trying to get him to stop looking at me that way, and also to try and get him to stop pushing around the edges of my mind, like he was trying to find another way in. I swear it felt like I could actually visualise him sticking his fingers under my tent, trying to find a hole in my flimsy barriers. If it was possible I would have stepped on his hand for even trying but unfortunately it didn't work like that. As my metaphor wasn't physically real.

He gave me an annoyed look and at first, I panicked slightly thinking he might have found a way in without me knowing. But when he nodded down to his lap and flicked two of his fingers at me, gesturing for me to come to him, I knew he was being demanding again.

So, with a sigh I gave him what he wanted. I unbuckled my belt, one I knew I didn't need to keep on, but did because, well I hated flying of any kind. Ironic seeing as my husband had wings I know, but what can I say, the cosmos must have had fun with throwing that one my way.

The second I was within arm's reach Draven whipped out a hand and snagged me, tugging me the rest of the way and catching me midfall.

"You know I am working on trying to be more graceful and less clumsy…you know, now I am queen and everything, but I have to say when you do things like that, you kinda make it impossible." He pulled me closer to him and buried his head in my neck taking a deep breath and breathing me in.

"I like you clumsy, it means I get to be the one to catch you," he murmured against my skin making me smile, one he couldn't see.

"Yes, but I am queen now and have an image to uphold," I informed him in a fake posh and regal voice.

"You're my queen and the only image you need to uphold little wife of mine, is that of you naked in my bed," was his reply and I had to say, it was a good one. But then if a reply could create butterflies to start kickboxing in your stomach, then it was always going to be a good one.

I, of course, had one better…or should I say, *funnier.*

"That's an unusual Queen's image Draven, but whatever you say…so tell me, will it be made into a painting to hang in the family gallery or should we just go with a tapestry to hang in the great hall for all to see when we have royal feasts?" I said pulling back to see for myself his reaction… he didn't disappoint. He threw his head back and roared with laughter then pulled me closer to him, to cradle my head to his chest and kissed my hair before whispering to himself,

"My beautiful, funny queen." I swear hearing this made my insides melt as I relaxed further into him. By the Gods he was sweet. So sweet in fact, I had turned in my seat to run my fingertips down his cheek and jawline before stretching my neck so I could follow the trail with little kisses.

"I think it safe to say that an image like that is for her King's eyes only and one I must say I am greatly looking forward to enjoying again and *soon."*

Yep, definitely a melty insides moment.

CHAPTER NINETEEN

WANTED CONFESSIONS AND UNWANTED PHONE CALLS

We soon arrived at Glasgow airport as it was only a short flight from Birmingham. Draven refused to let me sit in my own seat for landing, telling me that his arms could take place of my seatbelt and instead, he could take my mind off it by whispering sexual promises in my ear. I teased him, letting him know my thoughts and questioning whether he was in heat or something as I was sure seatbelts weren't supposed to keep skimming against your intimate parts. He just laughed and joked,

"All part of the service, ma'am." Then the second our wheels touched the tarmac he said in a professional 'Captain's voice,'

"Thank you for flying Draven air, safest way to travel for fearful little flyers." After this it was now my turn to burst out laughing. Yep, had to be said, my husband was a pretty funny guy when he wanted to be.

The other thing I noticed in this time was that Draven looked about as pleased with himself at making me laugh as I usually did when making him laugh. And this was yet another moment that I felt the need to say again, what a perfect day.

"How far until we get there?" I asked once we were in yet another expensive car, only the difference with this one was it was a massive four-wheel drive and Draven was driving.

I had been surprised to see that the second I had been led down the steps by Draven, a man exited a black car that looked like a heavy duty, military vehicle, one that looked like it had a baby with a luxury Mercedes Benz. Almost as if the expensive millionaire's business car just woke up one morning and decided to become an off-roading beast on four massive wheels!

"M' laird." A man with a heavy Scottish accent said at the same time tossing the keys to Draven, who caught them without looking.

"Thank you, Douglas."

"You're driving?" I asked him in surprise and I didn't know why exactly, as it wasn't as if I had never seen Draven driving before. But it had been a while and I was kind of getting used to us being chauffeured around. Not because I was quickly becoming spoilt or anything, but mainly because I was getting used to having Draven all to myself in the backseat. Especially when it included times like making our way back to the hotel and Draven telling the driver to take an hour in doing so, before the privacy screen went up.

Oh yes, those were good times.

He didn't answer my question with words, just with a bad ass grin before taking my hand and leading me over to the passenger side. Then he shifted me to the side as he opened my door before gripping my waist as he easily lifted me inside. I had to say, I was certainly grateful for this part considering the vehicle looked to be about seven feet tall! The ground clearance alone looked as though we could cross bloody rivers and I knew there was no way I was getting up into that thing without a stepladder. It was that or tripping, scrambling, and scratching my way in, which let's face it, was never a sexy look.

This instantly reminded me of the time I had tripped and fallen head first into Draven's lap before we had become a couple. Back when I thought Draven pretty much hated me.

"Now that is one look I would very much like explaining," Draven said after he took his seat behind the wheel with ease. Damn those long sexy, strong legs of his. But secretly not damning them at all and only wishing to see them naked again. Preferably on his knees as he powered into me from behind. Jesus Keira, get a grip woman, I scorned myself, for I felt like I was in heat or something. Of course, none of this was helped by what Draven had been trying to do to me when we were coming in to land.

"What makes you think it's a look that needs explaining?" I said trying to act calm and cool, which was a mission in itself after a flicker book of sinful thoughts had just passed through my mind's eye.

"You're blushing, Keira," he informed me and damn it, he was right.

"Just cold cheeks," I said trying to pass it off as nothing

but the bitter Scottish weather. And like Draven had said there would be, there was a cutting wind outside, which made me thankful for my warm hoodie.

So naturally, thanks to the weather, I thought I had gotten away with it. Well, that was until Draven being Draven decided to prove he was right. And he did this by reaching across the centre console and running the back of two fingers down my cheek.

"Sorry sweetheart, but I am calling bullshit," he said after pulling back and smirking like a cocky bastard. It was only then did he start the engine and I jumped at the sound of its deep rumble.

"What car is this?" I asked trying to get away from his interrogation, but he was having none of it.

"Nice try, Keira," he told me making me huff in response.

"Fine, I was just thinking about the time when I face planted into your lap," I said in a begrudging tone, one he started to chuckle at.

"Ah yes, a day I will never forget."

"What do you mean by that?" I asked as he pulled out of the private airfield, first nodding to the guard on duty before joining the main road and its traffic.

"Well, I don't think many would forget the day the girl they were obsessing over literally falls into their lap…*face first.*" He whispered this last part to his side window as he pulled out of a roundabout once it was clear. Of course, thanks to my Vamp super skills I heard him, and he knew this when I growled. Yes, now I was the one sounding animalistic and I had to say, it felt good when you were annoyed. Although, it would have felt even better had

Draven not been chuckling because of it. I probably sounded like a cub or a kitten compared to the King of the jungle over there.

"Yes, well if you enjoyed it so much then why were you so angry with me?" I snapped back at him and this time when he looked at me, he was in utter shock.

"Angry at you? Keira, why would you ever think I was angry at you?" he asked sounding dumbfounded and now I was the one looking at him in shock.

"You're joking, right?" I asked making him frown.

"Draven I was right there, you looked furious!" Draven heard this and made a face as if what I was saying was impossible. I laughed without humour and said,

"You know, fisted hand, tense jaw and a cold look of indifference as you glanced my way…ring any angry bells?" Once I had finished and my question was out there he now looked thoughtful, as if he was trying to replay the same events for himself. Scanning back through what must have been the biggest library in the world for a memory bank.

"No," he stated firmly making me frown.

"No?" I questioned shaking my head slightly as if this would help in making sense of him. This time he looked at me and repeated,

"No, that is not what happened."

"Draven I was there and…"

"Yes, you were and like many times back then, you totally misunderstood my actions for ones against you, instead of ones made *because* of you."

"I don't understand," I suddenly admitted because what he just said didn't really make sense to me.

"No and evidently you also didn't that day," he said

clearly frustrated but I couldn't understand if it was with me or himself.

"Keira, I was angry yes, but not with you… *never with you.*" He added this last part in a soft voice, this time looking at me. But my own look told him I obviously needed more here, so thankfully that's what he gave me…*more.*

"You have to remember, back then I couldn't simply take what I wanted… no doubt just as I couldn't when you walked into my life back two thousand years ago in the past," he said bitterly, and I noticed the way his grip hardened on the leather steering wheel.

"But at least back then I was known as King, even to mortals. But in this world, in this time, what do you think would have happened had I simply taken you, plucked you out of your life the first second I saw you back in that forest?" he asked, and I knew we had been here before. But no matter how many times I had heard him say the same thing, about stealing me away when he wanted to, I still found it hard to believe. Not because I *didn't* want to believe him, but more because I desperately *wanted* to believe him.

So, I gave him my answer as to how I thought I would have reacted.

"I don't know, thought I had died and gone to heaven?" He gave me an unconvincing look before saying,

"As nice as that is to hear Sweetheart, I think we both know that wouldn't have happened."

"Then obviously all the mirrors you are using at home don't work properly and are clearly broken," I told him and inwardly smiled to myself as at least if this was the case that would then account for all my bad luck then.

I at least managed to gain a small smile before he went

serious again, which was when I caved in and decided to be sensible too.

"Okay so yeah, I probably would have freaked out, no matter how annoyingly sexy and hot you are," I admitted, this time getting a bigger grin and I didn't know whether it was hearing me calling him sexy or that I had just admitted he was right.

"Keira, what you saw back then wasn't anger directed at you. But it was frustration and anger stemmed purely from my own restraints. Can you imagine what it must have been like... for no, you couldn't possibly know," he said half to me and half to himself.

"Oh no, I couldn't possibly know what it was like to want someone as..." I started to say but he cut me off with both a serious look and his serious words,

"Keira, I had been waiting for you for *thousands of years,* you had weeks, a few months at most. So, no, you couldn't possibly imagine what it was like. What it was like to finally feel your lush little body pressed against mine where I wanted it to remain. But what happened... I was forced to do nothing, when all I wanted to do was lock the fucking door, keep you in my lap and order my chauffeur to keep driving until I had you as far from your life as I could, thus making your life mine to control... So that little wife, as you now know, was why I was so fucking angry when my sister interrupted that dream." By the time he was finished I was in complete shock and feeling emotions so strong, I couldn't help but snap out an order.

"Draven, pull over." He shot me a look and frowned.

"Keira?"

"Draven, stop the car," I said again but now his look went from confused to worried in a heartbeat.

"Why? Is it what I said…? Come on Keira we can talk about this…"

"Stop the car!" I shouted interrupting him as I felt myself almost shaking. Thankfully, he saw how much I needed this, whatever *this* was to him. So, he indicated and pulled into the layby with speed, hitting the brakes with enough force that I slapped a hand to the shiny, expensive dash. Then, before he knew what was happening, I was releasing my seatbelt and climbing over his brand-new car, not caring one hoot about the pristine leather interior or where I was putting my dirty boots.

He seemed frozen by my actions as if utterly stunned as he watched me climb over the centre console and position myself over him, straddling his lap. Then I placed both my hands on his face, framing the perfection in front of me and as I watched his eyes melt into purple, I knew that I had been wrong before…

Because now it was perfection.

"Because I love you!" I told him desperately before taking his lips with my own and kissing him as if I would die if in that second, I didn't. I crashed into him and kissed him like I needed to get deep enough to possess him. Like I needed to brand myself to him and praying to the Gods that, in that moment, he even had some small concept, even a slither, of the endless amount that I loved him.

It took him a moment of stunned shock before he reacted and when he did, as usual he took over the kiss, as was his way. I felt one arm quickly imprison me to him, as his forearm pressed against my spine, securing me to his upper body in a near bruising hold. Then his hand held my neck, tilting my face so that he could go deeper and the second the connection hit new depths, he growled his approval in my mouth.

I was holding his head to me, with my hands embedded in his hair and in my impatience, I raked my nails against his scalp, tugging on the strands as my fingers made fists.

"Gods woman!" he said finally after letting me come up for air. I was panting in his lap with my forehead held to his. He had his eyes closed as he wrapped both arms around me, enveloping me and hugging me to him as his own hands formed fists in my hooded sweater.

"So, was that what you had in mind?" I asked him when I finally caught my breath, one Draven had stolen from me. He moved back slightly so that he could see me better.

"I only ever had *you* in mind, my Love," he told me, making me fall forward so I could bury my head in his neck and mutter my confession,

"Oh Draven, I wish I had known."

"And I too now see the error of my ways," he admitted.

"You do?" I asked curiously.

"I admit my reasons for holding you at arm's length to begin with was out of protection, but I would never, and *I mean never*, have wanted you to feel as though I hated you, Keira...*never,"* he told me squeezing me on this last whispered word, as if he was back in time and speaking this vow.

"Is this why you...?"

"Jumped on you?" I finished for him.

"Not that I am complaining here," he said holding both his hands out to indicate all that was me, still sat straddling his lap. Then those same hands came to rest on my hips as if not yet ready to let me go.

"Well, let's just say I liked the picture you painted as a better alternative to what happened that day and I couldn't exactly give into the impulse whilst you were driving...no matter how talented you are behind the wheel," I added making him grin and telling him the reason why I basically couldn't wait to kiss him.

"I wish we had the time for me to show you my other talents behind the wheel but alas..."

"Alas...really Draven...tell me, did you pack your club or are you just hoping to find a really big stick to hit me over the head with when you want to drag me back to your cave?" I teased making his lips quirk up at one side as he fought off a grin.

"Oh, don't you worry Sweetheart, I have everything I need right here to punish unruly little wives into doing as they're told, no club whacking needed." At this I moaned as he decided to show me exactly what 'weapon' he was talking about when he banded an arm around my waist and lifted his hips, pressing his hard length in between my legs. But being me and not wanting to give in that easily, I came back with a cocky reply,

"Whacking...well at least that *is* a word used from this century." He growled, this time playfully before pulling my head to one side and dragging the hood of my sweater off my shoulder, so he could nip at my exposed skin.

"Like I said... *unruly wife,*" he said into my neck, reminding me of my new nickname.

"And like I said...*Caveman,*" I teased him back and only stopped when his nipping turned into a bite. It didn't hurt but was a primal warning as he held my flesh in his teeth. Then he grabbed my wrists with each hand and restrained me by holding them at my lower back. I swear I felt my girly bits flutter as he pulled back and gave me a heated, dominating look that said he was about two heartbeats away from surging into me...

But I was only one heartbeat away from begging him to.

So, there we were, on the side of a Scottish road, locked not just by our bodies in this silent showdown but also with both our heated looks. A gaze that was seconds from igniting the electrically charged air around us and exploding in a world of motion.

But in the end, it was the sound of Draven's phone ringing through the speakers of the car that stopped us. At first, I didn't think he would answer it and half of me didn't want him to. Christ, I knew we were newlyweds, but we were acting more like a couple of horny teenagers!

"Sometimes I hate being King," he admitted astonishing me before he let go of my wrists and then lifted me back into my own seat. Thus putting an ice pack on my aching and raging libido.

"Speak!" Draven demanded after tapping the fancy touch screen on the dashboard. Then he put it into gear and turned to me and mouthed one word,

'Seatbelt.' I tried not to smile when I gave him a cocky salute, making him roll his eyes at me. But then his lips quickly gave him away as it was obvious...he liked my brand of humour.

But then this was when all humour stopped and quickly fled me. And why did this happen?

Because the man on the other line spoke and unfortunately sealed my fate,

"My Lord, I have Lucius on the other line for you as was requested." And my first thought and regrettably my first reaction went hand in hand and therefore couldn't be stopped.

Because not only did my whole-body tense but I also shot my already paranoid and suspicious husband a panicked look.

Then I screamed only one thing in my mind…

'Oh shit!'

CHAPTER TWENTY

NOT YET A TALL TOWER BUT INSTEAD TALL TALES

"My Lord, I have Lucius on the other line for you as requested." The voice seemed to echo in my mind even though it was one I hadn't heard before. Well, whoever they were, two things I was now certain of, one was they were definitely not Scottish and the second and most important one…

I was so screwed.

Which had me questioning my sanity for why I even cared who the person was, whether he be Scottish or not, he was obviously about to hand my ass over to Draven on a plate. This was the only important thing right now.

"Excellent," Draven said making sure he was looking at me to gauge my reaction. Okay, so now I knew why Draven hadn't brought up the conversation of me and Lucius before now and I had stupidly believed it had to do with my spoken love for him that night. Well, it was like Draven had taught me back in the early days,

Assumption is the mother to where all mistakes are born.

And this was the mother of all mistakes!

Because obviously he had this planned from the start. So now after foolishly giving him the reaction he was looking for, that being when he saw my wide eyes of clear panic and my whole body tense, I looked away.

"Put him through," Draven ordered sternly obviously liking my reaction as much as I liked giving it…which was absolutely fff'ing zero!

"For fuck sake Dom, what has happened to her now?" This was Lucius' way of saying hello and I couldn't help my reaction as I scowled at the screen as if I could see him there instead of the unflattering contact name Draven had given him.

"Oi!" I snapped, making Draven at least look slightly amused, which was definitely a step up from murderous. So, as annoying as Lucius' greeting was, I would take it as a positive.

"She is safe and by my side," Draven replied slicing me a look.

"Well, as much as I enjoy witnessing the unbelievable in this immortal life of mine, this still doesn't account as to why you demanded my call," Lucius commented sarcastically, and I had to give it to him, damn but he could play it cool like a freaking Jedi master!

"Because I would like you to explain to me …*in detail* … what it was you were doing with *my* wife shortly before you followed her through the same door she walked through when re-joining me," he asked emphasising certain words to make his point clear, *as in crystal.*

It definitely had a distinct 'lie and I will crush you' vibe that was for sure. And with the sound of his cutting question, it was like a fist being rammed through my chest and clutching my heart, preventing it from beating until I heard Lucius' reply.

Of course, when it actually came it didn't relieve the pressure in my chest, no it simply increased it to a point I gasped for air.

"I take it this means that she hasn't told you, like we discussed she would?" Draven frowned and gave me accusing eyes. I couldn't believe what Lucius was saying! Was he really about to betray me like that and so easily? I mean I know that he didn't want to take Draven's memories to begin with, but I didn't expect this. Christ, but he wasn't even putting up a fight.

"Keira," Draven's voice brought my panicked eyes back to his serious ones and I swallowed hard. I shook my head as I still didn't know what to say. How could I tell him what we had done?

What I had done.

"I...I..." This was all that made it past my lips before Lucius released a heavy sigh and started speaking once again. And once again that fist tightened with such force that I had to close my eyes just to relieve the pressure put there by Draven's hard look of disappointment.

"I am sorry to tell you this, but confess I am far from sorry about what occurred by my hand," he stated, and my mouth dropped open in shock. Jesus, but did he have a death wish?! This is certainly not the way I would have started this, that was for damn sure. Grovel yes, openly boast…that would be a resounding NO.

"What happened?!" Draven snapped, losing patience.

"Well as usual, our little Keira girl getting herself into trouble."

"Lucius!" Draven said his name as a warning, one spoken as a demonic growl that was too close to the edge.

"Very well, I was walking out of the restroom only to find some asshole in a cheap suit coming on to your wife." The second Draven heard this his possessive nature took over and his fist slammed into his side window, cracking it with an audible thud. This made me wonder if it was reinforced or bullet proof or something, because I swear that it should have shattered from the force of Draven's fist.

I jumped in my seat and let out a shriek in surprise at both Draven's outburst and at what Lucius was saying.

"Come Again?!" Draven asked in a deadly tone having to force the words past his barely contained fury.

"Naturally walking out the door to hear her repeating herself with force how she wasn't interested, and in fact newly married, he decided he had a death wish after all."

"Lucius, my patience." This was said by Draven as a warning that he was close to losing his shit, right alongside with his demonic temper.

"Does it matter what he did, the fact remains is he touched her and for that I took matters out of her hands and with it, *his firmly off her."* This time when Draven hit out, the window wasn't up to the task of remaining in one piece any longer.

"Draven!" I shouted which was ignored when Draven growled,

"What did you do?"

"What do you think I did, give him an address of a good tailor and send him on his merry fucking way...give me some credit old friend, I slammed the door using his face and gave him a new nightmare to fear," Lucius snapped sarcastically making me stare at the screen in wonder at where this easy lie had come from. Had he been expecting this call?

"And that was?" Draven asked, somewhat now comforted in knowledge that someone who had touched me without permission had walked away with a broken nose and forever haunted by a new unearthly predator.

"A threat from a demon he would never forget and from the piss stain soaking his trouser leg, I would say it would be enough to prevent the same offense happening again in the future...his dress sense on the other hand is a lost cause I am afraid, although the piss on his pants was a significant improvement," Lucius commented sardonically.

"Good. And what of his mind?" Draven asked, now definitely on the calmer side of the fence thanks to hearing of Lucius' effective brand of punishment.

"I took away his ability to tell anyone of his near fatal and suicidal endeavours and he can count himself fucking lucky I didn't do this by ripping out his fucking tongue instead of just controlling his mind." I shuddered at the thought and was counting my lucky (and hopefully un-cursed stars) that this didn't actually happen.

"You did the right thing and for that I am in your debt." Lucius scoffed at this and said in a more serious tone,

"No. You are not." And with those four words he was conveying much more than just a casual 'Mah, don't mention it, what are friends for' type of thing. No what he was actually saying was, that I wasn't just Draven's to protect and I knew this when Draven raised a brow in question. Then after a silent moment to give his words greater thought he spoke.

"No, I suppose not." Hearing Draven agree with this made me bite my lip as the guilt washed over me.

"Of course, the question still remains as to why I am only hearing about this now?" Draven asked once again turning accusing hard eyes to me and it was only when he focused his gaze on my bitten and currently abused bottom lip, that his expression softened slightly.

"Because it was at her request," was his curt reply and I couldn't help my reaction when I forgot myself by shouting,

"Lucius!"

"I am sorry Pet, but as I told you at the time, it is your husband's right to know. I gave you time to do this yourself, but I did so with a warning that I would not lie should the occasion arise, and I am sorry sweetheart, but that occasion arose as I knew it would," he informed me, and I swear even *I* was half way to believing him and I was bloody there!

He was that good.

"Why didn't you tell me?" Draven asked me, and this quickly became the flaw in Lucius' plan. Because no matter how rock-solid Lucius' lie sounded, it was about to come crashing down and crumbling on impact if it all relied on my ability to lie.

"If I may interject at this point and say that I believe her reasons were of a noble sort," Lucius interrupted, and I swear I said three hail Mary's in my head at this and thankfully ignored the insane urge to wave my hands up and down like demented jazz hands.

"Explain!" Draven demanded turning his attention back to the screen.

"She didn't want to ruin what was a family occasion so soon after your wedding and added to that, what already transpired the night before, well then I can't say I blamed her from wanting to do so privately and after the incident." Draven looked back to me and said,

"And far from being within distance of ripping his offending tongue out for myself, no doubt." Now this thought made me shudder and finally it was a reaction he could account for, given the circumstances Lucius had painted of course.

"And well, there is that," Lucius said on a chuckle.

"So now you know all that transpired," Lucius added after a moment of silence.

"Now I know," Draven agreed with a nod.

"Good, now will that be all, so you two can get back to your fucking honeymoon or is there someone you wish me to kill before I go?" Lucius asked on a pissed off growl that made Draven laugh.

"Königssee or Transfusion?" Draven inquired.

"Business before pleasure my friend, you know this," was Lucius' reply.

"Then we will have to visit," Draven said making Lucius laugh once before he stated firmly,

"No, you won't."

"No, we won't," Draven quickly agreed light-heartedly.

"Khoda hafez." Draven said reaching out to end the call when Lucius replied,

"And with you." Then he tapped the red phone icon and we were alone once more.

"What did that mean?" I asked in a quiet voice, one reserved for gauging what mood Draven would now be in after all Lucius had shared.

"It means 'let the Gods be with you' in my home language."

"Persian?" I asked to which he nodded.

"Why didn't you tell me?" he asked after a silent moment had passed between us. This time I didn't feel panic when speaking because Lucius had pretty much said all that was needed to say. This included my reasons why...something Draven obviously wanted to hear from my own lips.

"Why do you think?" I replied using my 'isn't it obvious' tone.

"I can't say I am not disappointed..."

"Draven I..." I said his name as a plea, but he held up a hand to stop me.

"...But I understand your need to protect me from such information, especially at that delicate time with your family present." I released a sigh of relief and muttered a quiet,

"Thank you." Turned out, my relief was very short lived.

"I have not finished Keira," he warned making me shut my mouth and wisely decided to let him speak and not to argue.

"I do not understand however, why you chose to continue to keep it from me and it now begs the question of when you would have told me, if at all?" Okay, so maybe I wasn't out of hot water just quite yet. I swallowed down the hard lump named guilt, swiftly followed by another called lies.

"When is ever a good time to tell you something like that? Last night before we made love, after we made love? In the shower, when once again we made love? Or this morning which was a start to a beautiful and perfect day where you would then whisk me away on a surprise honeymoon...?" I let my sentence end there for a moment and watched as realisation sank in.

"Seriously Draven, when is a good time to tell my new husband that some dickhead and probably leader of the asshole convention he was attending, tried it on with me only to nearly get his head ripped off from one very pissed off vampire?"

"Come here, sweetheart." he requested once I had finished speaking. So, I did as he asked, unbuckled my seatbelt, one in the end that hadn't been needed, as we hadn't yet moved from the side of the road. Then once again I made my way over the centre console, now with the help of his hands reaching over and grabbing my waist. After he settled me again in his lap he then pulled me close for a much need hug, *one needed on both sides.*

"I understand your reasons and as Luc said, they are noble ones," he said speaking over my head as he held my cheek to his chest. Then he placed both hands at my shoulders so that he could push me back enough to see my face. He even had to duck his head slightly due to our height difference.

"But that does not mean I will tolerate this in the future

and if anyone is demanding enough for another death wish to be granted for touching what is mine, then *I* will be the one who deals with it and the offending hand it belongs to, no matter what the occasion is or has been. Am I understood?" Hearing his serious voice cutting through all reasons I may have had ready, I simply bit my bottom lip and nodded.

This turned out to be a wise choice.

"Good, then we have no need to speak further on the matter. Now kiss your King and sooth his frayed nerves, little one." This time it was a demand, not a request and it was one I was more than happy to comply with.

This time when I kissed him, it wasn't the usual urgent and lustful battle we both fought but it was soft, slow and sensual. By the time I had finished kissing him soft and tenderly, he placed his forehead to mine and whispered,

"What am I to do with you, little wife of mine?" he asked making me nip at his nose playfully before saying,

"I don't know but Pip tells me restraints are fun." At this he finally let go of any remaining frustration or anger by releasing a contented laugh.

"Now that is an intriguing idea and one I might put to practice, you know, seeing as we are staying in a medieval castle."

"I meant fun for me," I teased back and again he laughed.

"Oh no sweetheart, for your vixen days are over on this honeymoon," he informed me grinning.

"And why is that?"

"Because I have a new role for you to play."

"Which is?" I asked knowing he was drawing me into his game, one I knew I would enjoy playing.

"My tied up little submissive blonde beauty," he said and when my mouth dropped in surprise, he took the opportunity presented to him. And this time when he kissed me, it was a heated lust filled battle...

One he most certainly won.

CHAPTER TWENTY-ONE

SWEET THINGS, THINGS ARE SWEET

A little time later and one window fixed thanks to supernatural magic mumbo, we were back on our way heading towards I had no clue where. I tried to press for information, but he would just grin to himself and shake his head, telling me no.

So, I sat there getting both lost in the beautiful Scottish countryside and the not so beautiful minefield that was my mind. It was a strange mix to be silently drowning in, as it felt like oil and water, guilt and relief. On one hand, I hated that I had started off married life with a lie. Especially after having to also lie just before it, so that I could get away with disappearing on my own quest through time. And on the other hand, I was just glad that Lucius had covered for me, *yet again*, and in doing so, keeping something huge from Draven.

But no matter how much I tried to tell myself it was for the greater good, it still sat within my stomach like a lead weight, rocking inside me every time I moved. In fact, it felt like we both spent more time lying to each other than speaking the truth.

Was this really to be our future?

"That looks like a heavy mind," Draven said shaking me from my dangerous and torturous thoughts. I wanted to reply with 'you have no idea' but thankfully refrained.

"I am just excited to see where you're taking me." At this he laughed and quickly informed me why.

"Keira, I have seen you excited, many times in fact, so trust me when I say that, Sweetheart, this doesn't look like one of those times," he said looking at me side on and he was right, I didn't look excited. Because the truth was I was too nervous to be anything else. My mind was being plagued by questions like…what if he found out? What if it happened again? And more devastating still, what if I lost him to his demon side…*forever?*

But throughout all these collective questions, not one of them included the question of my safety. Because I still held on to the certainty that Draven's demon wouldn't hurt me, no matter what Lucius thought.

"I guess I am just processing everything that has happened these last few weeks, well weeks for me anyway," I told him because for once this wasn't exactly a lie. He gave me a nod and looked thoughtful for a moment whilst he followed the road with his gaze. It had started to rain but that wasn't enough to take away from its natural essence. The raw beauty in the never-ending rolling hills of rusty browns, patches of heather and different shades of green. The jutting rock formations that looked like blue-black spires trying to penetrate the Earth's crust.

The glassy lochs and rivers we drove around, with the dark grey roads framing the landscape, winding through it and following its natural flow.

"Do you miss it?" His question caught me off guard.

"Miss what?"

"Persia," he stated softly without looking at me and it was almost as if he could still see it for himself. As though instead of the wet, green and lush landscape spread out in front of him, what he was actually seeing was years into the past. The majestic sandstone palace set amongst the endless desert, all topped off by the burning orange sun that kissed the domed rooftops.

So instead of answering him, I asked him the same,

"Do you?"

"Yes," he answered without question and I felt the tug in my heart for how hard it must have been for him. To stand by and let humans take over what had been his home since the beginning, that had once been his palace, only to see it fall to ruins.

It had to be said, that being an immortal sounded pretty cool to most, but it definitely came with its downsides and for Draven, then this must have been a big one. But I had never once asked. I had never even thought of what it must be like for him. How hardy and thick skinned you must have to become to continue only to watch the world around you change and finding it a necessary evil to be forced to change with it. Which made me suddenly feel bad for teasing him about how old he was.

"I am sorry," I told him, this time making him look at me in surprise.

"Why would you be sorry?" he asked, so I told him.

"Because I never stopped to think about how hard it must be for you." He gave me a questioning look, so I carried on explaining.

"You know, being forced to make decisions based on what is best for other people, for humanity, for your own kind and having to leave what was your home…I can't imagine how many times you have had to do it and what it must take out of you every time you do. All that time…" I let my sentence trail off as I shook my head, trying to force my thoughts around the concept.

"Sweetheart, look at me," he said in a tender tone that told me with only three words that what I had said meant a great deal to him. But even if his tone hadn't been enough, when I looked at him, his eyes certainly did.

"I must confess it has not always been easy. To live among humanity watching it close to destroying itself time and time again and most of that time, being forced to do nothing to aid in ending innocent people's suffering."

"You couldn't help?" I asked to keep him talking.

"By the Gods I wanted to, a lot of my kind often does, but I was not put on Earth to help control the greed of man but only there to maintain control and order of my own people. It is freewill for people to choose which side to fall behind and even if they do not, they can sometimes be free to leave. It is the unfortunate times when choice is not their own…this is always the hardest to ignore." I knew what he was saying. And to stand by and do nothing was often thought of as being just as bad as the act itself. But in this case, it was a law he could not defy and a line he could not cross. Not unless instructed otherwise and usually by the Fates.

Because in the end, Draven was governed just as we all were. It was just that his orders came from a higher power than everyone else's. And boy must that have sucked.

"That must have been so hard to endure," I said sympathising with him, if only understanding a drop in an ocean of memories. Memories he'd have to live with for eternity.

"It certainly wasn't always easy, and I must confess that there were times when whispered secrets were spoken in the ears of the right men in power. But in the end, fate had the final say. For it was always in your destiny to learn from mistakes made. For land to be conquered again and again, until even its history becomes a blurred image of what it used to be. When fact and fiction started to merge and inevitably the truth becomes lost through years of being told," he said, and I could imagine this to be true.

Because no matter how many artefacts or written pieces of evidence the world found and dug up, in the end, you could only really speculate where the breadcrumbs of time would lead us to. Oh, you could make educated guesses until the cows came home on what historical evidence showed you, but unless you were really there, then no one can be one hundred percent certain and call it fact.

After all, that important scroll you just found with what you think holds the hidden link to cracking some historical code, could in fact just have been an ancient version of the town's crazy person, that spoke to cats, believed in fairies and thought smoking avocados was a good idea.

Yeah, so being with Draven certainly made you look differently at the world's history, that was for damn sure.

"I regret many things during my time on Earth's plane,

Keira, but do you know what I regret the most?" he said once again bringing me out of my thoughts consumed by the past. I loved it when Draven shared parts of his past life with me, making me feel as though I could almost see it for myself, something I longed to do. But right now, with him talking about the bad times and with it his past regrets, I wasn't sure I was ready for it.

As it turned out, I was more than ready for it.

For what he gave me next wasn't just sweet, it was…

Well, it was perfect.

"I regret every second of it I spent living without you," he told me lovingly, making my heart melt at his confession.

"Dominic." I whispered his name, the one I hardly used and therefore reserved for the sweetest moments. He reached for my hand and gave it a squeeze when I told him,

"I have the same regrets…although my combined seconds are considerably less than yours." I added this last part to lighten the mood and I know I achieved this when he joked,

"Yes, well that's what happens when you're practically a Caveman." I giggled, and the rest of the journey was spent laughing and teasing one another now that the serious side of life had been filed away and unfortunately, saved for another day.

———

After driving for about two hours, I decided that I had to give into my bodily needs and tell Draven I needed a toilet break. I don't know why he found this amusing, maybe it was because the words I used were,

"Can we stop somewhere, only I really need to go to the little girl's room and tap a kidney." A lip twitch later and we soon pulled off the main road and into a petrol station.

"I will fill up, whilst you...how did you put it, tap a kidney?" he teased after he had pulled up to one of the free pumps and had come around to my side to help me out of the ridiculously high car.

"Okay handsome." I said making him grin as I reached up and kissed his cheek...well, after pulling on his neck first so he would get the hint and give in to me being a short ass. I then turned around and as I was making my way into the store, I couldn't help but notice the other people that were staring at Draven.

One was a young guy about to get into his car who stared in open shock at both Draven and his car, probably knowing how much it cost. There was also a couple and it was obvious they weren't here for a holiday like we were. For starters the girl who was filling up, what was obviously her car, on account of the pink racing stripes, was wearing what looked to be a supermarket uniform.

The guy who was sat in the passenger seat was staring down at his phone, completely oblivious to the fact his girlfriend was now freely staring at another guy with her mouth nearer to the floor than her forehead.

It was at that point that I turned around to see for myself the mouth-watering sight she was laying witness to and yep, it was mouth-watering all right. Draven was reaching for the pump after just pushing his sweater up his forearms, giving us both a little taste of what heaven lay beneath all those clothes.

But thankfully, I knew from experience all of the exotic

sin that was concealed beneath. But for an outsider, well, all she had was the glimpse of tanned skin you wanted to lick, a pair of strong hands you wanted all over your body and the face of a God, with the body to match. Oh, that and her imagination, which I knew for a fact would never have hit the mark.

I swear watching Draven filling up the car at a petrol station should not have been as sexy as it was...it was verging on the ridiculous. Of course, it still didn't mean it wasn't true, I thought as I walked through the store looking for the toilets.

I had just finished and was washing my hands in the sink when the same girl walked in. She took notice of me, nodded once a silent hello and after I did the same, she stepped into a cubicle. I then checked myself in the mirror, seeing my hair was still half up into a messy knot, with the rest of its length resting down my back. My lips looked a darker pink thanks to being kissed most of the night and my pale skin was blushed from coming in from the cold. My eyes also looked a darker shade than they usually did, with the blue getting lost to the grey.

I shrugged my shoulders at myself, feeling as satisfied as I ever would, before stepping back into the store. I saw Draven walk in through the doors at the same time as he was slipping his phone into his back pocket, telling me he had no doubt just taken a call before coming in here.

He scanned the room and visibly relaxed when he saw me. We were about to meet in the middle when I spotted the sweet aisle and I winked at him before side stepping out of sight.

"Fancy something sweet?" I asked him when I felt him

approach from behind and with a hand at my belly then pulling my body back a step into his own.

"Always," he answered almost purring the word against my shoulder after he drew my hooded sweater to one side. I giggled and warned just as playfully,

"Draven behave, this is serious business here."

"Yes, I can see that," he said with a grin as I started picking up bags.

"Oh cool, Haribo Starmix, I love these! Oh, but wait if we get these then we have to get the sour ones too…ah but then if we do that, then which do we choose, jelly babies, wine gums or fruit pastels…Oh decisions, decisions," I said tapping a finger on my lip.

"Why not just get them all?" Draven asked as if this was the most natural thing in the world. I shot him a glance, looking up over my shoulder.

"We can't get them all!"

"Why not?"

"Because that would be greedy and…hey, Draven what are you…?" I let my question trail off as it became obvious what he was doing when he grabbed all five bags and made his way over to the till. Just then the girl was coming out of the bathroom and when she saw that her sexy petrol station, dream man was standing next to me, her face said it all, 'Lucky Bitch'. It was in this moment when her asshole boyfriend started tapping his watch at her and throwing his hands up in the air through the store window, that I had to disagree with her…

I was the *luckiest* bitch alive.

Draven stepped up to the counter and this was when I got a craving for something else. Which was what happened when you have been out of your home country for a while and you suddenly have the urge to buy everything you knew you couldn't get back home.

"Oh, and crisps!" I shouted.

"Crisps?" Draven enquired and the cashier, an older guy in his late fifties smirked.

"I mean chips, dear..." I patted him on the chest and said to the cashier,

"It's alright, he's American," making him laugh and Draven shake his head in that amused way of his. Of course, I knew he wasn't American, but I think the poor guy would have been a bit confused had I said he was Persian.

"Third aisle, opposite the drinks," he told me making me realise that a drink would also be good. So, with a big grin I held up a finger to indicate one minute, which turned out to be three, because really, there was an awesome choice.

"They have Ribena!" I shouted enthusiastically the second I made it back to Draven, happy that there was no one else stuck behind us in a queue. The cashier smiled and said,

"I take it they don't have that in the States either?"

"Nope, they don't even have cordial and no cheese and onion Walkers in sight...it's a crime really." I joked referring to the bag of crisps I had added to my personal treasure trove, making the cashier laugh. I could feel Draven staring down at me as if he was seeing me for the first time, which was getting harder to ignore.

"So, you kid's here for a holiday?" he asked in a friendly way and I had to stop myself from bursting out laughing when he referred to Draven as a kid. I mean, even if he wasn't thousands of years old, he still looked like he was in his early thirties.

"We are actually on our honeymoon," I said excitedly curling myself into Draven's side and resting a hand on his chest, one I felt rumble slightly under my palm after I had said this.

"Oh, well congratulations!" The guy said beaming at us.

"Here, in that case, let me give you one of these flyers, I don't know whereabouts you're staying, but there's a medieval banquet on the grounds at Balmoral Castle...full costumes mandatory mind you." He added giving me a wink, because hey, I was a girl and what girl didn't want to have the excuse to dress up as a fairy-tale princess.

"Wow, that sounds great, thanks!" I said taking the flyer from him. Draven gave him a silent nod in thanks and reached into his back pocket, getting out a dark brown leather wallet. I don't know why but seeing something so simple like Draven owning a wallet had me suddenly itching to see what was inside. Did he have anything personal in there, like pictures? Did he carry ID, like a driving licence?

"Keira?" Draven said my name and I realised I had been staring at the wallet still in his hand long after he had paid the man. He was sliding a black and silver card back into the only free card sleeve of his wallet, when I finally snapped out of it.

"Well, I hope you two enjoy your honeymoon and all the best for the future," he said smiling and after a thank you and good day, I was out the door with one hand in Draven's and the other clutching on to the flyer the cashier had given us. I was also happy to see that my bag of treats was in Draven's other hand.

"You have a very friendly nature towards others," Draven mused aloud making me stop mid crunch, as it had taken me all of about five second to tear into my bag of crisps.

"You fink so?" I asked talking with my mouth full and saying screw the whole ladylike manners thanks to snacks that felt like they had been sent from the Gods. He smirked and said,

"I don't think. *I know*. You definitely have a way with people, they seem openly relaxed when you're around." I thought on this as I swallowed and said,

"Draven, I am just polite as my mother taught me to be. Now here, stop saying silly things and try the best crisps… sorry, chips, you will ever have!" I said reaching across to hold the bag out to him.

"Sweetheart I don't think…oh, okay…" Draven said after I gave him no choice because I had picked one out and was forcing the savoury snack in to his lips, so he had no choice in the matter. The second he tasted it, his eyes went wide, and I knew I had lost Draven to the junk food taste bud monster…better known as 'The munchies'.

"You like?" I said feeling smug and sounding it too.

"Mm, actually, they're not bad," he admitted, and I was shocked.

"Are you seriously telling me that you have lived all this time without once trying junk food?" I asked stunned.

"Well the word 'junk' doesn't exactly sell it to me, sweetheart." I laughed at this because well yeah, he was kind of right. I mean who would want to try something called, 'Crap Cuisine' or 'Shit Snacks'?

"Okay, so I will give you that one, but well lucky for you I am here to educate you in all things bad for you…well, to eat anyway," I said, adding this last with a coy smile. He raised a brow at me and asked,

"Oh really? Then please tell me, what is next on the menu?" This was when I grinned at him, held up a finger to indicate a minute like I had in the store, as I then dipped a hand in the bag, making it rustle. He laughed at my behaviour, once again shaking his head like he had just married a loon and bloody loved the fact!

"Sugary drinks that will rot our teeth," I said pulling out a cold bottle of my childhood favourite, blackcurrant flavoured drink and giving it a little shake at him. At this he faked a groan, making me chuckle as I could still see he was trying to fight off a grin.

After this we spent the next few hours chatting and eating the bounty of sweets Draven had bought me. Which included times like teasing Draven with jelly hearts, sugar-coated fruit pastels and sour cola bottles. I would reach over, offering them to his mouth and then pulling away just before he could bite them. This ended with him capturing my wrist, bringing the sweet to his mouth before taking both it and my finger inside for him to suck. Needless to say, after this I continued to tease.

It wasn't a surprise to find that Draven had a sweet tooth, as I remembered what he had been like when we had bought Ella candy from the supermarket. Talk about the saying 'kid in a candy store' Draven gave it new meaning, if you swapped the word Kid for Sugar Demon that was.

Then the teasing carried on when I saw a sign I couldn't pronounce and when I tried, Draven just chuckled at me and shook his head in amusement.

"Fesshy...bridge?"

"Feshiebridge," Draven corrected, even doing so with a hint of an accent.

Then after a short while, he turned onto a dirt road that looked to be privately used. This was when my excitement started to mount.

"How is it you have never been to Scotland before, when it is so close to where you grew up?" Draven asked me, and I gasped.

"Close...Draven it must be over a five-hour drive!" Again, he laughed and said,

"And?"

"Well, I wouldn't exactly call that close, honey." I replied but the second I watched him tense, I was left wondering what it was that I just said to warrant that reaction.

I didn't have long to wait.

"What did you say?" he asked, his voice sounding gravelly as if he suddenly needed to clear his throat before speaking.

"I said it wasn't close?" I told him in a questioning tone, shaking my head and by doing so silently asking him what he meant.

"You called me honey." I felt my hands drop in my lap and again that fist around my heart was back.

"Oh...I...well I don't have..."

"I liked it," he said stopping me before I could take it back and vow not to call him it again.

"I have heard you call others by the endearment and wondered if I would hear the sweet word from your lips, only this time being directed at me," he said surprising me.

"I'm sure I have called you honey before, Draven," I said in my defence and suddenly feeling bad that I never had before. Then again, thinking about it, when did I ever really call him any other name but Draven and on occasion Dominic. I never even shortened it to Dom like others did. I never called him sweetheart, like he did with me... *frequently*... or love, darling, honey, not even a babe or baby in sight. And now with that tender look on his face I found myself questioning why not? It was clear he liked hearing it, this made abundantly obvious when he stunned me with his next words.

"You have called me honey only one other time and that was when we spoke our first vows together and you became my wife for the first time...however it was my understanding that you were a little inebriated at the time, so I am not sure it counts," he teased granting me a grin.

"You remember that?" I asked in hushed tones, still deep in my shock.

"Of course, I remember everything when it comes to you," he said like this should have been obvious. I blushed and looked down at my lap as I smiled to myself.

"I see my girl likes the sound of that," he said and again, doing so with a sweet endearment calling me 'his girl'. So, my grin grew bigger when I said,

"I see *my man* likes that I liked it." And yep, holy cow but did he like the sound of that! I am not sure I had seen a grin so big on him before and was that...no, was that a slight blush I saw on him also? Okay so yeah, I was certainly onto something here with the loving pet names.

"Your man does...*definitely,"* he said almost purring the last word making my insides do that melty thing again.

"He is also looking forward to your reaction when seeing what lies ahead," he added nodding back to the windscreen and now instead of giving Draven my full attention, my head snapped to the front. The second he rounded a corner I gasped at the majestic sight.

Because there, high up and tucked close to the hills and mountains, was something that had Draven written all over it. And that something was Gothic and grand and like something out of another world.

Which is why I said the first thing that popped into my head.

"You really do have a tower!" Then he gave me a bad ass and sexy grin and said,

"No baby, I have several."

CHAPTER TWENTY-TWO

FINDING FORTUNE

O kay, in the past when Draven had ever mentioned having a tower to lock me in, I really shouldn't have doubted him. Because what faced me now wasn't just a large stone manor house that might have resembled a small castle-like structure that I had been expecting. Because really, who owned an actual castle these days? Most of them had surely been turned into hotels and wedding venues or buildings owned by the National Trust as tourist attractions.

But oh no, when Draven said he had a castle, then what he really meant was, he had a bloody big, humongous castle! I swear the place even had battlements and turrets, well don't get me started on the turrets! But most of all it had towers and as he'd said, he had many. I mean, I counted at least four of them from way down here, that and a massive square tower that stood taller than the rest at the centre.

The castle was situated on a hill, higher up than the road

we were currently on. It was then flanked by even higher hills at both sides that swooped down in front of it into a V shaped valley. But it was the mountain at its back that was incredible. It jutted out as a grey presence in the sky, looking as menacing as its owner could be. It was clever really, because with the patched grey stone it was built from, looking at it from a distance, you would have never known there was even a castle there. Which made me ask the question,

"Does anyone know of this place?" To which Draven replied by giving me a cunning look.

"Clever girl. No, humans don't know of this place and if they happen to stumble across it by pure chance then as soon as they pass back through the gatehouse, they lose their memories of it ever being here."

"Wow, I guess that comes in handy when you get those random people that come knocking on your door trying to sell you a hoover." He laughed hard at this and also when I added,

"Must be a bitch trying to get mail though, or a pizza delivery."

"Indeed, which is why we try not to burn our oven pizzas," he said reminding me of our first 'date' and the black frisbee that had been my dinner at the time. I gave him a warm smile knowing it was sweet of him to remember. Although according to him, he never forgot anything when it came to me. Well, I guess he was on a mission to prove this statement.

"It's incredible how its cut into the rock face like that," I said with wonder lacing my words.

"You will see that from here it casts an optical illusion as the hill it sits upon is a large flat piece of land. But yes, the back corner towers and part of the keep have been cut into the mountain," he told me, nodding to the side as if we were right in front of it.

I could see the winding road we would have to travel on to get up there and now the robust and heavy-duty vehicle started to make sense. But still, I had to say it wasn't as bumpy as I would have imagined.

Oh, who was I kidding, I couldn't have imagined any of this if I had tried in a million years and that included the road. One that thanks to years of been driven on, had now formed two dirt lines either side of a small green mound in the middle. One that was obviously all that remained natural on the road after years of abuse from mean, heavy beasts like the one Draven was driving. Well, one thing was for sure and that was I doubted that he ever drove his Aston Martins up here or any of his other fancy sport cars.

"What car is this?" I asked out of the blue and Draven laughed because of it.

"What?" I asked even though I had an idea what he was going to say.

"Just that we have been driving now for about three and a half hours and just before we arrive is when you choose to ask me about the car." Okay, so I could see his point. However, I didn't say this. No instead what I said was,

"Wow, has it been that long?"

"Well, you did fall asleep for an hour of it," Draven mused smirking.

"No, I didn't, it was like ten minutes at most," I argued because even though I knew he was probably right, it was still fun saying that it wasn't. Draven didn't disappoint.

"It's true, I was worried at first that it might have been a sugar induced coma but then you started snoring and this thankfully put my mind at ease." At this I gasped in fake outrage making him shoot me a sexy bad boy grin over his shoulder.

"I didn't eat that many!" I said in my defence, but then the smarmy bugger just nodded at my lap where yes, unfortunately evidence would suggest that I might have made a pig out of myself, thanks to the dusting of sugar that still covered my denim thighs.

"Naturally I didn't want to say, as I was hoping that when I rip your jeans off later, that some of that sugar would transfer to your skin for me to lick off...now I see I will just have to improvise." This made me bite my lip to at least try and hold back the massive grin that wanted to invade most of the lower part of my face.

I failed.

"Oh, I see she likes that idea," Draven said, pretending to speak to himself. God, but I just loved it when he teased me like that and I liked it even better when he was doing it in a bed, so that we may add a bit of play fighting to accompany it.

"You know too much sugar is bad for you, so don't go getting addicted now," I said thinking this was a good one but what Draven said next was way, way better.

"Oh, don't worry *Sweetheart*, I already have one addiction and I don't ever plan on swapping it for another." Then he winked at me making me close to swooning. I mean how you could even swoon in a car was beyond me, however it was happening.

But then the smarmy side of Keira didn't want to leave it at that, so I said,

"You know I don't think there is anything bad about being addicted to knitting, the sweater you made is quite lovely on you and don't listen to others, it really is an underrated hobby for a man. There's nothing to be ashamed about..." I said patting him on the arm in a patronising way before carrying on.

"...Hey, is that why you collect weapons, is it to counterbalance the girly, oops, I mean *manly* hobby...be honest here, are we over compensating for something, *Sweetheart?"* At this I could take it no more as I burst out laughing, at yes, my own joke. But it was the look on his face that did it. I laughed so hard I even slapped my hand on the dash. Which meant I missed the heated look he gave me when I called him by another endearment, his current favourite to use for me.

"Gods, I fucking love you, you mad beauty! I swear that if I don't get you naked and under me soon I am going to come just by watching you laugh!" he said fiercely and soon I was choking back my laughter and trying to remember how to breath and still look normal...as in not gasping like a fish out of water just because my husband said something, that right now made me want to orgasm.

"Now behave little one, or I swear I am going to drive this car off the hillside if you keep distracting me by looking adorable and cute," he growled playfully, and I couldn't help myself when I asked,

"I thought I was turning you on?"

"Does it look like I am lying, sweetheart?" he stated looking down at himself and motioning with a hand to his lap. My gaze quickly homed in to the evidence he was taking about. And yep, it was right there, every glorious inch, making its way down his thigh and pressing, what I can imagine was uncomfortably, against his jeans.

"But…but you…" I started to stutter for words, still in shock at how hard he looked just from seeing me laugh.

"But?"

"You called me cute and adorable…no one finds cute and adorable sexy," I argued because as far as I was concerned, they didn't, did they…or was it just my own self-doubt talking? I found out pretty quickly it was, when Draven swore again on a growl,

"Well, I fucking do."

"Have you …you know…always thought it was…" Okay so I knew I was fishing here but it was so worth it when he understood what I was asking and replied instantly with,

"With anyone else, no, not at all. But with you, yes, all the God's be damned time," he finished on a growl.

"Really?!" I asked again getting high pitched this time.

"Enough to drive me to distraction on a daily basis, and sometimes to the point where I want to either kiss you senseless or gag you, just for a minute's respite so you would have mercy on my diminishing control." Okay, so big wow and a firm ten points for me then.

"Now we are going to talk about something else before I seriously stop the car and make full use of this vehicle's spacious backseat." I swallowed down my grin and asked again,

"So, what car is this again?" His shoulders tensed, and he snapped his head around to face me and warned,

"I thought I told you to stop being cute." At this I laughed, held up my hands in surrender and said,

"What? I was being serious, pinky promise and scouts hon…"

"Keira, stop it." he said cutting me off after groaning to himself and scrubbing a hand down his face. This was when I had to put a fist to my mouth to bite on, just to stop myself from the raucous laughter that would soon erupt… *again.*

"Alright, so I know it's a Mercedes, as I recognised the badge on the front grill but why does it look like an expensive tank?" At this it was his turn to laugh. And whilst he was momentarily distracted, I really, *really* tried not to look again at his lap to see if it was still there, but what can I say, I have zero willpower when it came to Draven.

Which is why I could confirm…

With absolute certainly,

It was very much still there. And in all its hard and wonderful glory. Man alive, but how I wished we were at his damn castle by now, seriously this was like the longest driveway in history!

Thankfully my mind was pulled out of the sexual fog it was quickly falling into when Draven spoke.

"It's the new Mercedes-Maybach G-Class 650," Draven told me now that he was satisfied that it was in fact *a real question.* I looked around at all the comfort and technology that an endless stream of money could buy you, feeling like I was once again out of my league here. I kind of missed the simple things, like my rusty-patch truck. Poor big blue, she was certainly being neglected and I think the last time I saw her, some of the door trim was hanging off and one of the lights had entered the eternal darkness.

"I bet big blue would be great getting up here," I said making Draven snort, which was a very un-Draven-like sound.

"And what do you mean by that?" I asked folding my arms across my chest and feeling defensive about my big truck. Okay, so it was nowhere near as big as this one and it sometimes had trouble starting if it was cold, but still, she still had good bones…just a weak battery, which was usually like most people, just on a Monday morning.

"Sweetheart, you cannot expect me to continue to let you drive around in that thing much longer?"

"Uh…*continue to let me*…Draven, I hate to tell you this, but you don't get a say," I told him firmly after mimicking his own, ridiculous words.

"I think you will find I most certainly do decide which vehicle *my wife*, who is at this moment in time pregnant with *my child*, is going to be driving around in." I opened my mouth ready to deliver my argument when he held up a hand to stop me and carried on talking.

"…and I can tell you now, it will be a damn sight better and more to the point *safer*… than that truck you adorably named big blue." Once he had finished his little speech my mouth dropped open as it seemed it was obviously the day for it. So much so I was well on my way to declaring it 'Open mouth, shock day'.

Okay so I grant you, it wasn't exactly catchy or have a nice to ring to it, but it certainly fit with the day's events.

"But you were the one who sold me the car in the first place," I told him as was the first part of my argument.

"Yes, and trust me, if I could have gotten away with just giving you what I originally wanted to give you, I would have. But let's just say I learned early on, that you felt yourself duty bound enough to work for what you received in life and were not the type to accept handouts. No matter how much I wanted to intimidate you into accepting it."

"You're joking!" I shouted in a high-pitched, screeching squeal coated with utter disbelief.

"I can assure you I am not. If anything it was Sophia's idea to appear to advance you the money, and to appease me, I played my part to ensure you bought something that was safe enough for the time being, …I had just wished for more time beforehand so I could get something better than all the utter shit he had on his forecourt."

"And what would you have 'forced me' to have I wonder, as it would have looked a little strange giving your new waitress, one you made a hobby out of ignoring, a brand new car!" I said getting snippy and at the same time wondering why. But then as sweet and protective as it seemed to be, it was controlling and demanding and also not going to happen.

"I don't give a damn how it would have looked Keira, my main concern was getting you from A to B, and above all, doing it safely. And in those very simple parameters, it does not include breaking down on the side of the road, alone and without a phone…*twice.*"

"You knew about that?"

"Yes, I knew." He ground out his response.

"What was his name again, Edison Tucker…or was it Eddie to you?" he asked in a bitter tone, one that made me wince. But to this I had no response. I knew he had backed me into a corner and sometimes, it was best to just throw in the white towel and let him win…especially when he had his jealous pants on combined with his jealous ass kicking boots.

"Okay fine, but I get to choose, and it won't be anything expensive!" To this he finally swapped his jealous scowl for a smug look of victory...yep now came the victory pants, with no more need for his ass kicking boots.

Damn, I just wanted him naked, I thought annoyingly.

We continued to make our way up the winding road towards what I could now see was an ornate gate house, I found myself wondering how he knew of Eddie. So, I asked him.

"How did you know?" I said tearing my eyes from the two smaller grey towers and battlement wall in between that mimicked the castle higher up behind it.

"I know about everything that happened during that time," he informed me in a calm voice that was the complete opposite to the hard flex in his jawline.

"You do?!" I asked again, this time in astonishment. But we were making our way up to the massive, heavily gated arch in between the towers. And it was exactly as you would imagine an imposing castle entrance would look like. The only thing it was void of was a drawbridge hanging over a surrounding moat. Even its thick, horizontal flat bars of iron that crossed over vertical ones looked like something right out of a movie. And this wall of metal squares all came down to deadly looking spikes at the bottom, spikes that were currently half embedded in the earth.

One thing was for sure, it certainly didn't look inviting.

But Draven simply rolled to a stop and gestured with one hand at the barrier, flicking all his outstretched fingers upwards once before the gate started to move. I watched silently as it lifted and started to disappear through the arched stone walls that were sandwiched both sides of the gate. Then once it was clear, Draven put the car back into drive and we continued forward.

I could now see that the land started to even out slightly and the road was now winding through a wooded area with a thick blanket of trees on both sides.

"Ten months is a long time, Keira," Draven said cutting through our awkward silence with a sombre tone.

"What are you…"

"After you left the lake house that day and after you had told me some of what you had endured during our time apart, well let's just say that finding out everything that happened to you in your search for me became my new hobby. And as it turns out, there is a lot you can discover in ten months…*in great detail.*" I had to say hearing this didn't exactly give me the warm and fuzzies!

"Draven I…"

"It's alright Keira, I don't blame you and I am not arrogant enough to believe it's solely the fault of the Fates that played us. No, I am to blame, I know this and with this knowledge, I therefore must carry that burden for the rest of my days. One that still haunts me knowing of the danger you were in because of my mistakes."

"Oh God Draven, you're killing me here!" I shouted on a groan, but he shot me a stern look and I instantly felt like kicking myself for being so stupid. I knew I had majorly hit another nerve when he snapped,

"Please don't say things like that Keira, not after what recently just happened!" I released a heavy sigh and said,

"You're right, it was an insensitive slip of the tongue and not one I meant literally. But Draven, you have to move past this. I know what happened between us was shit, more than shit, it was *fucking hell...* for both of us and that includes recent events... but Draven, sweetheart, it's over now. We won. We are together, we are happy...well at least I was until about five minutes ago when you started talking about forcing a brand-new car on me." When I had finished my little speech, he looked at me and I don't know what part of what I said surprised him the most. The fact I swore, the fact that I called him sweetheart or that fact that I just ended my little speech with a jokey tease.

"I will tell you what, how about I make you a deal?" I said after his thoughtful moment of silence. He raised an eyebrow at me and asked,

"What kind of deal?"

"I will let you buy me whatever car you want, your choice, but in doing so I never, and I *mean never again* want to hear you blaming yourself for anything that happened in the past...do we have a deal?" I asked waiting with a held breath to see what he would say. And when I had finally managed to achieve that grin back, I knew that it was worth saying goodbye to big blue. But then I panicked and quickly told him,

"But I get to keep big blue and she doesn't see anything close to a crusher or junk yard." At hearing this I could now add his booming laughter to my list of achievements.

"Alright love, I promise not to bring up the past and in return I will let you keep your truck but only because I agree with you."

"You do?"

"Yes, for I too, couldn't see anything get crushed that

you had owned. And I have too many memories of you in it to ever see it rusting away in a junk yard...I think I would rather rip out the front seats than have the knowledge of anyone else sat in them after you." At this I laughed and said on another chuckle,

"I think that would be a little overkill on the obsession front, Draven." But his reaction to this was a strange one as he stared out of his side window for a moment and muttered something under his breath. I couldn't be one hundred percent certain, but I was almost sure I had heard him whisper, 'you have no idea'.

"So, what car is it to be?" I asked, trying to change the subject and okay, so I had to admit, I was kind of getting excited about having a new car. I had never had a new one before and it would be nice to have one that wasn't old enough that the radio still played cassette tapes.

"I don't know, maybe I will get you one of these," he said nodding to the console to indicate the massive car we were in.

"Uhh...and how much was this car?" I asked knowing it would have way too many zeros.

"Five hundred."

"WHAT! You're saying this car cost you five hundred grand!?" I screeched in astonishment. He chuckled at my outrage.

"Please tell me that was in Yen?" I joked again this time making him laugh before telling me,

"No, dollars."

"Draven, that is a crazy amount of money for a car," I complained.

"Keira, sweetheart, you do get that I am a very wealthy man?" he informed me, and I cringed at the thought.

"Yes, evidence would suggest so," I said dryly, again making him smirk.

"Then you also get that because of this, *you* are now a very wealthy woman," he added and this time my head snapped to his as if he had just yanked it on a string.

"No, it doesn't!" I argued hating the idea of him thinking this.

"Oh really, how so?" he asked in a teasing tone, obviously enjoying my reactions far too much.

"Because it's your money and I didn't earn a penny of it," I argued back.

"So, are you telling me, if it was the other way around, that I, as your husband, wouldn't be entitled to any of it?" Oh, damn him but he had me there and he knew this when I said stubbornly,

"That's not the point."

"I think you will find that in this case, it is a very *valid* point," he said on a laugh.

"Fine you're a millionaire, can we move on now," I said moodily and probably looking like a narky teenager right about now.

"No, I am a billionaire, many times over and no, we can't move on now," he told me firmly, but it was my turn to shout again.

"You're a billionaire!?"

"Yes, and now, so are you," he stated just like that. Just like we were discussing the bloody weather or something!

"No, I am most certainly not!" I huffed.

"Yes, you are sweetheart."

"Draven!" I said his naming in warning to drop this but of course, this was Draven we were talking about, Mr Bossy himself.

"Keira, listen to me now, as I am only going to say this once and then we will move on and we will do this by you accepting what is now fact..." He paused to look at me to check that I was still listening. So, with my arms crossed over my chest, I simply nodded for him to continue without saying a word, because seriously, what was the point?

"The moment I first met you, your fate was sealed and with that not only came my love but also my fortune. I have lived many lives to accumulate such wealth, most of which still grows through years of investments. What I am saying my dear, is that I could live the rest of my immortal life without another day's work in the business world and still be the wealthiest man on Earth."

"Are you serious?" I asked unable to help myself and really commit to the silent treatment...how long did I last, about forty seconds?

"I am very serious. Even if the banks closed tomorrow and even if the stock market crashed, as I know from experience that does happen and even if property prices plummeted. I would still be a very wealthy man and I couldn't spend it all even if I tried." Hearing all this and yes, it confirmed it...today was definitely mouth hitting the floor day!

"But if all that happened, how would you...?"

"Still be wealthy?" he finished off for me.

"The wealth I own is not just in bricks and mortar, it is not only in numbers on a computer screen or stacked paper notes in a vault. Over the years I have accumulated thousands of rare pieces of art. Even furnishings in the many homes I've lived in seem to become antiques in the blink of an eye." Well yeah, this I could imagine and not only after seeing inside Afterlife but also his grand home in Venice… now that place had been full of antiques.

"Even when simply buying a book years ago, it has made me money today, because it happened to mark the start of the 'Gutenberg Revolution' and the age of the printed book in the West. That same book today is now worth thirty million dollars alone…and Keira, I have many very old libraries."

"The Gutenberg Bible," I muttered to myself and in doing so gained an approving smile from Draven. But I was quickly thinking back through my past, remembering when Sophia first mentioned it. It was when she had been talking about gifts on the rooftop in her private Arabian nights tent. It was also painfully back when Draven and I weren't together, and it was the first time I had seen him in almost a year. Of course, my focus had quickly shifted to more important things like Pip's birthday.

"Jesus." I hissed through my teeth as I tried to get my head around all he had just said.

"Keira, think about it, I am thousands of years old and for most of that time I have been a King. I've had years upon years to amass such a wealth and although I am used to the finer things in life, for I have never been without, it simply means that even though I no longer rule in your mortal world, it doesn't mean I am powerless." I knew what he meant. It was the way of the world, as it has been throughout history. Just because you weren't King, with a shiny age-old title, it didn't mean you weren't high up on the food chain.

And Draven, well from the sounds of it, he was at the very top.

"I understand," I told him in a steady tone, one he frowned at.

"Do you though?" he asked pausing to look at me before carrying on.

"Because what comes with my wealth is also the power to do good. I may not be allowed to intervene in human life but that doesn't mean I can't do my part in other ways."

"What do you mean?" I asked intrigued to know.

"I have hospitals built, schools, shelters... all of my companies hold fundraisers and millions get donated to charities all around the world every year."

"You do?!" I shouted making him laugh

"Of course, I do. If I recall you used to have lectures in one of the buildings I had built... what did you think I did, just have it all in a mountain sized vault somewhere so that I could swim in it?" he joked, and I shouted,

"Like Scrooge Mcduck!" He gave me a look that said it all.

"Who?"

"Draven come on, you pretty much just described him, all you were missing was the red jacket, top hat and cane." All of which he would look good with I thought with a cheeky grin.

"I am going to take a wild guess here and assume you're not talking about an *actual* person." I laughed and said,

"Not unless you know of any supernatural beings that look like a cartoon duck obsessed with money, then no, he's not real." He gave me a sideways grin telling me once again, that he found me funny.

"So, getting back to the reason for this conversation. Keira, I have to know that this is something you will eventually come to terms with?" I frowned and then asked,

"But it just doesn't feel right, taking something I haven't earned and letting you just continue to pay for everything," I confessed and again I could see him fighting a grin.

He then stared out the window for a moment as he continued to drive through the wooded area looking thoughtful.

"Alright, what if you worked for it then?" he asked, and I couldn't help it but the first thought I had was a naughty one.

"Behave, vixen," he rumbled, and I gave him my best innocent look.

"What?"

"I don't need access to your mind with an expression like that. What I mean is why not help me in business, help me make decisions, which investments sound good…"

"And which charities we can help?!" I shouted getting excited by the idea. He laughed at my sudden enthusiasm.

"But of course, the thought of getting a new car makes you argue but the thought of giving away millions to others, is what makes you giddy," he said shaking his head to himself.

"I know, seems almost ironic I am half Vampire and not half Angel, doesn't it?" I mused making him smile.

"You will always be my Angel, sweetheart." I gave him my best 'I love and adore you' eyes in return. Then my mind quickly slipped back into a love induced fantasy where I would turn up for my first day of work.

Draven could be at his desk in whatever office he used the most and I could walk in all smart and sexy. Maybe get myself a figure hugging suit, with a tight pencil skirt dress under a smart jacket and some stiletto heels. Wow, I would love to see his reaction when walking in dressed like that, but more importantly, I would love to know what he would do after seeing it.

Alright, so I had to admit, working for him would certainly have its perks but it wouldn't be what I classed as an actual job. Because no matter how professional I tried to be, which clearly from my first lot of naughty thoughts, wasn't that much better, could Draven be professional? Could he really have me working with him in such a close and personal way and not sexually touch me?

Draven quickly brought me out of my sexually self-induced haze when he said,

"Now speaking of your new fortune, I would like to show you one of your new homes…" Just then I looked ahead to where he was nodding, and I couldn't help but gasp in wonder. If I thought it looked amazing from miles away then now, well now it looked like we were entering a gothic fairy tale realm.

And here Draven was King.

This was his realm.

He proved this when he said…

"Welcome to Domhnall Castle."

CHAPTER TWENTY-THREE

A BETTER MAN

"Wow…Draven you have a Castle," I said in utter awe at what now faced me. He grinned at me before getting out of the car. He had parked in front of a grand entrance that looked like its own separate building. Three of its walls were open arches and the fourth was attached to the main part of the castle with a sweeping stone staircase before it. I still had my mouth slightly open by the time he made it round to my side of the car. Therefore, he opened the door still to the sight of my utter astonishment.

"We have a castle," he corrected me with a grin after unbuckling my seat belt, lifting me from the car and placing my feet on the gravel driveway. Then, with him still looking down at me, he tilted my head back, so I had no choice but to tear my eyes from the dream it felt like I was stood in.

"Do you like it?" he asked me in a soft, tender way that made me realise that my answer was important to him. This was when I knew that this place, like Afterlife, obviously meant a great deal to him.

"I think it's perfect," I told him honestly, one he could read in not just my answer, but also my expression and in return his was one filled with satisfaction in a heated purple gaze.

"You know not the joy that answer gives me," he told me smiling.

"Now come, let's get you inside, out of this cold," he added as he rubbed my arms which helped keep me warm. Then he took my hand and led me up towards the imposing entrance. As I walked I couldn't help but look up at the towering building made of carved dark grey stone blocks. The building, as a whole, was made up of curved towers, topped with cone shaped rooftops in a lighter grey and straight walls topped with notched battlements in between.

"It's incredible," I whispered as I let him continue to lead me by the hand up a fan of large stone steps. These led up to the square structure that held a massive arched wooden door at its centre, one adorned by curled iron hinges, forged strips of metal and hammered rivets.

The whole scene made me feel as though I should be wearing some medieval gown. The ones with a long flowing trail of red velvet that would follow my every move and with my long hair in loose waves down my back like Maid Marion or Lady Godiva… but minus the horse or the being naked part of course.

I could see Draven's grin, one he wasn't even trying to hide as we reached the door, only to have it opened by none other than a butler. Yes, that's right, Draven not only had a castle, but he had a suited butler to go with it! And not just any butler, but one who wore white gloves, a grey waistcoat and a black suit jacket with tails at the back...the whole caboodle!

"Mack, it's been too long, my friend," Draven said in a friendly and easy-going manner, telling me that Mack, along with the castle, also meant a great deal to him.

"Aye it haes, m' laird," he replied with a massive grin on his face and a very heavy Scottish accent. He looked to be middle-aged and even though he was smartly dressed in a tailored suit, one surely even Lucius would be proud of... that was where all the typical butler appearance went out the window. In fact, it looked like a rough biker had decided to play dress up for someone's wedding or a fancy-dress party.

He had a wide, messy silver mohawk with shaved lines at the side of his head and a shaped beard that was longer at the chin tapering down to a point, with a thick moustache that joined it. I could also see his neck was tattooed but couldn't make out the design as he was wearing a cravat style tie. He had warm jade green eyes that had laughter lines at the sides when he smiled, telling a person that he had a jolly personality.

"'N' this 'ere mist be yer bonny queen, aye?" he asked making me want to giggle at how happy his accent sounded, and this combined with his deep baritone voice, well, I found it fascinating.

"That it is. Mack, I would like to introduce you to my wife, this is Keira," Draven said taking my hand and placing it in the crook of his arm.

"Keira, this is..." Draven started to say in return but was quickly interrupted by Mack's exuberant manner,

"Noo, noo, laddie, ah think ah kin tak' it from 'ere whin

introducing meself tae a bonny lassie," he said holding out his hand for me to shake making Draven roll his eyes in good humour. Okay, so I only ended up understanding half of what he said, which again made me want to giggle, which this time, I couldn't help.

"Aye she's a sweet wee thing…A'm Mack at yer service mah lassie," he said first looking to Draven after hearing me giggling and then back to me to finish introducing himself. I looked down at his hand to realise that the gloves he wore were in fact, fingerless white biker style gloves, that showed off the smaller tattoos he had inked on his knuckles and black painted fingernails. Well, he was certainly a butler with a twist. And it kind of had me asking myself, if this was Draven's butler, then what would Jared's look like if he had one? Would he be your typical English posh sounding butler named Jeeves?

The thought was a funny one.

"I am pleased to meet you, Mack," I said making him gasp dramatically before gripping onto my hand as he pulled it to his chest, over his heart. I shot a confused look at Draven to see him looking slightly amused but more than anything, just obviously used to this behaviour. Even when he smacked his free hand to the top of his head, pushed back his hair and said,

"Whit a sweetheart she is!" he proclaimed theatrically and once again, Draven although smirking, looked totally at ease with Mack holding my hand to his chest, as though I was precious.

"Yi"ll need tae loch this one awa' m' laird," Mack said and this time I didn't understand a single word other than 'My Lord'

"Yes, I intend to do just that, Mack," Draven agreed with...well, whatever it was Mack said. Then he gave me a wink and let go of my hand before moving to the side so that we could enter.

"Ah dinnae blame ye," Mack said looking down at me with a wicked grin.

"I trust everything is ready for our arrival?" Draven asked, still keeping me tucked to his side as we walked through the grand entrance with Mack walking slightly ahead.

"Aye is m' laird, Yer tea is nearly duin." Draven nodded and was about to say something in return but then stopped when I fell behind a step.

"Keira?" he said my name in question when he looked down at me to see I was looking around in awe. I mean the place was unbelievable! It was all highly polished wood that matched the layered, square wood panelling on the walls. Then there was the barrel-vaulted ceiling, also made from panels of polished timber and walls decorated with tapestries depicting battle scenes and Scottish mountains.

"It's...this place...it's...Draven it's incredible," I told him utterly flabbergasted and trying to find the right words were near impossible. He smiled down at me in that adoring way of his and now I found something better to look at than the magnificent building around us.

Then Draven did something that although wasn't out of character, it was still surprising. He suddenly scooped me up into his arms, making me yelp in a startled way and he turned back to Mack who had looked back over his shoulder to see what all the commotion was.

"I'm sorry Mack but dinner will have to wait, I have

something better I wish to eat." Then he strode past with speed leaving Mack chuckling behind us.

"Oh my God, Draven I can't believe you just said that!" I cried in horror and utter embarrassment. But Draven just laughed at me.

"He's a demon sweetheart, therefore I don't think that act is lost on him," he teased making me smack his shoulder in admonishment.

"I don't care if he is a bloody world champion in the act, I still don't want him knowing when we are...when you are...doing...well, *that!*" I said completely failing in the end at giving him a very deserved reprimand, one to which he just looked smug at.

"Oh sweetheart, we both know that if there were such a thing as a world championship, who would be holding the gold," he teased back in a cocky tone. I had to bite my lip first so as not to laugh before I delivered my witty reply.

"A demon with big lips, tingling lube for saliva and a vibrating lizard tongue?" I teased back making him throw his head back and roar with laughter.

"I wonder if I should worry about your dirty little mind, *my wicked little queen,*" he mused making me shout,

"Worry about me?! You're the one announcing to your staff that you're about chow down on your wife!" I told him making him chuckle.

"Chow down...not how I would have described it, sweetheart," he said with a raised eyebrow.

"Oh, enlighten me, my King, what would you have called it, um?" He gave me a bad boy grin, lifted me higher and whispered words closer to my lips,

"Feasted and devoured comes more to mind." Hearing

this I swallowed hard and then asked him only one important question,

"Then why aren't you running?" To this I received a growl of approval before he tightened his hold on me.

Then, he ran.

Many orgasms later, Draven finally let me come up for air and I did this panting into his neck. I was naked on top of him and he had a hand resting on my bare cheek which he was still cupping possessively. His other hand was stroking my hair down my back and the feel of his rising chest was close to lulling me into a peaceful sleep…well that and like I said, the multiple orgasms he'd just given me.

"I think it's a clear vote," I murmured against his skin.

"What's that, my beauty?" he asked, sounding sated and content.

"You definitely won the gold," I said feeling his chuckle vibrating beneath my body before I heard it.

"I'm glad you think so, sweetheart," he muttered softly, his words smiling for him. My own smile however he could feel against his neck before I kissed him there.

It turned out that when I asked Draven why he wasn't running he had taken that seriously, which meant I barely saw anything of his castle as he raced me through its hallways and grand rooms. Not even when he had me through the bedchamber door did I even get chance to look around before he was tossing me to the bed, ripping away my clothes and spreading my legs for the *'feast and devouring'* to commence.

Which meant at that point, other than throwing my head back and seeing stars bursting behind my closed eyes every time I came, I didn't really see anything else. Well, that's not strictly true, as there were also the tartan sheets in reds and greens that faced me when Draven flipped me over before driving into me from behind. Now that was when I really screamed and came calling his name...his real name.

Needless to say, this was when Draven ended up roaring his own release.

Which brought me to now and having the sudden urge to take in our new surroundings. I pulled back from Draven and felt his arms tense around me as if he thought any minute now I was going to leg it out of the room. I looked down at him, still with my forearms resting on his chest before leaning down to whisper

"Chillax honey, I am just checking out my new pad." Then I kissed his nose and pushed off him, so I could sit up. I flicked my loose hair back over my shoulder as I took in the room. I felt him shift behind me so that his back was to the headboard. Then I shivered as I felt him gathering all my hair in one hand, after lifting me closer to him, so my back was tucked against his front.

"You keep calling me honey and we won't make it down for dinner at all," he whispered back in my ear before moving my hair away so that he could leisurely kiss my neck.

"Draven, if you keep doing that then not only will we not make it down to dinner, but I will never get a chance to check out our bedroom," I told him in a breathy tone, or should I say closer to breathless.

"Our room," he whispered against my neck as if he

really liked the sound of that. So now I had to wonder how many nights he had spent in here asking himself how long it would be until he found me and could share it with me.

"I have waited so long," he said, and I froze in his hold. Then my silent freak out began as I asked myself, had he just heard what I had being thinking?

"Keira, what is it?" he asked because obviously my reaction was a dead giveaway, something was wrong...or depending on his answer to my next question, it most certainly could be.

"Can you hear my thoughts?"

"No, why?" He seemed taken-aback by my sudden question making me relax once more against him.

"Because I was just wondering how many nights you had spent in this room asking yourself when we would finally meet," I told him, and his reaction was a curious one. His hand came up to my cheek, so he could turn my head to look at me. His dark eyes seemed lighter, less black and more very dark brown with a purple ring around the iris that seemed to be glowing.

"This is good."

"What is?" I asked as it was clear as day I was confused here.

"You must be unconsciously opening up your mind to me." Oh no...this was anything but good!

"Don't worry, I can't read your mind, not unless you choose to let me," he said giving my tensed shoulders a reassuring squeeze.

"I don't understand, then what did you mean by opening up to you?" I asked hoping I didn't start doing this unconsciously.

"What I mean is that I am becoming attuned to your other senses, that you're letting me read your feelings."

"So, you could read my panic then?" I asked light-heartedly, now that I knew he couldn't read my *actual* thoughts or hear them more like.

"Yes, that and you tensed so hard in my arms, it almost hurt." I laughed before calling him a liar.

After this I finally got my wish and took in 'our' room, which was 'new' to me, not so much for him. And boy, what a room! Or should I say, bedchamber because that was exactly what it was. I shouldn't have been surprised to see that it wasn't that dissimilar to our room at Afterlife. Only the differences were more the building and outer shell itself than the decor.

And like our room back home, it held a massive fourposter bed which we were currently still sat in. But it was different to our huge bed, with it carved tree trunk sized posts and thick curtains. No, this one looked more like four carved church spires with ornate patterns that formed spikes at the top, ones that reached up to the high, vaulted ceiling. The stone on this side of the castle seemed to be paler and I can imagine this was down to not having to battle the elements for hundreds of years like the outside.

Opposite the bed, that was void of curtains, was a massive stone fireplace that was probably big enough for me to stand in. This surrounded by an intricate frame, carved from dark mahogany. Four spindles on each side held the mantle and above it, a large carved screen showing yet another battle scene. Inside was a metal basket with logs piled ready to be lit and this stood on four curled black wrought iron legs.

The rest of the room was wood panelled in the same dark mahogany with pale stone walls. There were a few pieces of antique furniture dotted here and there. Like the bedside tables that held two matching stained-glass lamps, a writing desk pushed against one wall and a small table and chairs that sat near a bay window.

The leaded glass windows cast diamond shapes along the pale floor, and they were framed with thick velvet curtains the colour of red wine, held back by massive brass bars that held a shield of amour at the ends. There was also a large red and green tartan rug at the foot of the bed and another by the window under the table and chairs. It was the same pattern that was on the bed and cushions on a burgundy, leather wingback chair that sat in one corner next to a small side table.

Over by the other corner there was a stone framed door of panelled wood, lighter in colour this time and I was suddenly itching to get up and see what lay behind it.

So, I did.

Or at least I tried.

"Where are you trying to run off to?" Draven said wrapping his arms around me.

"Trying be the operative word here, Draven." I remarked comically.

"If you must know I am trying to discover more of our room…if you would let me." I told him shooting him a 'fake' disapproving look over my shoulder. He grinned and then at the same time, nodded his head and released his hold on me. I granted him a wink before I grabbed his discarded shirt from the floor to put on like a robe. Then holding the two ends together to cover up my nakedness, I turned back to him on the bed to see him in all his own naked glory. It almost made me say, sod whatever was behind that door and go running back to him.

He didn't seem to care about his naked state or feel the need to cover it up like I did and with a body like his, I was very thankful for this fact.

I decided if I was ever going to focus on the reason for me leaving all that deliciousness that was Draven's sun-kissed skin over hard muscle, then I would first have to turn away from him.

"So, may I enquire as to the verdict of your inspection... does it please you, my queen?" Draven asked in that deep velvet voice of his that for some reason had me licking my lips.

"Draven, it's amazing!" I told him, astonished that he even needed to ask.

"I am glad you think so."

"Of course I do, I mean look at this fireplace for Pete's sake. You could roast a bloody cow in that thing," I said gesturing enthusiastically to the fireplace making him laugh. Then I walked over to the door and paused a second before opening it.

"Can I?" I asked looking back at him to be sure. Now this question had him really laughing and looking astonished that I would even ask. He nodded through it all and I smiled at him before opening the door. Then I shouted,

"It's a bathroom!" Like this wouldn't have been the obvious choice at all. Not surprisingly Draven's laughter continued because of this.

"But of course, what were you expecting, love?"

"I don't know, but let's just say you don't know how

happy I am not to see a chamber pot under the bed," I told him, making him laugh even harder this time.

"I think you will find this castle comes well equipped in all the modern-day luxuries, bathrooms at the very top of that list," he said making me giggle.

"Phew, cause I gotta say, not a fan of doing my business in a bowl on the floor," I informed him making him chuckle before shocking me by saying,

"No, me either, sweetheart."

"Well, it's a damn sight easier for you," I stated bitterly making him lift an eyebrow at me before asking,

"Is that right?"

"Well, it's like I happened to mention to your two-thousand-year-old younger self, I am not a natural born squatter," I told him and this time when Draven burst out laughing, he did this long, and he did this hard. To the point where I think I brought tears to his eyes.

"Now, I would have paid good money to see my reaction to that," he informed me when he finally caught a breath. I had my hand to my hip and said,

"Well, obviously I didn't just blurt it out like over dinner or anything, no at the time I was actually telling Pip as she was trying to get me to hurry up. Then next thing I knew you were there behind the screen, thus completing my shame," I told him and this time he fought his laughter by biting his bottom lip, his eyes bright with mirth.

"I am sure I found it adorably funny as I do now," he told me sweetly.

"Well, it wasn't exactly the look I was trying to achieve at the time."

"No?"

"No, I was trying to seduce you remember?" At this he growled, and I had an 'oops Keira moment' forgetting that I was telling my very jealous husband this. But instead of back tracking my mistake, I only cocked my hip out more and waved a finger at him like he was a child.

"Now we have talked about this and it is utterly ridiculous for you to be jealous of…well, of you!"

"Come here," he ordered with a growly voice, but I was having none of it. So, I stood my ground in sight of his irrational behaviour and said,

"No, not until you stop being utterly…ah!" I ended up abruptly cutting off this sentence thanks to Draven bolting from the bed to tower over me in a heartbeat. I backed up a step and he in turn took two towards me, placing his hand at the wall I was now up against. A hand that was level with my head and attached to a very strong and muscular arm that was caging me in.

"You're mine Keira, in this time or any other. You belong to this man that stands in front of you now, not a man of the past with the same name or one more ancient. Not any other version of me you thought you knew," he said with a voice so thick and deep it felt as though he was close to shaking from it. His jaw was hard and unforgiving, as though he almost looked pained from the force of his words. Like somewhere deep down he was battling with himself and the visions of me being with his younger self.

I had to admit that I didn't understand it, well that was until he told me why and this was when it felt like the Earth had stopped spinning and everything in my world stopped.

Stopped because what he gave me was beyond beautiful.

It was pure love.

But before he gave me that beautiful love, I first had to ask the question,

"Why is this so hard for you, Draven?" I asked raising my hand to his cheek and feeling a silent victory when he leaned into my touch. He closed his eyes and softly uttered his reasons why.

"Because in this time I am *your* Draven...the Draven being with *you* has made me and has forged my soul forevermore..." He paused a moment, raised his other hand to the other side of my head, leaned in close and whispered the rest of his sentence with his forehead against mine,

And by the Gods,

It was so lovingly beautiful...

"...Making me the better man."

CHAPTER TWENTY-FOUR

GARDEN OF DEATH

After this Draven and I seemed to pass through our days in a state of marital bliss. I hadn't encountered another strange demonic freak out from Draven and I didn't know whether this was down to not letting him get close to my birthmark again, or that the strange hellish storm had passed.

Obviously, I was hoping for the latter of these two.

We had been here a week now, but it had only felt like a few days. To be honest, it was just nice spending quality time together, just the two of us and now for the first time without any prophecy shit lurking over our heads like a dark cloud of doom. Of course, this didn't mean that it was incident free but at least what did happen I could blame myself for...or at least blame my tortured mind.

The day started out simple enough as Draven had given me a tour of the grounds surrounding the castle. This included a beautiful walled garden that was filled with wild flowers that weren't cut or trimmed or pruned to fit with whatever man-made design was thought as being royal enough for a castle. No, this was simply a beautiful, natural piece of the world that reminded me of the children's novel by Frances Hodgson Burnett, The Secret Garden.

All there was to tell you someone had intruded on this little slice of heaven was the stone pathway, a few stone archways and a cute half-moon shaped bench that had been made to fit half way around a huge weeping willow tree. I remember Draven grinning at my excitement when I saw it, grabbing his hand instantly and pulling him through the green curtain.

"Gods, it's beautiful," I uttered in awe, looking all around as I had never seen one so big. The way it cast long shadows against the lush green blanket of grass as the sun tried to penetrate through the long weeping branches.

"No," Draven said coming right up close to me and tilting my head back with a crooked finger under my chin.

"It's only beautiful when you are under it, speaking of its beauty," he said before leaning down to steal a kiss. Then he picked me up around the waist, hugging me to him before walking me backwards so that he could stand me on the low bench. This managed to put me slightly taller than him and it was lovely to be able to seek his lips with ease. Then, before I knew what was happening, the only sounds to be heard were that of nature, our heavy breathing and the sharp sound of my zip being pulled down.

Once loose he then peeled back the jacket over my arms, trapping them behind me.

"Draven." His breathy name sounded from my lips as he gripped my jacket with one hand fisted at my back, whilst

the other yanked my top down before freeing one of my breasts from the satin and lace cup. Then he groaned the second it was free in his hand before he pulled hard on my makeshift restrains, making me arch my back, pressing my breast up into his waiting mouth. I let my head fall back as a loud moan of pleasure rippled not only through my lips but also along my throbbing clit.

And right there, looking up at the canopy of green, Draven made me orgasm so hard with his teeth around my nipple and a hand down the front of my jeans, I was soon shuddering in his arms. Once I had come down from my high, I started wondering why, after slipping his hand free of my underwear, he started to button up my jeans.

My face must have said it all because suddenly he pulled me close, and told me,

"I will take you sweetheart, but here, under this age-old willow, I want this forevermore be *your* place and *yours* alone, for the beauty it holds is nothing compared to the beauty you just gave me watching you come undone by my hand." Then he proved just how much he had enjoyed himself when one finger at a time, he sucked them clean with his mouth, groaning at the taste of me.

And this blissful moment, over the last few days, was one of many.

Well, minus the one hiccup and that was to fall upon me that night…

The night of my living nightmare.

I was back in the gardens, but this time I was alone. But that's the thing about being alone, it is not only the feeling of being lost in a place but more about being lost in the prison of your mind that can sometimes be more deadly...because how do you fight against yourself?

But that night, I was to find out that I wasn't just fighting myself, but I was also fighting,

A new Demon obsession.

I don't know why I had decided to venture out so late at night, but it felt like I couldn't sleep, even in Draven's arms. I vaguely remember leaving our bed, looking down to see him still asleep and reaching out to brush back a fallen piece of his hair. He looked so peaceful in sleep, an almost innocent glow to him. As though it was solely his angel that rested, whilst the beast lurked beneath the surface, lying in wait.

Waiting for the chance to take what he deemed his...

Complete control.

But right now, the beast was contained and what was left was the sleeping Angel in our bed, one I was about to leave. Because something had woken me. I looked back to the window where I had first seen the light and quietly shifted from the bed. I walked on bare feet to the window and saw a flickering light in the distance, only now it was moving away, as if someone was carrying a flaming lantern through the grounds.

I placed my hand on the glass, feeling the beads of condensation dripping down my fingers. It was ice cold and for a moment I felt stuck there. I tried to pull my hand back, but it was as if something wanted me to stay. Suddenly the light started to flicker brighter and I could see the silhouette of a man turn towards the window.

I couldn't be sure from this distance, but it looked as though he raised his hand to his mouth, first to indicate my silence at seeing him. Then he made a motion for me to follow him. It was at this moment that my hand was suddenly released from the glass and the compelling need to do as he asked nearly overwhelmed me.

So, I moved through the room, taking heed of his warning not to wake Draven and padded barefoot across the wooden floor. I casually picked up the flimsy nightgown I had been wearing before Draven had removed it to make love to me. Then in a dreamlike state, I slipped from the room still naked with the silk and lace clutched in my hand, trailing on the floor behind me.

"Dress for me." A voice suddenly spoke in my mind and without knowing what I was doing, I did as I was asked, slipping the long gown over my head. It was more like a long dress of tight lace across my chest and easily showcasing my erect nipples through the pattern. This joined the layers of black silk under my aching breasts that flowed down to my bare ankles. My hair was loose and fell like a curtain of golden waves down my arms and back, making me shiver whenever the ends would tickle against my bare skin.

As I walked down the dark hallway, one I knew would lead me to the right staircase, I could feel eyes watching me. I turned to see that even the grand pictures on the wall were judging me, some even willing me to go back. Telling me without words that this was wrong. The moonlight breached through the window, casting shadows on their painted faces and their glassy eyes of disappointment stared at me as I continued on, despite their silent warnings.

Somewhere deep in my mind I knew I wasn't dressed for going outside and told myself that I was only there to have a look. But the second I was faced with the front door, I found myself sliding back the locks, knowing I would go further. The echo of metal grinding against metal was so loud in the silent room, my hands nearly slipped from the latch as they shook.

I took one last look at the empty hallway behind me, staring into its vast darkness as it suddenly became elongated, twisting all its walls around and becoming a tunnel. There at the end was fire licking at the woodwork, licking out its orange forks at anything that would ignite to fuel its rage. This was enough to get me running through the door and into the calmer night.

I jumped as the door slammed behind me thus sealing my fate to continue. Looking down at the pale steps I then looked back up at the moon, to see it peeking out beneath the rolling clouds. It seemed just enough for me to be able to see my surroundings and where I knew I must follow…

Back to the weeping willow.

I closed my eyes, inhaled a deep breath and took my first step into the unknown. The smell of the garden was different at night, as though you could almost taste the early morning dew as it penetrated the air. It was so serene and calm… peaceful even, that I was getting lost in its dark beauty before I even noticed what I was doing to it.

But as I continued to walk down the steps, I couldn't help but notice that in my wake I was leaving behind crusted black footprints, as if my bare feet had infected the stone.

And this wasn't just my feet as I looked up to see that as I passed each bush that framed the stone wall of the stairs, each started to die and crumble in on itself.

What was happening?

I couldn't make sense of it right now, so I decided not to even try as I carried on until reaching the bottom. Then I turned to where I knew the lantern and its carrier had disappeared to and I knew it was through the gardens. At first when I had started following this compelling force, I had felt almost in a drug induced state, but then once I stepped outside again, it was as though I was released from its power.

No, now I was doing this on my own, I knew deep down I should have gone back. But then again, was it safe or was it just as dangerous inside as it was out? I didn't believe I had walked away from a living inferno but only the essence of one. But surely, I was safer inside with Draven…

Wasn't I?

Asking myself these questions seemed to be the only thing keeping me going as the further I went, the darker the scene before me became. Like the stone steps had done, now the grass beneath my feet turned to dry dirt, branching out and cracking under my feet with every step. The beautiful colourful flowers, seemed to either wither up and die, or if I happened to touch one, it would turn black and freeze the edges into a deadly shard of ice.

I couldn't understand what I was doing?

Maybe the man would know, maybe this is what he wanted me to see. Suddenly I found myself desperate to know so I took off running. I came to the stone path, that dotted its way through the grass, leading me to a stone arch.

The second I stepped on the first slab my feet sank a little, as if I was walking on wet sand. I ignored the feeling and ran to the arch, tripping a little and catching myself on the corner of the stone to save myself from landing.

The second my hands touched it, the stone blocks turned to black glass, cracking like heavy footsteps on a lake. I instantly let go and this was when I finally turned around contemplating heading back once more. The second I did I gasped, my hands flying to my mouth in horror as I took in the death all around me. When walking through, only certain parts of the garden would die but now, well now it looked like that infection had spread out over the entire thing, and I...

I was the disease.

This was when I decided to turn from the deathly sight of what I had done and run through the archway. The second I did I screamed in fright when I heard the cracking continue until it shattered, raining deadly black shards all around me. I threw my hands up to protect myself from the deadly projectile pieces and the second before they could cut into my back, I felt a presence surround me. I opened my eyes enough to see that a black cloak of some kind had whirled around my body as if providing me with a barrier against the destruction.

It happened in a blink of an eye and then,

It was gone.

I raised my head up slowly as if expecting to be faced with my unknown protector, but all I saw was the sinister night. I looked back to see what had happened to the glass to find it had all fallen in a line, as if hitting a wall and instead of bouncing back, it simply fell.

"Come to me." I jumped when I heard that luring voice only this time, it wasn't in my mind. I looked up to see where the voice had come from in the open space and focused quickly at its centre where the huge tree sat.

The voice had come from inside the weeping willow.

So much of me didn't want to go in there but I swear it was like pushing against a vault door as my will wouldn't seem to let me just run away.

"Come see me." The voice hummed again in a gravelly way that sounded like it was trying hard to appear soft, when any minute now I knew it would roar at me in anger. This was what I feared, almost as much as I feared to move. But in the end, move I did as my feet took me closer towards the tree. At first it seemed unaffected like the rest of the garden, only with long hanging branches now darker in the night, creating a wall of darkness surrounding what lay hidden behind it.

Then as it started to rain, I felt my gown begin to stick to my body as if it was suddenly made of latex, looking as though someone had just painted my skin with oily black paint. I could hear the wet crunch of leaves beneath my soles as I imbedded them deeper into the grass and the sound of rain dancing on the earth's many surfaces. I finally made it to the thick blanket of branches, now swaying as the weather had taken a darker turn. I reached out, ready to cast them aside to grant me entrance when I heard the thunder cracking the sky in the distance.

"Come closer." The voice returned, louder now I was closer to it and it spoke as if it could feel my reluctance. Then with a deep breath I lifted my arm up, catching the branches and stepped inside.

I don't know why but the second I was out of the rain I felt colder, which didn't make any sense. However, I barely had time to wonder this for long as now I looked ahead and saw a large shadow perched up in the tree. The moment I saw him my automatic response was to take a step back. The second I did I saw his head turn toward me in a slow dangerous way. Then I saw him extend out an arm and he beckoned me forward.

"Come closer," he repeated, and I saw a long talon tipped finger reach out towards me before curling in on itself. It was only now I could see that I wasn't exactly faced with a man. Oh, he had the right shape but even in the shadows I could see the differences. Starting with the horns coming from his forehead and curling back on themselves, twisting up again to reach the sky. I took a single step forward and then wisely stopped.

"Tut, tut, little Alice," he told me, sounding almost playful in a creepy way and now shaking that same finger at me in reprimand.

"Th…at's…that's not my name," I told him stuttering on the first word, wondering why he called me that. The second I said it, his hand snapped out and grabbed the thick branch overhead as he leaned his body down through the gap in the tree. Once there and slightly closer he told me on a demonic growl,

"I know who you are!" I frowned back at him and then jumped when he suddenly bellowed,

"NOW COME HERE…where I can see you…*all of you!"* he ordered at first with a demonic roar, which sounded as though it dragged up Hell itself. Then he ended it with more of a silky promise, with only an underlining presence of who he really was.

Of course, neither of which compelled me to do as he asked, so instead I stumbled back until I could feel the branches at my back. But then came the thick drips of oil weeping down my arms and I looked back to see that the branches had also now changed. Now they looked like long drips of tar running down each branch, as if it was bleeding black tears of pain.

I backed away from it and before I knew what I was doing I whipped back around to face the demon.

A demon that wanted only one thing…

Me enslaved.

CHAPTER TWENTY-FIVE

ENSLAVED

I took in the sight of the demon and shuddered, holding myself around my belly, shivering in the cold. He cocked his head at me, as if asking himself silently what I was doing. It felt as though he was studying me and who knows, maybe trying to find my weaknesses. Either way the look felt far too deadly and I felt as though I had no choice but to tear myself away, before it consumed me.

I looked back at the branches of the willow, now looking more like thick long charred limbs, dripping with black blood from a source above. It stained the earth around it, attacking life and burning it like acid. This was when I found myself questioning again, had I done this?

"Am I...killing the earth?" I asked the looming figure above me, still situated in the dead branches of what was the twisted tree. He was now lounged out, one leg bent and the other stretched out in front of him. A strong muscular arm was resting casually against his bent knee and I could see the spikes of bone that grew up through his forearm as if he was wearing skin and bone gauntlets. His long jacket high up at the collar but cut off at the sleeves so his huge arms were bare. I could just make out straps across his large bare chest, as if this was holding his jacket together and allowing it to move freely with his torso. His legs also looked encased in some type of material but from down here I couldn't tell you what it was and even then, I would probably have to touch it to be certain.

But what was I talking about, I didn't want to be anywhere near this beast!

"You think you have that power, little human?" he asked in a mocking tone, answering my question about the earth and what I was doing to it.

"I...I am half Vampire," I told him, and he growled a snort of annoyance before snapping,

"You are a mere pup! A kitten with sharp teeth. One to be played with and nothing more...*you make him weak!*" I swallowed hard when he snarled this last part.

"I...I...don't know..." I started to say, backing away slightly when I saw him swing his legs around so that he was sat on the edge. He rested both hands either side of him and he leant forward.

"You know of whom I speak, for I know you to be no fool...*Keira,*" he said, curling his lips up and giving me a flash of demonic teeth when he uttered my name. The whites glinted even in the dark and I could see a row of fangs with two larger ones where a person's canines were found.

"Well, you may know my name, but I don't know you and it's clear you know nothing about me other than that name!" I shouted as my hands balled into fists at my sides.

Then I heard the wood splitting and I homed into his hands as his talons curled, growing longer and cutting into the wood.

"I know of your sweet little pussy that has a King weak at the sight of it!" he snarled down at me, straining his neck forward.

"How dare you!" I shouted, and I don't know why but I followed through with my first impulse and when glancing down I suddenly spotted a palm sized rock on the ground. Before I could stop myself, I picked it up and threw it at him.

His hand snatched up, catching it in the air before it could hit him, being now only a hand's length away from his face. Then he turned his head like a confused beast would, bringing it closer to look at. I couldn't tell if he was mesmerised by the rock in his hand or just shocked that I had thrown it at him in the first place. I knew it was the latter of these two when he finally looked back at me and grinned.

Then, before I had chance to react, he pushed off the branch and landed on his feet right in front of me. I froze in shock with only my head able to move as I looked up slowly, doing so until my neck strained back as far as it would go. By the Gods he was tall, the size of Ragnar at least. I moved to take a step back, but his hand snapped out, capturing the top of my arm in a bruising hold.

Then with the rock still in his hand he raised it up and I flinched, automatically thinking he was about to bring it powering down over my head. He smirked at this as I could see the glint of his teeth again, his other features however, were still mainly lost to the dark. Then he continued to raise his hand up and as if to prove a point at how indestructible he was, he bit into the rock. My mouth fell open as he simply chewed the stone as if it was nothing but an apple. The rest of the stone didn't even break, it now just had a piece missing with teeth mark grooves on its inside.

This was when I tried to get away from him, knowing that with very little force, he could take a bite out of me just like that rock. This was why he did it, as a warning, telling me his teeth could cut through my flesh and bone as easily as biting into an ice cream. He tossed the rock aside, and with a mere flick of his wrist it was powering through the air as though just fired from a cannon.

"Let go of me! You're hurting me!" I shouted up at him as I fought against him to free myself. The instant I told him he was hurting me he did the complete opposite of what I expected. I had thought he would have tightened his grip further but instead, he loosened it so that I still couldn't escape but at least it no longer hurt. If anything, it seemed as though he was just unsure of his strength in this world. For it was fairly obvious to assume he was from Hell.

"You cannot fight me," he stated on a growl and I wanted to say, well duh. I mean not only was the guy huge and basically looked like the Devil on steroids, I was also pretty sure strength wasn't his only demonic party trick...not if that rock was anything to go by.

"You think I would even try!?" I asked him, lacing my words with both sarcasm and anger.

"Then why run?" he asked, and I couldn't help my reaction. I snorted. I swear the second the sound was out it was like it was the first time he had ever heard it. I don't know why my reaction seemed so foreign to him or such a surprise. But he even recoiled from it.

"That sound, *I know that sound,"* he said cryptically to himself and he seemed momentarily stunned.

"I...please, please just let me go and I will..."

"NEVER!" he suddenly roared at me, getting lower down in my face so I could even taste his breath and it too was like the early morning air.

He snapped his teeth as he saw me flinch back, pulling on his hold to try and get away from his rage. The second he saw my fear something seemed to snap within him and he raised a hand to my cheek. I tensed again as it started to come closer and a low growl of warning rumbled from him. The sound was a familiar one, but I dismissed the urge to dig too deep into my memories to find it.

This time I decided it was wise to remain as still as possible, as though you would when being slowly approached by what could be a dangerous animal. I had a strong feeling that with this creature in front of me, if I was to run, he would only end up enjoying the chase.

So, as much as it pained me and went against every reflex I had, I remained still as he came closer. I closed my eyes tight waiting for the first feel of his fingers against my skin. Then the second I felt his touch, I froze, almost as if waiting for the pain...*a pain that never came.*

I could barely believe that a being such as who faced me now could be this gentle. But as he curled his finger in, his deadly black talon tucked the sharp end away from my face, so it wouldn't catch on my skin. Then when all was safe, he ran the back of it down my cheek, leaving a cool trail in its wake.

"Even through my claws I can feel your cold skin

quivering against me," he told me, this time with his voice a much softer rumble.

"Like your human milk flowing into the black river that surrounds my home," he said in a strange tone that at a guess, could have been in awe.

"And like that river, one touch is all it takes to damn your soul, imprisoning it for all eternity with a single finger holding the key." I swallowed hard and bit my bottom lip, and his once black cold eyes void of white, now turned into that of a demonic, Hellish sun swirling as they gazed at my mouth.

"Tell me my quivering cream, is that an invitation?" he asked cocking his head to the side. The second he said this I let my lip slip from my teeth and he scoffed at this. Then with his hand still close to my face, he ran his claw along my jaw and all the way across my lips, this time using the sharp end. My breathing stopped as the second I gasped, I felt the sting. I could now feel the small drops of blood pooling around his nail and once it overflowed down my chin, he pulled his hand back. Then he raised it up to his face, first inhaling the scent, by taking a deep breath and making his massive chest rise.

I licked my lip and tasted the copper tinge, swallowing it down quickly to rid myself of the metallic flavour. He groaned long and low in a grumbling sound, one building from his chest and rising up in a silent howl as he threw his head back. It was almost as if the frequency of the sound was too high for us humans to hear but maybe there was demonic dogs down in Hell whining at the sound.

Then he raised his hand up and offered his own hand to

himself in a dramatic way, as if it was an offering from a higher power.

I felt myself tense as I watched in fascinated horror as his finger now coated in my blood disappeared into his mouth. The second my blood must have hit his tongue, this time he did howl, and it was so deafening I swear my ears were now bleeding as was my lip. It was a demonic sound unlike any other I had ever heard and given my past few years history, I had heard many. It was almost as though it had different layers to it.

Then he brought his focus back to me and the next words he spoke, I may have not understood their meaning, but I knew that they meant a great deal to him.

"Sarrat irkalli ma sebu wardum..." He spoke in some ancient sounding language as if speaking to someone else, like this was a vow he was making. Then in a blink of an eye and a tug on my captured arm, he twisted me, spinning me around so that my back was plastered to his front. A massive arm banded across my torso, holding me easily against him and I could now feel his long jacket curling around the bottom of my legs, as if it was also alive and needed to touch me.

And like this I could now feel that his bare skin was more like armour because it was hard and ridged...but surely flesh couldn't be that solid, could it?

I was about to let out a scream when I felt a hand clamp securely over my mouth, his talons now tapping gently against the side of my head, curling and catching in my hair. Then I felt him lean down, close to my ear as I was held immobilised against him. Once his lips were at my ear he finished the rest of his ancient sentence in hushed tones and a throaty whisper. Then, once finished he released my mouth, now resting his hand at my hip, curling it round my flesh in a possessive way.

Again, I had no idea what it meant, which was why I asked,

"What…what do you want with me?" I tried to keep my voice as steady as I could but now that I was so close, I felt all my bravery leave me in a whoosh of air, one that got expelled once he yanked me into his body.

"You are the enslaver and I want to punish you for it," he told me simply and when I didn't reply quickly enough, I felt his talons drag against my belly, tearing into the silk but thankfully not my skin.

"I don't know what you're talking about," I told him, but this obviously wasn't the right answer as he growled in my ear.

"I…"

"You keep him in a cage and what I want is the fucking key back!" he snarled before I could start to beg him to release me.

"No, I…"

"He belongs to me and I will take him back. I will release him from your slavery and set him free. Only then will he be strong enough to defeat you," he said snarling this promise, making me shake in fear.

"Defeat me? Why, why would you want to kill me?" I asked him this time forcing the words to sound stern.

"If I wanted to kill you I could crush you in my arms until your bones snap like the death you brought to this place." As if to prove his point he gave my body a painful squeeze thankfully releasing me just as quickly when I cried out.

"No, I need him to see you weak and on your knees before him. For you will answer for your crimes at the foot of his kingdom and at the foot of his rightful place." Suddenly it started to become very clear that whoever this demon was, he felt I had wronged him by taking someone from him. Was it Draven, did this person want him back in Hell?

This was when my heart nearly stopped as I finally knew what I had done.

"My mark...I...brought you here...didn't I?" This was when his hand reached up and with his elbow bent outwards, he cupped the back of my neck before tapping on the birthmark hidden beneath my hair.

"You released me from my prison and now it is time I free the King from his. I will drag him back to Hell so that we may rule the underworld together."

He paused to pull me tighter, then curling a hand around my breast he squeezed, grazing his thumb claw across my erect nipple. I gasped before crying out at the bite of pain.

"Then we will watch as you fall and what will you do..." he paused to lick up my neck before delivering his final threat...

"...*when you have no wings to catch you?*" Then he let me go suddenly and I fell forward into the grass. I quickly scrambled away before turning, flipping to my bum so that I could face him.

But he was gone.

He had vanished from sight and all that was left was the remains of my nightmare world as it started to evaporate around me. Then I heard his voice again but like before, there was no body to go with it.

"Run home, my little slave," he said in my mind and I did just that. I scrambled to my feet and ran from this place as fast as I could. But the world around me was moving as I was. It was travelling past me in a whirl of shades of darkness so that I felt trapped by the shadows. I turned for one last look back to see him standing there in the shadow, a looming force of the destruction I knew he would soon bring to my life. All around him the world blurred, swirling like the cutting wind had the power to carry it away. I was almost frantic at this point and it was only when he lifted an arm up that I could see, he was pointing my way home. I turned to look in the direction he was pointing to and then in the distance I could see the castle.

And finally, I could hear him calling my name.

"KEIRA!" I could feel a sob break from my lips as I shouted for him,

"Draven, Draven...DRAVEN!"

And finally, I reached for the outstretched hand through the fog of death, and the second I did I heard his voice one last time threaten my mind and sanity with a warning he wanted me to deliver.

"Run home and tell the King..." I didn't wait to hear the end of it as I clasped my hand in Draven's. I opened my eyes, but I wasn't quick enough, for the sound of his voice still lingered in my mind.

The voice of a Devil...

"I will be coming for him...soon."

CHAPTER TWENTY-SIX

DOMHNALL CASTLE

That was the night I screamed Draven's name and woke from quite possibly the scariest nightmare I had ever had to date. And this was saying a lot considering I had been living with nightmares both in sleep and reality for quite a while now. One of those even nearly killed me...*thank you Lucius*. Okay, so that was back when he was an asshole but still, he had nothing on this last nightmare demon!

And yet, despite all of this, I still hadn't told Draven what happened in my dream.

Not a single word of it.

I would like to say I knew the reasons for this, but the truth was, I simply didn't. Of course, from past experiences, I knew that I should have told him. Yeah, that would be the smartest thing to do, but I guess I just kept asking myself, what if it was all in my head.

But then wasn't asking myself that question like taking a

step back in the past, one filled with an empty darkness? A void that wouldn't be filled with answers until Draven was to enter my life.

Yes, so I had woken that night with blood dripping down my chin from a cut in my lip. But what if the reason for that too was that I had bitten it too hard in my sleep like Draven had thought. Like I said these were all valid points against the argument in my mind, but if that was the case then why the next morning did I find the unanswerable?

It was just before I stepped into the shower and I felt a sharp pinch in my foot. I sat down on the toilet and lifted my foot to see that not only were they covered in dirt but also a tiny drop of blood pooled around something that had cut my heel.

"It…it can't be…" I uttered in whispered disbelief.

But as I pinched the small piece and pulled it from my foot to hold up to the light from the window…*I knew what it was.* The second I saw it I gasped, dropping the piece and it fell to the floor in slow motion. It hit the tiled floor with a tinkering sound and lay there against the white floor like a dark teardrop. Like a single drop from a black river in Hell against a pool of milk.

So, if it was just a dream, then how was it that evidence still lingered, pointing to the fact that it wasn't? Did dreams from Hell really have that type of power? Okay, so it was questions like this that plagued me and continued to do so for the remainder of the day, which was why I was so thankful when Draven said he had a surprise for me. Well, as long as it didn't include going anywhere near the damn willow tree, then that was just fine with me.

I was just finishing plaiting my hair off to one side when

Draven walked in with a rolled-up blanket under his arm. I gave him a questioning look and then said,

"Is it that cold out?" When really what I wanted to say was 'oh my god, I worship your body, and can you just throw down the blanket so that you can make love to me on it'. But no, I went with the weather question. Which was surprising considering he just looked as though he'd stepped off a GQ magazine shoot advertising men's designer clothing.

He was wearing pale blue jeans that were rough and frayed around the pockets and knees. To this he'd added a light grey roll neck cashmere sweater pushed up his forearms showing a hint of the white shirt he wore underneath. Dark brown boots that matched his expensive watch, completed the look. Well, that and the blue and green tartan roll under his arm.

He gave me a wink and then took my hand in his. As I was passing the bed I grabbed my maroon coloured jacket that was lined with a grey fur type material, meaning it was lovely and warm. It also meant that it went with the rest of my outfit that was as simple as it gets. Dark grey jeans and a thin ribbed top that was a white with maroon coloured sleeves. To this I had just kicked on some converse that had cute little skulls on and I was good to go.

"So, are you going to tell me where we are going?" I asked but he just shook his head and remained tight lipped on the matter. Of course, it soon became obvious when just before we walked out the front door Mack appeared with a basket in hand.

"Are we going on a picnic?!" I shouted enthusiastically making Mack laugh.

"Aye she be easily pleased," Mack said making Draven smile down at me and reply with,

"Which pleases me." I bit my lip going shy at the compliment. Then we walked out the door as he was now fully equipped to begin a very romantic date.

A short time later I found myself in a pretty meadow not far from the castle so that it was all still in view. Draven had laid out the blanket and dropped the basket suddenly before grabbing me from behind and lifting me up in his arms. I squealed in surprise and burst out laughing when he dropped to his knees as if I was too heavy. I smacked his shoulder when he shifted me so that I was straddling him. Again, he pretended as though my hit had been a mortal wound and fell to his back, making sure to drag me with him. Then he groaned as though in pain, so I leant down, and whispered over his lips,

"Poor Baby." The next thing I knew his groan turned into a sexy growl before he spun me so that I was now on my back being covered by one sexy, turned on male. Then he did the same thing he did to me under the willow tree, only this time…

He followed my release with one of his own.

"You know it's a good job your skills don't just stop at being a sex god, otherwise people might have seen the despicable and sinful things you just did to me." Which included, biting my neck and drinking my blood before spreading my legs and quenching another thirst of his. Then he ended by contributing his own mess to the one he made by finding his release inside me.

He laughed and repeated,

"Sex god?"

"Obviously that's the part he focuses on," I muttered as if I was speaking to someone else, making him chuckle again. Then he threw his hands up in the air and said,

"Hey you said it...*baby.*" He added this pet name on a purr and I had to say, I could totally see why he had jumped on me because of it, as I only ended up wanting to do the same thing to him.

After this we cleaned me up, well Draven cleaned me up, whilst I just fell back and covered my head with my arm in shame as I moaned with my embarrassment. Then he heard my stomach rumbling. A sound that ended up making him laugh again, before he leant down to kiss my groaning belly.

"Oh dear, time to feed my pet human," he teased making me laugh.

"Don't you mean Pet Vampy human?" I corrected making him wink up at me before saying,

"Oh yes, I forgot..." pausing so that he could climb his way slowly up from my belly until his lips were over mine. His hands were either side of my head, but he was holding all his body weight above me, he then lowered himself doing a press up and finished his sentence,

"...You are a Vampire baby...*my vampire baby,*" he added before granting me a kiss, smiling against my lips when I growled at him but secretly loving it.

Then he fed me, and I loved this too.

It turned out that our picnic was all the things I loved, like BLT sandwiches without the T, and with extra mayo. There were also cheese and onions crisps that I had gone crazy for in the petrol station, that he must have had sent for. Of course, there were other things too of the posher variety that reminded me of an afternoon tea in a fancy hotel in

London. Little cream cakes, truffles and chocolate macaroons, sat delicately in a black box. Finger sandwiches sat in another and I picked one up, waving it at Draven and said,

"No crusts… these be what my people call *fancy sandwiches.*" He burst out laughing, and I don't know what he found funnier, what I had said or the strong northern accent I had put on when saying it.

"You funny girl," he said making my insides feel all smushy.

After this, and after I had made a pig of myself, Draven popped open a bottle of champagne and unclipped the two glasses from the basket.

"Would you like to hear about our castle?" he asked after he had positioned me in between his legs so that I could lean back on his chest. And therefore, I could still see the beautiful building for myself. Then he passed me my glass before picking up his own.

"I would love that!" I said in excitement.

"So over there…"

"Oh wait, first can I ask, what does Domhnall Castle mean?" I said interrupting him making him chuckle because if there was something Draven was used to when with me, it was me asking lots and lots of questions. To be honest, I was surprised I hadn't yet asked him this but then again, I had asked him about a million other things since we had been here.

It was everything about the place, which included the beautiful masterpieces that adorned the walls. The exquisite vases, the colourful tea sets, the stunning grandfather clocks, some taller than Draven and others sat on small half-moon tables in hallways. I had wanted to know where he got it all and find out if anything had meant something special to him. But most of the time I was just left disappointed as there was never really a story behind it.

"The name Domhnall was chosen because it means 'ruler of the world' in Gaelic," he said, and I turned to face him to see that for once he looked embarrassed. I smirked and couldn't help but ask,

"And did you choose that?"

"Fuc...I mean no, Keira I didn't choose the name," he said nearly swearing in front of me, something I knew he only did now when he was angry or very turned on...or trying to make his point, like on the drive up here.

"Then who did?" He raised an eyebrow at me as though it was obvious, which was why I said,

"Sophia."

"Yeah, Sophia," he confirmed dryly.

"So, you have had it a while then?" At this he laughed and said,

"I had it built, Keira." At this I gaped at him and said,

"But it must be..."

"It's over a thousand years old, sweetheart," he told me tenderly.

"Wow...that's...that's..."

"Old?" he finished off for me in an amused tone.

"Well yeah."

"It's well maintained," he told me, making me snort.

"Like you," I teased making him nip at my neck warning,
"Behave my little Vamp baby."

"With you at my back looking sexy as sin, no chance." This time he growled after burying his face in my neck.

"You're the one that is sexy, although I don't know what I find sexier, your clothes on or half off whilst I thrust into you," he said pressing himself against me in a tighter hold.

"Well, I know which I prefer," I told him making him chuckle against my neck.

After this the playful teasing continued in between Draven describing to me the different parts of a castle and explaining what they were for. Like the square cut out pieces along the tops of the walls being called crenels and the upright sections being merlons, this known as the battlements. On the inside was a path you could walk along and when he asked me if I would like to see it, he chuckled when I said,

"No thank you." He knew the reason being my fear of heights, something he then teased me on. Then he pointed to the small slits for windows and told me they were known as Loopholes. These were usually used for shooting through or providing light and air in the towers. He also told me that the larger section of the castle, which was like a massive square tower at the centre, was known as the 'keep' or stronghold. This was also where our bedchamber was on the top floor.

Thus, why Draven thought the need to remind me about his thing for towers or more like his thing for getting me into them. This was proven when he whispered along my neck,

"I knew I would finally get my way and lock you in one, one day."

"Don't get cocky Draven, it doesn't become you," I told him in reply.

"So, I was thinking, I know it might end up being a bit corny, and well not your thing, so I totally understand if you don't want to go but..." I started after a short time of comfortable silence.

"Ask me sweetheart," he said, giving me a break.

"Well, I was wondering if you wanted to go to that medieval banquet thing with me?" I asked kind of feeling a little embarrassed and more like I was asking him on a date. Which I kind of was, but still it felt weird with him being my husband now. After he had been silent way too long I quickly added,

"Nah, maybe not, it might be a bit silly...forget I mentioned it." And I hated to admit it, but I was kind of disappointed when he did forget I mentioned it, as he never gave me his answer. Nor did he bring it up again. I can't say I was surprised, I mean dressing up in a costume and spending the evening with complete strangers...make that *human strangers*. Well then yeah, this might have been asking a bit much for my supernatural king.

"Are you ready to go in, I don't want you getting a chill?" he asked with his hands at my belly, rubbing small comforting circles there. I smiled to myself because I knew even though I was wearing a coat, Draven would still worry. After all, I was pregnant. Gods, but sometimes I would forget, and I know that sounded terrible, only it just felt surreal somehow. And in my defence, I had only just had it confirmed a little over a week ago.

I had asked Draven a few days ago how long we were planning on staying in the castle, after first assuring him that I was still very much enjoying myself. If I was honest, probably a little too much as I would have been happy to stay forever. That was if I had everyone I missed living here with us…because let's face it, the place was certainly big enough. His answer had been a whispered,

"As long as we wish."

This had been lovely to hear and if I were honest, I hadn't really given our future too much thought. Well in my defence, up until recently I had thought that our future would be considerably shorter. So little factors like 'where would we live' hadn't really come to mind. What with the whole, 'Doomsday' thing and the little matter of 'End of the World' and of course there was the 'Keira, as the Chosen One it's up to you to save everyone on the entire planet, we hope you're okay with that and hey, sorry we as Fates suck ass and can't tell you a damn thing but cryptic shit'. Okay, so with my 'lost in my thoughts' rant over and moving on to much nicer things like…the future.

And top of that list right now was where we were going to live.

So, regarding this, I had to admit that I still had no clue. But I knew if I was to choose, which I found out from Draven later that I could, I would still choose Afterlife. Because to me that was home and although I knew it couldn't be forever, for the time being it was the perfect family home. Or it soon would be in about eight months' time, I thought with a grin. One that Draven of course wanted to know the reason behind.

"Just thinking about the future."

"Then I am a blessed man indeed if that is the thought that puts a smile on your face," he told me softly making me melt against him once we were back inside.

"What would you like to do now?" he asked, and this was when I had a great idea.

"I know, we could watch a movie together, you know maybe pop some corn, snuggle on the couch and...what, what is it?" I asked as he started frowning. Then he dropped a bombshell on me and told me of the one thing he didn't own.

"We don't have a TV here."

"What!?" I screeched in disbelief. He winced and then shrugged his shoulders.

"But you do own one...right? Like in one of your other homes?" I asked making him frown and correct me,

"Our homes."

"Yes, yes okay, I will rephrase that, do we have a TV in any of our other homes?" I asked again, only this time he didn't focus on my question but more on the way I asked it, as in saying words like 'we' and 'our'.

"Draven, focus," I said trying not to laugh at the fact I could turn him on with saying something so simple.

"No."

"No? As in no, you can't focus or as in, no, we don't have a TV, I am really that old fashioned and prefer to read books by the fire, drinking brandy from an overly big glass and smoking a pipe, in my spare time?" I said making him roar with laughter before pulling me in for a hug. Turned out my husband thought I wasn't just funny, he thought I was very, very funny, something he told me whilst rubbing his chin on the top of my head.

"The latter, only without the pipe but definitely with the brandy," he teased back. So, I pulled back from the hug and demanded,

"Draven! We have to get a TV!"

"We do?"

"Yes, unless you want to see me go insane over the next year and yes, that is all it would take, in fact, scrap that, it would probably only take a month, and especially if I don't have a mountain of college work or an actual real job to go to, keeping me occupied." At this he smirked and said,

"I can keep you occupied," he told me, and I didn't know if it was as a tease or not. He saw my sceptical face and then gave in.

"Alright love, I will get you a TV." I hugged him back and said,

"That's all I ask." Making him chuckle.

"Oh, and don't you mean you will get *us* a TV, Mr Hypocrite."

"I am sorry sweetheart, but that one is just all you."

"Oi! You never know, you might enjoy it," I said making him pull a face.

"Come on, I will show you." I said playfully grabbing his hand and pulling him down the corridor. We saw Mack on the way and he was about to say something when I said,

"Sorry Mack, we can't stop, I am a woman on a mission."

"Aye right ye are lass…ye be a lucky man m' laird," he said making Draven chuckle and I shouted back,

"Not that type of mission!" Now making Mack laugh in that deep baritone voice of his.

Then I dragged Draven into one of the drawing rooms, although I wasn't actually sure why they were called drawing rooms, as it wasn't exactly brimming with art supplies. However, it did have some very comfy sofas, one of which I was leading Draven over to right now. Then I looked at the angle of the room, making sure it was right, turned a few times to look at the other couches and said,

"Yep, this will do nicely." He gave me an amused questioning look, one that he added to with a raised eyebrow when I practically pushed him back into sitting on the couch, demanding at the same time,

"Right sit there."

"You know I like it when you're bossy." I rolled my eyes and he grinned up at me, telling me that he wasn't taking me seriously. I sat down next to him, and held out my hands in a square, mimicking where the screen would go.

"Right so picture this, the screen is there so that we get no glare from the windows if we watch it in the day but then at night, we turn off the lights, cover ourselves with a blanket and I curl up to you like this…"

"Now I am liking the sound of that…but tell me, will you be naked?" I moaned, lightly smacking him on the chest and saying,

"Not unless you get one for our bedroom, then no, now concentrate." He gave me a bad boy grin and curled his arm tighter around me.

"So the lights are off and it's dark all around us, a horror movie is playing, and then suddenly the killer jumps out stabbing the stupid girl that always runs up the stairs instead of out the front door, and I jump and need your arms around me to feel safe…so okay I have also probably spilled popcorn all over the floor because this is me we are talking about and…"

"Stop, Keira." Draven said interrupting me and suddenly I was in his arms as he looked down at me with heated purple gaze,

"Keira, you had me at 'I want'." Then he kissed me, and little did he know that in his near future he would soon discover that a sentence very similar to that would be said in a film I would make him watch.

Oh yes, this was going to be fun.

CHAPTER TWENTY-SEVEN

THE GIFT OF ART

I t was four days later when Draven made good on his promise, surprising me that it took him that long. Not that I was impatient, but just that usually when Draven said he was going to do something, it was normally as soon as Supernaturally possible.

However, during this time Draven managed to keep me plenty busy as it seemed he had got it into his head to take me sight-seeing every one of those four days.

We went to other castles, drove along the stunning coast with its dramatic cliffs and spectacular views. We also visited cute picturesque towns, went hiking, at which Draven found great amusement as it clearly wasn't my forte. But one of the best trips out was when Draven drove us to Edinburgh for the day, which took a few hours to get there.

We went in Edinburgh castle where Draven would protect me against the flood of tourists and at the same time giving me a personal lesson on its history but only the fun stuff that I wasn't sure if many people knew. Like how it was built on an extinct volcano and that Castle Rock had actually been inhabited for around 2865 years, although Draven assured me it could have been more.

He also told me how St Margaret's Chapel was one of the oldest surviving buildings in Scotland and how the Scottish crown jewels were lost in the castle for over 100 years. I laughed when he told me this, saying,

"I am surprised that hasn't happened to you yet, considering how old you are… I am not sure I would even remember my first name after all that time, let alone where I put my crown," I teased making him roll his eyes at me.

"What, it's not like it gets used very often, maybe other people will forget it as well," I said in jest. However, instead of the laughed reply I was expecting, Draven just pulled me back against him when we were waiting in a queue for a drink. Then, as he wrapped an arm around my belly, he whispered a promise in my ear,

"Then I will have to start calling you this in bed just before I come inside this hot little body I own." Then as if to prove his sexual point, he lowered his hand so that his fingers were just skimming the edge of my waistband, toying with the lace of my panties.

"Catherine," he hummed in my ear and I nearly choked, coughing back a gasp as the lady behind the food stall shouted,

"Next!"

Now this made Draven laugh.

I had to admit that over the past few weeks, I couldn't remember a happier time. I don't think I had laughed, giggled, chuckled, smiled and teased so much in my life. Of course, the sex had to get mentioned which, with Draven, was always amazing no matter what he did to me. But seeing as our sex life had never been in question before, then this time, it was all about the smiles.

Because if there was one thing in our relationship that had always been lacking, it was spending quality time together, just being a couple. Going out on dates, whether it be to a restaurant, or a simple walk in a park somewhere. Hell, our first meal out together was after my crazy serial killing ex had stood me up, so it was kind of tainted because well, we weren't exactly together then…oh and you know, like I said, the 'killer ex' thing.

But now, just getting the chance to do all the usual stuff, even if that just included the simple things like our picnic, it didn't matter because for the first time, I was actually starting to feel like…

Well, *like Draven's wife.*

And right now, as he walked me into our bedroom with his hands covering both of my eyes, it just felt like another one of those times.

"You ready?" Draven asked me and the excitement in his tone was an endearing sound.

"I was ready the second you took my hand in the library," I told him, because if we weren't out at the crack of dawn and only getting back when it was dark, then this was where we spent most of our time. Something about Draven having work done and ceilings restored in other parts of the house.

I had even teased him, asking why he couldn't just fix it himself, you know, with his mumbo jumbo superpowers. To which he hadn't looked overly impressed with my description, as I got another raised brow directed my way and a stern,

"Keira." Which basically said it all. Okay so it didn't, which is why I asked him again, this time rewording my sentence to say,

"Oh, mighty God of mine, why not just grace us with your strength and otherworldly talents and fix the damn ceiling yourself?" Which finally had him laughing.

His answer had been a simple one,

"Because I am no artist."

And as it turned out he was right, his drawing skills sucked. I know this because for some reason I got it into my head that I needed proof of this. So that night at dinner, I had Mack find me a pencil and paper, and forced Draven to draw random things. Needless to say, that after drawing a bird that looked more like a plane with eyes, a beak and only one leg, I knew it was a lost cause.

He was right, he sucked, as in big time and I don't know why but this made me ridiculously happy. He asked me why and I told him,

"Because you're annoyingly good at everything! Hell, I teased you the other day about knitting for a hobby, but I bet if you took it up, you would be whipping up baby blankets by the dozen, so yes, I am happy to see you were right... sorry baby, but you can't draw for shit." I said after reaching over and kissing his cheek as he chuckled at my funny comment.

And to prove this statement I looked down to see the last

thing I had asked him to draw. I stared at what clearly looked like a penis and snatched it from under his palm. Then I held it up in front of him and said,

"Really Draven? This is your banana?" Then I pointed to the bulbous head he had drawn at one end and he replied with deadpan seriousness, informing me,

"That's the bananus." At this I snorted a laugh and couldn't stop myself from blurting out,

"Sounds more like you just gave a banana an asshole to me!" To which he threw his head back and burst out laughing and this made even more so, when we turned to see Mack had come in the room the second I had said it.

He held up his hands and said,

"Ah dinnae want te know." Then swiftly made his exit. I turned back round to Draven with a look of horror and said,

"Please don't tell me he just got the wrong idea and now thinks I want to introduce fruit into our sex life?" Now this had Draven roaring with laughter and yes, even to the point where he had to wipe the tears from his eyes.

Something he had to do again when he saw my face drop in utter shame, when I woke next morning to the sight of a fruit bowl sitting at the end of the bed.

"Draven, you little shit!" I had shouted before throwing an apple at him, making him catch it, bite it in that sexy way, before throwing the apple aside and stalking towards me.

That morning sex tasted like apple and there wasn't a banana in sight…well,

There was Draven's.

But getting back to my surprise and the reason he had found me with my nose in a book in the library.

"Let me see!" I said excitedly reaching up to pull his

hands from my eyes. Then once he did I squealed with delight.

"It's a TV at the bottom of our bed!"

"Well, unfortunately I had to get rid of the fruit to put it there, I hope that's okay...Oww," he moaned, teasingly rubbing his arm after I had playfully hit him.

"So, didn't fancy it in the drawing room then, yea?" I asked with a grin.

"Oh, there is one in there too," he said, and I beamed up at him before confirming this was true and getting a little high pitched at the end.

"There is?!" He nodded down at me giving me a soft smile.

"Of course, there is, you had me at 'I want' remember." Hearing this sweet reply made me throw my arms up, reaching his neck so that I could pull him down for a kiss. Then once I had finished showing him how thankful I was, I decided to tell him.

"You're too good to me, thank you honey," I said tenderly over his lips, making him groan against me.

"So, if we have one downstairs, why one for the bedroom as well?" I asked turning back to the ultrathin and no doubt mega expensive TV that was now at the end of our bed.

"Well, you mentioned that if I wanted to watch it with you curled into me naked, then I would have to get one for here as well...so this one is actually more for me," he said with a wink making me giggle.

"I also have another surprise for you," he told me and then took my hand, led me to the bed and told me to get comfortable. So, I did as I was told, kicking off my slippers and arranging the pillows so that they would be comfortable.

I then watched as Draven walked to the door, opened it and said,

"Alright Mack, you can come in now." I frowned wondering what he was up to this time and I had to bite my tongue against warning him that it had better not involve fruit. Thankfully, it didn't but it did involve food and not a bit of it healthy.

Draven had obviously taken my words about getting a TV very seriously, as Mack walked in our room pushing a trolley that looked as if he had first robbed it from a Cinema. It had everything on there, from bowls of popcorn, nachos, striped bags of sweets and a wide array of chocolate bars, including the legendary Cadbury's Crunchie bar. I nearly wept with joy.

Of course, I thought nothing could top this, that was until Draven produced something hidden under his jacket on the chair. When he brought it closer this time I squealed before launching myself at him. He caught me as I jumped off the bed, wrapping my legs around his waist and peppering him with kisses.

"I love you!" I shouted making Mack chuckle as I threw the DVD over my shoulder so that it would land on the bed. Then Mack left the room muttering something about being easily pleased, which was all in good humour, but neither of us were really listening. Not as soon as my little kisses had turned into very intimate kisses, that required my hands either side of Draven's face, so I could tilt his head and deepen the kiss.

He didn't need to ask me if I was pleased because I showed him and this time doing so in an even more intimate way...one that still required my mouth.

Oh yeah, he got that I was happy pretty quickly and the reason why, because there now sat on the bed waiting for us, was my second favourite love story of all time.

The love story of Jane Eyre.

And my first favourite love story…

But of course,

It was our own.

CHAPTER TWENTY-EIGHT

MOVIE HEAVEN

A little time later and we soon found ourselves curled up under the covers and as Draven had requested, we did this naked.

"I remember that look," Draven commented and when I asked what he meant, he nodded at the screen. It was the part when Jane Eyre first travels to Thornfield Hall and she looked terrified. And I kind of had to say, I could relate. I also remembered walking into Afterlife's VIP the first time as Draven did, but I can imagine my memories of this time were quite different to his.

"Tell me Keira, did you also think that I had an insane wife locked away in one of my towers somewhere?" he asked playfully.

"An insane wife no, but maybe a seduced sex slave or two," I replied with a smirk. He gave me a pretend look of shock and whispered,

"And now I only have one seduced sex slave to warm my

bed, whatever will become of me and my reputation as a scoundrel?" he teased back making me growl.

"I think you will live...or at least you will if you don't ever speak of there being another woman in this bed again." At this he roared with laughter. Then he pulled me closer and hummed sexually in my ear,

"You are and always will be the only woman I want in my bed, sexually seduced or as a willing slave, for I am not picky which, as long as you stay where you are needed," he told me making me shiver against him, only this time it wasn't with sexual desire like he thought.

No, unfortunately it was hearing the word 'slave' that did it, even if it was only said so in jest. My mind was instantly taken back to my nightmare, one that was still yet to explain itself. Or more importantly, explain why had there been the physical evidence left over from it...surely a thing like that wasn't possible?

"Keira?" Draven saying my name dragged me away from my dark demonic tormentor who had secretly plagued my thoughts.

"And if I tried to run from my sexual tyrant of a husband?" I enquired making his eyes seep into purple liquid before answering me, as obviously he liked the idea.

"I think you have seen my chains Keira, or do you need reminding of what they look like?" I shuddered in his hold at just the thought. He grinned down at me and chuckled,

"And now my shy wife is back once more." I didn't say anything but instead looked back at the telly blushing.

"I will never forget those shy, doe eyed looks you used to give me. The way my presence used to make your pulse quicken and the sound of you drawing in a shuddered breath with every stolen touch I took." I blushed at his words and when I wouldn't look up at him, he forced the action upon me. He reached my chin and hooked his finger under it, bringing up my face to look at him.

"You made me feel like a tyrant. Like some wicked master trying to steal you away from the world so that I may make you mine and enslave your heart." I bit my lip at what his words did to me and asked him shyly,

"Is that not what you wanted to do?"

"Fuck yes!" I giggled at his outburst.

"I have told you many a time of how I wanted to pluck you from your world and chain you to my own, so that I may have you whenever I wanted you. Which, after one sweet taste of your lips, I soon discovered was all the damn time!" It was like listening to the confessions of an obsessed stalker again. Then he reached down, picked up my hand and started playing with my wedding ring.

"I wanted to brand myself to you, body, mind and soul. So that everyone out there, human or not, all knew that you belonged to me and would do so for all eternity." This time I could see for myself the sincerity not just in his words and the intensity in which he spoke them, but also in his deep purple gaze.

"And now, I have my wish," he added finishing this statement with a kiss.

We continued to watch the movie and as usual I got suckered in to one of my favourite love stories of all time.

"This is one of my first favourite parts…" I uttered on a heavy sigh. Draven wrapped his arms closer, pulling me back against him and said,

"As this is one of mine," he said running his fingertips up

my neck and then down to skim across my breast and definitely not speaking about the film. Much to Draven's disappointment I told him,

"Ssshh, this is where they finally meet and AHHH!" Suddenly I jumped a mile as the horse suddenly reared up out of the fog, scaring both her and me half to death. My automatic reflex kicked in and I gripped onto Draven's arm tighter as though I had just been startled by a zombie movie not a period drama.

Draven burst out laughing and I scowled at him but with his arms holding me, his hands stroked down my back. He had paused the screen so now all it showed was her frightened face, one that had mimicked my own.

"She faces a God and an army in Hell, but a horse throwing its rider scares her…tell me sweetheart of mine, what am I going to do with you?" Draven asked me after first talking to himself or the Gods, who knew.

"I don't know, protect me if we ever go to a farm?" I said making him start roaring with laughter. After this he re-started the movie with barely a look and soon I was gasping for a different reason.

"Well, that was rude," he commented making me look back at him in surprise. He was of course referring to the part when that 'thrown rider' had just called Jane a witch, telling her to get away from him.

"Like you can talk!" I said strangely defending Mr Rochester. He raised an eyebrow at me asking me without words to explain my outburst.

"Oh, come on, remember how you used to treat me… remember when I fell into you the first time I was in the VIP. You looked at me like you wanted to throw me out of your club yourself." The look he gave me was one of astonishment.

"Is that what you think?"

"No, it's not what I think, it's what I know...I was there remember," I said feeling like we were once again digging up the past and I was already starting to regret it. Especially when I'd asked him in the car not to speak of it again. But what could I say, I think deep down because of his cold treatment towards me back then, it just seemed to stay with me. Like it had imprinted on my mind, with such an impact at the start, that because of it I was always trying to find ways into his mind. What had he really been thinking back then?

So once again he told me.

"Then let me enlighten you. If I looked at all strained, angered or irritated by your presence standing there in front of me, *after once again nearly falling at my feet,* then the tense emotion I had shown was one I solely directed at myself."

"What do you mean?" He looked up as if to ask the Gods for help on this one as his irritation grew before he levelled me with a hard look.

"What I mean is that every second I was with you I was doing so fighting myself for control. I swear my palms would itch at just the sight of you! I wanted to grab you, throw you over my shoulder and snarl 'mine' to the world, before taking you to a place no one would ever find you. That is what I fought against and in doing so, saved you any fear you would have gone through finding yourself my prisoner."

"Oh," was all I could manage to say after that.

"Yes, *oh,*" he mimicked after his outburst. Yep, he was definitely getting annoyed at having to obviously keep repeating himself. So, after a moment of silence that lingered between us, I decided to cut the tension.

"I would have liked to have seen you back in those times," I told him, as I watched Mr Rochester dressed like a gentleman. His tight waistcoat tapering down strong shoulders into a slim waist.

"In those times?" Draven enquired, clearly interested in what I had to say next. I nodded at the screen as he had once done and said,

"You know, from the 1800's, all suited and booted sat upon a horse in the grounds of some old English Estate...*or a castle,*" I added making his lips twitch as he fought a smile.

"Well, I can't say that the thought of seeing you also in a *tight...*" He paused saying this with a quick tug at my waist, tightening his hands around me to emphasise his point before continuing,

"... fitted corseted dress, with your skirts billowing in the wind as you ran towards me across those vast green lands... yes, that is a sight I would want to see myself indeed." I grinned contentedly and snuggled closer to him, telling him without words this time, that I liked what he'd just said.

"Keira...you're biting your lip again," Draven whispered behind me as though he was speaking from the shadows of a dream. It was a little time later and another of my favourite parts. Of course, I had watched every adaptation of this story, but my all-time favourite was unbelievably, the one Draven had bought. I think it was probably because it was the longest, being that it was on two

disks. No doubt thinking that he would get me naked next to him and squirming for nearly four hours, which of course, he did.

But to be honest it was my favourite because I think the actors played it that way. It wasn't about anything else, the grand house, the side characters, the fine costumes worn, nor the clever filming or even the skilful directing. No, it was only about the two people on screen and their ability to convince you long enough, into not only believing in *their* love but more importantly, of the true love that would one day find you, as it did for Jane.

"It's the part where she saves him from the fire…it's the part where he wants to kiss her for the first time, listen to what he says…"

'What, are you going without saying goodnight, Jane… you just…you just saved my life.' Mr Rochester says played well by actor Toby Stephens.

"But he just told her to leave…" Draven said sticking up for Jane again.

"Ssshh." I told Draven as he interrupted the magic on screen. Then I couldn't help it, having seen and read it over a hundred times before I start mouthing the same words being said.

'We might at least shake hands…' he said reaching out for her, but anyone watching knows that he wants more from her than just her hand. Which is confirmed when he speaks and again and my lips seemed to follow in a mind of their own.

'I knew you would do me good, the first time I met you, I knew I wouldn't mind being your debt…' he said as he caresses her hand, both of them silhouetted in the shadows

with only the romantic glow of the few candles behind them. Then, as if embarrassed, the actress Ruth Wilson, who plays Jane, and acting just as well as her co-star, lets out a nervous laugh before replying,

'There is no debt, Sir...' then after repeating herself more seriously this time, she tries to pull away. And it was at this point that I always wondered why, as she knows even then that she loves him. But after being with Draven, I now knew how frightening that intensity could be. So, she tells him that she is cold, using this as her reason to get away. But it was what he did next that always melted my insides.

He takes hold of his dressing gown and stepping closer to her, wraps it around her, now with them being too close and face to face, the intensity of the scene grew. Now with only a hair's breadth away from each other, he tells her,

'And we agreed that you would never be cold again.' Then he pulled her slightly, holding her captive by gripping the lapels and then he tests her,

'Well, if you must leave me...you must.' At which point he let her go and, in that moment, I always thought that was a test, one she had unknowingly failed by leaving. I released a big sigh once it showed her back in her room, safe for now and unknowing of any of the horrors she would have to endure at the hands of love.

Back then, I could sympathise.

"You love this story, don't you?" Draven asked the obvious and I said,

"I don't know why but the story just...well it just stayed with me above all others."

"Mm, I wonder why?" he mused, and I wanted to tell

him why, but I stopped myself before I would voice the words…

'Because I think it was fate.'

No instead I continued to talk about the movie.

"Of course, that's not what was written but most of it was the same." Draven made an amused sound behind me and I turned to look at him over my bare shoulder to enquire what he meant by it.

"Just how many times have you read this book, my little librarian?" he teased.

"A few," I said giving him my vague response and not admitting how many times I had read it or watched it. I knew he knew I was lying when he laughed again, only louder this time.

After this, it was the time when Mr Rochester leaves and I couldn't help but say,

"I know what that feels like," in a small voice at seeing Jane's gutted expression. Draven growled low behind me and his hold around my torso tightened but other than that, he didn't comment as we continued to watch the movie. And once again, I wanted to kick myself, knowing I had just spoken my thoughts aloud.

As I watched the montage of clips of Jane struggling with her loss and battling her inner feelings for Mr Rochester, it made me realise just how much this movie mirrored many of my own feelings and fears. The sad tortured way he forced her to feel things for him, when sat among his own kind, surrounding himself with beautiful women dripping with wealth and living a life full of virtue. But it was the way his eyes would seek out her own in a room full of these people, confusing her even more on what it was he saw when his gaze beheld her?

Even watching how the mad wife cries and screams into the night, howling like the beast she is, makes me think of all those times I myself was faced with all those strange questions lurking inside my mind. Asking myself who and what he really was behind the closed doors of his club?

Not long after this point we reached the part where she asks him for her wages, and Draven pulled me back tight to his frame and whispered once more in my ear,

"Oh look, another stubborn woman that won't take money from the man who loves her and wants to give her everything."

"Behave," I warned back, bending my elbow and poking him with it in his belly, but secretly loving the sound of his voice speaking tenderly in my ear. Then came the part when she leaves, and Draven couldn't help but get his own back and say,

"And now she leaves him...*I know what that feels like."* And like he did, I ignored his comment as I knew he had made it in reference to my own earlier.

We watched it a while into the second disk when I felt him tense behind me. It was the part where finally she was returning home after her Aunty had died. At first, I couldn't understand why this part was affecting him but then I remembered what this story meant to us.

What it meant to me.

Of course, unbeknown to me at the time, it was Draven's first secret message of love to me, marked in a simple but effective way with my lost hairclip. A message I wouldn't discover the full meaning of until the time was right.

The second he saw her about to speak, he did a beautiful thing, starting with when he paused the screen. Then when reaching around to caress my face, he spoke the beautiful declaration of hidden love, not just for her but also for me.

"Thank you, *Keira,* for your great kindness. I am strangely glad to get back again to you; and wherever you are, is my home, my only home." I looked up at him, giving him a beaming grin when he adapted the line to include my name and once he had finished, doing so by sealing his words with a kiss.

"I think I am not the only one who has read this book more than a few times," I told him after first having to swallow down the emotional lump his sweetness had caused.

"Well, the moment I saw it I knew I had to read it again, this time trying to see it through your eyes," he confessed.

"And what did you surmise, I wonder?"

"Well, of course it gave me hope."

"Hope?" I questioned.

"Yes, hope that not only was I dealing with a hopeless romantic but that I was dealing with one obviously willing to overlook certain dark aspects should we say, of the man she would fall in love with." Yeah, he could say that again! Now, I wondered how Jane would have reacted if Mr Rochester's secret had been that he was actually a supernatural king. Oh, and instead of having a crazy wife locked away, he just had a murdering, stab happy waitress named Layla who wanted to see her head mounted on a spike.

I am thinking poor Jane would have done more than go running off to the moors, and more like hitching a carriage ride to the nearest port and saying sayonara to England, to forever become a nun and pray for her immortal soul.

"And you got all that from a book?" I laughed at my own question.

"Keira, you saw me as a demon who hunted you down and chased you on my rooftop, pinning you to a door. Then I kissed you, took what I wanted and the next day you woke and the first thing you did was come back to me. So yes, I believe it was a fair statement made and an assumption proven correct, don't you?"

"Okay, so maybe you have a small point." He laughed and said,

"I think you will find it is an ocean sized point there, love." Again, I chose to ignore him and continue watching until my real favourite part started to play out.

I couldn't help but feel so sorry for her. Watching her emotional turmoil raging within her, trying to break free but kept under sacred guard, locked to her chest deep within her heart. The way he pushed and pushed at her, making her believe for as long as possible that she would have to leave him. For he was to be married and she knew she could torture her soul by staying around to watch that happen.

The similarities of our combined stories were mounting by the second. I remembered back to only my second day in his bedchamber back at Afterlife. Standing by the door, readying myself to leave after the torturous task of telling Draven the horrific story of my past.

But Draven wouldn't let me, no instead he pushed against my barriers of self-preservation and started tearing them down with each step he made towards me. He was like a man on only one mission and just like Mr Rochester was now, it was to prove his love. To prove his worth. To prove that once and for all there was no other that held claim to his heart.

I found tears streaming down my cheeks as I watched it all play out and I held my breath so that the sob wouldn't erupt at the sweet memory of it all. I watched her own tears fall as mine did now. I wanted to ask her, if you knew of the pain that was coming, would you still do this? Would you still let yourself fall into the abyss of your heart? The endless love that never seems to catch you but only seems to embrace you as you fall gently into the night. I wanted to ask her...

Was it worth it?

I looked towards another bedroom door and saw the memory of ourselves flickering there like a projection from the past. The way we were back then, the way I was so frightened and unsure. Was this another trick? Was he just trying to get me to stay, like Mr Rochester was doing now? My answer came in the form of Draven's thumb, wiping away my tears. He too looked towards where my mind had wandered, and he must have seen it for himself.

He surely could see the same emotions that were played out that day...the day he finally made me his forever. Because this ring was just a symbol like the ones hidden beneath our skin. They didn't define our love or mean that we would be together forever, destined to love one another till death do us part. Being married and saying the words didn't mean he was finally mine or I his.

But that day had.

That day I didn't run from him or his love for me, had meant only one thing to him...

He got to keep me forever.

And as I looked back at the screen and watched the brief happy times they shared before reality ripped it all away from them, then right then I saw the same thing for me and Draven. I saw those brief moments of happiness were neither tainted by death or threat, capture or sacrifice.

We were simply two people in love and wanting to get lost in the comfort our entwined souls created. You didn't have to be supernatural to experience that type of love, for it happened every day. That feeling you get when you finally meet the one. It was unlike anything you had ever felt before and if you thought you knew what love was before it, then it merely left you feeling foolish for even thinking it was love.

The sheer pain you felt when they weren't with you, had you nearly forgetting how to breathe and had you clutching at your chest as though you could feel a part of you was missing.

And a part of you was missing.

Sure, you may in time be able to live through it and carry on, but deep down, you would always know that for the rest of your life, you would walk the journey alone and incomplete. A piece of you missing and the place you knew where to find it, you weren't allowed to go. Not until it was your time.

I didn't know it back then, in that dark place waiting for my tortured lost soul to be saved from myself. From the memories of pain that I was holding onto or the feeling like no one would ever truly understand me. The day Draven would eventually come back to me, back from not only his own metaphorical death but for one that felt raw and real enough to be my own.

But come back to me he did.

As was the way with true love.

Like Jane making her way back to Mr Rochester. Draven had found a way back to me. He had found his way home.

And now looking back at the man I loved with this amount of emotion near bursting from me,

I knew that this…

This was finally our time.

CHAPTER TWENTY-NINE

TIME WARP

"**I** can feel your soul near glowing with your love for me and you don't know what it means to me to witness it." Draven's voice was deep and rough as if he was finding it difficult to speak, so I replied with the only words that needed to be said right in that beautiful moment,

"Make love to me." He didn't say anything to this as his actions said it all. He simply turned me in his arms and placed a hand gently to my cheek before running it up through my hair. I closed my eyes the second I felt him bringing me forward close to him for a kiss. It wasn't demanding or raw or possessive. No, this time, it was gentle and soft, caring and tender. It was the type of kiss that tells you, the world has stopped and the only two hearts beating are the ones you can feel beating for each other.

I felt him slowly pull away at the covers, shifting my body to face him fully and breaking our connection for only a second before his lips were back to mine. His hands were everywhere but not just sexually. Over my shoulders, down my arms, entwining his fingers with mine to squeeze once, twice, a third time before letting me go so that they could caress my back. It was tenderness in every touch and his fingers left invisible prints against each part of blushed skin he touched with his heat.

And all the while Jane Eyre continued, and her own love story became a backdrop to our own. But the difference was clear, she was yet to experience the trials of love and tests put before us. But me...well I had already conquered mine and the man in my arms now was my prize.

"Look at me, I want to see your soul light up for me," he murmured softly and the second I did he finally joined our bodies. I cried out at the pleasure of it all, then I reached up, framed his face in my trembling hands and said,

"You don't just light up my soul, Dominic..." I paused reaching up further and whispered over his lips fiercely,

"You set it ablaze." I then ended up swallowing his response with a kiss, whatever it would have been. His hands reached down, held onto my wrists before raising my arms above my head to hold me still so he could continue to slowly make love to me. It was a maddening pace but one that was so beautiful, that it didn't last as long as Draven's sexual drive normally pushed me. No, this wasn't about sexual gratification or the high from riding the wave of an orgasm. This was about letting our bodies speak to one another in the best way two people in love could. It was about letting our souls touch the fire that burned and sparked around them as our vessels connected.

"Come with me, let us fall together," Draven demanded softly, and I could only nod my answer as I already felt the building need chasing up from my core. Every long pull of his length away from me was followed slowly by an even greater feeling of him going back in for more. Every drag created along my nerves to fill the void, was done so with such tender care, that I was close to begging him to take me hard.

But after only a few moments more of him licking my nerves with his steely shaft, I was crying out in his arms and found him doing the same. He buried his head down next to mine, turning it so his release was being called against my cheek. I felt him coat my insides with his seed, one I was blessed to know had already taken root within my body.

"I love you, Keira," he whispered against my cheek before kissing me there, no doubt tasting the salty tears that had escaped through the strength of our lovemaking. He raised himself up and looked down at me, now framing my face with his own hands. The look he gave me was simply one of wonder, as if any minute he expected me to merely fade away as if it had all been a part of his dreams. I covered one of his hands with my own, slipping two of my fingers between the gaps and I closed my eyes telling him the only thing he needed to hear from me...

"I love you, Dominic."

"Well, there is another pretty big reason not to forget this story," I said after we had calmed our loving storm back down to a simmering breeze and in doing so I nodded back at the telly. Draven laughed above me before falling to his side and taking me in his arms. He looked back to the screen and saw that it was the part where Jane was sneaking out of Thornfield Hall and leaving Mr Rochester for what she assumed was forever. Draven gripped me tighter and his next words, stole my breath.

"I know how that feels." He may have been mimicking my earlier statement again, but this one referred to many more heart-breaking times. I couldn't even say which time he was referring to, considering if it wasn't through my own doing but that of others, this was when I realised, I had indeed left him more times than he had ever left me.

"And thankfully, we both know how that feels," I told him once Jane and Rochester were again back together.

"To have you back in my arms after so long of living in the darkness without you, consumed by a fear that I had lost you forever…yes I would say I too thought it must have been a dream."

"But now it is time for another dream to be lived and experienced, one of which that up until recently, I hadn't known was also one of your own." I shifted on my side to look at him and asked,

"What do you mean?" Then before he could answer me, his phone rang as if on cue. He winked at me before getting from the bed to retrieve it from his pocket. I swear the sight of his naked bum sent a little spasm down against my already sensitive channel.

"Is everything ready?" Draven asked as way of answering his phone. I frowned, wondering what he was up to this time and seriously wondering that if it was anything like my surprise today, then would it be possible to burst from so much joy?

"Excellent, give us ten minutes," he said then waited for

the other person to finish and I was just questioning what would be happening in ten minutes, and also who he was talking to. I didn't have long to wait as the next thing he said finally gave me a name.

"You have done well Sophia, I am proud of you." After this he hung up and turned back to me now sporting a rather large grin.

"What was all that about?" I asked as he came back to the bed. He didn't tell me, no he only continued to grin before he suddenly whipped the covers off me.

"Hey!" I complained, something he ignored. No once again instead of explaining his actions he just picked me up off the bed and walked with me in his arms to the bathroom.

"Do I smell that bad?" I joked making his lips curl up at one side.

"It's time I got my little Queen washed, as we have things to do," he told me finally, although this didn't really give me much to go on.

"And that being?" I asked but again his answer was a secretive one. Only at least it did kind of answer my earlier question about bursting from joy, especially when he replied,

"Another surprise."

Ten minutes later and after one of the quickest showers ever, I was stood back in our room in a fluffy bathrobe still looking at Draven expectantly, waiting for him to tell me what he was up to. Although I had to say the sight of him dripping wet with a towel hanging low off his hips and rubbing another one over his hair was somewhat distracting in my mission to find out. Especially the way the action made his delicious muscles bunch at his biceps and shoulders. Jesus but even his back was ripped.

"So, are you going to tell me?" I asked finally shaking myself out of my sexually induced Draven haze.

"Nope," he answered, throwing the towel he had been using on his hair casually off to one side.

"But I will tell you what sweetheart, I might let you see your dress when it arrives…and speaking of which, here it comes, along with some other…"

"Pip! Sophia!" I shouted as his sentence was cut off when the two of them burst into the room. Well, Pip did the bursting bit and Sophia sashayed in after her.

"Tooty Preggers!" Pip shouted making Draven's lip twitch and Sophia groan. Then it took me half a second to realise what the surprise was thanks to what they were wearing. My head quickly snapped to Draven and in total shock I uttered,

"You're taking me to the medieval banquet?!" Draven just grinned at me, obviously enjoying my reaction and then closed the distance between us. He cupped my cheek as I looked up at him adoringly before he lowered his head, so he could grant me a sweet kiss.

Then he said,

"We shall see." Which only ended up confusing me more as soon after that he left the room, saying,

"If you will excuse me ladies, I will now leave my wife in your capable hands." And I had to wonder where he was going considering he was still only wearing a towel.

But I didn't ask this, no instead I turned back to the girls and said,

"Oh my god, I think he is taking me to that banquet." To which they both just laughed. Well, Pip squealed a giggle and Sophia chuckled sounding like the Angel she wasn't.

"Wow, you guys look…"

"Utterly amazeballs with supersonic range?" Pip finished, and I grinned at her and said,

"Totally."

Sophia wore a beautiful gown of red velvet and gold embroidered oak tree leaves that were interwoven with tiny red crystals. It was in the typical medieval style dress that was cut across the breasts and full sleeves that covered her shoulders and fanned out into a great teardrop shape by her hands. It was a full skirt, that must have had a petticoat underneath to give it that much body. As for her beautiful black hair, half of it was twisted back over a little net cap of pearls that sat at the crown of her head and the rest cascaded down past her shoulders in lovely loose curls. She looked as though she had just stepped out of an Anne Boleyn movie.

Now Pip on the other hand looked as if she had just climbed up from Wonderland and out of a rabbit hole finding herself in a sweetshop. In fact, I think this was one of her most outrageous outfits yet, and it was definitely her most colourful. It was funny because the only colour missing from her dress was black, which she had chosen to wear over her eyes instead and for probably this reason. It looked as though a candy factory had first turned into a transformer, had then tried to swallow her, only to end up choking so had to throw her back up with all the sweets still attached!

The only remote thing about it that was authentic was the shape and cut of the dress being that it was similar to Sophia's. The bodice part was patterned in candy pinstripes, in a rainbow of pastel colours, this matched her tights that could be seen thanks to a large section of the long dress cut out at the front. In its place was a huge net tutu in layers of fuchsia pinks, lime greens and pale blues, all of which sparkled with a hem of silver sequins around the wavy edges.

But this wasn't the craziest part, nor was it her ice cream shoes that had colourful cupcake shaped heels and cherries at the toe. Or even her massive baby pink wig that was up and around her head in a massive cone that was at least a foot high. To this she had added a massive stuffed bow of white latex with candies glued to it.

But again, like I said this was still pretty tame for Pip, that is if it hadn't been for the flowing pink gown cut like a curtain either side of the tutu and nearly completely covered in sweets! I mean it even trailed along the floor behind her and I just had images of her being chased by a gang of kids at a children's party. Although, knowing Pip she would have loved it.

But I was ashamed to admit, my first thought had been what were all the humans going to think when we all turned up at this banquet thing. Suddenly I couldn't help it but I kind of started to wish we were now having our own here.

It wasn't because I was ashamed to be seen with her, not in a million years. That was Pip and you loved her for who she was, not who everyone else thought she should be. No, what I was afraid of was anyone coming close to hurting her feelings, which I knew from speaking with Sophia, this had happened before. Although she had also told me that since she was now decreed 'The Queen's' best friend, this had magically stopped happening. Something to do with the threat of what upsets my friends, would also upset me…And the King would not tolerate that.

So, I was definitely calling this a perk.

A perk however that had no effect in the human world.

"When did you guys get here?" I asked getting giddy just at the sight of them both. Sophia shot Pip a look first, which was a dead giveaway that when this happened, there was always something I should know but was being kept from me.

So naturally, I wanted to know.

"Alright guys, come on, spill it," I said putting a hand on my hip.

"Spill what, nothing to spill here, nope, nothing, nada… nothing to see here folks, time to move along…so what do you think of my hair, awesome right?" Pip said with a twirl of her foot as she pointed her toes like a naughty coy child.

"Smooth, really smooth," Sophia commented dryly, and Pip raised a sugar sprinkled coated fingernail to her blue painted lips and started biting it.

"Well come on, what do you expect, she's the Dr. Claw to my Inspector Gadget… I mean she is intense and has MAD interrogation skills…Haha, get it…not a fan eh, fine then but it's still those shifty eyes, no offence Toots," she added blowing me a kiss.

"Oh, jeez thanks, none taken." I muttered as Sophia commented sarcastically.

"Oh yeah, just like a member of the Gestapo, gosh I don't know how you survived."

"I know right, don't think I don't see you eyeing up my candy tits now," she said wagging a finger at me and I don't know why my first thought was…isn't that the only place she didn't have sweets dripping off her. Unless there was something I was missing and if that was the case well, Adam was certainly in for a treat later. Which reminded me, I still had my own treat to give Draven, thanks to Pip's handmade sugar corset she gave me at my hen do.

Now knowing of Draven's recently discovered sweet tooth, I was definitely looking forward to that night!

But right now, what I was looking forward to even more, was seeing my new dress and knowing what everyone was up to.

"So, you're not going to tell me what's going on?"

"Nope"

"Not a chance." Both Pip and Sophia answered together making me groan.

"But you get to see your dress," Sophia added.

"Oh, and we get to play human dress up again YEY!" Pip shouted after Sophia and this time I really groaned, then felt the need to correct her, like I felt I had to do around everyone these days,

"Don't you mean human *Vampire* dress up?" To which they both just shrugged their shoulders at the same time, like some comedy duo.

"Nah." Pip answered this time for them as a collective unit.

"I am never going to get taken seriously as a vampire, am I?" I asked with a slump of my shoulders.

"Nope" Pip said swiftly followed by Sophia's,

"No, not really" I rolled my eyes at them and said,

"You guys are spending way too much time together." They both just laughed at this, and again, it was just another thing not to take me serious about.

Then my human/little respect Vamp self was made to sit down whilst my two crazy best friends went to work on dressing me for a night of the medieval past, and of course what music did Pip click to play whilst they worked…

The Time Warp.

"Seriously Pip if you don't stop 'jump to the left' and 'taking a step to the right' every time you brush her hair then it will end up being more knotted than before she got out the bloody shower!" Sophia said referring to Pip dancing behind me. Of course, what she forgot to include on this list were the hands on the hips and pelvic thrusts she was also adding every time the chorus came on.

"Yeah well, at least I have an actual brush this time, seriously you should have seen the shit I had to deal with back in Persia, I thought I was going to cut it off whilst she was sleeping!"

"Oi!" I shouted moaning, one that was ignored of course.

"But then she would have strangled me with it, so I said to myself…I said Pipper, just walk away and find a horse to take your frustration out on," she finished, and I said,

"Yes, she would have strangled you…but wait, did you just say a horse?!"

"I know I am going to regret this but explain, Pip." Sophia said first giving me a sideways looks as if to say, 'here we go'.

"Well, I cut its tail off of course," she said as if this was obvious behaviour, which even for Pip I was struggling to see. I blinked a few times, shook my head and this time it was me and Sophia that were both speaking at the same time,

"Come again?"

"You what now?"

Then as if it explained everything, she just lifted all my hair up and said,

"Duh." And that was it.

That was our explanation.

A little while later and a lot more crazy from Pip, I was now staring at the finished product and again was dumbfounded by the reflection now staring back at me. My gown was truly like something out of a fairy tale and suddenly I found I didn't even want to leave the castle, as it certainly fit with the fantasy. No, all I wanted was to see Draven dressed in an outfit from the same time period after entering his grand ballroom and for him to see me like this before asking me to dance.

Maybe this was something I could ask for a New Year's Eve party one year or something?

Well even if not, then at least we had tonight and staring at myself right now I found I couldn't wait to know what Draven would think.

My dress was a different style to the others as for a start the corseted top had a sweetheart neckline instead of just the classic cut across my breasts. I wondered if this was because I was curvy in this area and therefore this style suited me better, showcasing them, rather than just squashing them flat.

It looked as though two dresses had been made together with the front section of the dress being a rich Cadbury's purple colour. This went down from the tight corset to my feet flaring out at the bottom into a wider section.

The whole of the shimmering purple taffeta was

decorated with a luxurious black velvet Damask brocade in a classic medieval style. The rest of the dress was a soft plain black velvet, that hung down, and flared out over my petticoat underneath. Its sleeves came down past my knees and were folded back to reveal the purple, patterned material underneath. This looked like overly large cuffs so that my hands could be seen and not get lost underneath all the lush fabric. The same exquisite purple material could also be seen at the large hood that swooped down from my shoulders, looking more like a cape because of the way it hung.

I was just wondering how I was going to walk without tripping up over the massive train that followed my every move, making this dress bigger than what I wore for my wedding. It was definitely a medieval statement, that was for sure, as it was most certainly fit for a queen.

My hair, done by the dancing Pip, had been braided in different sections then wound around the crown of my head framing a riot of loose barrel curls, that fell down my back like a waterfall. Even my make-up had been done to look the part, with smoky purple shadow and heavier eyeliner flicking up to points at the edges. My lips were a deep matt red colour that seemed to be stained on as it wasn't going anywhere fast. Great news then for kissing handsome Kings.

Over all, I barely recognised the girl who had looked in the mirror this morning.

"I guess we'd better get going if we want to make it in time, I don't know how long a drive it is…what…why does she now look like she is storing a couple of golf balls in her mouth?" I asked Sophia, referring to Pip who looked like she was trying to stop something from exploding from her mouth. It was that or she was holding her breath like a kid does, where they puff their cheeks out, looking like a blow fish impression.

"Pip no, don't do it..." Sophia warned but I swear she looked like she was going to blow any minute. Then, before she could say anything else, she ran to the door still with her hands over her mouth. Sophia inhaled a premature sigh of relief when just as she pulled a hand away to open the door, she quickly blurted out,

"See you at the party...which is downstairs as Draven wanted it to be a surprise for you, so that instead of going to a different castle for a night in the past, he decided he wanted to show you what it was like in his castle playing king and queen with you, blonde preggy queenie, by his side. He has been keeping this a secret for days having Sophia make the arrangements as he lied to you about having work done on the castle, so you wouldn't find out!" My mouth had dropped open at all she had just blurted out and I turned to Sophia to see her head lowered as she rubbed her temple in that disappointing way. But with Pip still having her back to us she simply said,

"Sorry, I didn't make it...See ya!" Then she ran out the door before another word could be said.

"Is that all true?" I asked once me and Sophia had just recovered from all...well, all of that.

"You mean the truth bomb that just went off?" she replied making me snort a laugh.

"Did he really do all that, just because I mentioned about going to a banquet?"

"No, he did all that because he loves you and wants to make you happy. He did all of that Keira, because after everything you have done, and all you have endured for simply loving my brother, well honey, he did it because... *you deserve it."* Hearing this I practically threw myself in her arms and hugged her to me. She made a little 'humpf' sound at being caught off guard but as she hugged me back I only had one thing to say to her...

"I love having you for a sister."

CHAPTER THIRTY

A DRAVEN FOR EVERY ERA

I had to say that after Pip's wonderful outburst I found myself even more excited about the night ahead and especially as we were walking though the castle making our way to the party. It was so easy, given my surroundings, to get sucked into the past and I found myself wondering how it would have been if I had met him at some banquet back then. How would it have played out if I had been introduced to a man like Draven, lord of this grand castle? Or maybe I was getting ahead of myself, or should I say, more like ahead of my stature.

What if I had been a penniless servant, coming here seeking employment? What if like back when I worked the VIP, I simply found myself serving him? And in fact, that was the way it was always meant to be, no matter which time period we had found ourselves meeting in. A servant, then a concubine in the past and now a waitress. Well, evidence was pointing closer to that theory than the grand lady I looked like right now.

"Hey, what's that look about?" Sophia asked, walking the way that a grand lady should look. She had the walk down to a fine art, with her skirt not getting in her way like mine was.

"I was just thinking about the past." I told her making her smirk before saying,

"You mean you were thinking about Dom in the past," she guessed, and I nodded.

"Do you want to hear my theory?"

"Yeah." I said, after a moment of silence fell between us once I had expressed where my thoughts lay.

"Okay, come on, I will tell you on the way." I frowned and said,

"On the way...I thought we were..." She grabbed my hand and started pulling me down in the opposite direction to where we had been heading.

"I want to show you something that I think you are going to like." Okay, well I would have shrugged my shoulders if I'd had both my hands free, so instead I just agreed and let her lead me off. Then she let go of my hand as we could see a door at the end of another long hallway. I hadn't been this way before and Draven hadn't shown me, which had me more than a little curious.

"I think that no matter what time you were destined to meet, that it was always written to be a certain way. Think about it, even back in Persia, Dom held you at arm's length to begin with...well okay, he cracked pretty quickly, but that was down to circumstances," she said with shrug of her shoulders, as though she was looking back at that time for herself.

"You really think so?" I asked wondering if this would have been true.

"I do. I know my brother and much better than he thinks I do. I know that even if he had met you five hundred years ago, then he would still have acted the same. As much as he likes to think himself the type to just take what he wants without question, I knew the first moment he met you this would not be the case. Now, maybe if he was solely ruled by his demon, then this may be so, but his angel is what holds the real power and you my dear, bring that part out of him more than any other...giving him more power over his tested will." When Sophia had finished she had given me a lot to think about, most of which I didn't really have time to process because we had come to the door at the end.

"Now you wondered what Dom was like back in the past?"

"Yeah, why?"

"Then walk through that door and go see for yourself," she said nodding to the door, grinning as though not only was she giving me something she knew I wanted, but also because it was also naughty.

And the second I opened the door I was stunned by what I saw, for she was right, in this one large space, there was a Draven for every modern era I had missed.

"It's...it's him, it's Draven," I said in whispered awe making Sophia laugh. Then she grabbed my hand and said,

"Come on, let's sneak a look." Then she pulled me into the long wide Gallery that was filled with every period style portrait of Draven I could have imagined. And each of them was beautiful in their own right.

"The first one is from 1426 I think, anyway when I

suggested the idea he hated it but being that I am spoilt, he soon gave in," she said referring to the first painting of his side profile, something that she told me was of the style this early on in portraits. Oh, it was Draven alright but if you asked me, they hadn't gotten his nose right, but his jawline was dead on the money.

As we moved along Sophia would tell me about dates and time periods, often saying how he would put it off for tens of years, sometimes even reaching at least seventy years before he agreed to do another one. Talk about persistence, nagging someone for seventy years and getting what you want by the end of it is an achievement in my book.

There were paintings of him in different styles, wearing what was no doubt considered fashionable for a man of his wealth back then, but no matter the outfit, the continued theme through them all was that natural air of confidence he wore like a weapon against the evils of humanity.

But as I gazed at them all, ones that spanned throughout the ages, it was the one in the centre of the room and the largest of the collection that I was utterly captivated with. It was by far the best and took up the size of the entire height of the wall.

The room was filled with paintings of different sizes, some being just the torso and head, some being in a sitting position against a back drop of fields on a summer's day or others more sinister where he would be wearing full battle gear, with the war painted on the background behind him, as though he had just slipped out of the fight to get his picture taken before running back in there with his weapon held high.

There were others in all his finery, with lavish materials

draped over one shoulder and gathered there by a clasp, or large fur lined jackets over slashed doublets in royal colours. In one, he was even wearing a wide brimmed hat and a short cloak hanging down off one side. But it was that same one I kept coming to and I wondered was it because it was the only one where he was sat upon a mighty black steed, reminding me of my ancient Draven.

Reminding me of my King of Kings, *Arsaces*.

And like the day that he found me in the desert, he reminded me as he was now in this picture. Positioned straight on his horse, those proud almost arrogant features that a man of high position possesses. He was also wearing dark armour, that obviously fit with the time period and hanging down by his side was a sword, one he had his hand resting upon the hilt, as if at the ready for the fight.

"Ah yes, I remember this one."

"How come?" I asked knowing there was a story behind it. She laughed once and said,

"Because it is the only one he likes." Okay, so in the end not so much a story, but more of a statement. But even so, I was shocked.

"He doesn't like any of these?" I asked in astonishment.

"I think seeing as you have been here nearly two weeks and you haven't yet seen this room, that is evidence enough. But even without it, I know because he has told me enough times throughout the years," she said smirking.

"But why, I think they are beautiful. To be able to see him as he was, to get to see him through all the years I have missed…Sophia, this is like another gift to me." Sophia gave me a warm smile and took my hand to give it a squeeze before shocking me still.

"Why do you think it was that he gave into me in the first place?" I frowned as I didn't understand what she was trying to get at. This time she gave me a mischievous grin and told me.

"Because my argument was a sound one."

"And that was…?" I asked waving my hand around telling her to roll on out with it.

"You."

"Me?" My voice said it all…disbelief.

"I told him that one day his Chosen One would come into his life and when she did, she might find it difficult knowing he has lived so many lifetimes before her own, that this…" She paused to cast a hand out down the gallery before continuing,

"…This all might make it easier on her and that one day, she might even consider it a gift from the past."

"Oh Sophia…to think that even then before you knew me you had my back… that you were thinking of me." Sophia gave me a slight shrug of her shoulders as if it was nothing on her part, but I knew this wasn't true. For starters, she had battled Draven over doing this for hundreds of years, at least. That wasn't just worth my thanks, it was worth a bloody knighthood!

She was about to say something else when I heard her phone ringing. I was about to ask where she would even keep her phone in a dress like that, but then she surprised me. I watched as she reached into a hidden compartment on the skirt of her dress that the folds concealed nicely.

"What? Even girls in those days needed pockets," she said with a nod to the nearest picture with a grin, before answering her phone.

"No, that's not right, I said the dressed salmon first… okay, okay, I will be down there to deal with this shortly," she snapped clearly annoyed.

"Well, it's lucky the guests have only just started to arrive and won't be sitting down to dinner for an hour, so you had better hurry!" Sophia said then she ended the call and said,

"I have to sort this mess out. Do you want to come with me or stay here and wait for me?"

"I can stay here?" I asked making her laugh.

"Of course, you can, Keira, it's your castle now, remember?" I smiled at this but then with a reluctant glance at the door, I asked,

"But what about your brother, won't he be angry if he finds out?"

"Honey, one look at you in that dress and he'll have you another castle built if you asked him for it…trust me, he will get over it very quickly." I laughed at her comment and watched as she walked down the gallery, then I shouted before she could get too far,

"Hey, Sophia!"

"Yeah?" She stopped to look at me just over her shoulder.

"Thank you… not just this but you know, for everything." She gave me a warm smile and said,

"I should be the one thanking you."

"Why?"

"Because I love any excuse to piss my brother off!" I laughed at this and said her name in reprimand making her laugh again. Then she spun on a heel, making me wonder again just how she did it in a dress that big. She then lifted an arm up in the air, with her back to me and shouted,

"Demon, remember!" So, I shouted back,

"Yeah, me too!" To which she replied calmly but loud enough for me to still hear her,

"No, you're not!" And then the door closed behind her beautiful dress and its even more beautiful owner, leaving me alone with many different Dravens from the past.

I gave him one last look upon the horse surrounded by the gilded frame and continued down the gallery to the portraits I hadn't yet seen. It soon became obvious to see that the skill level increased as time went on. And I think by the time I reached the one where he was dressed like something out of a Jane Austin novel, I was near panting at the sight.

In fact, I was so lost in my sexy fantasies about him, I hadn't really noticed until now that dotted here and there were different antiques situated around the room and usually in between each painting. It was only now that I started to piece it together, although you would really need to be studying each one to realise it and well, I could easily make a profession out of studying Draven.

But why I had missed it and why many others would, was because usually in a portrait you are supposed to be focused on the person's image and the background was there just to set the scene. However, in this case and on finer inspection, I noticed that the antiques in the room were also the ones from the different paintings. Like a blue and white vase that sat on a narrow side table and even the table itself was in another painting I had seen. I laughed as I noticed one portrait that even had one of the earlier paintings in the background of another, hung there behind him on the wall. It was clever in the way it was done and very subtle, but it was without a doubt Draven.

There were other things too, like clocks, carved boxes, a Chinese style fruit bowl, making me giggle because of the other day and the fact that Draven had actually pulled a prank on me.

But what really drew me in was a sword on the wall, hung just within reach on brass hooks. I walked back over to the centre picture to see that yes, it was as I thought.

It was the same sword.

I don't know why I was so drawn to it, but I was. Maybe because out of all the items in the room that were mirrored on the walls, this was the one thing that he had actually been touching. So, I don't know why but I found myself walking back to it, and before I could stop myself I was reaching up to touch it.

It was fairly simple in its design, not really being too ostentatious or anything. It was more like a sword that you could see belonging to a Knight and one that wasn't used for show. It was silver and black, with a T bar across the blade that was attached to a black round handle that was embedded with silver strips. The handle finished with a round shield that looked to hold his family crest in polished gold.

I couldn't help but run my fingertips along its long length marvelling in this being something Draven himself had used, defending his land and his people. I was about to stop there when the picture flickered in my mind's eye and I found myself reaching for the handle like Draven would have done. My fingertips skimmed the twisted metal design and then came across something that didn't feel right. Something that shouldn't have been there,

A switch.

"What is..." My voice was cut off by my own actions or should I say the result of them, as I had put pressure against the round button I had found. The second I did I heard the distinct sound of locks sliding back from their casings and then I watched in shock as the large centre picture I had been obsessing over swung open slightly. I let go of the sword in slow motion, almost as if I was too scared to move too fast in case the painting fell and crashed to the floor.

Yes, that would be bad and a major 'oh shit' moment.

I don't know what I had just done but somewhere in the rational side of my brain, one reserved solely for 'oh shit' moments like these, I wondered if it was for security reasons. I knew galleries all around the world had security in place behind each of their paintings, locking them in place to prevent them being stolen.

Was this what that was?

For some reason I didn't think it likely, for I doubted he would be worried about burglars coming in here and nicking portraits of himself. Hell, from what Sophia had said, sounds like he was close to inviting them in and giving them away.

Either way, I needed to go and check to see what damage, if any, I had caused this time. So, I walked back over towards the painting and the closer I got to it the more it started to look like a large door. It was slightly ajar with only enough space to put your hand through so that you could pull it wider, something I hadn't yet had the courage to do. I knew that it was probably just some hidden passage like in Afterlife, as that place was filled with them. No doubt for Draven to spy on his people to make sure there were no traitors lying in wait.

But even still, I didn't know what to do next. Of course, I knew what I wanted to do and that was to step inside and see where it could lead. However, I knew that from past experiences what could happen when I would just wander off and usually it came with sharp teeth snapping at me from behind bars.

But really, would Draven have a dungeon or temple in a place like this? Surely it couldn't be a requirement for every home he lived in. I could just picture the realtor's face when telling her his requirements. This thought made me giggle aloud but done more so out of nervousness. I looked back down the hallway where Sophia had just left and remembered that she did say she would be back in a few minutes. So, if anything did go wrong, at least I had that as a backup plan. And also, she had said that this was my home now too, so surely whatever was behind this painting was also mine by default...right?

Okay, so after convincing myself that it was a good idea and my curiosity basically winning out over all past events and twisted my logic on any reasons why I shouldn't, I slowly snuck my hand through the crack and pulled back really slowly. It was as though at any minute I was half expecting the picture to crash to the floor like I had first dreaded happening. I mean, it wasn't like something like that would go unnoticed, it was the size of a freaking car for Christ sake!

But this didn't happen, no instead it swung open with ease and once it went past a certain point, it must have triggered a switch or something, as lights started to flicker on. I could see the old style wrought iron lamps had been fitted with the marvel of modern day electricity. Well, when

Draven said this place came with all mod cons, he hadn't been kidding as even his spooky hidden spaces came with easy day living accessories such as the light bulb.

Surely that was a step up for me, because as a rule, all bad situations I got myself into in the past normally started with flaming torches on walls or crazy angry exploding lamps like back at Afterlife when I had been lured there in my sleep. Another one of Sophia's interfering ways of trying to push Draven in the right direction...that being, *my direction.*

So now, with the warm glow of light bouncing off whitewashed walls, I could easily see steps leading down to a dark space, telling me that it went a fair way down. So, with only my dangerously curious nature leading me, I took my first step...

Into one of many unknowns.

Past and Present Demons

CHAPTER THIRTY-ONE

PAST AND PRESENT DEMONS

As I walked further inside I was happy in the knowledge that I wasn't going to trip at the bottom and break my neck. Because I soon discovered that as I walked further down, a motion sensor would trigger the lights. I also discovered that this must have been a section of the castle that was built into the mountain, as it was clear from the rough walls this tunnel had been cut out of the rock.

It was a bit tricky at first, trying to manoeuvre both myself and my dress down the steps without causing bodily harm. But thankfully the steps weren't steep, and they weren't narrow. I also kept looking behind me and found comfort in the small slither of light from the hidden doorway, that at least I wasn't locked in down here.

Wherever here was?

I don't know how long it took me before I could see the last few steps opening out before me in a staggered fan shape, but it was obvious that it was leading into a large room. This time instead of electric lights switching on and flickering bulbs flooding the room with light, it was once again my arch nemesis…

Flaming torches.

Yep, this was when I knew my seemingly innocent curiosity could possibly take a turn for the worse, as I watched the walls start to ignite. Overly large wrought iron candelabras looked as if they had been first sliced in half and were embedded into the wall with carved stone hands holding them in place. These were alive with the dancing flames captured inside small teardrop shaped glass lamps.

But it wasn't the light that had me gasping, no it was what it now illuminated, and the sight had me taking a staggered step back. It wasn't just a room I was stood in, it was in fact a cavern sized space that one sound would have sung with an echo.

But again, it wasn't even the size of the place that was staggering, but more like what filled it.

Because I had finally found,

Draven's private vault.

This should have been shocking enough but it wasn't. Because it was what filled the space that stunned me and the lack of wealth. As this wasn't a vault for money, it was a sacred vault of all Draven's worldly possessions that meant the most to him.

I knew this the second I was faced by the heavenly figure everything seemed to be centred around. A great marble statue of who I knew was his mother, Sarah. It was breathtakingly stunning in all its fine detail and it could almost be believed that any minute she would come to life, lifting the veil of stone from her divine figure.

I stepped further into the room and looked all around in utter astonishment. Shelves filled to the brim with rolled scrolls, too many to even fit in the space without spilling onto the floor. There were also large trunks piled high and dotted around the space. I was so curious that I gently lifted the lid to one, flinching when the old hinges creaked.

"Oh my god," I uttered as I saw notebook after notebook, all crammed in there with different covers, but the age looked to be the same. Which is when I looked up and counted the trunks, asking myself if they were what I thought they were?

I knew the only way to check and even though it felt wrong, I still found my hand reaching for the top one.

'April 3rd, 1877

'This morning I found myself gazing from the window again, getting lost in my torturous thoughts. The dispute about owned land was an annoying murmur

in the background, one I wanted to dismiss as soon as possible.

Something I did far sooner than my patience usually stretches to, and this was done with what I knew was a sharp tongue lashing out as I followed through with my impulse. But then again, I found I had no patience for such things these days and wondered if it wasn't time to move on again. Start somewhere afresh and if possible, discover a new piece of this tainted earth that hadn't yet been butchered by the human race.

My sister continues to drive me to distraction with her constant annoyance at my foul mood, one brought on by yet again the pressure to find my Electus that surrounds my soul. I often find myself writing about her and plaguing my mind with questions as to who she could be. With her presence a constant in not just my journals but also in the prison of feelings that I keep locked away in the hellish pits of my mind.

All I have left to hope for is that she won't keep me waiting much longer.

For I fear for my angel's sanity and my demon's control.'

I dropped the book the instant I read those last words and then looked up slowly at the tower of trunks all stacked in a corner.

"Oh my god," I said again, only this time in complete disbelief. It was true, *all of it was true.* Draven hadn't just been waiting for me for thousands of years, but he had *really been waiting for me.*

I don't know why this had hit me so hard, hard enough to place a hand to my heart as if to check it was still beating and this wasn't just all a dream. But to hear it from Draven's version, one long before he met me, had an effect that rocked me to my core.

I found myself asking just how many pages were in this room that held hope to the existence of me? How many more tortured words were written somewhere in this room speaking of the only name he knew…his Electus?

In the end I had to tear my eyes from the sight of what I could assume were catalogues of journals spanning throughout the ages, for fear that I would give into my impulse again and grab one.

So, instead I looked around the rest of the space and saw other things that also caught my interest. Like an array of small statues on plinths and a charred wooden throne as if there as a symbol of a torched past. Even paintings, none of which were of himself, but ones of horses he must have owned.

Then there was a row of stone mannequins against the wall, all wearing different styles of amour like an army of frozen warriors, ready at the front line of battle. Even a few broken pieces of furniture and pottery were dotted around the edges. But with every single piece I found myself desperate to know why, how and when?

I don't know how I felt about finding this place, but I knew now that I had wished for Draven to have been the one to have shown it to me. Not only so that he could have been the one to explain to me the stories surrounding all of these things. Things that meant something to him. But mainly because right now I felt like an intruder.

I turned back towards the way I had entered, noticing that framing each side stood stone centurions that looked as if they were the vault's guardians. They even had their weapons raised high and spears crossed over the threshold.

Yep, suddenly this place didn't seem like such a good idea as all the objects around the space started to cast flickering shadows across the dirt floor. I felt like I was in Aladdin's cave, only instead of jewels and mountains of gold to find, what lay in here were too many lifetimes' worth of secrets to be told.

So, I decided enough time had passed as the last thing I wanted was Sophia not knowing where I was if she came back...or worse still, Draven finding me down here after searching everywhere for me.

But as I made my way back towards the entrance something made me stop and I looked back at the room one last time. As I did this, something happened as one of the lights further back suddenly came to life, making me wonder if there had been a delay in the ignition or something?

Well, whatever it was, I could now see that the space went even further back than I had originally thought. This was when something shimmering caught my attention and unfortunately, it was enough not to leave.

I knew what I should have done, but this didn't seem to register as my feet were already taking me closer to what it was. The closer I got I could see that the flickering flame on the wall was reflecting off a strange pool of water. It looked like some kind of old well and from where I was stood it looked as though that water was close to spilling over the edge of the small stone blocks that surrounded it.

I decided to take a closer look as if something was telling

me I needed to. This time it wasn't just my curiosity that was pulling me forward, but something else, *something deeper*. Like a voice was speaking to me without words, tempting me with a glimpse into not my future but Draven's.

I found myself getting closer. So close in fact, that before I knew it, I was stood only a foot away. But then the clear water started to change as if some sort of black substance was being released below and merging up to the surface. I squinted as I could see something down there shining, something white that every now and again was catching the light. I got down on my knees by the edge without even thinking about my dress or the fact that I should no longer be down here.

It was as if something was speaking to me now, telling me to just reach down and grab it. 'Take it, it's yours' it said over and over. To the point where I was just about to reach in and…

And thankfully, before the impulse to do something so stupid could take full control of me, I started to pull back. Only now as I did this the once clear water started to ripple as if something had been dropped in the centre. Swirls of black liquid mixed into a darker shade, making it now almost impossible to see beyond the surface.

"What on earth…?" but that was the wrong thing to ask, as the second I uttered the words a shadow started to emerge as if rising closer to the top. A dark shape, barely even seen in the obscure water but the closer it got, the more visible it became.

However, the second my mind started to process what it was, I was too late. I barely had time to scream as suddenly a demonic arm shot out from the water and grabbed my face before suddenly pulling me under. The last thing I saw was a pair of demonic eyes of Hellish sun looking back at me, grinning sadistically through the murky depths.

The beast had wrapped an arm around me, capturing my body as I fought for escape. But with the strength in those arms, I knew it was impossible and I was running out of air. The only thing that saved me from gulping in all that water when I screamed, was the demon's hand that had clamped firmly over my mouth and nose.

I knew this was it, the demon had been granted his wish. Because now I recognised the face from my nightmares, only this time I knew I wasn't dreaming. Because you can't die in your sleep. You can't feel the air as it's being sucked from your lungs with your need to breathe as it becomes desperation. Draven's arms weren't around me, holding me safe in a tight embrace on the bed until I managed to fight the monster away and back to reality.

No, because the truth only now started to hit me, pounding into my soul and into my heart like the death that would soon follow.

That night of the war. The night Draven had no choice and no will of his own before he plunged that dagger into my chest.

Now I knew that Draven killing me had never been the prophecy after all.

It was never about that.

I knew this when a memory hit me and infected my mind like the water that was now drowning me.

I finally understood what it was that my demon said to me that night. Both his ancient words and barely spoken whisper being a threat of my future, one taking place right now.

A sentence that said it all,

'Queen of the Netherworld and seventh slave, you will come to me and I…*I will make you my slave in Hell.'*

A threat, from who I know knew was...

Draven's Demon.

To be Continued

ABOUT THE AUTHOR

Stephanie Hudson has dreamed of being a writer ever since her obsession with reading books at an early age. What first became a quest to overcome the boundaries set against her in the form of dyslexia has turned into a life's dream. She first started writing in the form of poetry and soon found a taste for horror and romance. Afterlife is her first book in the series of twelve, with the story of Keira and Draven becoming ever more complicated in a world that sets them miles apart.

When not writing, Stephanie enjoys spending time with her loving family and friends, chatting for hours with her biggest fan, her sister Cathy who is utterly obsessed with one gorgeous Dominic Draven. And of course, spending as much time with her supportive partner and personal muse, Blake who is there for her no matter what.

Author's words.

My love and devotion is to all my wonderful fans that keep me going into the wee hours of the night but foremost to my wonderful daughter Ava...who yes, is named after a cool, kick-ass, Demonic bird and my sons, Jack, who is a little hero and Baby Halen, who yes, keeps me up at night but it's okay because he is named after a Guitar legend!

Keep updated with all new release news & more on my website
www.afterlifesaga.com
Never miss out, sign up to the
mailing list at the website.

Also, please feel free to join myself and other Dravenites on my Facebook group
Afterlife Saga Official Fan
Interact with me and other fans. Can't wait to see you there!

facebook.com/AfterlifeSaga
twitter.com/afterlifesaga
instagram.com/theafterlifesaga

ACKNOWLEDGEMENTS

Well first and foremost my love goes out to all the people who deserve the most thanks and are the wonderful people that keep me going day to day. But most importantly they are the ones that allow me to continue living out my dreams and keep writing my stories for the world to hopefully enjoy… These people are of course YOU! Words will never be able to express the full amount of love I have for you guys. Your support is never ending. Your trust in me and the story is never failing. But more than that, your love for me and all who you consider your 'Afterlife family' is to be commended, treasured and admired. Thank you just doesn't seem enough, so one day I hope to meet you all and buy you all a drink! ;)

To my family… To my amazing mother, who has believed in me from the very beginning and doesn't believe that something great should be hidden from the world. I would like to thank you for all the hard work you put into my books and the endless hours spent caring about my words and making sure it is the best it can be for everyone to enjoy. You make Afterlife shine. To my wonderful crazy father who is and always has been my hero in life. Your strength astonishes me, even to this day and the love and care you hold for your family is a gift you give to the Hudson name. And last but not least, to the man that I consider my soul mate. The man who taught me about real love and makes me not only want to be a better person but makes me feel I am too. The amount of support you have given me since we met has been incredible and the greatest feeling was finding out you wanted to spend the rest of your life with me when you asked me to marry you.

All my love to my dear husband and my own personal Draven... Mr Blake Hudson.

Another personal thank you goes to my dear friend Caroline Fairbairn and her wonderful family that have embraced my brand of crazy into their lives and given it a hug when most needed.

For their friendship I will forever be eternally grateful.

I would also like to mention Claire Boyle my wonderful PA, who without a doubt, keeps me sane and constantly smiling through all the chaos which is my life ;) And a loving mention goes to Lisa Jane for always giving me a giggle and scaring me to death with all her count down pictures lol ;)

Thank you for all your hard work and devotion to the saga and myself. And always going that extra mile, pushing Afterlife into the spotlight you think it deserves. Basically helping me achieve my secret goal of world domination one day...evil laugh time... Mwahaha! Joking of course ;)

As before, a big shout has to go to all my wonderful fans who make it their mission to spread the Afterlife word and always go the extra mile. I love you all x

ALSO BY STEPHANIE HUDSON

Afterlife Saga

A Brooding King, A Girl running from her past. What happens when the two collide?

Transfusion Saga

What happens when an ordinary human girl comes face to face with the cruel Vampire King who dismissed her seven years ago?

Transfusion - Book 1

Venom of God - Book 2

Blood of Kings - Book 3

Rise of Ashes - Book 4

Map of Sorrows - Book 5

Tree of Souls - Book 6

Kingdoms of Hell – Book 7

Eyes of Crimson - Book 8

Roots of Rage - Book 9

Afterlife Chronicles: (Young Adult Series)

The Glass Dagger – Book 1

The Hells Ring – Book 2

Stephanie Hudson and Blake Hudson

The Devil in Me

OTHER WORKS FROM HUDSON INDIE INK